"Quit hanging on to the handrails...Let go. Surrender. Go for the ride of your life. Do it every day."

—Melody Beattie

Chapter One

Manhattan, 1986

"Here you are, Charlotte," the woman said, setting down a plate of pancakes in front of a four-year-old girl with chocolate-brown curls. "Shaped like bunnies, just the way you like them."

"Thanks, Auntie Anna," the child said, watching as Anna poured syrup on top of the pancakes. Then she looked up at her. "Auntie Anna…are you my mommy?"

Anna dropped the knife she was using to cut up the child's food, sending it clattering to the floor. After taking a moment to regain her composure, she bent down to pick up the knife. "I'm your aunt," she told her as she straightened up, resting her hands on top of her apron. "You know that. Why are you asking…about that?"

"Mrs. Finn…that man who came to see her called her 'Mama'. So I thought that you were my 'Mama'," Charlotte answered.

Anna remembered that Cheryl's son had come to visit from Chicago a few days ago, when Anna asked her to watch Charlotte while she went to work. "That man is Mrs. Finn's son," Anna said as she sat down across from the child. "That's why he calls her 'Mama'. Now eat your breakfast," she requested, tucking a loose strand of gray hair behind her ear. She blinked at the bright sunlight streaming in through the kitchen window, trying to steady her shaking hands. *She's getting older,* Anna thought as she poured herself a glass of juice. *I won't be able to hide the truth from her forever.*

If I get to keep her that long.

1987

Charlotte took several gulps of air, trying to catch her breath. She could feel her heart beating faster and faster and she couldn't slow it down. Leaning against a park bench she squinted in the darkness to try and see better. Once she'd calmed down a bit she curled up on the bench, looking up at the full moon, a sight that always made her feel better. It was the last image in her mind as she drifted off to sleep.

The next morning she woke up to see several strangers huddled around her, staring at her in concern. Charlotte jerked up in terror, shrinking back against the bench.

"It's alright, honey," a woman with dark hair and large glasses soothed, kneeling in front of the bench. "We're not going to hurt you."

Charlotte looked at her and the two other woman and suddenly began to cry. "I want Anna," she sobbed. "But...she's gone."

The dark-haired woman held her hand out to her. "I know of a place we can go that will help us find Anna," she said kindly. "My name is Sherri, and I work at a children's shelter, a place where I help kids like you every day. Don't worry, sweetheart. We'll find Anna."

Charlotte accepted her hand and let her lead the way out of the park, from the two bystanders, and down the sidewalk. She kept her eyes straight ahead, trying not to be afraid.

"What's your name?" Sherri asked as they walked down the street.

"Anna says it's Charlotte but I like Charlie. That's what Mrs. Finn calls me."

"Charlie it is then," Sherri told her as they walked the crowded streets of downtown Manhattan.

Suncrest Children's Center, 1989

"Who cares if it's your birthday?" Tommy sneered as Fuller shoved Charlie roughly, up against the brick wall. "No one wants you anyway."

"Yeah," Sarah chimed in, looming over Charlie. Sarah was thirteen and always lording it over the younger kids, particularly Charlie. "When are you going to realize Anna's never coming back for you? You talk about her all the time like she's so great...but where is she? If she loves you so much why is she leaving you here?"

"You know what I think?" Fuller asked the others. Fuller was ten, and known for being a bully along with Tommy. "I think that *Anna* doesn't even exist, that she just made her up," he jeered at Charlie.

"Yeah!" the others chorused in agreement.

Fuller stepped up to Charlie until he was two inches from her face. "I want to hear you say that Anna was never real."

"No," Charlie told him, standing her ground. "She is real. She was like my mom."

"You don't have a mom," Fuller growled. "That's why you're here."

"That's why you're here too," Charlie pointed out.

Fuller's face colored deep red and he grabbed Charlie by the shirt. "Admit you're lying," he snarled.

"Never." Charlie looked from Fuller to the other kids leaning against the fence. She was outnumbered, as usual, and she was the youngest and the smallest...but she was also the most fierce.

"I'm not lying!" she yelled, shoving Fuller as hard as she could, then jumping on his back. "Anna is real, and she loves me! Nothing you say can change that!"

Charlie was sent to bed without dinner that night as punishment for fighting. Though she received a bloody lip and scratches on her arm, she was the only one disciplined. No one ever believed that she was constantly targeting for bullying and teasing; they just saw her as a troublemaker.

But all the time she was laying in bed gave her a chance to think, and find a way to finally hatch the plan she'd been working on for the two years she'd spent at Suncrest Children's Shelter, and it only had one goal: securing her freedom.

When the lights had been turned out and she was sure everyone was asleep, Charlie broke into Mrs. Bowers' office, the lady who ran the children's shelter. Mrs. Bowers kept emergency money in a turtle-shaped jar-Charlie had been sent to her office enough to know-and it was easy enough to break open. She eagerly grabbed as much cash as she could, stuffing it into the small duffel bag she'd taken with her that night she'd been separated from Anna; it and its contents were her only possessions in the world. Then she quietly crept down the hallway toward the back door, her heart in her throat until she'd safely gotten outside.

Charlie ran down the sidewalk, deeply breathing in the cool night air and tasting the sweet scent of freedom. And she knew exactly what she would do with her new-found independence.

She reached the train station-she'd grabbed a map of the city on the way-in record time, looking around the semi-crowded station full of strange-looking people. She stood on her tip-toes as she got to the ticket window, scarcely getting a reaction from the clerk. Then she boarded the train, looking around in amazement and wonder; she'd actually done it. After two long years of waiting for Anna, dealing with bullies and adults who didn't really care about her…she was completely free.

As the train pulled away she watched as the Manhattan skyline slowly began to disappear, her nose pressed up against the cold window pane. With each mile she was farther away from New York…and every bad thing that had ever happened there.

New Jersey, 1991

Charlie knew all the regulars at the park by heart: the joggers, the dog-walkers, those who sat on the benches to read the paper and eat their breakfast before hurrying off to work. Her routine didn't go unnoticed either; everyone knew about the young girl who spent so much time at the park…but no one was curious enough to investigate it further.

That was until one morning, in early June. One of the joggers Charlie recognized approached her; she stood out from all the rest, with long wavy red hair. None of the joggers had ever approached her before; most people stayed away from her, for which Charlie was grateful. So when the young woman approached her she felt incredibly apprehensive; there was no way she was going back to a children's shelter.

She said as much when the woman began to talk to her. "I'll disappear before they can catch me," she told her fiercely. "No one will ever find me."

"That's what you're afraid of?" the woman asked curiously. "That you'll have to go back to a shelter?"

Charlie nodded vigorously. "I won't."

The woman nodded thoughtfully. "What if I make a deal with you?" she asked after a moment. She held up a quarter. "Heads, I leave you alone and go on my way, not mentioning you to anyone. Tails you come with me and get a free milkshake...but you have to spill your life story."

"Why are you so interested in me?" Charlie wanted to know.

"Because, like you, I'm in this park every day, and every day I see a young girl sitting alone on a bench who's as skinny as a rail. That makes me curious."

"How do I know you won't cheat?" Charlie asked, staring at the quarter.

The woman handed her the quarter. "That's how."

Charlie took the coin and reluctantly tossed it in the air, catching it quickly. "Tails," she said with a sigh.

A short while later she was sitting in a coffee shop, enjoying a large strawberry milkshake and a muffin. She kept looking at the woman across from her, who introduced herself as Melinda Booker. She was very pretty, young...and Charlie immediately felt at ease around her but couldn't figure out why. As promised, she began to tell her story...the parts she remembered of it anyway.

"My name is Charlie, and I don't have a last name. I'm not even sure when my real
birthday is...I just celebrate it the beginning of every June. Anna never told me the day."

"Who's Anna?"

"My aunt...she was a lot older than you, she had gray hair. She took care of me. I stayed with Mrs. Finn across the hall when Anna went to work. She called me Charlie, but Anna didn't like it. Anna would only call me Charlotte."

"You don't remember having parents?"

Charlie shook her head. "No. Just Anna. When I was five people came after us...and I don't remember all of what happened except that I ended up alone. I never saw Anna again." She looked down at the table.

"I'm sorry," Melinda told her softly. "I know how hard it is when we can't be with the people we love anymore."

"You do?" Charlie asked with interest.

Melinda nodded. "My mother...she passed away last year. And even though I'm grown up I still needed her, loved her. So I know how sad you must be."

Charlie just looked at her in amazement. No one had shown such kindness to her, or really seemed to understand before. She started to feel even more at ease than she already did. "I was sad...after Anna was gone I had to go to the children's shelter and it was horrible.

The other kids were mean and I got beat up a lot...so I decided to escape."

"The shelter here in town?"

Charlie shook her head. "In Manhattan."

"*Manhattan?*" Melinda asked incredulously.

"Yep. Got on a train and came here. I've lived in the park ever since."

"All this time?" Melinda asked quietly, unable to hide her surprise.

Charlie nodded. "I'm friends with bagel vendor, he gives me a bagel for breakfast every morning. He also gets me fruit." She looked at Melinda. "Please don't send me back to a shelter."

"I don't intend to. Instead...how would you feel about coming home with me?"

"With you?" Charlie repeated. "You...would want me?"

"Absolutely. Charlie, do you know what a licensed foster parent is?"

Charlie shook her head.

"It's a person who has children came stay in their home until their parents or guardians can be found," Melinda explained. "They take care of you just like a real parent would. That's what I am, Charlie...and I'd be honored if you'd be my first kid. What do you say?"

Charlie looked at the kind woman, and realized why she felt so at ease. She didn't look like Anna...but she acted like her. Like someone who would really care. "Alright," Charlie agreed after a moment. "I'd like to come live with you."

1992

"The state of New Jersey grants Melinda Booker, guardian of Charlotte, the formal adoption of the minor child," the judge stated, looking from Melinda to Charlie, who embraced one another.

As they were leaving the courthouse they were stopped by Charlie's social worker, Fran.

"It was highly irregular...but we've set up a temporary identification for Charlotte, giving her a
social security number and a record of her existence so she will be able to get a valid driver's license when it's time," she informed them. "And, according to the state of New Jersey, her date of birth is June 1, 1982."

"Thank you," Melinda said, shaking her hand. "I know there's no record of Charlie's birth…but it's a mystery we intend to pursue so she can have answers one day."

After a celebratory dinner and a trip to the movies to watch *Aladdin,* Melinda tucked Charlie in that night, in the room Charlie decorated herself. "What happened today was just a formality," she said, brushing Charlie's dark hair out of her eyes. "You've already been my daughter for a year, and this was already your home. But now it's official, and the whole world will know and no one will ever be able to take you from me. And you finally have a last name." She grasped Charlie's hands. "I know there's a lot we still don't know but we'll find out together. We have plenty of time." She ruffled Charlie's hair affectionately. "You are an extraordinary ten-year-old, Charlie Booker. Tougher than most adults. You've spent so long taking care of yourself…now it's time for someone else to take over, let you finally be a kid."

"Sounds good…Mom."

Melinda froze. It was the first time she'd ever called her "Mom" and not "Melinda". A smile broke over her face, tears glittering in her eyes. "Goodnight…daughter."

1997

"It's been five years since we started looking," Charlie said into the cordless phone, plopping onto the couch. "It's okay, Mom. I wanted to find Anna…but it's like a needle in a haystack. I don't know anything else about her, anything that would help us find her. Maybe we should just focus on tomorrow instead," she suggested. "I'll be fifteen…"

"…which means you want your learner's permit," Melinda finished. "I know, I know. I promised you we'll go to the DMV and we will…but I was really hoping your birthday present would be answers." She sighed in frustration.

"Relax," Charlie told her. "I'm happy with the way things are. I finally have a normal life, remember? School, friends, dates…"

"…getting grounded for breaking curfew, getting a navel piercing without my consent, skipping class," Melinda continued. "Yes, you're acting pretty typically alright. Which reminds me…I've got a late night tonight, so you're on your own for dinner. And there had better be no wild parties in my absence," she added sternly. "If I get another call from Mrs. Waters-"

"Will you chill already?" Charlie interrupted, rolling her eyes. "That was *one time*. Mrs. Waters needs a hobby."

"Fine. I'll be home as soon as I can. Love you."

"Love you too." Charlie hung up, then turned the phone back on to order a pizza.

She fell asleep early in her room watching episodes of *Buffy the Vampire Slayer* she'd taped so she could re-watch them as much as wanted. When she woke up a couple of hours later something felt off. It wasn't a specific feeling, just a general uneasiness. She put on her bath robe and padded down the hall. "Mom?" she called sleepily, wondering if she fell asleep in front of the TV in the den again. She passed the hall clock and saw that it was midnight.

When she reached the living room she was that it was empty. Before she could react the
phone on the side table begin to ring. Charlie picked up the phone, which was next to a framed photo of her and her mother taken two years ago at Disney World. "Hello?"

"Charlotte Booker?"

Charlie frowned. "This is she."

"This is Officer Horton of the Jersey PD," he told her soberly. "I'm afraid your mother's been in an accident."

1998

*I never thought I'd be back here and look at me. Sitting on the same park bench Mom found me on seven years ago-*Charlie squeezed her eyes shut as she laid down on the bench. It had been a year but it still hurt unlike anything had hurt before. Melinda Booker was the only family she'd ever had, and now she was alone once again.

Except Anna, she reminded herself, opening her eyes to look up at the stars. *But it was so long ago it doesn't feel real. Mom's who felt real.*

But Melinda wasn't here now. She gave Charlie a home, a family, a last name...but now it was up to Charlie to keep going, to revert back to her self-sufficiency. Which meant she had to keep running.

Social services had been looking for her ever since her mother's funeral, and Charlie had to stay on her toes ever since. She'd been all over the area, trying to stay one step ahead of them, but she was getting tired. She knew the park was the first place they'd look, which is why she'd stayed away. But since tonight was the one-year anniversary of her mother's death she had to come here, to this bench. To the spot where her whole life changed.

Tomorrow I turn sixteen, she thought, closing her eyes. *And I have to leave. They'll find me if I stay here, and there's no way in hell I'm going to a shelter or to foster care.* The only solution was to go back to New York, see if she could track down Anna and find out about her past.

She only stayed in New Jersey as long as she did because she couldn't let go of her home. But she had to now if she wanted to survive. *I'm so sorry, Mom. I have to run again.* She got up from the bench and looked around the park one last time.

I love you...good-bye.

Brooklyn, 2000

"Come on, Rocky," Charlie said, holding her hands up in the air, slowly backing away. "You know how it's been."

"I know how it's been for all of us," Rocky sneered, showing his gold tooth. He advanced toward her, which forced Charlie to back against the boxcar. "I've got three kids at home. All you have to feed is your own sorry ass."

"Give me a week," Charlie told him. "I'll get it by then."

"You can get me a grand in a week?"

Charlie thought about all the ways she could and it made her sick to her stomach...but
she didn't have a choice. Everyone knew crossing Rocky was a mistake, a dangerous mistake. She nodded. "I can," she said, hoping she sounded convincing.

"Bull!" he yelled, slamming his hand on the metal next to her, making her flinch. "You
couldn't get it for me in three months. There's no way in hell you can now."

"So that's it then? We're done negotiating?"

"Oh yeah. We're done." Rocky grabbed her by the shirt and shoved her hard against the boxcar.

Charlie managed to pull her knife out of her back pocket and sliced him on the arm, causing him to yelp in pain. She began to run, not getting farther than a yard when three guys appeared, all taller and stockier than Rocky.

Charlie felt her breath catch in her chest and was reminded of her time at the children's shelter, when she was outnumbered before.

Just as she knew then, she wouldn't stand a chance...but there was no way she was just going to lie down and give up. If she went down, she went down fighting.

"You want a chase, boys?" she muttered under her breath. "I'll give you a chase." She took off, the men right on her tail. Her heart pounding, she silently vowed to give them the chase of their lives.

***

Bob Holden walked past the abandoned boxcar he passed every night on his way home, hunching his shoulders in the sudden wind. As he got closer he noticed the door that was usually shut was now partway open.

Light from a nearby streetlamp illuminated the darkened car, revealing a huddled shape on the floor. Bob stopped, seeing the women's tennis shoe on the foot that dangled over the side. His eyes traveled up to the blue jeans, faded leather jacket, and the long bleached-blonde hair hanging down the girl's back. *Must be homeless,* he thought, reaching out to shake her shoulder. Then he froze.

Even in the dark he could see all the blood, the bruise-covered face, and the arm bent at an odd angle. Reaching up to the girl's neck he was relieved to find a thready pulse.

Taking out his cell phone, Bob hastily dialed 9-1-1. "I'm at Lincoln and Brazelton, the old train yard. There's a girl whose been beaten, badly."

After he hung up he gently rested a hand on the unconscious girl's shoulder. "Help's on the way," he told her. "Just hold on." He noticed something laying next to her, something glinting from the light of the nearby street lamp, on top of a blood-sprinkled pack of cigarettes. He reached over and picked up a silver locket with a thin, bloodstained chain and carefully placed it in his pocket.

Bob rode in the ambulance with her to the E.R. at St. Joseph's, watching the EMTs work. When they arrived at the hospital he talked to the police in the waiting room, who reported the girl had no I.D. on her. Because of that, Bob decided to stay so she wouldn't be alone.

The doctor emerged an hour later, reporting that she needed emergency surgery. Bob continued to wait, knowing fully well why he couldn't leave.

Bob was later told the surgery had successfully stopped the internal bleeding but that she'd been beaten so hard her organs had been bruised. Amazingly enough she hadn't suffered any neurological trauma, so she would regain consciousness. But her left arm had been broken in three places, she was covered in bruises and cuts, and there was evidence that she had been beaten before on multiple occasions. Bob was also told if he hadn't gotten to her when he did she would have bled to death.

Though she was in ICU Bob was allowed to sit with her. He watched as she laid in the bed, looking so small and fragile-though he knew it wasn't true; the doctor said she'd put up a hell of a fight. *Bastards,* he silently fumed. *Whoever did this to her is my next job,* he silently vowed. It didn't matter that she was a stranger; she was a kid, and no kid deserved this. Especially not a girl. A girl who reminded him so much of-

Suddenly he heard coughing, and he sprang up from his chair. Before he could call out for a nurse the girl opened her eyes and looked up at him in confusion.

"It's okay," he told her. "You're in the hospital. I'm going to get a nurse, okay?"

She managed to shake her head. "Water," she rasped.

Bob picked up the pitcher and filled a small cup, gently lifting it to her lips. She drank a few sips and pulled back when she was finished. Then her eyes abruptly went down toward her neck.

Bob pulled the necklace out of his pocket he found laying next to her in the boxcar. The clasp had been broken on the silver chain but the locket remained in tact, with the initials "C.B." engraved on the back. "You're C.B.?" he asked, carefully laying the necklace in her palm.

She managed a nod. "Charlie," she croaked out. "Booker."

"It's nice to meet you, Charlie Booker. I'm Bob Holden, and I'm the one who found you."

A shadow quickly crossed her face. "They wouldn't stop...tried to run...they caught me..."

"It's okay now," he soothed. "You're safe."

She nodded. "Got...what they wanted. Won't...bother me...again."

"Bother?" Bob repeated in disbelief.

"We're even now," she explained, squeezing her eyes shut as she adjusted herself on the bed. "Owed them money." She opened her eyes and looked up at him. "My fault," she whispered.

It all made sense. The girl looked as if she'd been living on the street and hadn't had a decent meal in ages. Bob knew how the city worked for the homeless. *Borrow and steal to survive,* he thought bleakly. *You get a loan from a punk, you can't pay him back so he takes it out of your hide, beats you to a bloody pulp.* "You listen to me, Miss Booker," he said, pulling up a chair. "No matter who you owe, this-" he gestured to her injuries "-is never okay. Understand?"

She shook her head. "I'm not a good person," she blurted.

"Why? Because you borrow from thugs to survive? That doesn't make you a bad person, Charlie. That makes you a survivor."

The nurse came in then and stated that Charlie needed her rest. As she left Bob walked over to Charlie. "Can you do me a favor?" She nodded. "Give me their names." Charlie stiffened. "Please," he told her. "Nothing bad will happen to you if you tell me. I promise."

After a moment's hesitation she spoke up. "The only name I know is Rocky, Rocky Westover. The others were his...enforcers."

Bob nodded. "Okay. Get some rest. I'll come check on you tomorrow."

"Thank you," she told him sincerely. "For helping me...saving my life."

"You're welcome," he told her. "Get some rest now."

After he left Bob took out his phone and punched in a familiar number. "It's me. Give me everything you can on a Rocky Westover."

***

Bob went back to the hospital the following evening to find Charlie awake after sleeping most of the day. He knew she was on painkillers but seemed to be coherent enough to talk. Before he could say anything she started telling him everything about her life, and he listened patiently. Bob was astonished by everything she'd been through in the short eighteen years of her life. He interjected now and again with questions, trying to put it all together.

"Normally I don't open up like this," Charlie told him once she'd finished. "But I am on all kinds of meds, and you did save my life..." Her expression sobered. "You asked me who did this," she said, her hazel eyes intense. "I want to know why."

"If I tell you the truth you won't believe me," he told her. "I'll tell you when you're stronger, you have my word. Right now you need to focus on healing."

"One more question then." She paused. "Why are you so interested in me?"

"That I can answer. You remind me of my daughter," he told her simply. "The rest can wait till later."

"You're not obligated to keep visiting me," she told him quietly.

"Don't look at it as obligation. It's more of-" He broke off.

"What?"

"Making up for the past."

Weeks went by and Charlie began to heal: her bruises began to fade and she started to get stronger. Bob was a frequent visitor, her only visitor, and they spent their time talking or playing cards. Charlie enjoyed talking to him. It was completely ridiculous…but it was what she imagined having a father would be like.

She knew he was probably just substituting her for his daughter but she didn't care; it felt good to have someone around. Bob talked about his childhood, his education, and what kind of music and television he liked but he never mentioned his daughter in further detail or what he did for a living.

He did, however, offer her a place to stay when it was time for her to be released. His sister, Rita, had an apartment near him and when she heard about Charlie she immediately wanted to help. Rita was divorced and had a son in college, so she had the room.

Charlie was overwhelmed by their kindness but didn't hesitate; reaching out to her the way they did reminded her of Melinda.

She still had a cast on her left arm but she could walk, and with a little help from a nurse makeup hid the worst of the healing bruises on her face. Bob was there to pick up Charlie as soon as the discharge papers were signed and they went straight to Rita's apartment, where she was immediately fussed over and cooked a nice, hot meal of homemade lasagna and garlic bread. Charlie hadn't had anything homemade or any hearty, substantial food for that matter since she'd lived with her mother.

Rita was a lot like Bob, just as kind and reassuring. She was six or seven years younger than him, about forty-five and talked a lot about her son, Jack, who was away at Columbia. She was very warm and hospitable, helping Charlie get set up in what was to be her room after dinner. In all the fuss Charlie could almost forget her questionable past and just pretend to be an ordinary kid. She also decided it was time to wean herself off smoking, a habit she'd wanted to kick as soon as it started three years ago. Now it felt like she could.

That feeling didn't last long. Charlie woke up screaming that night after dreaming about the attack. She also slept fitfully-as usual-haunted by her numerous mistakes and bad choices, as well as the recurring nightmare she'd had since she was a kid but always woke up forgetting.

In the days that followed Rita wanted to talk to her about it but Charlie wasn't used to divulging information from her personal life, though she felt as comfortable with Rita as she did with Bob. She did confide, however, that she'd only finished up through ninth grade in school, having quit when she disappeared off the radar of children services after Melinda's death. She also admitted her love of reading to Rita, who showed Charlie her book collection and told her she was welcome to it any time. She also told Charlie about free tutoring offered at a community center downtown, and the option of getting her GED if she was interested.

For the next several weeks Charlie spent most of her time at the community center receiving tutoring. Though she'd been out of school for a while she'd always had a quick mind and was a fast learner, soaking up information as though she were a sponge. She planned to take the GED test at the end of the year. Her other goal was to find a way to pay Rita and Bob back for all they'd done for her as soon as possible.

A month passed and Bob took Charlie out for coffee one night, Charlie sensing that he had something important to share with her. It turned out she was right; he finally wanted to talk about his daughter, and his job.

"I wanted to give you a chance to get settled in," he began, pouring sugar into his steaming mug. "But now I think it's time I lay all my cards out on the table. I know almost everything about you now, so I think it's only fair that I tell you everything about me.

"You know I grew up here in Brooklyn. I went to college and met my sweetheart, Izzy. We got married after we graduated, and I got my first job in the corporate world. Two years later we had Michelle, or Shelley as we called her.

"Shelley was bright, talented, and incredibly intelligent but I'm ashamed to admit that I didn't always have a lot of time for her. I always so focused on work, on getting ahead, that I neglected my family. So much so, that when Shelley was sixteen she ran away.

"Izzy and I were frantic, going to the police and starting searches; we even offered a reward. I did everything in my power to find her, though I had little in the way of connections or resources. Six months passed...and she was found in the river." His voice broke slightly. "No one knew the details of what happened and Izzy and I fell apart.

"I couldn't let it go; I had to find out what really happened. I became obsessed, eventually driving Izzy away. But I couldn't stop. So I went looking for help, and I found it a year later. I met a man who told me about his line of work. He had resources, connections...and he offered to train me, teach me the same line of work so I could get the answers I needed. It took time, but I learned and we worked together until we found out the truth. We found out who was responsible."

"Did you track them down?" Charlie asked in interest.

Bob nodded. "Charlie...I'm a bounty hunter," he confessed.

She could only stare at him. "You're a...what?"

"A bounty hunter," he repeated. "For the past ten years, people have hired me to find
people, and they pay me when I deliver. I paid the man who trained me."

"Not that I know a lot about staying inside the law or having wholesome values or anything...but is that legal, exactly?"

Bob shrugged. "No different than any other under-the-table job I guess. And I use discretion when choosing a job. I do have limits, boundaries I won't cross."

Charlie thought about that for a moment. "What did you do?" she asked finally. "When you found those men?"

"Brought them in to the authorities, believe it or not," Bob told her. "Although it took
everything in me not to-" He broke off with great effort. "But it's not always that heavy. People hire me to find a roommate who bailed and skipped out o rent or a deadbeat behind on child support, or even someone who backed out of a corporate deal. I have all the resources and connections I need, just like my trainer did. I'm good at what I do because I had a good teacher; the man I met really felt for me. He also became a good friend, and didn't just help me with work-he also helped me to stop being so consumed with guilt. And that's something you'll have too learn someday."

Charlie flinched at his words but let them slide; she had other things to digest. "That's why you want to know who beat me up," she said slowly. "You wanted to find them."

"I did find them," he told her quietly. "That's why I'm telling you all of this now. You say the word and I'll bring them right to you."

Charlie frowned. "But I'm not a paying customer-"

"This one's on the house," he assured her. "You might've been a stranger then but I used to be a father and when I saw you that night-" his face darkened "-all I saw was someone's daughter."

"Except I'm not," she pointed out softly. Then she cleared her throat. "I don't know what to do," she told him honestly. "I'm no judge, jury, or executioner. Yes, I'm angry, yes, I went through a nightmare...but I wasn't an innocent girl stalked by a predator. It wasn't a random crime; it was business. It's no different than the bank taking back your house when you can't pay the mortgage. I borrowed money, I couldn't pay it back-not for the first time either-and they collected."

"They nearly killed you," Bob reminded her quietly.

"And then they went home to the families they have to support. That's the way it works, Bob."

"It doesn't have to be that way for you anymore. You have options now. But even so...beating on a teenage girl-legal adult or not-is a crime in my book, period. And if you want you have the chance to get justice, make sure the cycle stops."

"I'll think about it," she promised quietly.

"I can accept that." He paused. "Can I ask you something?"

"Sure."

"You borrowed money often, right?" Charlie nodded. "Was it for more than just to live?"

Again, she nodded. "But it wasn't for drugs or anything like that. It was to fund my search, to find Anna. I want to know where I came from, find out who I am."

Bob nodded thoughtfully. "When do you take your test?"

"My GED test? The end of the year. Why?" she asked curiously.

"Talk to me then and I'll tell you," he promised.

***

"I know you'd pass," Bob told Charlie proudly. "And I knew it wouldn't take you to the
end of the year either." He raised his glass, clinking it with Charlie's and Rita's.

It was September, two months after Charlie had come to live with Rita, and a month after Charlie's conversation with Bob at the coffee shop. Charlie passed her GED test after studying relentlessly, and Rita cooked a large meal to celebrate, acting the whole time just like a proud parent. She took pictures of Charlie holding her certificate and bragged on her all through dinner.

After helping with the cleanup, Charlie and Bob sat on the small balcony, looking up at the stars. "I have an offer for you," he told her after a while, "one you don't have to take me up on but it's something to consider. Rita's not fond of the idea-to put it mildly-but you're old enough to make your own decisions."

"What's up?" Charlie asked curiously.

"Now that you have your GED you could go on to college, and since you've said you see me as a surrogate father that's what I should encourage," he told her. "But you're not a typical eighteen-year-old, in any way. You've done a lot of living, experienced horrors most people can't imagine. It's made you tough, and it's made you smart. Add that to the stellar intellect you already have…and you'd be a natural."

"At what?"

"At what I do."

Charlie focused on him, making sure she'd heard him correctly. "You think I should be…a bounty hunter?"

"I think you could be anything," he told her honestly. "I'm suggesting this because you're quick, you've got great instincts, and you can take care of yourself. Everything I'd look for in a partner."

Charlie just stared at him.

"I'm not getting any younger," he explained. "I'm going to need someone I can trust as my right-hand…and I'd like it to be you."

"You're serious," Charlie said in disbelief.

Bob studied her carefully. "People don't get into this line of work without a good reason. It's usually the people who've experienced nightmares firsthand, who know they'll never be able to fit comfortably in a regular nine-to-five gig. I had a horrific event in my life that changed me…and this is all I know now, this is the life I want to lead, giving people what I needed before I had the experience. And you…you've had a rough go of it in life, had to learn very early on that you have to have money to survive. This will get that for you, and open the door to anything you want: school, travel, a career in a specialized field suited for your skills. But, most importantly, it'll pay for your search and give you access to resources you didn't have before, help you establish life-long contacts that'll come in handy no matter what you decide to do. Afterward you can go on, maybe into a special ops job or for an agency...or earn enough to solve the mysteries of your past, go to some island, and lay on the beach all day, finally able to have fun and enjoy life without having to worry about survival. The possibilities are endless. But it's your choice. You can go in a completely different direction; I know you'll do well in anything you choose. You have Rita's and my unlimited support, no matter what you decide."

Charlie tried to digest everything he'd just told her. "You've briefly told me about what you do...but I still don't know what all it involves. Other than you mentioning the term the only time I ever heard it used was in the movies or on TV. I never knew it was something people really did...and if I had, I would've imagined-"

"Bottom-feeders?" Bob suggested. "Greasy men who lived in the gutter, parasites, criminals who broke the law?"

"No," she told him hastily. "You just seem so nonchalant about it, and even though Rita's not a big fan of it she does too."

"What do you think about it?"

"Honestly? I like the sound of it," she confessed. "It's definitely outside the box, unusual, and it does seem well-suited for someone who's had a less than ordinary life," she told him. "Like you...and like me."

"Are you saying you're accepting my offer?"

"I'm saying I'm trying to figure out how lucky one person can be," she said finally. "I had Anna, Melinda found me and became my mom, you and Rita treat me like family...maybe my life hasn't been a complete crap hole after all." She shook her head. "I know it'll sound corny...but I never thought anyone but Melinda would ever believe in me. So thanks, for proving me wrong." She gave him a hug.

"Anytime," he said, patting her on the back.

The next morning, as Charlie was getting dressed, Rita came in to talk to her. Rita was an attractive woman, with the same dark hair and eyes as her older brother. Rita and Bob were Italian on their mother's side, which explained Rita's chef-like abilities, and accounted for them
using that language when they argued. Charlie noticed they'd been doing it a lot more often lately, and was pretty sure she knew what it was about.

"My brother's a good man," she said bluntly, sitting on the edge of the bed while Charlie brushed out her long, bleached-blonde hair, "and a good big brother. He's been a hard worker all his life, he loves his family, and he's a lot more generous than he'd like to believe. He's decent, loyal, and keeps his promises, which is a rare thing these days. But there are some who don't believe that, who label him a criminal based on his profession all because he's taken a path few could understand, because they don't know where he comes from, where he's been. I do, which is why he's always had my support. I will stand by him and defend him as long as I have breath in me." She looked up from the edge of the pillow sham she'd been playing with, eyeing Charlie. "That being said, while I accept him I don't always approve of everything he does, the danger he puts himself him that I deem unnecessary. I also don't approve of his decision to extend this job-this lifestyle-to an eighteen-year-old girl who's seen her share of violence, trials, and heartache for a lifetime."

Charlie avoided Rita's eyes as she fastened her necklace around her neck.

"Bob tells me you've made a decision," Rita told her quietly. "About working with him."

"I have." Charlie walked to the closet to grab a pair of boots.

"I suppose it wouldn't do any good to try and talk you out of it, would it?"

Charlie shook her head, still not meeting Rita's eyes.

"It's not just your safety that you'll have to worry about," Rita warned. "There's a certain stigma that follows the job description. You'll be segregated, criticized, and you'll have to develop what Bob has termed his 'own code of ethics and morals', instead of always following the law. You'll have to be careful not to get caught and-" She broke off, looking at Charlie worriedly.

Charlie walked over to her, finally meeting her gaze. "You've been so kind, opening up your home to a complete stranger and treating me like family. I don't want to disappoint you, or do anything to upset you...but I need to do this, Rita." She laced up her boots.

"May I ask why?"

Charlie sat next to her on the bed. "You said whenever I felt comfortable opening up to you about my life and my past I could. I wasn't ready then, but I think I am now." She took a breath. "When I was sixteen I lost my virginity to a guy twenty years older than me, whose name I didn't even know, in exchange for a place to sleep one night. It was the middle of December, snowing like crazy...I couldn't make it in the park like usual and I had no money for a motel. And it went downhill from there. I've had sex for food, clothes, a place to crash, even antibiotics when I got sick once. I'm not proud of it; I hated it. I spent a long time feeling guilty and ashamed...so I started borrowing money from guys like Rocky. I didn't have any skills to get a job; I only had a ninth grade education. I did manage to get a job as a waitress once but it didn't last long because of cutbacks. I did what I had to do to survive...and I want it to be different now. I've hardly ever had anything normal, Rita. I've never-" She broke off. "It was different when I had Melinda. I finally had what other people had: a family. Also a roof over my head, an education, friends, even a few dates. But after she died I lost all of it; I had to go back to what I knew best: my survival skills. I want a chance to have more...and working with Bob can do that. You know he'll look out for me if I need it, and I can use it as a stepping stone: save up for college, see the world, maybe even meet someone someday, if he doesn't mind damaged goods. This is my shot. I want to take it." She paused. "And I think it's safe to say that I haven't exactly been living on the right side of the law the past few years anyway."

Rita just looked at her. "You deserve to have a shot," she told her softly. "More than anyone I know. And I love my brother, respect him very much and always admired the courage and strength it takes to do what he does...even if I don't always approve. So if you're sure this is what you want, then this is what you should do. I'm not your mother, and would never try to replace her...but I love you just the same."

Charlie wrapped her arms around her. "Thanks for understanding," she told her, squeezing her eyes shut. "I can't be that sixteen-year-old girl again. I won't."

"I don't want you to be," Rita said as she started to pull back. "I want you to be free."

"I am. And don't worry; I'm used to criticism and segregation," Charlie assured her with a small grin. "I'm a former street urchin, remember?"

Rita hit her on the arm playfully. "You're a lot more than that," she told her softly.

Charlie left shortly after and met Bob in town a couple of hours later at a diner, drinking the coffee he ordered for her. "We have a job," he greeted her, sliding a manila folder across the table. "His name's Dwayne Curtis," he continued as she began to look through it. "His ex-wife hired us to track him down. He got the summer home in the divorce, she got the boat."

"Let me guess. He took the boat too?"

Bob nodded. "You in?"

Charlie closed the folder. "I'm in."

Bob lifted his mug. "Welcome aboard."
Charlie grinned, lifting hers as well.

Chapter Two

Queens, Present Day

Josh ran up the second flight of stairs, breathing heavily. As though he needed a reminder that he was out of shape, his breath started coming in short gasps and his sides ached from the exercise his body wasn't use to receiving. When he got to the second floor he took off down the hall, sneaking a glance behind him as he ran and keeping his ears open for the sound of rapid footsteps other than his own.

He hastily unlocked the door to his apartment when he reached it, running in and quickly re-locking it behind him. He leaned against it, closing his eyes and trying to catch his breath, relieved by his narrow escape.

"Don't you just love fire escapes?"

His eyes flew open and he saw his pursuer seated calmly on the couch, smiling at him pleasantly. "You really should close your window next time," she added sweetly.

Josh groaned, burying his face in his hands. "What do you want from me?" he mumbled.

"You know exactly what I want, Mr. Crawford, or you wouldn't have ran," she replied, standing. "I've been instructed by your former business partner to give you these papers to sign, dissolving the partnership." She held out a thin leaflet of paper.

"Who are you?" Josh demanded.

"I'm Charlie Booker, and Mr. Allen hired me to persuade you to do the right thing and walk away. If you sign these right now he gives his word that all of it will stop: the phone calls, the threats, the invasions into your personal life. It's up to you."

"Up to me?" Josh echoed in disbelief. "None of this is up to me! It's my company too, and he's forcing me out!"

"After you embezzled thousands of dollars in the middle of a recession, violated the agreement you signed going into the partnership, and hassled his family to get to him," Charlie reminded him. "You failed to show when his lawyers summoned you, so he resorted to your kind of tactics-making your life miserable. When that didn't work, he hired me."

"Why you?" Josh sneered, reaching behind him with his free hand to grab a football-shaped paperweight off a shelf. "You look younger than my sister."

"He hired me because I'll get the job done, one way or another." She walked up to him until they were inches apart. "You have two choices, Mr. Crawford. Sign the papers now and finally get some peace or refuse, and I deliver you to Mr. Allen himself. And I can assure you, there will be nothing pleasant about the experience."

"Is that so?" Josh's hand closed around the object and tried to swing it forward, aiming toward Charlie's head, but he didn't get that far; Charlie quickly reached out and punched him in the nose, following with a kick to the stomach.

"Bitch!" he yelled, doubling over. "You broke my nose!"

"I told you, I'll get the job done one way or another." Charlie bent down to his level. "Now I suggest you take this-" she held up a pen "-and give me your John Hancock or Mr. Allen will break a lot more than your nose." When Josh didn't move she shrugged. "It doesn't matter to me what you decide; I get paid either way. But I'd like to be finished with this before the sun comes up."

Josh winced as he straightened up, groaning loudly. "Fine," he grunted, snatching the pen from her fingers.

After he signed the documents Charlie tucked them in her leather jacket and backed toward the window. "You made a good call. Mr. Allen wants to pass along his insistence that you stay away from his him, his family, and the company. If you don't...you'll be hearing from me again." She nodded briskly before hopping out of the window.

The drive home to Brooklyn went by quickly enough as she sped along on her Harley Sportster, enjoying the crisp, clear night. Driving the bike on a night like this was one of her favorite things to do, making her want to push the envelope until she felt like she was flying in the moonlight.

It was after midnight when Charlie finally got back to her apartment, collapsing on the couch with a groan. *Another eventful day of chasing bottom-feeders,* she thought as she closed her eyes. *Awesome as usual.* She heaved a long sigh and got back up, heading toward the bathroom.

After showering she studied her reflection in the mirror, carefully looking at the latest scar she'd acquired from the slight injury she had the week before. This one, unlike some of the others, was quite noticeable and wouldn't be hidden since it was right under her chin. She was used to it, however, adding to all the others she'd accumulated over her lifetime.

She towel-dried her wet, coppery locks, grateful that it had finally gown back past her shoulders after the mistake of a bob she got several years ago. After a long time of being a chameleon, she'd finally settled on red, keeping it that way for the past two years. Then she stopped combing out the tangles, realizing she was thinking about her hair like a frivolous female...all to avoid what she dreaded thinking about instead.

Never able to sleep right away after finishing a job, Charlie took a six-pack and turned on the TV, watching but not really paying attention. A few hours later she was finally able to turn in, crawling under the silky sheets of her large four-poster bed and closing her eyes. *Three fifteen,* she thought. *Not too bad when it's usually six a.m.*

After a fitful five hours Charlie woke up, lingering feelings of uneasiness all that she remembered of her disconnected, disturbing dreams. She got out of bed, quickly dressing in her active wear on her way to the kitchen, where she made her usual protein shake and granola. Afterward she left the apartment for her daily run.

Her run usually consisted of two miles at a nearby park, though this morning she felt more energized than normal and made it three.

She cranked up her ipod in an effort to drown out all the conflicting thoughts and uneasy feelings about the day ahead, pushing herself onward.

After her shower Charlie called Mr. Allen to let him know the situation had been handled and that she'd fax the documents to his office. Mr. Allen, however, requested she deliver them in person so he could pay her fee. Surprised at his thoughtfulness, Charlie promised to stop by late that afternoon.

She spent the remainder of the morning in her office-which was the spare room across the hall from her bedroom-catching up on paperwork and sorting files. She had a unique system of keeping everything in order, knowing someone could never be prepared for the information
needed at a later date. She also had a catalog of all her contacts and resources, which she kept in a lock-box.

As she was finishing up her eye caught the framed photos, one on each side of her desktop: the one on the left was the one of her and Melinda at Disney World when she was a young teenager, and the other was of Rita, herself, and Bob standing in front of the main building at NYU. Charlie was in her cap and gown holding up her diploma, flanked by Rita and Bob on each side who had their arms around her shoulders and were grinning as broadly as she'd been.

Her insides clenching, Charlie picked up the photo and thought back to her time at NYU. It had taken her five years to save up enough to enroll for online classes, and Bob and Rita were both thrilled when she did. She still worked to pay for books and ongoing expenses, including rent for her apartment. She'd only imposed on Rita for three years-she couldn't do it for any longer than that-and it was an interesting challenge, to say the least. *College student by day, bounty hunter by night,* she thought ruefully. *I bet no other student could put that on a résumé.*
When she graduated last year she thought everything would change...and it had. Just not in the way she anticipated.

After lunch-turkey on wheat-she changed out of her ripped jeans and T-shirt and into black dress pants and a deep blue button down shirt. Throwing on her leather jacket-despite the fact that it was early July-she went downstairs to hail a cab, not exactly dressed to drive the bike.

While stuck in traffic her phone rang and Charlie answered, already knowing who it would be. "Hey Jack," she greeted him, watching as the cars started to move again. Jack Larson was Rita's son, the one who'd been away at college and whose room Charlie had taken over. Over the years she and Jack had gotten very close, their relationship being what Charlie imagined a brother/sister relationship to be. When Jack got married Charlie had been a bridesmaid, and when Charlie graduated college he'd taken all the pictures.

"Charlie." He sighed. "Is there any way we can just skip today?"

"It'd be nice," she told him. "But I don't think it works that way."

"It's hard to believe, isn't it? That this is all really happening."

"It is," she agreed. "Even though we knew…it still felt abrupt. How's Megan doing?"

"Better," Jack answered. "Now that she's out of her first trimester there's no more morning sickness, which she's thrilled about. She had a checkup yesterday and everything's good."

"Good to hear. Tell her we'll start planning the baby shower whenever she's ready." Charlie paused. "Have you heard from him?"

Jack laughed bitterly. "The bastard actually called this morning and wanted to know where he could send a bottle of wine, as if it's some kind of party." He let out a long breath, as if trying to calm himself down. "Some father," he muttered. Then he cleared his throat. "Are you almost here?"

"Almost. I'll see you in fifteen," Charlie promised, then hung up.

The cab dropped her off at 2012 Vanden Court and Charlie started up the narrow sidewalk, looking warily at the large building in front of her. She pushed open the glass door with the words *Harmon & Morris* printed across in white lettering, and the receptionist escorted her down the hall.

Charlie walked into a large room with picture windows and a solid oak table with high-backed chairs surrounding it. Jack and Megan were sitting at the far end, gripping hands while the lawyer sat across from them, looking over his paperwork. Suddenly they were obscured from Charlie's view, when someone blocked her way and caused a shadow to fall over her.

Charlie hugged Bob wordlessly, squeezing her eyes shut for a long moment. When she let go they walked toward the table, their arms around each other's waists.

"Now that everyone's here we'll get started," Rita's lawyer, Mr. Parkman, addressed the group when everyone had been seated. "Mrs. Larson's will is fairly straightforward. She didn't own any property, and her bank account was drained due to her...medical expenses over the past year. She left her car to her brother, Robert Holden, and her personal items-family photos and keepsakes-to her son, John R. Larson and his wife, Megan Hunter Larson. There are several pieces of jewelry she left to who she named her surrogate daughter, Charlotte Booker. The rest is detailed in the letters she left for each of you." He stood, passing the letters out.

    Charlie opened her envelope, pulling out a letter that contained Rita's elegant script.

Taking a deep breath, she began to read:

June 2010

Charlie,
    It's so hard to believe it's been ten years next month since you walked through my front door and into my family. You were so young and yet so old at the same time; everything you'd been through aged you past your years. But I still saw the girl inside, the girl who just wanted a place to be safe and for someone to want her. What I didn't realize was what I was missing too-I didn't know I had an emptiness inside me over all the regrets I had in my life, not until you filled it. We healed each other, you and I, in a way that made us family. And like any mother, I've been so proud of you. You've grown into a wonderful woman, and though I was never crazy about the line of work you and my brother share you're very good at what you do and you've helped a lot of people.

    I know you had plans after you graduated. You wanted to change your career, go in a new direction, and take me to Europe to celebrate. You also told me you decided to give up your search into your past for answers because you were perfectly content with your life and felt incredibly lucky to have found another mother in me...so you felt there was no point in going back. But then I was diagnosed with lymphoma and you abandoned all your plans to help me. You and Bobby both worked overtime, taking on dangerous jobs, to help me financially. And while I'm grateful to you both it was such a large sacrifice, particularly for you. I don't want you to give up on your dreams, Charlie. You have the opportunity now to break free and do anything and everything that you want. You can go to Europe or the tropics, travel the country, or use your hard-earned education to do things you never would've thought possible ten years ago. It's time to go out and make yourself happy.

I'm leaving you my mother's bracelet, the silver-and-turquoise one you always admired, along with all of the trinkets and treasures you and I accumulated over the years. I wish I had the money I always meant to leave all of you but...well, you know what happened. But I do have one more thing for you, something I hope you'll seriously consider.

A couple of months ago I found out about a man, a P.I., who specializes in finding biological relatives. He might be able to help you find out who your parents were or at least why there's no record of your birth. I know you wanted to let it go but everyone deserves to know where they came from. Just think about it, alright? It doesn't change anything between you and me; nothing ever could. Take care of yourself, sweetheart, and live the best life you can live. Thank you for all that you have done for me but mostly, thank you for walking into my life.
Love you always,
Rita

Tears were flowing freely down Charlie's face by the time she finished, lowering the hand-written pages. Then she noticed something else in the envelope: a small white card covered in more of Rita's writing:

T.J. Mackenzie
Mackenzie Investigations
2142 Marcus Blvd., Manhattan

Charlie replaced the card and the letter in the envelope and tucked it inside her jacket. After they'd all finished reading-looking as devastated as Charlie felt-Mr. Parkman continued with the will, covering all the legal aspects. Charlie wasn't listening, however; all she could do was stare at the envelope and think about everything Rita had written.

Since no one lived nearby they decided to go to a small coffee house two blocks over, not yet ready to separate. At first no one said much as they all stared into their mugs but finally Jack broke the silence by talking about the time he wanted to be a superhero when he was a child, complete with the cape-and the ability to fly.

"I tied a towel around my shoulders like a cape and climbed up on the railing on the back porch, thinking if I believed it enough I'd be able to fly like Superman.," he began with a smile, remembering. "Mom came out just in time before I plummeted off the third story of the apartment we lived in then. She grounded me for a week and took all my comics away; I'd never seen her so mad. Finally, when she calmed down, she told me why it had upset her so much-that she couldn't stand the thought of ever losing me." His smile faded. "And now we've lost her," he said softly. Megan reached over and squeezed his hand.

Jack's story prompted others from everyone at the table. Charlie especially liked hearing Bob's stories of when he and Rita were kids; she liked trying to imagine what Rita had been like as a child. According to Bob, she'd been just as fearless, just as fiercely protective and determined as she had been as an adult. Charlie didn't expect anything less.

Pretty soon the conversation drifted to babies, sobering Jack and Megan who were both devastated that their child would never get to know its grandmother. Megan announced, however, that if the child turned out to be a girl she would inherit her grandmother's name.

As Charlie looked around the table she felt incredibly grateful to be a part of this family. Though she didn't share their DNA, none of them had ever made her feel like that mattered.
Especially Rita, who'd gone out of her way to include Charlie and give her the love and support she never expected to have again.

An hour later they left the coffee shop, and after an emotional good-bye with Jack and Megan, Bob and Charlie headed to the park. Sitting side-by-side on a bench they stared out at the water, watching the ducks swim across the lake. "Punch in the gut today, wasn't it?" Bob asked after a while, still staring ahead.

Charlie nodded. "Definitely." She let out a long sigh. "I really wish we'd gotten to go to Europe like we planned," she said softly. "She was so excited about it-" She broke off. "Did you know she found a P.I. for me?" she asked abruptly. "Thought it would help in the search."

"No I didn't." Bob looked at her, clearly surprised. "I thought you decided not to keep-"

"I did. But Rita thought I deserved to know the truth."

"A P.I. though?" Bob frowned. "Between the two of us we have extensive resources, lots of connections. We weren't able to find much of anything."

"Apparently this guy's supposed to be special," Charlie told him with a shrug. "Besides, we mostly focused our search on Anna. This is a more direct route."

"Your birth parents?" Bob looked thoughtful. "I wonder why she didn't say anything to me."

"Oh I don't know. Maybe because you can't keep your trap shut around me," she said wryly, giving him a half-smile. Then her expression sobered. "The last thing we talked about was me letting it go...then she mentions it in her letter, about why I told her why I wanted to stop looking. How many mothers do people get in a lifetime? Usually one. I had two, three if you count Anna, though I barely remember her. Why should I go looking for another one?"

"Because it's about more than just tracking down your biological mother," Bob replied. "Or your biological father. It's about answers, Charlie. It's about finding out why you ended up with Anna in the first place and why she disappeared because it caused the chain of events that led you to that boxcar and me finding you-" He stopped. "Yes, you had good sprinkled in along the way: Melinda, becoming family to Rita, Jack, and me, making a life for yourself, getting a college education...but you've also had a lot of unnecessary heartache and were deprived of stability and a decent childhood. Don't you want to know why?"

Charlie considered it a moment, all the horrors she faced at such a young age. As hard as she tried to move past all the things that had happened there was no denying how much easier she used to think it would be if she had something definite to blame it all on. Now that she was older she realized it wasn't about blame exactly, but it would be nice to be able to hold someone or some event accountable. "Yes," she admitted finally. "I guess I do." She let out a long sigh. "I guess I'm heading to Manhattan tomorrow."

"Good. Let me know about this guy, see if he knows about more than catching cheating husbands."

"I will," she promised. "I know what to look for."

They stayed a while longer, until Charlie realized she needed to get going. "Mr. Allen wants me to deliver his paperwork in person," she explained, standing. "I've got a lot to take care of before then, other jobs I'm wrapping up, so I need to get a move on."

Bob rose also, giving her a hug. "Just remember, you do have family, kid. No matter what happens."

"I know. And I couldn't ask for a better one." Charlie pulled back. "Heading back to Brooklyn?"

Bob nodded. "Final things to take care of, then I'm meeting Jack and Megan back at my apartment later, probably some time this evening. You'd be invited too but I know how busy you get these days."

"Maybe I wouldn't be if someone hadn't retired and could share the client load," Charlie said in mock annoyance.

"You'd really want a sixty-one-year-old partner?"

"If it's you? In a heartbeat." Then she shook her head. "I'm just giving you a hard time. After twenty years of this you definitely deserve to be free. Go lay around on an island somewhere," she told him. "Someone I know suggested that to me once."

That caused him to smile. "Maybe one day I will."

When she got home she took advantage of the time she had to finish up what she'd started earlier. She was trying to finish up everything so her plate would be empty once she saw Mr. Allen, giving her time to focus all her attention on seeing the P.I. and starting up the search again. After a couple of hours she was ready to take the documents over to Mr. Allen. As she was leaving the downstairs lobby, something caught her eye.

A small package had been stuffed into her mailbox.

Charlie walked over, checking the postmark. It was local, but there was nothing else on it to indicate who had sent it. She quickly ripped into the package, her curiosity piqued.

The first thing she saw was a bright pink feather. Frowning, Charlie pulled the item from the box to discover it was a long, pink feather boa. There was another still stuffed into the box, only it was yellow.

Charlie just stared at the boas for a long moment, images flashing through her mind. She pulled out the small card, knowing who it was from before she even read it:

For our trip overseas, we'll look perfectly sophisticated in these...ha ha. I got them because of that day, do you remember? When I first I had treatment and was afraid of losing my hair you brought these over along with a bunch of ridiculous wigs and we had a fashion show. That helped me more than anything, just clowning around with you. I know what these doctors are saying...but I don't care. We will go on our trip, and we'll look completely fabulous when we do. Don't worry, you can still have the yellow one since I know how much pink revolts you. This time next month we'll be in Paris!
Love, Rita

The date on the postmark indicated how long ago it had been sent, back when Rita was in the hospital and Charlie was frequently out of town working. *She must've forgot about sending it,* she thought, gingerly fingering the feathers. As she did the memory washed over her, the day Rita had been talking about, and suddenly she knew there was a stop she had to make on the way to see Mr. Allen.

    Charlie had the cab drop her off at Rita's old apartment. She hadn't lived there in quite some time; when she wasn't in the hospital she'd moved in with Bob. But for Charlie this place would always be her home, the first home she had since living with Melinda. This was the place that held the most memories.

    After speaking with the super, who she was on a first-name basis with, Charlie found out it had yet to be rented out so he let her inside, leaving to give her privacy. She started walking around the empty rooms, carrying the feather boas she brought with her.

    She stopped in Jack's old room, the room that became her room for three years, leaning against the door frame. She could stare at the spot where the bed once was, remembering her first night in that room and her all talks with Rita. She could still see the concern in Rita's eyes when Charlie told her she decided to work with Bob. She also saw the hope when they'd discussed the possibility of college one day.

    There were memories everywhere, in every room. No matter how much time had passed since she'd actually been in the apartment she could still feel Rita just by being there.

    It was getting time for her to leave, so she walked over to the front door and hung the pink feather boa on the doorknob, wrapping hers tightly around her arm and shutting the door behind her.

Chapter Three

Curtis Allen lived in Breckinridge, in a large estate in a private neighborhood. When Charlie arrived she was promptly escorted by the housekeeper to what appeared to be a parlor.

Charlie had felt out of place every time she'd had to come to Mr. Allen's home; though she made a good living, the Allens were rich enough to make her feel like a pauper. She'd never felt entirely comfortable in posh surroundings. Still, it had been very generous for Mr. Allen to offer to pay her in person; most people sent her checks in the mail and they weren't always on time. Charlie was grateful for his punctuality.

As she waited she thought about the case, about how far Mr. Allen would go to protect his interests. It wouldn't be hard to side with him; Josh Crawford was a piece of work, resorting to ludicrous tactics to keep what he thought belonged to him. But, as a cardinal rule, Charlie never got personally involved in her work, never taking one side or another. She did what she was instructed to, collected payment, and was on her way. The circumstances leading up to it or the consequences afterward were not her concern. *Lesson one from Bob,* she remembered.

A short while later Mr. Allen entered the room, smiling warmly. He was known for being quite the ruthless businessman, but he was also a very charming host as well as a generous benefactor to his employees. "Good afternoon Miss Booker," he greeted her, shaking her hand. "Sorry to have kept you waiting."

"Not a problem sir," she said, sitting down across from Mr. Allen at his insistence. She handed him a folder containing the requested documents.

He looked through them, making sure everything was in order. "I appreciate your diligence," he told her, placing the file on the small table next to him. "You've made this whole...matter a lot easier to deal with. For that, I've included a bonus." He handed her a check. "I also appreciate the fact that I don't have to have an unpleasant...encounter."

"Thank you sir," Charlie told him sincerely, the total figure catching her eye.

He invited her to stay for a drink to celebrate the positive outcome of the job but Charlie politely refused, ready to be on her way. Mr. Allen offered to have a car take her home but Charlie was fine waiting for the cab she called. She did, however, allow Mr. Allen to escort her out.

They stood at the start of the circular drive, Charlie thanking him once again for his kindness, and chatted briefly as they waited. As Charlie listened to him talk about the history behind his estate she noticed something fifty yards away that immediately caught her attention.

An object was catching the sun in the shrubs lining the property, an object that didn't belong. Most people wouldn't have noticed it but it didn't get past Charlie's trained eye. At once she understood.

She turned toward Mr. Allen, thrusting out her arm. "Get down!" she yelled, diving toward him. They both hit the ground and Charlie pulled out her .45, just as shots were fired.

***

After leaving a shaken but unharmed Mr. Allen with his security team, Charlie went after the shooter, who was wounded after Charlie shot him in the shoulder. She ran along the edge of the Allens' property, pleased to see there was nothing but open land on the other side of the bushes, giving someone virtually nowhere to hide.

She followed a blood trail to a pair of trees, surprising the shooter who'd taken a rest. *Amateur,* Charlie thought as she trained her gun on him and he stood, his hands raised. *Which means it's not hard to figure out who hired him.*

It didn't take long for the shooter to confirm what Charlie already knew, that he'd been hired by Joshua Crawford. Naturally Mr. Allen was out for blood and offered Charlie double to track him down. She agreed, but was secretly frustrated that the job wasn't over, silently cursing Crawford.

Since he wasn't the brightest bulb in the chandelier, Crawford's apartment seemed like the first logical place to look. To her surprise Charlie discovered the place was deserted. She used her contacts to find out his bank account had been recently emptied and his landlord reported he skipped out before paying his rent when she questioned him.

By the end of the day Charlie had a good idea where he might be, after some digging. Her hunch took her to Manhattan, and this time she was on her bike, speeding through the crowded streets, weaving in and out of traffic to make good time. She didn't want to give Crawford a chance to wise up and hightail it out of state.

She drove past Central Park to a club on Fifth, owned by one of Crawford's former associates, who was known to give Crawford a hideout whenever he needed it. *And he definitely needs it now,* she mused.

Charlie skipped the main entrance and went around back, spotting a fire escape that led up to a loft above the club. She climbed up carefully and opened the window, her gun ready.

The loft appeared deserted until she got to the kitchen, where a half-eaten pizza was in an open box on the counter. *Still warm,* she thought as she touched the box. *Meaning the squatter is still here.*

Carefully walking down the hallway, Charlie was on complete alert. The guy didn't have to be a genius to be dangerous. She noticed the door at the end of the hall was partway open, and she carefully entered the room.

It too appeared empty. As she inched toward the adjoining bathroom she felt the hair on the back of her neck stand up. She spun around quickly, her gun aimed.

Crawford was aiming a gun of his own, his hands shaking. "You can't leave well enough alone, can you bitch?" he snarled.

"Sorry. I tend to take it personally when someone opens fire in my vicinity." Charlie quickly appraised him. "You and I both know you know less about firearms than a Girl Scout, so
why don't you lower that thing before someone gets hurt?"

"What makes you think I'm not a crack shot?" he countered, making no move to lower his weapon.

"You're practically convulsing, for one," Charlie replied. "And you're a coward. That's why you didn't go after Allen yourself; you sent someone else to do your dirty work, though he was barely more apt for the task than you." She eyed him steadily. "As for me, I can assure you that I'm a hell of a lot better than a crack shot. I've spent twenty hours a week at the shooting range for the past ten years. Not to mention, I've had a few live targets in my line of work…so
let's make this simple. Drop the gun and come quietly or I'll shoot you and you can bleed all the
way to Breckinridge."

"What if I give you a trade?" he asked suddenly. "You let me go and I'll give you what you want most."

Charlie couldn't hide her amusement. "And what, may I ask, is that?"

"To find out who you really are, Charlotte Booker."

Charlie froze. "What did you say?"

"I've asked around," he told her. "I take it personally when someone breaks my nose."

"What is it you think I want to know?" she asked, trying to keep her voice steady.

"First things first. Do we have a deal?"

"You don't know jack," she said irritably. "All you're doing is trying my patience and itching my trigger finger." She moved her gun slightly, aiming at the lamp next to him. When it shattered, Crawford dropped his gun, yelping in surprise.

"Reach for that gun and this time it'll be your forehead," Charlie promised, aiming at him once more. "You have two seconds to spill your guts or I'll bring you back to Allen full of holes."

"Fine!" he yelled. "I heard someone named Jonas talking, said you only got into this business to find out where you came from. That and to punish some sharks who beat the hell out of you when you were a kid."

Charlie felt her breath catch in her throat, but showed no sign of emotion. "Jonas who?"

"I don't know, he just goes by Jonas. He said you had a partner who took care of the guys for you so you wouldn't get your hands dirty, and it freed you up to start poking around. He knows what he knows about you because you tracked down his brother's ex once, and he really admired you. Jonas got curious and wanted to know more…so he started talking about what he did know that night until this old guy working at the bar came up, joined the conversation. He said he overheard what we were saying…and that he knew you."

"You got a name?"

"Stevens," Josh told her. "Just Stevens. What he said was, 'That sounds like my girl, turned out just like I thought she would'. Jonas asked of he was your old man and he just laughed. Before he left he told Jonas to 'never mess with his Ace'."

"Is that all?"

"That's all."

"And how, exactly, does that give me answers to my past?" Charlie demanded.

"Because I remember what bar he works at," Josh replied. "Keg & Ale, on Fourteenth. Across from the old cannery."

Charlie's head was swimming with questions as she delivered Crawford to Mr. Allen, barely even noticing the amount on her bonus check. Mr. Allen thanked her once more, and she nodded, stuffing the check in her pocket. As she turned toward the door she caught a glimpse of Crawford, standing there pale and looking terrified between two of Mr. Allen's employees. She felt no sympathy for him whatsoever and walked away without looking back.

On the way back her mind started working overtime, trying to organize her all her wandering and questioning thoughts. Her first instinct was to bring Bob in on this but ultimately felt it'd be better if she had something substantial to tell him first. After all, she had no reason to
take Crawford seriously; most likely the mysterious bartender would be another dead end.

She was also starting to think about Rocky and his associates, something she hadn't done in a long time, and it was making her queasy. *Just another reason not to feel bad for Joshua Crawford, for opening that old wound,* she thought angrily.

There was still time before last call so Charlie made her way to Keg & Ale straight from Breckinridge, pleased that the crowd was thinning out. To her disappointment, however, the bartender was a woman, who appeared to be about ten years older than her. As Charlie walked over she nodded to her in greeting. "What's your poison?" she asked, wiping down the far end of the bar with a dishcloth.

"Scotch," Charlie replied, taking a seat. As the woman poured it for her Charlie looked around, then turned her attention back to the bartender. "Is there a bartender who works here named Stevens?"

The woman nodded, sliding the drink over to Charlie. "He's on vacation this week."

Charlie slid several bills across the counter. "Could you tell me what you know about him?"

The woman looked at Charlie with interest, pocketing the money. "Are you another ex-wife? You're a lot younger than the last one."

Charlie shook her head. "I'm not an ex-wife. How many are there?"

"Three, that I know about."

"Does he have any children?"

"Not as far as I know." She leaned forward. "Stevens has worked here for several years, longer than I have. He's always been pretty mysterious about his personal life...so of course there are rumors. Some think he was a former agent of some kind because he's got kind of a businesslike manner, really professional. And because he's so secretive. Others think this job is a cover, so he can look like an upstanding citizen when really he's working under the radar, shady business and all. Other than that, his exes showing up demanding alimony are the only eventful things about his life. Everything else is a mystery. He doesn't really talk about much of anything...except once, when he was talking about Charlie."

Charlie froze. "Charlie?" she repeated. *Crawford's not as thick as I thought,* she thought in surprise. *He might've actually come across a decent lead.*

She nodded. "I remember because Stevens never talks to the patrons if he can help it, unless she happens to be wearing a short enough skirt," she said wryly. "But one night some were talking about her and Stevens seemed to know her, or know about her anyway. He said-" She broke off, suddenly understanding. "You're Charlie, aren't you?"

Charlie nodded. "I need to know what Stevens said about me."

"Not much. He called you his girl but the way he said it...he didn't sound like a father exactly. More like a mentor, and you were his protégé. Or something like that. He never mentioned you again."

"Is there any way you can get in touch with him?" Charlie asked quickly, her heart rate accelerating.

"He didn't list any contact information but he did list his address. Mercer Apartments on Madison, a few blocks from here. Oh, and his first name's Andy if it helps."

"It does." Charlie finished her drink and dropped a few more bills on the counter.
"Thanks."

***

It was three a.m. when Charlie broke into Stevens' apartment, moving in carefully. The first thing she noticed was how spotless it was, and how bare. There wasn't even a television in
the living room.

She began to look around, rifling through any papers she came across. *No photos, no keepsakes...nothing. No evidence at all that he has a past or any kind of personal life.*

She searched all the rooms, including one that appeared to be an office. She logged onto the computer but everything was encrypted, and her tech wouldn't be awake at this hour. She settled for turning her attention to the nearby filing cabinet.

Her first thought was that it was all too easy, especially when she discovered the cabinet wasn't locked. She started looking through all the files, not finding anything interesting until she saw the last one.

It was simply labeled "Ace".

Charlie leaned against the wall, opening the manila file folder. She was completely unprepared for all the eight-by-ten photos that fell to the floor, so she bent down quickly to retrieve them. As she started to pick them up she noticed something incredibly familiar: a shot of Melinda's apartment complex. The next one was of Melinda and Charlie at Disney World riding the carousel, taken fifteen years ago.

She hurriedly looked through all the others in shock; they were all surveillance photos, ranging from Charlie as a small child with Anna all the way until now. The most recent was of her exiting the church with Bob, Jack, and Megan after Rita's service.

Suddenly feeling like she was suffocating, Charlie ran out to the balcony to get some air, leaning over the railing and breathing in deeply. Desperately trying to regain control of her spinning-out-of-control mind, she closed her eyes and commanded herself to think like a professional.

I've been under surveillance since I was three or four years old, by someone so good at it that neither Bob or myself noticed it, and tailing and surveillance is an important part of our job. This man obviously has a vested, personal interest in me and refers to me as "Ace".

What the hell does all of it mean?

She went back inside and looked through all of the photos again, focusing on the ones of her with Anna. *I'm probably four in these...which means there's still nothing about before that, who had me then or how Anna got me. But now I have a photo of her, which means I can finally track her down.* She started to fold the photo of the two of them leaving the apartment one morning and tuck it in her jacket when she noticed there was writing on the back:

Marianna with Ace
1987
Placement Terminate

Marianna. I've got a name...and this might be right before Anna disappeared. Charlie stuffed the photo into her jacket, thinking. *He won't miss this...obviously he set all this up for me*

to find, and follow the breadcrumbs like a good little girl. He better believe I'll track him down and when I do...we're going to have a nice long chat about him following me my whole life.

She knew that Bob would want to be in on this, investing just as much time and effort over the years as she had about her search. She also knew he had a lot to deal with right now and that this wouldn't be a small event; it'd take everything he had-just like it would for her-and that was too much to ask of him right now. Also, Stevens was making it personal, focusing on drawing her in; everything was lining up too neatly to think otherwise. *Not to mention, Bob and I are great at what we do. If we couldn't find anything before, it's because there was nothing to find.*

Too exhausted to bother driving home, Charlie checked herself into a motel to try and get at least a few hours of sleep. *I'll see that P.I. Rita recommended a little later, let him start handling the biological relatives part while I start looking for Anna again and go after Stevens. Stevens' better hope I calm down enough not to break both his kneecaps for spying on me and the people I care about for most of my life.*

She settled in the uncomfortable bed, her body letting her know just how much it needed
the rest while her mind continued to tick away, having no intention of slowing down. *I've got to try and turn it off...*

All in all it had been a hell of a day: the reading of Rita's will, the shoot-out at the Allens', having to track down Crawford again, finding out about Stevens and wondering what his connection to her might be...

Basically, just another day at the office.

Chapter Four

"Anna?"

The call was left unanswered in the darkness as Charlie looked around the park desperately. There was no sign of her anywhere, no sign of anyone-

Then she could hear it from far away, the distinct sound of a woman's scream. Charlie knew who it was at once and wanted to go to her, to get her away from the bad people who were making her scream and sound so scared...but she made a promise, a promise she had to keep. Instead of running back she stayed where she was, squeezing her eyes shut as the screams slowly faded away into the night...

Charlie bolted upright, blinking as the morning sunlight poured into the large gaps of the shabby motel blinds, streaming directly into Charlie's eyes. She sat where she was for a moment, breathing rapidly. For the first time she'd actually remembered some of the recurring dream she'd had most of her life, the dream she always assumed had been about Anna and the last time she saw her. Usually the images were so disconnected that they immediately became fuzzy whenever she woke up. *But not this time,* she thought with a shiver, still able to feel the fear and desperation though she was now awake.

Doing her best to shake the disturbing thoughts and images from her mind, she dragged herself out of bed and proceeded to take a shower in the grungy bathroom, standing under the low-pressure trickle of the water. As she bathed her thoughts drifted back to the dream she had, the memory she was starting to remember, giving up on not thinking about it . *Someone had Anna, was taking her away from me...somehow I escaped, even though I was just a little kid. And she was screaming...* If the person responsible turned out to be Stevens, he was a dead man.

She dressed quickly and tucked the card with the P.I.'s name and address on it in her pocket, along with the photo of Anna and herself she'd swiped from Stevens' apartment. Then she left the motel.

After stopping at a smoothie shop for a liquid breakfast, Charlie drove across the city until she found the strip of offices she was looking for. She walked down the shrub-lined sidewalk to the door on the end with silver letting that read *Mackenzie Investigations*.

There was a college-age receptionist with short blonde hair sitting behind a counter, speaking on the phone when Charlie walked in. Charlie walked over, reading the name plate in front of the girl that said "Amber Hunt" and waiting patiently for her to be finished with her call.

"Hi," Amber greeted Charlie a short while later, hanging up the phone and studying Charlie with amusement, who was well aware that it looked like she was wearing yesterday's clothes since they were rumpled and her long hair was still damp. "How can I help you?"

"Someone recommended Mr. Mackenzie to me," Charlie told her, staring back in a way that her know she clearly wasn't intimidated. In fact, disapproving looks from other women was quite the norm for Charlie and she didn't mind in the slightest, especially since she knew she could drop-kick any of them with her eyes closed. "Is there any way I can see him?"

"Your name?" Amber asked professionally.

"Charlotte Booker."

"I'll check." Amber picked up the phone and quickly made the call while Charlie waited, looking around. *Must be nice to be legit enough to have a public office,* she mused. *I could just see what my letterhead would read: "Charlie Booker, Bounty Hunter Extraordinaire".*

"Okay," Amber told Charlie as she hung up. "He'll see you. End of the hall."

Charlie walked down the narrow hallway, noticing the door at the end was slightly ajar. She stood in the doorway and saw a man sitting at a cluttered desk, typing rapidly, and she cleared her throat. "Mr. Mackenzie?"

He looked up from his computer. "Charlotte Booker?" he asked, standing.

She nodded. "But call me Charlie."

He extended his hand. "Nice to meet you, Charlie. I'm Thomas James Mackenzie. But call me T.J."

Charlie shook his hand, then he gestured for her to sit in one of the chairs across from his desk. As she did she was momentarily distracted by his piercing blue eyes. "I hear you specialize in tracking down biological relatives," she began, "and that's what I need."

He nodded, turning his attention back to his computer. "What are your adoptive parents' names? Do you have any idea what agency they used?"

"Actually, my story's not that typical. It's pretty complicated...and pretty unbelievable, to tell you the truth."

"I've got time," he told her. "Start with what you know."

Charlie told him about her earliest memories of Anna, continued on with the basics of her life until now, when she discovered all the photos of her in Stevens' apartment. She gave all the names, dates, and specifics of everything she knew and went on to talk about what she did for a living. She expected some kind of reaction but T.J. just continued to listen, nodding and
making notes on a legal pad as well as typing in the computer.

She also told him how strange she thought it was that with all the resources between Bob and herself that they couldn't come up with anything in ten years and now, suddenly, she stumbled upon answers with little effort. T.J. seemed to agree that Stevens was the key, that he was purposely leaving her clues though neither of them could figure out why, or why now.

T.J. was a credit to his profession; he didn't seemed shocked by any part of her story. *He must get a lot of strange cases,* she mused.

"To recap," he said when she'd finished, "there's no record of your birth that you've found, and you're not a hundred percent sure you were even born in Manhattan. What about the woman who lived across from Anna?"

"Cheryl Finn," Charlie supplied. "She died five years ago; by the time I tracked her down it was too late. She'd moved several times after living at the same apartment complex as Anna. Her only surviving relatives were distant cousins-her son died in Desert Storm. I tried to speak with some of them but no one knew anything about Anna or me." She paused. "Stevens has given me a start when it comes to Anna…but this is a two-person job. Normally I'd ask my partner but he's retired and has a lot to…handle right now. Someone very close to me recommended you, so I thought I'd seek you out and see if you'd be interested. Are you?"

"Absolutely. This could be the most…intriguing case I've ever had," T.J. told her. "With our combined resources we should be able to pull it off."

"I appreciate it." Charlie stood. "It could get a little dicey, so I'm willing to pay double your rate."

T.J. looked at her thoughtfully. "You don't have to pay me double if you do me a favor."

"What's that?" Charlie asked curiously.

"Have dinner with me."

Charlie was completely caught off guard. "Excuse me?"

"Relax," he assured her. "It'd be strictly business. There's a case I'm wrapping up and I could use the input of someone with your skills."

Charlie visibly relaxed. "Oh. Sure, then."

T.J. raised an eyebrow. "Thought I was asking you out, huh?"

"That's what it sounded like," Charlie said defensively. "It wouldn't be entirely ethical, but outside observers think I compromise my ethics every day."

"I doubt that. But then, normal people rarely seem to understand abnormal careers. So. Meet me at Beretti's? It's a little Italian restaurant on Third in the Village. We can also update one another on whatever we find out today."

"Sounds good. But remember, someone's photographing my every move," she reminded him. "Which means they'll get you too."

"I don't mind. I've always wanted to know what it was like on the other end of a camera." He grinned. Then he took out a card and wrote a number on the back. "That's my cell," he said, handing it to her. "Call me if you need to get in touch."

Charlie nodded, pocketing the card. "I will. Thanks for agreeing to work with me, Mr. Mackenzie."

"T.J.," he corrected her. "Mr. Mackenzie is my old man."

Charlie gave a small smile. "Got it. See you tonight...T.J."

"Much better. I enjoyed meeting you, Charlie."

As Charlie left the office she had the strangest feeling that there were underlying innuendos in their conversation, and that possible flirting had somehow taken place. *That's insane,* she chided herself as she got on her bike. *We're both professionals. T.J.'s just a friendly, attractive man and I've been out of the dating world so long I probably think someone performing the Heimlich maneuver would be a way to come on to me. That's all.*

She refocused her energy on searching for Anna, giving Anna's full first name to her contacts and faxing them copies of the old photo. She also sent everything else she managed to procure from Stevens' apartment, getting word out that she wanted to know everything there was to know about Andy Stevens.

Charlie returned home that afternoon, still waiting to hear about the feelers she'd put out. She took another shower, since the one in the motel that morning hadn't done much good, and blow-dried her hair out straight-something she didn't usually do. She walked to her overflowing closet, looking past all her gear and work clothes to try and find something suitable to wear to a nice restaurant. Charlie didn't go out much but when she did it was mostly to casual places: bars, diners, movie theaters. Since she didn't date often, or have business meetings in fancy places, she didn't have a lot of need for dresses.

As she was rifling through the hangers she stopped suddenly, pulling out a deep purple
halter dress she'd completely forgotten about. Rita bought it for her on her twenty-fifth birthday, and Charlie could still hear her saying "every woman should have at least one killer dress". Blinking away tears that pricked the corners of her eyes Charlie stepped into the dress and zipped it up, pleased it still fit. She studied her reflection in the mirror for a long moment before fastening the necklace Melinda gave her around her neck and slipping the bracelet from Rita Jack had dropped off while she was away that morning onto her right wrist. She quickly

applied some eye makeup, grabbed a small bag, and went downstairs to hail a cab.

Beretti's was a small, upscale restaurant across from an impressively large, Victorian house that had long been empty by the looks of it, the yard completely surrounded by a wrought-iron fence. The restaurant had the same older, classy feel about it on the outside as well as in, as Charlie noticed when she awkwardly entered. Not used to the dress or the sling-back heels, she made her way over to the smiling hostess and told her she was there to meet Mackenzie.

Smoothing the material over her hips, Charlie followed the hostess to the back of the restaurant, where T.J. Mackenzie was already seated.

With his amazingly blue eyes and thick, dark hair, T.J. reminded her of someone she used to know; she'd noticed it the second she walked into his office earlier that day. *Maybe that's why I'm acting so weird around him,* she thought as she neared the table. Normally she was calm and collected in all situations-ever skillful, methodical, and businesslike. Even in high-stakes situations she kept a level head, propelled only by adrenaline and her instincts. But around T.J., a man she didn't even know, she felt completely off-balance.

T.J. rose from the table as she sat down, smiling pleasantly. "Glad you could make it," he greeted her. "I took the liberty of ordering a bottle." He gestured to the center of the table.

"Thanks," Charlie told him, watching interestedly as he poured each of them a glass. *He's...a gentleman,* she realized in awe. *They do exist.* She quickly took a sip, hoping to feel less out of place.

The waiter appeared a moment later and Charlie selected the tortellini primavera. Thanks to Rita, who'd completely educated her about Italian cuisine, Charlie had grown to love Italian food and was familiar with many dishes.

Charlie was about to ask about the case when the waiter reappeared, bringing a basket of freshly baked rolls and butter. Charlie eagerly helped herself, always having found herself addicted to fresh bread. As she ate she noticed T.J. was watching her with a peculiar expression. "What?" she asked self-consciously.

"Nothing," he assured her, beginning to eat his own roll. "It's just most women I know don't-"

"Stuff their faces full of bread?" Charlie finished wryly.

"That's not exactly what I meant," he told her with a smile, sipping his wine. "It's just been a while since I've been around a woman

who has no objection to carbs. Kind of refreshing, actually. But then, something tells me you're not like most women." He put down his glass and
pulled out a file and handed it across the table to Charlie. "The case I'm working on," he told her. "I've got it about wrapped up but I could use a fresh perspective."

Charlie abandoned her rolls and opened the file, expecting a cheating spouse case or maybe a missing persons. What she wasn't expecting was to be staring at her own face and her name printed underneath. Her hands started to tremble as she leafed through the file that
documented her life-the second one she'd come across in less than twenty-four hours-but it only contained the parts she already knew. It still didn't reveal her birth parents or mention Anna or Stevens...but it did mention everything else: Suncrest Children's Center, Melinda, when she lived on the street, records from when she was admitted to the hospital for the beating in the boxcar, and the past ten years of being a part of Bob and Rita's family, as well as her work.

She finally lowered the file, trying to find her voice. "The photos and the documents date back to three months ago," she stated flatly. "Apparently Stevens isn't the only shadow I have." She dropped the file on the table. "This was a lure to get me here. You knew who I was the second I walked through the door, the moment you heard my name. You didn't seem surprised to see me at all...in fact, it was almost like you were expecting me. I've got to admit; you're good. You played the whole thing flawlessly, asking for the details of my case when you already knew everything. The question is, " she began, leaning forward, "who are you really and who hired you?" she asked, staring at him unblinkingly. Her instincts were now on alert, causing her body to go rigid as she contemplated her next move.

"My name is T.J. Mackenzie." He dropped his driver's license on the table. "I really am a private investigator in Manhattan. I'm sorry for the subterfuge but I figured if I came clean right off the bat you wouldn't be ready to listen. I also wanted to hear what you had to say, how much you knew. Then I had to call the person who hired me, who gave me explicit instructions to make contact whenever you showed up, before I said a word to you about the truth."

"What's the truth?" Charlie demanded. "Did Stevens hire you?"

T.J. shook his head. Before he could say anything further the food arrived, the server setting the dishes on the table before disappearing. T.J. hesitated for a moment, as if trying to anticipate what she might do next. Then he took a deep breath, leaning forward. "When Rita Larson was admitted to the hospital earlier this year she had a roommate. A roommate who saw your picture and immediately knew who you were. She was released before Mrs. Larson and never saw you, but she heard a lot about you and told Rita about me so she would pass the information along to you. She wanted to leave it up to you instead of just popping up in your life. She hoped you'd track me down one day and when you did, she wanted me to give you that file. That's pretty much everything she doesn't know about you. She also wanted me to give you this." He produced a wallet-sized photograph and handed it to her.

Charlie took the old photograph with the worn edges and stared into the face of a teenage girl with dark hair and hazel eyes, dressed in a tennis outfit. The big, curly-permed hair was definitely an eighties trademark, as was the style of the uniform. Other than the hairstyle, she looked a lot like Charlie as a teenager.

"Her name is Diana Sullivan," T.J. told her. "She's my neighbor." He paused. "She's also your biological mother."

***

Charlie felt like she was suffocating.

After bolting from the restaurant, she ran across the street and leaned heavily against the wrought-iron fence. She had no idea how to process all the new information she was continually being bombarded with. Work was one thing, and easily handled. It was completely different when it was about her personal life.

How can this be? Bob and I worked our asses off for ten years, trying to find out about my life. Now in less than two days I'm being hit with answers left and right...and tonight I find out who my mother is? Why now?

Other questions circled her mind as well, all relating directly to Diana Sullivan. It made her feel like she was going to implode.

T.J. caught up with her, studying her carefully. "You look like you're going to be sick," he said in concern, holding his hand out to her. "Come sit down."

Charlie let him lead her to a nearby bench off the sidewalk, feeling like a fool. "I'm sorry," she told him. "I don't think I've ever been a basket case in my life and tonight-" She broke off, shaking her head.

"It's my job to be observant, to read people," T.J. told her. "Much like your job. I can tell you right now, I haven't thought you were a basket case for one second. I've done my homework on you...and you're an extraordinary person, who's had an exceptionally rough life. All of the sudden you're hit with the truth...it's bound to knock the wind out of you. And I didn't help, with my pretenses. But Diana was very specific and she's a good friend-"

"What's she like?" Charlie interrupted quietly.

"Unpredictable," he answered quickly. "Always has you guessing. She's funny, outgoing, smart-loves to read-quick-witted, and very loyal. She befriended me when I was having a rough time, right when I moved in to the building, and she's been really good to me ever since. So when she hired me to find her daughter I jumped at the chance to pay her back for her kindness over the years. She wanted to do it sooner, but I think she was gun-shy, trying to work up the nerve."

"Why?" Charlie wanted to know. "Why did she let me go? How does she know Anna? And how does Stevens fit into this? Is he my father?"

"Slow down." T.J. held up his hands. "One thing at a time. Diana was seventeen when she had you, and her parents forced her to give you up for adoption. She wasn't allowed to hold you, touch you, or even name you. No one would give her any information about what would happen to you, except to assure her she was doing the right thing and you'd be placed in a good home. She never knew anything that happened after that. She searched for you for years but she never found out anything. She never knew you weren't adopted, nor does she know why. She doesn't know who Anna or Stevens is, or how Anna ended up with you in the first place. She also doesn't know who was after you that night."

"What about my father?" Charlie asked.

"She won't tell me anything about him. Just that he's not Stevens."

Charlie tried to think of what to ask next. "Why was she in the hospital? Is she alright now?"

T.J. hesitated. "Diana's a paraplegic," he answered. "She was in the hospital because she gets infections sometimes. She's fine now."

"A paraplegic?" Charlie asked in surprise, thinking of the girl in the tennis uniform. "What happened to her?"

"I think these are all questions you should be asking her. She can explain it all better than I can."

Charlie's heart skipped a beat. "She wants to meet me?"

"If you're willing, she asked me to set it up."

Charlie nodded. "I want to meet her."

"How about tomorrow afternoon?" T.J. suggested. "Here's the address." He handed her a card with Diana's address and apartment number written on it.

"Tell her I'll be there," Charlie said, putting the card and photograph carefully into her bag.

"I know you have a lot to think about. I just want to let you know that I really do want to work with you on this, help you track down Anna and Stevens and your biological father. If you're still interested after my charade."

Charlie nodded. "You were just doing your job; I can respect that. And being a good friend." She stuck out her hand. "I appreciate the help. And thanks for inviting me out tonight, giving me such a big piece of the puzzle. It really means a lot to find out who she is."

T.J. shook her hand. "You're welcome. I do feel bad that we never got around to eating our dinner, however."

"Since that was my fault, why don't I treat us to one of my favorite places?" Charlie asked him. "Do you like tacos? There's a stand not far from here that I go to when I'm working a job in the area."

"Sounds good," T.J. said, following her up the sidewalk past the old Victorian.

***

Later that night Charlie was sitting up in bed, looking at the photograph T.J. had given her. Now that she had a name she considered finding out everything there was to know about Diana Sullivan; it wouldn't be difficult. But since she was going to meet her the next afternoon she decided to hold off.

Instead she continued to stare at the picture, knowing there were no words to describe how it felt to look at it and associate it with the word "mother". Even though thousands of questions flooded her mind all she could do was look, gingerly touching Diana's face in the photo with her forefinger. Hours passed with Charlie sitting that way.

She slept little that night., anticipation keeping her awake the way it would a child waiting for Santa. As she got on her bike the next morning she was shocked that her hands were still trembling. *Keep it together.* she ordered herself. *You still have a couple of hours. Besides, you know there's somewhere you have to stop first.*

Letting herself into Bob's apartment, she was surprised to find him in his recliner, smoking a cigar and watching *Jerry Springer*. "You've got to be kidding me," she greeted him, tossing her keys on the coffee table and sitting on the couch. "Why the hell are you watching this crap?" Bob rarely watched television and when he did it was usually sports or the news.

Bob shrugged. "Beats fishing or whatever the hell it is retired people do. What brings you by so early? Work in the area?"

"What are you talking about?" she asked, taking off her jacket and tossing onto the cushion next to her, setting the file inside it on the table in front of her. "I do more than work."

Bob raised an eyebrow. "Who are you trying to fool?"

"It so happens that this isn't about work," she told him with mock indignation. "Exactly."

He turned off the TV set. "Okay, you have my attention. What, exactly, is this about?"

Charlie took a deep breath. "My biological mother."

It received the proper reaction; Bob nearly dropped his cigar. "Come again?"

She told him the whole story, everything she found out the night before. When she got to the part about Rita and Diana sharing the same hospital room Bob rose from his chair and went to stand by the windows, looking out at the back porch as she continued. When she finished he walked over to the bar and poured them each a drink. "I don't care if it is before noon, I think this calls for it," he said, handing her a glass.

Charlie accepted it gratefully, hoping it would calm her unusually jittery nerves. "Does it bother you?" she asked finally. "That I'm going to meet her so soon after-" She finished her drink, unable to complete the sentence.

Bob shook his head. "Rita wanted this to happen, which is why she sent you to that detective. And the way it's all working out...it's almost like it's supposed to."

"Since when do you believe in the whole 'meant-to-be' theory?" she asked, raising an eyebrow. "I thought we were both way too cynical to buy into all that crap."

"We are," he agreed. "But look at the way it's playing out: Rita sharing a hospital room with the woman who turns out to be your biological mother, who just happens to see a photo Rita had of you-"

"And it conveniently happened when I was out of town on a job and didn't even know Rita had been admitted again because she didn't want to worry me-"

Bob shrugged. "Maybe that just means it wasn't time for you to meet her yet."

"But I am now?" Charlie began to pace. "I can't ignore the timing of everything else, Bob. Like Stevens. Why did he pick now to leave me clues? Who the hell is he and why has he been keeping tabs on me my entire life?"

"That's something we'll figure out," Bob promised. "But for now, you need to focus on Diana. This is huge, Charlie. You're finally going to meet your birthmother. Not that long ago you gave up on the idea of that ever happening."

"I know, you're right." Charlie leaned back. "This is so unreal. And the P.I. really got me. I had no idea that I was the case he was working on. I'm losing my touch."

"We both are. Two people have been tailing you and we were as oblivious as a couple civilians." Bob shook his head. "Maybe he's former military."

Charlie shook her head. "I had him checked out; Gary just got back with me this morning. Gave me his background." She picked up the file and handed it to him. "Now you can't worry."

"And?" he asked, accepting it from her.

"He's clean," Charlie replied. "Everything he said checked out. He just a hell of a P.I."

"Do I detect grudging admiration?" Bob teased.

"I can admit when other people are good at what they do," she said defensively. "I don't think I'm the best."

Bob started to laugh. "Sure you don't."

Charlie frowned. *I don't think I'm the best,* she thought. *I think Bob is, I tell him all the time. I just don't...complement other people too often, that's all.*

"I'm pulling your chain," Bob told her, shaking his head. "I know you're not arrogant. You're just...not used to working with others. Aside from me of course," he added. Then he lifted his glass. "And you were a damned fine partner."

Charlie held up her empty glass. "So were you."

"So tell me more about this guy. Where'd he drop the bomb on you?"

"An Italian restaurant," Charlie told him. "Beretti's."

"Beretti's?" Bob repeated in surprise. "Fancy, shmancy. I'm surprised they let you in. Leather jacket's aren't exactly in their dress code." He sipped his drink.

"Ha ha. I worse a dress, genius. Give me some credit."

Bob nearly choked on his drink. "A dress? You?"

Charlie stood. "I'm leaving. I've had enough abuse today, thanks."

"Oh come on, be fair," Bob complained, standing as well. "In all the years I've known you I think I've seen you wear a dress twice-once to Jack and Megan's wedding, once to your graduation. It's interesting," he continued as he walked her out, "that the next time is for a date."

Charlie rolled her eyes, walking down the stairs. "You of all people should know a business meeting when you hear about one. Although it wasn't business for me, exactly, since I was the investigate-ee. Anyway, when we went to the taco stand-"

"Terrific Taco? The one you're always talking about?" Bob interrupted. "Although I don't know what's terrific about it; all it does is give me terrific heartburn." He grimaced.

Charlie looked at him knowingly. "I think that might have more to do with your...aging constitution."

"So we're resorting to age jabs now?"

"You started it-"

"Fine, fine," he relented, holding up his hands as they reached her bike. "Truce." Then his expression sobered. "You ready?"

"I don't know," she replied honestly. "I don't think anyone could be ready for something like this. I have no idea what to expect, or what she'll expect..."

"I wouldn't worry about that; she'll just be thrilled to meet you." He gave her a hug. "Good luck, kid. Let me know how it goes."

"You'll be my first call," Charlie promised, pulling back. Then she looked past him, back in the direction of Rita's old apartment, halfway visible from the parking lot. "I wish she were here," she said softly. "I wish she'd gotten the chance to know what happened, so I could thank-"

"She knows," Bob interrupted firmly, resting a hand on her shoulder. "She knows."

Chapter Five

It was nearly one o'clock when Charlie pulled in to Colonial Apartments, killing the motor and just staring at the large building for a long moment. Then she hopped off her bike and headed toward the double-door entrance.
She removed her sunglasses as she pulled opened the large-windowed door, glimpsing her reflection. Her expectant expression

stared back at her and she looked again at her jeans, leather jacket over her T-shirt, and loose ponytail. *It's not like there's a handbook that tells you what to do when you meet your birth mother,* she thought as she walked in. *No one tells you what to wear, what to say...*

Diana's apartment was on the ground floor, down the back hall off the lobby. Charlie looked at the surrounding doors as she passed, briefly wondering if T.J. was home. Then she took a deep breath and knocked on 6A.

It took a few moments and then the door opened, revealing a dark-haired woman in her mid-forties, sitting in a wheelchair. Her face lit up immediately upon seeing Charlie.

"Diana Sullivan?" Charlie asked, swallowing the lump in her throat. Diana managed a nod. "I'm Charlie Booker." She extended her hand.

Diana looked up at Charlie, emotion etched into every contour of her face. She took Charlie's hand and gently pulled her downward, wrapping her in a secure embrace. "My sweetheart," she whispered, stroking Charlie's hair.

As Diana held her Charlie felt something she didn't expect, something that coursed through her entire being. It was a connection; a piece of her soul that had always been missing was now securely put back in place. In that moment she knew without a doubt that Diana Sullivan was her mother and knew she had never wanted to let her go.

After they broke apart, both crying freely, Charlie followed Diana as she wheeled herself into her spacious living room. Charlie saw that the fireplace mantle was covered in framed photos, recognizing the one at the end. "That's the one T.J. gave me, of you in your tennis uniform."

"I was on the school team," Diana told her, gesturing for her to sit on the couch. "That was taken right before the county tournament my junior year. I didn't know it yet, but I was already pregnant with you." She looked at Charlie meaningfully.

"I have so many questions," Charlie blurted as she sat down. "I don't even know where to start. Normally I'm so organized and prepared-you have to be to do what I do-but now my mind's all over the place."

"Mine too. Why don't we start with me telling you a little bit about myself?" Diana suggested. "Give you some background."

Charlie nodded. "Sounds good."

"Alright. Let's see...my name is Diana Marie Sullivan and I was born on January 5, 1965 in Philadelphia. I'm an only child, and my family moved to New York when I was ten; my father was an insurance salesman and got transferred. My mother was a grammar school teacher, and I grew up in Queens. My parents-your grandparents-were Joseph and Ellen Sullivan."

"Were?"

"They passed away a few years ago," Diana explained. "My father had a heart condition that his constant smoking didn't help and my mother suffered from kidney failure. But we hadn't been in touch in years; we were estranged." She sighed. "I was sixteen when I told them I was pregnant. They were ashamed, horrified by what people would think...so they forced me to give you up. It was the hardest thing I ever had to do, and I hated them for it. As soon as I turned eighteen I left home and started working on tracking you down. But all the records were sealed and no one would help me. It was then I realized I wouldn't be able to find you by ordinary methods; it was going to take time. And money.

"I was a good student, and I got a scholarship to NYU. I knew a college education would go a long way in getting me a good job. It also gave me access to information about adoption. I learned everything I could, hoping to find a way to get through all the red tape and find out what happened to you.

"I graduated and started working as a paralegal. As soon as I had enough money saved I hired a P.I., but he couldn't find out anything because there was no record of your birth."

"Why is that?" Charlie asked.

"My father had a lot of connections then, because of his father-my grandfather was incredibly wealthy and influential-and paid off the hospital staff to make it look like you were never born. He was so preoccupied with what people thought, he didn't want any record of your existence on paper, no proof of my 'terrible mistake'." She shook her head in disgust. "Anyway, when the P.I. didn't find anything I hired another. I just couldn't let it go-I had to know if you were safe and loved-but I could never find anything. As time went by I knew you were getting older, getting attached to the home and parents you had, so I started to back down. I hoped, instead, that one day you would find me. And you did."

"You just knew? When you saw the photo of me that Rita had...you knew I was your daughter?"

Diana nodded. "I saw myself in you, and I could just tell. But I didn't want to force myself on you; there was the possibility that you could've been perfectly happy with your life and not wanted any interruptions. So I decided to leave you the right clues and let the decision be completely up to you. I hired T.J. because I wanted to know about your life, even if I didn't get to meet you. I hope you don't mind."

Charlie shook her head. "You wanted to find out about me as much as I wanted to find out about you. It's still so crazy...I've had four moms in my life."

"And all of them loved you. I could tell from the pictures. I found it very interesting, though, that T.J. couldn't find out anything about your life before you were four."

"I can't either. That's why I want to track Anna down and grill this Stevens guy."

"I'm sure you'll find them," Diana said confidently. "T.J. told me about what you do. It's very unusual...but he says you're very good at it."

"I had a good teacher." Charlie paused. "How much do you know, exactly? About my life after Melinda died, when I was on my own?"

Diana's face darkened. "He told me how you came to know Bob Holden and Rita Larson, showed me your hospital admittance records from the night Bob found you. What those animals did-"

"I made a lot of mistakes when I was a teenager," Charlie interrupted, looking out the window. "I did so many things that made me sick...I was young, desperate, and impulsive. I had to think on my feet and my rushed judgment led to colossal mistakes." She shifted her gaze back to Diana. "But Bob and Rita helped me turn my life around. Bob offered me a job, unconventional as it was, and things got a lot better for me. I got to go to college-NYU, like you-and I met people, almost started to feel normal." She smiled suddenly, feeling the urge to talk about someone she hadn't in a long time. "When I was twenty I went to this diner all the time and there was this guy who always came in the same time I did, for lunch. He always got the bacon burger and fries while I got a patty melt and a coffee, and when our orders got mixed up one day we started talking, and as the weeks passed we became friends. We started hanging out periodically...and then we started dating. I'd been living with Rita for two years at the time and it was the first time someone wanted to be with me just because they wanted me. And for the first time...I was crazy about someone."

"What was he like?" Diana wanted to know.

"Everything I wasn't," Charlie answered with a grin. "Patient, steady, thoughtful, generous, selfless, neat. And unbelievably kind. Definitely one of the good ones." Her smile faded. "But he couldn't accept my career choice, the life I led...and who I was. So he left, I stopped going to the diner, and haven't gotten that serious with anyone since. I haven't thought about him in years...until I met T.J. They look a lot alike."

"What was his name?"

"David Hart," Charlie said, surprised by how easily it rolled off her tongue after not speaking the name in eight years. "It's so weird, to talk about him again, be this open-I know it's strange, but I feel comfortable telling you about it."

"I'm glad. I want to know everything, all the personal details and milestones that wouldn't show up in a file. But if you're not ready for that, I'll settle for what I just heard, hearing about your first love. That's an important milestone."

"Speaking of relationships...could you tell me about my father?" Charlie asked hesitantly.

"I knew you'd ask," Diana said with a sigh. "It's not something I purposely want to keep from you, it's just hard to talk about. It was very-" She broke off abruptly. "I was your typical high school girl: I played sports, joined clubs, was fairly popular, had boyfriends. But when I was sixteen I met someone, someone a lot older. It was different than all the superficial relationships in my life-he was real with me. He treated me with respect, encouraged me, appreciated my opinion. He gave me the attention my parents never did." She let out a long breath. "I was young and naïve, inexperienced...and I fell for all of it."

"What happened?"

"I found out the truth. He wasn't the man I thought he was. He had...secrets. And when I told him I was pregnant he disappeared. There was no trace of him, ever again."

"At all?"

"As far as I know, no."

Charlie could tell that was all she was willing to say on the subject so she let it drop, even though it was the last thing she wanted. "Can I ask why you're-" She broke off, looking at her.

"-in a wheelchair?" Diana finished. "Sure. It happened a long time ago, when I was twenty-five. My friends invited me on a summer trip to the Gulf, and when I was water skiing I lost control. Sailed through the air, landed on shore, and hit my spine in just the right way to permanently paralyze me."

"I'm sorry," Charlie told her sincerely.

"Don't be. Like I said, it was a long time ago. I've adapted since then, lived a fairly full life. No more water skiing though. Or hiking, cliff-diving, or motorcycle rides-" She stopped, noticing Charlie's expression. "What is it?"

"All the things you liked to do...it sounds like you were an adrenaline junkie."

Diana laughed. "I suppose I was, though I never thought about it that way."

Charlie wordlessly pulled out her keys, handing them to Diana.

"A Harley Sportster?" she asked, inspecting one of the keys. "And a jet-ski and some kind of...is this to a four-wheeler?" She held up a small key.

"It was," Charlie replied. "Rita's son, Jack, had a four-wheeler and a jet-ski his wife wanted him to get rid of-they were both collecting dust-so he gave them to me," she explained. "Jack's been like an older brother to me, and he told me it was about time I started having fun and putting my daredevil tendencies to good use, instead of just relying on them for work. So I did, and I had a lot of fun...until the four-wheeler ended up at the bottom of a ravine. Long story, but I was fine. Kept the key as a souvenir, though, and missed it so much I bought the Sportster right after." Charlie took the keys back. "I guess we have something in common, huh?"

"Sounds like we do," Diana agreed. Then she paused. "Except that you're a stronger woman than I could ever be. Everything you've gone through, how far you've come...not everyone could handle what you had to handle. But you did it...and look at you now."

"Look at *me*?" Charlie echoed. "You had a kid at seventeen and were completely alone in it. You didn't want to let me go, and you've been fighting like hell ever since to get me back. And the way you've lived your life, on *your* terms. Besides, all us daredevils are strong." She winked and Diana laughed.

Charlie spent the rest of the afternoon at Diana's apartment, the two of them getting to know one another. When she finally prepared to leave she gave Diana another hug, then pulled back with great effort. "I'm glad I finally got to meet you," she told her, emotions apparent in her voice.

"So am I." Diana looked or her for a long moment. "I'm very proud of you Charlie. I really like your name," she added. "I didn't get to choose it...but it suits you."

"Thanks. You know, I got so distracted by everything we were talking about that I forgot to ask you something I've always wanted to know."

"What's that?"

"When, exactly, is my birthday?"

"June 6, 1982," Diana replied. "I'm sorry you spent your entire life not knowing." She followed Charlie to the door. "I'd like to see you again. I'd never try to replace the other important women you had in your life...but I'd love to have a relationship with you, if you're interested."

Charlie nodded. "I'd like that, a lot."

As Charlie was leaving, walking down the hall, she ran into T.J., who was just leaving the lobby and heading in her direction. "How'd it go?" he asked curiously.

For the first time in her life Charlie was so choked up she couldn't speak. Instead she
gave T.J. a hug, surprising them both. Charlie knew she hardly came off as the touchy-feely type.
"Thank you," she managed, unable to say more.

To T.J., it was more than enough. "You're welcome. She's a hell of woman, isn't she?" he asked as he pulled back.

Charlie nodded, eager to cover up her awkwardness. "I don't know what I was expecting but I wasn't disappointed." She took a step back. "Anyway, I should get going. I still have a lot to find out."

"I can help you with that." T.J. handed her a card.

"'Buxom Cabaret'?" Charlie read in amusement, eyeing the red card with a black silhouette of a shapely woman.

"Stevens' most recent ex-wife, Lydia Travis, is a cocktail waitress at the club. She's willing to talk to us about him; apparently she's scorned, big-time, and wants to unload. It's not much, but it's a start."

"When does she want to meet?"

"Tonight, after closing," T.J. replied. "About two-thirty a.m."

"I'll meet you around two." She extended her hand, able to act more professional now that her burst of emotion had passed. "Thanks again, for everything."

He shook her hand. "Happy to help. I'm really glad you and Diana finally got to meet. See you tonight."

Charlie took her time driving home, trying to absorb everything that had taken place in the past several hours. All of it seemed like a dream, something far too fantastic to possibly be real. She'd waited her whole life to meet Diana and now that she had...there weren't words to describe how it felt, what it was like. Trying to process it all was close to impossible, so she gave up trying. Instead she settled for driving around the city, watching the setting sun start to disappear behind the Manhattan skyline.

***

"Bring your ones?" T.J. called as Charlie drove up next to his car, a shiny black '69 Chevelle. He was casually leaning against it, obviously waiting for her.

Charlie just shook her head as she killed the engine and got off her bike, lifting off her helmet. She walked closer to the car to get a better look, whistling as she did so. "Now *that* is a car," she said appreciatively. "None of those carbon-copy foreign toys that try to compete."

"Try and fail," he agreed, looking past her to the bike. "And *that* is a bike. Not one of those Ninja screechers. How long have you had it?"

"About seven years. What about you?" she asked, still staring at the Chevelle.

"Ten years," T.J. replied proudly. "I inherited it from my grandfather. He took excellent care of it but I went the extra mile and had it completely restored. Money was part of the inheritance too," he explained. "And I put it to good use."

"Didn't have a major case load that year?" Charlie quipped.

"Hardly; I was twenty. Not even out of college." T.J. looked at the car fondly. "I was always a big fan of American muscle cars. It meant a lot to me that my grandfather left it to me." He looked at his watch. "We still have about half an hour before Lydia's shift ends. Want to go for a ride?"

"Sure," Charlie agreed wholeheartedly, walking over to the passenger side.

T.J. left the parking lot behind the club and drove out onto the highway, gunning the engine for Charlie's benefit. "What's your story?" he wanted to know. "What got you into bikes and cars?"

"When I was a teenager I lived briefly with this group of other teenagers, across from a garage. I used to watch the same kinds of cars go in and out every day, all similar and nothing special. Until this one day, when a beautiful old orange car pulled in and I was mesmerized. I had no idea what kind of car it was, since I knew nothing about cars at the time, but I knew it was special. One of the guys I lived with told me it was a Charger, either a '69 or a '70, and he said they didn't make cars like that anymore, with grace and class. After that, I wanted to know more so I always kept my eyes open for older cars, and when I lived with Rita she taught me everything I needed to know; she said where she grew up, women knew more about what made cars run than men. She definitely knew more than Bob." Charlie shook her head, smiling. "Anyway, I toyed with idea of getting one but a bike seemed to be a better option for me, so I could haul it whenever I needed to and get in and out of tight spots as quickly as possible. But I don't have to tell you about that," she added wryly.

"We could definitely swap war stories," he agreed.

And they did, on the way back to the club. T.J. talked about his cases, and Charlie talked about her jobs. It was immediately clear to them both how alike their professions were: the surveillance, the research, the connections made and resources acquired, the detective skills, thinking on one's feet, being capable of taking care of oneself, using a firearm, the danger, the adrenaline high, and being set apart from others.

Other than Bob and the associates they interacted with, Charlie didn't really know anyone that she had that much in common with, especially the men in her past. *It feels good for once to just be able to be...me, without having to explain. Even if it is just business.*

By the time T.J. pulled back up next to Charlie's bike he was laughing and shaking his head. "And I thought I was the only one who'd ever been chased down by a woman with a rolling pin."

"Apparently not; there was someone else out there who had the same crappy luck you do," she told him, opening the door.

It was two-thirty but Lydia still hadn't emerged from the building. Charlie and T.J. leaned against the front of the car, waiting. "Do you mind if I ask you something?" Charlie asked after a moment.

"Shoot."

"How did you and Diana get to be so close?"

T.J. appeared to be reflecting, thinking back. "I was twenty-four," he recalled. "It was raining the day I moved in; the movers lost half of my stuff...and I was in a pretty bad place. I'd just had to give really bad news in a case-missing persons-and I'd just gotten divorced, which is why I was moving. Anyway, I dropped one of the boxes in the hall and started yelling and cursing when I heard someone behind me say 'If it's that bad today, maybe I'll just stay in'. I turned around and saw Diana, watching me in half-amusement, half-understanding. I apologized and she invited me in for coffee and told me I might be in a rough spot then but they don't last
forever. After that I did work around her apartment-cases were slim at the time-and she'd give
me sketches in exchange; she's very talented." He shrugged. "And we've been friends ever since."

Charlie already knew most of what he was talking about, having done the background check, but she didn't know the details of his friendship with Diana and was glad to learn them now. "Wow."

"She means a lot to me," T.J. confided. "My family's scattered all over the country and I stay too busy to really have a lot of other people in my life-" He broke off. "Something you can relate to?" he asked knowingly.

Charlie nodded and was about to comment further when the back door of the club opened and a woman with spikey jet-black hair and a killer figure walked out, smoking a cigarette. She appeared to be in her mid-thirties but could've passed for younger. Her intense brown eyes narrowed when they focused on Charlie and T.J. "T.J. Mackenzie?" she asked hesitantly.

"Lydia Travis." T.J. pushed away from his car and walked forward, Charlie right behind him. "This is Charlie Booker."

"I know." Lydia opened her purse and pulled out a small black-and-white photograph and handed it to Charlie.

Charlie looked at the picture of the toddler child with dark curls, sitting in a baby swing with a small teddy bear.

"That's you," Lydia told her. "You were about two years old."

Charlie looked up at her in shock. "How do you-"

"Andy had it, hidden in a drawer," Lydia explained. "I found it six months after we got married. I confronted him, asked if he had a child I didn't know about but I couldn't get anything out of him, not for a long time. Toward the end of our marriage he came back home from a bender and started babbling about his Ace, going on and on until I asked him who Ace was and he said her name was really Charlie. I put two and two together, that Charlie was the little girl in the photo. I asked him who she was, why she was so important to him and he admitted she was a...project."

"Project?" Charlie repeated.

"I don't know all the details and, to be honest, I don't even really know how truthful he was with me. There are many reasons to suspect everything he ever told me, because as our marriage was ending he just didn't care enough to put up a front anymore. So this may or may not be true but...he alluded to working for the government at one point."

"Doing what?" T.J. asked.

"Don't know. He never elaborated and like I said, I now doubt every word that ever came out of his mouth. Except one thing."

"What?" Charlie wanted to know.

"I asked him once if he wanted kids-before I knew about you-and he told me he couldn't because he was sterile as a cotton ball. He showed me the test results-and it was done by my doctor, who I trusted, so it wasn't faked. So Andy is definitely not your father."

Charlie knew she shouldn't be surprised; Diana assured her that she didn't know who Stevens was so he couldn't have been her father. But, for some reason she couldn't explain, she felt slightly deflated upon hearing the definite news.

"I don't know what your connection to Andy is, but be careful in pursuing him," Lydia
advised. "There are lots of things he kept from me, but his true nature wasn't one of them. He's a driven man and always has been; by what I don't know, which is what can make him dangerous. I'm not proud to say it, seeing as how I married the man, but I think he could be capable of...a lot of things. So watch your backs."

T.J. looked at Charlie in amusement, who didn't share his reaction because she still going over everything Lydia had said. Then she turned toward Lydia. "Do you have any idea where he might be now?" she wanted to know.

"We don't keep in touch," Lydia replied. "But I know he had a cabin in Cape Cod where he'd go a lot, to escape. No one else knew about it, as far as I know."

"Thank you," Charlie told her. "I appreciate it."

The older woman nodded. "Not a problem. But remember what I said."

"We will," T.J. assured her. "Thanks again."

After Lydia disappeared back into the club T.J. turned to Charlie. "What do you think?"

Charlie was looking at the photo again, then raised her eyes to meet his. "I'm thinking there's no one more dangerous than a dedicated person with an agenda." She tucked the photo in her back pocket. "Which means something needs to be done, ASAP."

"My thoughts exactly." He looked at the calendar in his phone. "I've got something pertaining to a case tomorrow that I can't postpone, but Friday's good. What about you?"

"Friday works," she told him with a nod. "So you're up for a basically impromptu road trip?"

"Absolutely. This case gets more intriguing by the minute. Why don't you let me pick you up first thing that morning? We can fit more gear in a car."

"Sounds good." She started to walk. "You know, all this stuff falling into place...a normal person would be grateful, not suspicious. Mark of a true cynic I guess."

"You're not being cynical, you're being practical." T.J. walked with her. "It's obvious Stevens is setting this up for you to find him. Since we don't know why, we need to be prepared."

Charlie was in full agreement. "I really appreciate this," she told him as she mounted her bike. "It's good to have someone objective around since I'm personally invested in this job."

"Don't mention it."

"I'm serious, you're definitely getting hazard pay." She put on her helmet.

"Let me drive that bike sometime and we're even."

"Deal. See you Friday." She took off, waving over her shoulder.

Chapter Six

"Char-lie," a sing-song voice called. "Where are you?"

Charlie looked around to locate where the voice was coming from but could see nothing in the dark. She looked down at her shoe instead, noticing how the strap had broken on one of her sandals. They were the sandals Anna recently got her for her birthday...

"Charlie!" the voice cried sharply, as if it were closer by. But as Charlie looked, she continued to see nothing.

Then she heard laughter, soft at first then building until she couldn't escape it. It echoed in her ears so loudly that she covered them with her hands; it wasn't a pleasant sound, the way laughing should be. It was dark, menacing. Evil. Even as she closed her eyes Charlie could hear it continually ringing...

Charlie had been awake for a while Thursday morning, laying flat on her back in the middle of her queen-sized four-poster bed, one of the few indulgences she'd treated herself to within the last few years. She looked up at the canopy above her, made of a shimmery gray-black material she'd purchased while shopping with Megan, both on a mission that day to decorate-something Charlie had never gotten a chance to do on her own before. To her surprise, she'd actually enjoyed the experience, letting Megan help in her bedroom. Along with the shimmery canopy the bed had silky burgundy sheets, plump black-and-red throw pillows, and a silver satin comforter. The long curtains that covered her full-length windows matched the comforter over black vertical blinds, which cast a glow of patchy sunlight over her bed every morning. She also had two small, white bedside tables, a velvet ottoman in the far corner that Megan no longer wanted, and framed photographs all around the room, particularly on top of her stereo. Like all the others rooms in her apartment, it had Charlie's mark all over it.

Her mind slowly wandered from thoughts of her room to her dream once more, what she'd been thinking about when she first woke up an hour ago. *That night's trying to come back,* she thought as she rolled over onto her side. *I wish it would just happen already instead of taking its time and coming only in bits and pieces.*

Before she could get ready for her run and eat breakfast her phone rang, and she answered it eagerly, hoping for some kind of update. She was disappointed, however; since it was her landline, it was just a telemarketer.

As she got dressed in her bathroom she became curious as she thought about T.J. and the case requiring his attention that day. She then thought of her own job, glad that she had no current commitments so she could devote all her time and energy to her own personal case.

The park was more crowded than usual, the trails filled with mothers pushing baby strollers and elderly people walking their dogs, forcing Charlie to have to weave in and out around them. Not feeling particularly patient that morning, she became increasingly annoyed.

Her mood was anything but pleasant when walked through her front door, just in time to hear the landline ring again. Ignoring it, Charlie walked into the kitchen to get another bottle of water.

As she leaned against the counter, drinking, Charlie could hear the automated voice on her voice mailbox ask the caller to leave a message, followed by a loud beep. Since she assumed
it was another telemarketer, Charlie's attention drifted elsewhere.

Until she heard her name.

She ran across the kitchen and to the wall-mount on the other side, quickly snatching up the phone. "This is Charlie Booker," she said breathlessly.

"Miss Booker? I'm Gloria Winters," an uncertain woman's voice greeted her. "I got your phone number from a friend-"

Charlie sat on the couch, disappointed. Clearly it wasn't anyone calling with information; it was someone who probably wanted to hire her. *And I was just thinking earlier how glad I was to not have the distraction of a workload right now...* "What can I do for you, Ms. Winters?"

"Actually, I'd like to do something for you," Gloria told her. "The friend who gave me your number is T.J. Mackenzie. He got in touch with me because I work in the county clerk's office, and have been for the past thirty years. He was trying to find information on a woman named Marianna."

Charlie sat up straight. "That's right. We're looking for anything we can find on her."

"I did some digging into our records and I found out several Mariannas lived in the general area of the apartment complex T.J. said you resided. I checked but there wasn't a Marianna living in the apartment at that time; the only name that showed up on the landlord's records was Andrew Stevens."

So Stevens was paying for Anna's apartment, Charlie realized. *But why? How did he know her?*

"So I kept looking at the four women in the area named Marianna: Marianna Marsden, Marianna Blake, Marianna Riccoli, and Marianna Marquez. Marquez turned up in the system-she got a parking ticket in 1986 and had to come into our office to pay it. When she did she had to give us her address...and it was the address of the apartment."

Marianna Marquez, Charlie thought. *I finally know her real name.* "Thank you so much," Charlie told Gloria gratefully.

"I know it's not much but I thought it might help," Gloria told her. "She seemed to disappear after that; there wasn't anything else to find."

"It's enough to get me started," Charlie assured her.

"Good luck on your search, Miss Booker."

When Charlie hung up the phone she immediately picked it back up again, punching in a familiar number. "I've got a full name now, Marianna Marquez. Give me everything you can find."

In much higher spirits, Charlie decided to take a bubble bath for a change, setting her mp3 player up on the counter so she could listen to her favorite songs. *So Stevens is good for something after all, even if he is a blatant interferer,* she thought as she slid further into the bubbles. *I just wish the clues weren't so obvious, because that means the finale's probably coming soon...and I'm sure it won't be small.*

After her bath Charlie spent time pouring over her computer and talking on the phone, using the speakerphone option, putting together a file of information on Anna. She didn't have a lot to go on yet but was confident that would change; everyone-herself included-was working hard on this, not prepared to give up easily. Charlie was grateful for all the valuable contacts she'd made over the years with Bob's help, people who respected her and wanted to help her now when she needed it. Like Bob had told her in the beginning, you never knew what a goldmine of information you could access if you only knew the right people.

Thinking about Bob prompted her to call him and update him on the situation, letting him know she was going out of town the next day and hopefully would be returning with answers.

Afterward Charlie decided to take a break for lunch. Just as she was about to head into the kitchen her cell rang, and Charlie saw that it was Megan. "What's up?" she greeted her, flopping onto the couch in the living room.

"I was wondering if you wanted to spend my lunch break with me at the mall looking at baby stuff," she replied. "If you're not too busy."

Bob had filled both Jack and Megan in about Charlie's renewed search and what she'd discovered so far, including her meeting with Diana. "I can manage," Charlie assured her, rising from the couch and walking back into her bedroom. "I'll have my phone with me; there's not much I can do until I start hearing back from people. I do have to pack for tomorrow but I'll have time for that later." She opened her walk-in closet to find a pair of shoes.

"Great. It's a lot more fun when you're not by yourself. Then again, if my mother was here I'd never get a break."

Megan's parents lived in Michigan and didn't get a chance to visit often. Even though Megan often complained about how much her mother hovered and loved to interfere in her personal life, Charlie knew it couldn't be easy expecting your first child with your parents so far away, and now she no longer had a mother-in-law willing to step up to the plate. Because of that, Charlie took it upon herself to be Megan's go-to girl when it came to anything baby, including planning an upcoming baby shower and going to countless baby stores all over the area comparing and contrasting prices and deals. Charlie knew she was in over her head from the moment she volunteered; she knew less about babies and showers and Diaper Genies than Jack did. But even though she completely out of her element, Charlie soon discovered that she was enjoying herself and it could be fun. Even though she and Megan were already close it connected them even more and that meant a lot to Charlie. She also found out, to her great surprise, that she wasn't half bad at all the "baby stuff".

After letting Charlie know what mall, Megan hung up and Charlie grabbed her keys. She quickly went downstairs, sliding on her sunglasses in the bright parking lot. Then she started her bike and drove downtown, feeling the warm sunshine on her face. She started humming one of her favorite songs that had been stuck in her head for days, unable to remember the last time she'd felt like this. *Things are coming together,* she realized. *That's what's making me happy. Even the fact that it's all orchestrated by Stevens isn't going to take away from that.*

Megan also noticed the change in her mood when she arrived at the mall, and said as much. It wasn't as though Charlie was always in a bad temperament; she was just always so busy, so stressed that she could never just slow down and relax a bit. Especially lately, as she'd thrown herself blindly into work so she wouldn't have to deal with Rita's illness and eventual passing.

They decided to eat first, maneuvering their way through the crowded food court until they found what they wanted. They sat at a small table under a large skylight, talking as they ate. "Jack's getting promoted," Megan announced after Charlie asked her if anything knew was going on. "It's not official or anything yet but his boss invited us to dinner last night and started talking about it...so Jack's fairly certain that when he leaves tonight he'll be leaving as the new junior vice president of Harlon Publishing," she finished proudly, sipping her tea.

"That's great," Charlie said, raising her cup in the air. "He's definitely earned it. To all the normal nine-to-fivers, may they all succeed in climbing the corporate ladder."

"I'll drink to that," Megan said. "I wouldn't mind some climbing myself." Megan worked in marketing for a major food company.

When they were finished they walked across the mall to a small shop that sold cribs, bassinets, highchairs, and other kinds of baby furniture. As they were inspecting a particular crib, Megan casually brought up the subject of the next day. "Where exactly are you going again?" Though she recognized the danger in Charlie's profession, Megan had always admired and respected her for having guts she was sure she could never have. She was always curious about Charlie's jobs and where she went when she had to go out of town, liking the excitement in Charlie's tales. Charlie didn't expect this time to be any different; in fact, she expected more questions since it was about her personal life. She never minded; she liked the interest Megan took in her. It really did make her feel like she had a sister.

"Cape Cod," Charlie answered, bending down to look at the skinny legs on the crib, frowning. "This doesn't look sturdy enough," she observed.

"I know. Let's check out this one." Megan was already moving to the white one less than a foot away. "So this private investigator guy is going with you?"

Charlie nodded, surveying the new crib with interest. "This one would look really good in the nursery; it goes with everything you already have. Also-" she reached out and began to shake it "-I think it could handle a hurricane."

"I agree. I'm registering for it then." Megan scanned the price tag. "You want to go look at clothes a few stores down?"

Charlie nodded and they left the shop. When they were looking at onesies Megan wanted to know more about T.J.

"You sound like Bob," Charlie commented, looking through the racks of clothes absentmindedly. "There's nothing to tell. He's a P.I., who also happens to be the neighbor of my long-lost biological mother, and he's helping me with my search."

"He's also single, likes the kinds of cars you do, lives on the edge like you, and looks a lot like that guy you brought to my wedding."

Charlie stopped. "What exactly did Bob tell you?" she asked suspiciously, her eyes narrowing.

"He told us about the conversation the two of you had about this guy, and he was intrigued. Said you hadn't talked about anyone like that in a long time."

"Like what?"

"Like you want to know more."

Charlie rolled her eyes, walking the length of the aisle and stopping at stuffed-animal covered shelves in the back. "Bob's being ridiculous, and so are you."

"This isn't a bad thing," Megan pointed out, brushing her light brown hair back over her shoulder. "It'll be good for you to get to know someone-"

"This is just for work!" Charlie interrupted, exasperated. She picked up a small purple elephant, tracing its ears with her forefinger. "If he happens to be a nice guy that's a bonus,
because it'll make the job a lot easier."

"You mean it will make going out of town easier."

"Going out of town's a big deal," Charlie told her, handing her the stuffed toy. "This Stevens guy is on one long power trip, just waiting for me to react to whatever he throws at me. Facing him will be no small feat...and that's all I can say without endangering you."

"I realize what the two of you are trying to do," Megan assured her. "And I'm not trying to give you a hard time. It's just that you so rarely let yourself have a life outside work, meet anyone you have anything in common with. I just think that it would be good for you, that's all. Besides...it's doesn't help that he's insanely good-looking," she added with a grin, her brown eyes twinkling merrily.

"How do you-"

"Bob left his file on the coffee table when Jack and I stopped by," she explained. "And I couldn't resist taking a peek."

"You're worse than a thirteen-year-old," Charlie said, shaking her head as they walked toward the front of the store. "I guess next you're going to ask if he has dimples when he smiles."

"Does he?"

"Yes," Charlie grudgingly admitted.

Megan let the subject drop after that and they started to make their way toward an exit so Megan could get back to work. On the way Charlie's eye caught something in a store as she looked through the window as they passed and she insisted Megan wait just outside the store for a moment, until Charlie got back. She rushed inside to the corner of the store, picking out the item and bringing it to the check-out counter to purchase.

When she returned she handed the small blue-and-gray bag to Megan with a large smile on her face. "An early baby shower present," she explained. "I saw it in there and I couldn't pass it up."

Obviously curious, Megan pushed aside the tissue paper and pulled out a tiny black T-shirt with a drawing of a motorcycle on it underneath the words "Skip the tricycle and get me a Hog". She started to laugh.

"Cute, huh?"

Megan nodded. "I should've known not to expect a little lamb-suit from you," she quipped. "Thanks, Charlie. It's adorable." She put her arm around Charlie and they walked out of the mall and into the afternoon sun.

***

Charlie decided to go to the diner for dinner, the one she hadn't been to since she and David broke up years ago. As she walked inside she saw the place hadn't changed: red-backed booths lined the walls of the small restaurant and matching red stools sat in front of the high gray counter-top at the front. An old juke box sat in the back corner and neon-lit words covered the windows outside, casting the inside in a yellow-orange glow. It was also just as crowded as she remembered; she had to wait by the door until one of the stools at the counter opened up.

Without even looking at the menu, Charlie ordered her old standard: coffee and a patty melt. She ate fairly healthily as a rule to stay in shape, but didn't find the harm in indulging for at least one meal of the day. She sipped water while she waited for her food, casually looking around. She noticed the seat next to her suddenly become available. When her coffee arrived she added her sugar, stirring it in as someone else sat next to her.

"I hear the apple pie is good here," a voice came from beside her. "Probably because they use real apples."

Charlie nearly choked on her coffee. *I know that voice...but it can't be, not on the night I decide to come to this place for the first time in eight years...*

But it appeared that it could be. Sitting on the stool next to her was David Hart, the reason she stopped coming to this diner, the person she hadn't thought of in years until recently, the person who just disappeared from her life leaving it quite different from when he'd entered it.

He looked exactly the same, as if he hadn't aged a day. His thick dark hair was still shiny and smooth, with no hint of gray hairs or a receding hairline and his eyes...still the same beautiful blue-gray.

"David," Charlie greeted him when she finally found her voice.

"Charlie," he returned.

She could only stare at him in amazement. "I don't know what to say," she said finally. "It's been...a long time. I can't believe you're here."

"I'm always here," he told her. "For the last eight years...only now it's for dessert since I promised the wife I'd cut back on all the red meat." He gently patted his stomach though Charlie could detect no bulge.

Then what he said registered. "So you tied the knot, huh?" she asked conversationally, trying to ignore the slight twinge in her stomach.

He nodded. "Three years ago next month."

Before Charlie could ask anything else her order arrived and David chuckled. "Your usual," he said, shaking his head. "You still order that every night?"

Charlie shook her head. "This is the first time I've been in here in...a while. Whenever I go to another diner I order something else but here...it felt like I should get the old reliable." She took a big bite of her patty melt to emphasize her point.

"Actually, I was just about to say I never saw you around here anymore. Or anywhere for that matter. I wondered if maybe you might've moved away somewhere, to a different part of the country entirely. Or maybe jetted off to Europe, since you said Rita always wanted to go."

The twinge in Charlie's stomach intensified.

"So how is everybody?" David wanted to know. "Bob, Rita, Jack and Megan...do they have kids yet?"

Charlie was grateful that the waitress appeared to take David's order, though she knew she'd still have to answer him as soon as they were alone again. She took a large bite for fortification.

After the waitress left Charlie proceeded to tell him about Jack and Megan's baby, Bob's retirement, and, lastly, Rita's illness and passing. She could see the genuine sadness on his face as she told him and wasn't surprised; David had always been fond of Rita, and she him. He got along well with Bob too, though he didn't approve of his and Charlie's line of work.

After she finished talking about Rita she asked him about his life, and he told her he worked in the sales division of an electronics company ever since he graduated college and was
thinking now of writing a book, something he'd always wanted to do. He also talked about his wife, Kate, and how they met and their plans of leaving New York one day to pursue other career options.

They stayed and talked for hours, long after they'd both eaten-David insisted she try the apple pie and it was delicious-and played catch-up. The whole time they were there Charlie paid close attention to David and realized his life had gone exactly the way she'd known it would.

A direction completely different from her own.

When they finally exited to diner they walked down the street to where they had parked, coming across David's vehicle first: a blue Toyota 4Runner. "Wow," Charlie commented as they stopped. "Look at you all grown up and playing responsible businessman and husband."

He laughed. "It's not very exciting, is it?" he asked, gesturing to the car. "But it gets decent gas mileage and it's family-safe...for the future."

Suddenly the atmosphere grew tense; neither one of them had mentioned kids-other than to talk about Jack and Megan-though he talked about his wife and the future. Now everything became more serious, the gulf between their respective lifestyles growing even wider and putting everything that had ever been between them farther into the past.

"It's just for now though," David said in an attempt to break the awkward silence. "When I'm in my forties having my mid-life crisis, then I'll get the motorcycle."

Charlie wordlessly held up her keys. "Does that mean I'm already there?"

His eyes widened. "You didn't."

"I did."

"You were always talking about that, about getting one someday. Either that or a Trans Am." Then his expression sobered. "So how is...work?" he asked tentatively. They'd carefully avoided the subject of her job the entire time they'd been talking.

"It's good," Charlie said with a nod. "Just wrapped up a job recently and now I'm focusing my energy on my past, finally getting answers. I have some leads and am collaborating with someone...and hopefully I'll be finding something out soon."

He looked at her carefully. "How soon?"

"Possibly tomorrow."

"I know that look," he told her. "This is something big, and whatever you're doing tomorrow is risky."

She nodded. "No point lying about it."

"You never lied about it."

"Do you wish I had?" she asked. "That I hadn't been so open about it? Did that make things worse?"

He looked at her for a long moment before speaking. "You didn't do anything wrong," he said finally. "The problem wasn't you."

"What was it then?"

"I think you know," he told her. "Look at our lives, where we're at now. We're miles apart, Charlie. We were going in two different directions then, leading each of us to where we wanted to be. And that place wasn't together."

"No I guess it wasn't." She paused. "I just want to make sure you didn't resent me, for forcing all of it on you and expecting you to just deal with it. I never realized what I was asking, how different my life really was when for me…it was all I knew. It's who I am."

He nodded. "And there's absolutely nothing wrong with that. I think we both turned out pretty great," he said and Charlie nodded her agreement. "I never wanted you to think I wasn't crazy about you, that you didn't mean that much to me because the truth is, I'd never met anyone like you before and you meant-"

Charlie held up her hand to stop him. "You don't have to say any more," she told him. "That was plenty. And the feeling was mutual."

With that they decided to say good-bye, David pulling her into a tight hug. "It really was good seeing you again," he told her. "I'm glad you're getting close to the truth…and I'm glad you never stopped being who you are."

"I'm glad you haven't either." She raised her hand in a wave and started to walk away.

"If you feel like apple pie again I'll save you a seat," he called after her.

Charlie turned around, continuing to walk backwards. "I'll bring my fat pants," she called back and he laughed.

As she approached her bike she felt as though a burden had been lifted that she wasn't aware existed. *It's like Diana said…your first love is special,* she told herself as she out on her helmet. *And if I ever had any doubts before that I was his…I don't now.*

And that feels pretty good.

***

Charlie spent the rest of the evening packing her gear, the stereo on and a beer in hand as she did so. Since they had to be prepared for anything she had more than usual.

As she was finishing up her cell rang, and she walked over to the left bedside table to retrieve it. She recognized the number and answered quickly. "Mike," she greeted him, sitting on the edge of her bed. "You got something for me?" She was grateful that people in lines of work similar to her worked odd hours.

"Marianna Thompson Marquez," Mike told her, sounding as though he were reading. "Born August 24, 1941 in Boston, only child of

Maynard and Esther Reed. Married Daniel Thompson March 15, 1961 and moved to Atlantic City. Marianna worked in the casinos, Thompson was retired. He died ten years later from a stroke-he was a good twenty years older than her. Marianna left Atlantic City shortly after and moved to Jacksonville, where she met and later married Christian Marquez. Her parents moved down there for retirement, and Marianna ended up caring for them as they got older until they each passed away. Her marriage to Marquez lasted five years before ending in divorce. It was a nasty one too-Marquez had more money and got the high-priced attorney, so he got everything. Marianna stayed in Jacksonville until the early eighties; there's no record of her after that except for the parking ticket she got here in 1986. Other than that and her driver's license, there's no record of her: no record of work or taxes, property, or automobiles in her name. However she was surviving, she was doing it under the table and calling as little attention to herself as possible."

"What about after 1987?" Charlie wanted to know. "The last time I saw her? Where has she been all this time?"

"We're still working on it,' he told her. "But for right now, that's all we have. Oh and
we're trying to locate any relatives, but so far the only ones on file were her parents."

Charlie had been jotting down all the information while Mike had been talking, planning to add it the file she was starting on Anna. After thanking Mike she hung up with him, looking over everything she had written before walking across the hall to her office so she could file it in its proper folder. Then she called T.J. to give him an update but got his voicemail, so she left him a quick message.

As she settled into bed later she started thinking about the next day, trying to mentally prepare herself for anything. It wasn't difficult; she did it all the time since she rarely knew what to expect. But, yet, there was something different about it, something different she was feeling that never had before. Unable to pinpoint what it was, she closed her eyes and found herself falling into a light and-for the first time in years-dreamless sleep.

Chapter Seven

Around nine o'clock the next morning there was a knock on Charlie's door, just as she was finishing breakfast-grapefruit and whole-grain toast.

"It's open!" she called, drinking the last of her coffee and taking her empty plate to the sink. Then she headed to her bedroom, hauling her bags off her bed and down the hall.

T.J. was waiting in the living room, looking at the photos on the fireplace mantle. Since he investigated her Charlie knew he recognized Melinda, Rita, Bob, and Jack and Megan, as well as the friends she made over the years. Or acquaintances, if she was being factual.

He was wearing his usual rust-colored leather jacket while Charlie was wearing her black one. Their similar attire, profession, skills, and knowing Diana led to a path of commonality. *As well as our taste in cars,* she added mentally. But there were differences, too. T.J. was more positive than Charlie, a lot less weighed down.

And he was nowhere near as damaged as she was.

Unsure why her thoughts were drifting in the direction they had, Charlie cleared her throat. "This is all my crap," she announced, gesturing to the bags at her feet. "Are we ready?"

He nodded. "If we get going now we should make it by the afternoon."

Charlie was loading her bags in the Chevelle's trunk when her phone rang. She answered it without bothering to check who the caller was first. "Yeah?"

Silence echoed on the other end.

Charlie checked and saw that the caller was unknown. "I could have your number traced so fast your head'll spin, so you better start talking. Now."

"I have information," a frightened female voice replied. "About Anna."

"Who is this?" Charlie demanded. The line went dead.

Charlie shook her head, cursing under her breath as she hit the call button after scrolling through her phonebook. "I need a trace," she ordered, walking to the passenger door as T.J. looked on. "The number that just called. Yeah. Thanks, Lou." She hung up and got in the car, shutting the door. "I feel like I'm in a damned thriller movie," she muttered, strapping on her seatbelt.

T.J. started the car. "But the soundtrack's a hell of a lot better," he told her, switching on the stereo. Within seconds the sounds of Quiet Riot filled the car.

Charlie grinned despite herself. "Bring on the big hair," she declared as T.J. pulled out of the parking lot and headed toward the highway.

They had finished shouting the lyrics to "Cherry Pie" when they crossed the state line. T.J. informed her his stomach was growling so they exited the interstate and stopped at a diner. Though she'd eaten at one just the night before, Charlie had no objection.

She immediately excused herself to the restroom, where she checked her messages after using the bathroom. *Still no word from Lou, or mike or any of my guys searching for Anna,* she thought in annoyance. *I don't have time for these games…*

She fingered through her hair, pulling it back into a loose bun. When she re-joined T.J. he was already drinking his coffee, sitting at the counter. The waitress stopped by to take their order as Charlie sat down, ordering a steak burger with extra pickles and fries; her "usual" only
belonged in the diner back home.

To her surprise, T.J. ordered identically. Charlie looked at him in amusement as the waitress disappeared into the kitchen. "Fancy restaurants, fancy clothes, cab-riding, laid-back negotiator…leather-jacket-wearing, muscle-car-driving, eighties-hair-band-listening, down in the trenches private investigator, carnivore…which one's the real you?"

"Both," T.J. answered as the waitress refilled his coffee. "I'm a multi-faceted guy. But I'm pretty straightforward. By the way," he added, turning toward her, "I ran into Diana before I left and she told me to tell you she wishes you luck."

"That's nice of her." Charlie took a sip of water, not mentioning once again how strange it was to have someone new in her life who cared about her.

"It's an adjustment," T.J. said, reading her expression. "I'm sure it'll take some getting used to."

Charlie nodded. Then she took a breath. "I think we've gotten the subject of me well-covered. Why don't we talk about you?"

"You want to talk about me?"

"Well...I kind of have a confession to make. When Rita left me your name I ran a background check on you. Just to make sure you were legit."

"Understandable," he said with a nod. "Wouldn't have expected anything less."

"Would you have expected for me to do it twice?"

That got his attention. "Twice?" he repeated in surprise. "Once wasn't enough?"

"It was enough until I found out you'd been digging into my life," Charlie pointed out. "The night at the restaurant when you told me everything I wanted to be absolutely sure you were on the level, so I handled the second search myself."

He shook his head slightly, appearing amused. "Find anything interesting?"

"You pay more alimony then ten average guys put together," she told him. "You need a better lawyer."

"Actually, that was my call. The truth is...it was my fault the marriage failed," he admitted.

"Your fault?" Charlie repeated incredulously. "She had the affair."

T.J. raised an eyebrow. "So you have done your homework," he stated, sounding impressed. Then his expression sobered. "Yes, she stepped out on me but it was because I was never around. My cases took me everywhere, sometimes weeks at a time. That puts a lot of strain on the relationship."

"I guess I know about that. Kind of hard for someone to invest in you when you're always gone, huh? Of course, in my case no one stuck around long enough to really get to that point." She thought of David, and their conversation the night before. It was undeniable that there had been strong feelings there on both sides, but there wasn't the level of commitment to get past or accept the vast differences in their lives. And every other man she'd ever been involved with usually bailed before she could say "9 millimeter". "They wanted your sweet, average woman, and they found my career choice...intimidating. Didn't like that I was tougher than they were."

"Imbeciles," T.J. told her. "Too insecure to appreciate a strong woman. That's on them, not you. Any man with half a brain would be all over the chance to be with someone like you."

"And why's that?"

"Because you're completely original," he told her simply. "And that's worth ten 'sweet, average women'."

No one had said anything quite like that to her before, and it rendered Charlie speechless.

"And there's the fact that you know how to handle a gun," he continued with a grin. "In my book, there's nothing sexier."

Charlie smiled wryly. "You might be slightly biased about that." Then her expression became serious. "Thanks," she told him sincerely, for what he'd said earlier. "And for the record, your ex-wife sounds like a nutcase. At least from what I found out about her."

T.J. chuckled. "Too true, too true. You'd never guess how many times she's been remarried since we spilt up."

"Twice?"

T.J. shook his head.

"Three times?" Charlie asked in disbelief. "In six years?"

"Make it four."

Charlie burst out laughing. "Are you sure she's not secretly a celebrity?"

"No, just easily distracted."

Their food arrived then and they began to eat, trading war stories about their love lives. Charlie offered to cover the bill when they finished but T.J. insisted, so she headed out to the car.

Her phone rang on the way and she answered it immediately. "Lou? Tell me you've got something."

Instead of a reply the caller hung up and a few seconds later her phone beeped, signaling that someone had sent her a photo.

T.J. came out of the diner in time to see Charlie go white, then lean over the hood of the car and breathe in deeply, as though trying to calm herself down. He ran over to her, catching her phone as it slid from her grasp. She walked away, dazed.

He looked at the phone and saw a photo of a woman he recognized as Anna, appearing to be the same age as she was in the photos he found of her and Charlie when Charlie was a child. The only difference in her between those photos and the one he was looking at now was that she appeared to be no longer alive.

T.J. looked at the photo carefully, going into work mode. There was a date stamped at the bottom right-hand corner that read JULY 20, 1987. If the date was correct, the photo was taken not long after Charlie and Anna were separated.

Charlie had walked across the street and was leaning against a telephone pole, wearing an expression he couldn't interpret. T.J. quickly called one of his contacts in a tech lab and sent him the photo, telling him to put a rush on analyzing it. Luckily he owed T.J. a laundry list of favors and was more than willing to comply.

After he hung up he walked over to her, studying her carefully. "He's playing with you," he said finally. "We have no way of knowing if that photo's even real." Charlie remained silent so he continued. "It doesn't make sense for him to have had her killed and reveal it to you now. Don't you see? He knows you're close, which is where he wants you to be, and he's trying to get a reaction out of you, cause you to slip up. He's counting on you doing something rash without thinking it through." He took a step toward her. "Don't let him goad you into some kind of battle."

Charlie finally turned to face him. "I have no proof that it's real," she told him finally. "The intellectual part of my brain knows that. And even though there's a part of me that's terrified that this could be real I know the chances are slim; the timing of it all is too convenient. But I'm sick of this, dammit. I'm sick of this...man playing with my life. It's not enough that he's been secretly having me tailed all these years, knowing that all the private and special moments of my life were being watched by strangers, he has to resurface now and cause nothing but drama and mayhem...and possibly could be sending me into a trap. He's done enough, T.J. He can't just keep going on-" she broke off, running her hands back through her hair and taking a few steps backward.

"I think we might have to consider that Stevens isn't working alone on this," he told her quietly.

"That makes sense. I'm sure he can't do it all by himself. He must've hired-"

"I'm not talking about random men for hire," T.J. interrupted. "I'm talking about Anna."   Charlie stopped, staring at him. "What did you just say?"

"There could have been some elaborate plan to steal you from the hospital," he began in a rush. "You said she was left with nothing in the divorce. Maybe Stevens was looking for someone to help him steal you, willing to pay anything-"

"We don't know that Stevens is loaded," Charlie said impatiently, cutting him off. "We weren't able to get into his financial records. In fact, we haven't been able to find out much about him at all. And maybe we haven't been able to find out a lot about Anna either but...she wouldn't do that."

"How do you know?" he challenged. "You said it yourself-you were a kid. The truth is, you don't know much at all about Anna, about what she was really like or what she could have been involved in. She probably wasn't even your aunt. Maybe she's been in hiding all these years, for one reason or another. We can't rule anything out. At least wait until we hear back from my guy, find out if the photo's legit-even though we don't think it is-before you do anything you might later regret."

"What is it you think I'll regret? Killing Stevens? That sick son-of-a-bitch has some kind of obsession with me that set events in motion that shaped my life forever, if he's the reason Anna and I got separated and I believe that he is. If that's true...he's the reason everything happened the way it did. I don't know why or what the details were, and I don't care. The only thing that matters now is that he screwed with me for the last time. For being sick enough to try and make me believe he killed Anna, he's a dead man." She began to walk briskly to the car.

"Wait," T.J. called after her. "What are you going to do?"

"What do you think I'm going to do?" She went straight toward the trunk. "I need the keys," she told him.

"Think this through, Charlie. You can't run in there half-cocked, guns blazing."

"Why the hell not?"

"Because you're a professional," he said firmly, seizing her by the shoulders. "Take your personal feelings out of it for a moment and remember what the goal is: to find out what *his* goal is, why he's after you, and where you were the first four years of your life. Dropping clues out of the sky left and right about your past, clues that plainly lead back to him, going out of his way to set all this up, and now he sends the picture to screw with you even more...he knows exactly what buttons to push because he's watched you all your life. He's done nothing but try and manipulate you from the start, wanting to knock you off balance, let you go in unprepared. If you go in there purely on anger that's what he'll be expecting, and then he'll get the drop on you. What we need to do is the complete opposite, go into this as rationally as possible."

"It does seem like he might have something planned," she said slowly. Then she let out a long breath. "What you're saying makes sense. It would be to his advantage if I'm operating solely on rage; that makes me vulnerable and him the one who's in control." She paused. "And that's the exactly first thing I'd say if it were happening to someone else-never react with anger, never act on emotion." She shook her head angrily. "Damned asshole has me acting like an amateur."

"You're acting like someone with emotional ties, someone who's fed up with being someone else's guinea pig," he corrected. "All that means is that you can't think clearly about this, which is perfectly understandable. I doubt it'd be any different for me if I was in your shoes." He put a hand on her shoulder. "You're allowed to be human, Charlie."

"Thanks," she told him, swallowing hard. "For reigning me back in."

"No problem. I vote we hole up in a motel for a while, wait till my guy gets back to us and see if anything else we've been researching turns up something on Anna. Then we'll go, when we're ready."

"Alright," she conceded. "I saw a sign a mile back for a motel with free wi-fi, so we can
set up shop there."

Charlie couldn't help but be amused as she followed T.J. away from the check-in counter a short while later. "Dr. and Mrs. Jekyll?" she asked in disbelief as they walked to room eight. "Good thing the clerk was stoned off his ass."

"I never use my real name when I check into motels; job hazard." T.J. unlocked the door and let Charlie walk in first.

They each sat on a bed, set up with their computers and phones. After a few hours T.J. announced one of his contacts produced something and was e-mailing it to him now. Charlie ended her call and gave her undivided attention to the computer screen.

"He found her," T.J. said, looking at the surveillance shots. " 'Marianna Marquez'," he read. " 'Last seen outside Sydney.'"

"William Ford?" Charlie asked. "Who's that?"

"My contact in Australia. I've had everyone everywhere looking out for her, like you have, and we struck gold. He took this photo last month."

Charlie looked at the pictures, comparing it with the one she took from Stevens' apartment. The woman in Australia looked a lot older but it was definitely the same woman. "This guy's on the level?"

"Absolutely. Which means Stevens didn't kill her, as we suspected."

Even though she hadn't really believed the photo had been real it still felt good to see that Anna was alive and well. "How the hell did she end up in Sydney?" she wondered out loud. "If Stevens did get a hold of her, how did she get away? And how come she never tried to contact me?"

"Good questions," T.J. observed. "We'll keep digging."

They worked into the evening, stopping when T.J. got a call confirming what they already knew: the photo Stevens sent to Charlie's phone was a fake, as well as how it had been edited.
Meanwhile, Charlie found out that Anna had been a legal citizen of Australia for the past ten years, but her whereabouts before that still remained a mystery. After that they put the search for her on hold so they could plan and organize for the next day, be ready to expect anything.

They went out on the back porch at twilight, when the first stars were appearing in the sky, continuing to discuss the situation. They sat on the concrete, leaning up against the railing as they strategized.

"I've been thinking," Charlie said after a while, "about Stevens' connection to me. Diana doesn't know him, so it has to be through my biological father, the person who still remains a giant question mark." She looked at T.J. thoughtfully. "Why do you think Diana won't talk about him?"

"I don't know," he replied honestly. "She never has. I've gotten the impression that she's ashamed somehow, that he's too painful for her to think about."

"Lydia said there's a possibility that Stevens worked for the government. If that's true, I wonder if my father did too." She looked up at the sky. "I wonder if he was as sadistic as Stevens," she muttered.

Then she looked back at T.J. "What's your family like?" she asked suddenly. "Are they normal?"

"My parents were lawyers, both retired now and living in Palm Springs. My mother has a pet Capuchin monkey and my father spends his retirement going to antique stores to look at old hubcaps. My youngest sister is a Marilyn Monroe impersonator in Vegas and my other sister is an aroma therapist who lives in Minnesota with a man old enough to be our grandfather...so you tell me."

"They sound like fun."

"They are. I mean, they're crazy...but they're not bad people to be related to. Always been there for me."

"I've always wondered what it would be like, you know? To grow up in one house with your biological relatives, maybe a few siblings thrown into the mix, a couple pets...be born with a last name and a birth certificate and know everything about where you come from. But then I tell myself how fortunate I am, to have met the people I met who weren't my blood but chose to love me anyway."

"That's what makes you truly special," T.J. told her. "Most people go through life feeling like they're an obligation, because of DNA. You know differently."

They went inside after that and ordered a pizza, agreeing to go to sleep shortly after so they could get an early start the next morning. They sprawled on one bed, the pizza box between them, and watched a block of old sitcoms on TV as they ate. "You could have your own show," T.J. told Charlie, picking up a large slice. "Charlie Booker, Bounty Hunter."

"What about you? Mackenzie, Private I.?"

"Or we could put both of our names together," he suggested. "Instead of *T.J. Hooker* it could be *T.J. Booker.* "

Charlie laughed. "That's hilarious. Except then we'd have to be cops. I don't know about you...but I don't always live inside the law."

"Neither do I. Look for me the next time you get arrested and I'll do the same."

"Deal," Charlie agreed, and they both lifted their pizza slices in the air to toast on it.

While they'd been eating the sky clouded over and a wind had sprung up. When Charlie got out of the shower she noticed lightning, and a storm followed close behind.

The storm shook the old, tired building as lightning illuminated the dark room. T.J. and Charlie decided to turn in and they both laid in the dark listening to the wind whistling through the cracks in the windows.

"Charlie?" T.J. asked as the storm worsened, rain pounding on the dilapidated roof.

"Yeah?"

"Do you ever wonder what else is out there? Aside from work?"

"I used to," Charlie replied, staring at the peeling paint above her. "Rita and I wanted to go to Europe, start seeing the world, but we never got the chance. When I still had the jet-ski I went on trips to Florida and the Gulf and had a lot of fun…but survival's always been at the top of my list. I've never really had a chance to just be free."

"Neither have I," T.J. told her. "I used to think I'd make a good mechanic. Or maybe a dad."

"You want kids?" Charlie asked in surprise, rolling over to face the other bed.

"Thought about it. You?"

His brown eyes were staring at her unblinkingly, seeming to sort of glow in the darkness. She hadn't thought about having kids of her own that often, until encountering David the night before when she realized how close to that possibility he was…and how she'd never felt farther. "Not much," she admitted after a moment. "I'm not sure I'm mommy material. I would've liked
to be an aunt, though. Have someone to spoil with ridiculous gifts. I guess I kind of will be, when Jack and Megan have their baby." She paused. "It always seems to come back to family, doesn't it?"

"I think that means we're getting old."

Charlie groaned. "Awesome. Thanks for reminding me I'm a hop, skip, and a jump away from thirty," she complained.

"Just wait till you're here, then the real fun begins: senior citizen discounts, early bird specials, hearing aides, Viagra-"

Charlie burst out laughing. "You did not just say that."

"Maybe I did, maybe I didn't."

After they'd both stopped laughing they agreed to call it a night, listening as the storm died down outside. Just as her eyes began to feel heavy, Charlie felt something cold hit her between the eyes.

Blinking, she looked up to see that water was dripping from a hole in the ceiling, lightly at first but then turning into a steady trickle. Groaning, Charlie buried her head under the pillow.

"What is it?" T.J.'s voice came from the darkness.

"It's nothing," she assured him. "I'm-" She broke off as the ceiling gave way; now a tennis-ball sized chunk was missing, and the water that had pooled in that area now streamed down freely, pouring into Charlie's nose and mouth. She began to sputter.

While T.J. inspected the hole, which was growing larger by the minute, Charlie went into the bathroom to look for a towel so she could plug up the hole.

"You don't have to sleep there," he told her as she worked on the ceiling, which felt rotten. "We can trade."

"It's not a big deal; I'm not exactly a prissy princess. I can handle it."

"But you need your sleep," he reminded her. "A good night's sleep. We both do if we're going to be ready and on top of our game…so sleep here." He rose from the bed. "I'll sleep on the floor."

"T.J.-"

"You've got a waterfall in your bed," he interrupted. "Just take mine."

"Wait." She got down from the bed and walked over to him. "You won't get any sleep that way…why don't we both sleep in your bed?" she suggested.

"You don't mind?"

She shrugged. "As long as you're not a blanket hog."

A few moments later they were both settling into to bed, trying to get situated. "Do you have enough room?" T.J. asked as Charlie fluffed up the pillow.

She nodded. "I do. Good night. And thanks." She paused. "You know, someday I'll do something for you."

"I'll hold you to that. Good night, Charlie."

***

"Anna?" Charlie asked, tugging on the woman's dress.

"Not now, Charlotte. I'm on the phone," Anna chided, turning toward the sink in the kitchen and continuing her conversation.

"But Anna," Charlie protested.

"I know!" Anna snapped impatiently into the receiver. "But we had an agreement. You can't just waltz in here now and take her-"

"Anna!" Charlie shrieked, ducking behind her.

"What on Earth-" Anna broke off, looking up to see two powerfully built men enter the apartment. "You bastard," she whispered into the phone, dropping it and letting it hang by its cord. She scooped Charlie up in her arms and ran toward the fire escape.

After they carefully climbed down, Charlie still in Anna's arms, Anna looked around frantically to see if they were followed.

"Why are we running, Anna?" Charlie asked, burying her face in Anna's shoulder.

"There are people after us, very bad people," Anna answered, her eyes darting around nervously. "We have to get as far away from them as we can."

Charlie's eyes snapped open around dawn, trying to breathe normally again. *What was that?* she thought in a panic, her heart thumping loudly. But she knew what it was. It was the beginning of the dream she never remembered of the memory of that night with Anna, of how it all started. Though she couldn't figure out why it had come to her now, unless it had something to do with what Stevens tried to pull the day before.

When she finally calmed down she realized T.J. was curled up behind her, his arm around her while she was holding his hand.

We go to sleep on opposite sides of the bed and wake up spooning? she thought as she tried to disentangle herself without waking him. *What is that?* Behind her she could feel T.J. beginning to shift.

Not wanting to deal with the awkwardness that would inevitably follow, Charlie stayed where she was and pretended to be asleep while T.J. sat up and yawned, careful not to disturb her. He lingered for a moment before heading to the bathroom, and Charlie got up as soon as she heard the door shut. She changed, suddenly feeling like she was thirteen.

When T.J. exited the bathroom fully dressed, his thick dark hair still wet, Charlie wordlessly went in to continue getting ready. After she brushed her teeth she pulled out her .45 and tucked it into the back of her jeans, dropped her knife into her left boot, and stuffed an extra clip into her jacket pocket with her phone. Then she brushed her hair back over her shoulders, grabbed her sunglasses, and carried her bags out of the bathroom and out the door after T.J.

They wordlessly drove away from the motel and into the early morning light; the sky was clear, showing no evidence that there had been a storm the night before. Neither said much, stopping only once for breakfast at McDonald's. The stereo was on, mostly for background, but since they weren't really speaking it was louder than it should have been.

They continued on like that throughout the drive to Cape Cod.

***

When they were just miles from Stevens' cabin they got down to business, circling areas on the map for escape routes and hashing out the details. Once they were closing in T.J. parked about half a mile from the cabin, out of the way on a deserted street. He got out and unlocked the trunk, starting to get everything they needed together when Charlie came up behind him, taking a breath. "I think I should go in alone," she told him.

T.J. stopped, turning around to face her. "Why?"

"Because he set all of this up for me, which means I'm the one he wants to talk to," Charlie replied reasonably. "It's not a big deal; I've gone solo for a lot worse."

"But this is different," he reminded her. "You said it yourself: you're emotionally invested, and that affects your judgment."

"Which is why you'll be in the area. Keeping an eye out for any surprises."

"Fine." T.J. shut the trunk. "But I want to hear everything that's going on." He dropped a listening device in her right boot. "If I think you're in over your head, I'm coming in after you."

Charlie nodded. "Agreed." She handed him his gun. "See you when it's done." She started down the road.

"Good luck," T.J. called after her. Charlie waved over her shoulder.

The cabin sat on a hill overlooking the water, surrounded by trees. A red SUV sat in the gravel drive next to the large front porch. Charlie quickly walked the perimeter, and once she was sure the coast was clear she started up the back entrance, her gun drawn.

No lights were on inside but there were enough windows to illuminate the cabin's interior. Charlie cautiously walked through the small kitchen toward the narrow hallway, staying on alert. So far she hadn't seen any evidence that someone was staying there, except for the car
outside.

The hall ended shortly, the living room on the right. When she entered the room Charlie stopped in surprise.

Sitting calmly on the couch, reading the newspaper, was a man in his early sixties. His silver-streaked dark hair and weathered skin were what gave away his age, but his eyes were a strong, piercing azure blue unlike anything Charlie had ever seen. "Charlie," he greeted her pleasantly, lowering his newspaper. "So good of you to come."

Chapter Eight

"Why don't you have a seat," he suggested as though they were old friends, gesturing to the chair across from him. "I'm not armed," he added, eyeing her gun.

Charlie hesitantly lowered her weapon and sat on the edge of the chair, studying his calm demeanor suspiciously. "You went through a hell of a lot of trouble to get me here," she said finally. "Sending me a fake photo of Anna's 'death' was below the belt, even if I did see right through it."

Stevens looked at her, leaning forward slightly. "And you've never used questionable methods in your line of work to get what you wanted?"

Charlie bristled. "Not that questionable. And never to further my own agenda." Then she cleared her throat. "Can we just cut all the bull and get down to it? Who are you, how do you know me, and why have you been documenting most of my life?"

"My name is Andrew Stevens, I know you because of your father, and I've been keeping tabs on you all your life in case I needed you in the future," he answered promptly.

Charlie was surprised at his casual tone and by how eagerly he divulged the information. "Who is my father, and how do you know him?" she continued, unfazed. "Why did you go to so much trouble to lure me here? And why now?"

Stevens chuckled. "I expected you to have questions but you're a regular little interrogator. So businesslike and professional. If you want the truth…here it is.

"I was recruited out of high school to work for on a secret government project, based on my natural talent and skills. I could tell you about the project…but the less you know, the better. Anyway, about eight years into it I was assigned to train a new recruit, show him the ropes. He was fresh out of high school like I'd been, and soon we became friends.

"Not long after he turned twenty-five he met someone, someone I could tell he was crazy about but wouldn't say much about her. The one day, months later, he confided to me that she was pregnant. He also told me she'd lied about her age; she was only a junior in high school. I told him he had to end it before anyone found out but he refused, saying he was going to quit the project and do the right thing. What he didn't know was I had another task added to my job description. I couldn't let anyone quit the project, walk away with what they knew. If anyone tried…I had to make them disappear."

Charlie frowned. "That doesn't sound like the U.S. government protocol-"

"It wasn't," Stevens interrupted. "We weren't really working for the government, we were only told we were. In actuality we were working for an underground organization, which is why everything was top secret and no one could just walk away. I figured it out pretty quickly, but by then I was already in too deep to get out.

"I had a job to do, but I didn't relish the idea of killing my friend. So I blackmailed him instead."

"How?"

"You." Stevens looked at her, his expression resembling fondness. "I tracked your mother down and presented myself as an adoption agent. Her parents signed you over to me without hesitation. I took you and hid you, raised you for the first time four years of your life. And just as I knew he would, your father stayed in exchange for my promise that you were safe and one day he'd be reunited with you. But then...things got tricky.

"Things started going downhill and the men upstairs decided it would be best if the whole operation vanished, meaning no witnesses. We all split up and went our separate ways...and your father wanted to turn himself in to the authorities, expose what was really going on-"

"and you couldn't let him, because your hands were so dirty," Charlie finished. "So you held onto me."

"I couldn't take care of you while I was on the run so I found a relative, your great-aunt on your father's side. Marianna Marquez. I paid her to keep her mouth shut and take care of you, which she did. But she got attached, didn't want to give you up when I was able to take you
back-"

"Stop," Charlie interrupted. "Stop." She stood. "I think I've seen this movie before." She shook her head. "You are the most manipulative, twisted person I've ever met. And I'm from New York." She took a step forward. "You can spin a hell of a story. But it takes a con to know a con when they see one, and you're definitely conning me."

Stevens burst out laughing. "You're no one's fool, I'll give you that. What gave me away?"

"If you were really working on some top secret pseudo-government project they wouldn't have screwed around; all of you would be dead, no matter how good you were. But I know there's some truth to your story, and I want to hear the rest. Now." She folded her arms over her chest, glaring at him.

"I apologize for getting carried away; I did get some ideas from movies I've recently seen, and it's quite fun." He smiled. "Now that I got my espionage tale out of my system, I suppose it's time for the truth. I have not worked for the United States government, no matter what I've let people believe over the years. I might have let people assume thoughts in that direction to give me a past, as part of my cover." He paused. "Andy Stevens isn't my given name."

"Who are you, then?"

"I was born Hector Juan Montenillo."

Charlie stopped. "Montenillo?" she repeated. "As in the Brooklyn Montenillos who practically run the Eastern seaboard? The reigning mob family?"

"We were," Stevens said shortly. "We're only half as powerful now as we once were. We can thank your father for that."

"Why?" she demanded. "What happened?"

"My father is Antonio Montenillo, whom most referred to as the kingpin of Brooklyn before you were born, the man in charge. As his oldest son I was expected to follow in his footsteps, and I did for years. My father trusted me to hire men as needed and one day I met someone with promise, someone dedicated. He was young, eager, but he was steady and dependable. Trustworthy. So I took a chance on him. His name was Johnny Black, and we ended up becoming close friends.

"Then things started to get bad for the family, and we soon discovered there was leak somewhere; someone was feeding information to the cops. A rat who needed to be stopped. So Johnny and I worked together to track down the leak and take care of him, but we weren't really getting anywhere. Then a meeting got busted one night, a private meeting that only the inner circle knew about. I was confused, trying to figure out who the rat was…and couldn't believe it when it turned out to be Johnny.

"Johnny revealed himself to be a cop and arrested my father, who shouted for my brothers and I to run for it. Johnny had called backup and my brothers were caught. All because of a detective, who's life mission was taking my family down. And he partially succeeded: my father's still in prison, my brothers were killed resisting arrest, and Hector Montenillo ceased to exist after that night. I changed my name, became Andy Stevens. My uncle and cousins were the only ones who knew I was still alive; they're the Montenillos you've heard of now. My uncle took over."

"The detective-Johnny-was my father," Charlie stated.

"And because of him, I had to fake my own death so they wouldn't come after me. I couldn't even avenge my own family. My uncles and cousins were furious of course, wanted to strike, but I convinced them not to. I told them as Andy Stevens I could do a lot more damage flying under the radar. So they agreed to let me do it my way, and I did. I spent months researching the bastard detective who pretended to have loyalty toward my family and earned my trust enough to become my friend while planning the entire time to destroy us all. There wasn't anything interesting at first...and then I found out about Diana Sullivan, that she was pregnant with his child. So I came up with a plan as quickly as I could, before time ran out. I claimed to be an adoption agent and spoke to your grandparents, who set the whole thing up with me after I assured them you would be going to a good home, though they didn't really seem to care. They just wanted you gone, which made them completely oblivious to suspicion and they didn't bother having me checked out.

"I took you out of the hospital the day you were born and brought you here, to the cabin I'd just purchased and was hiding out in. But I wasn't the only one who had to stay low. Your father was at the top of the hit list in the underworld, now he'd been revealed as a cop, so he had to stay hidden for his own protection. He disappeared from sight, but once everything had settled down I contacted him, revealing that I was very much alive and that I'd taken you from your mother. I told him if he wanted me to give you back he had to come out of hiding, stop the ongoing investigation into my uncle and cousins. He agreed, and I held onto you until I was sure he'd back off. I raised you here for the first few years of your life and called you Ace, because you were my Ace in the hole. As long as I had you my family would be safe, which is why I didn't go with my original plan."

"And what was that?" Charlie asked, trying not to appear fazed by all the new information she was receiving.

"Keep you, raise you as my daughter, and not let him know until you were grown and were already a Montenillo. There'd be a lot of pleasure for me if I went that route but it didn't guarantee my family's safety. So I chose Plan B. Then I found out your father drank himself to death."

Charlie froze. "He's dead?"

"He lost his badge because he botched the case against my family, acting on my orders of course. He didn't have you or your mother..." He shrugged. "So I was stuck with a baby I didn't know what to do with. I'd been glad not to go with my first idea because I knew nothing about children and didn't think I could possibly put up with one for eighteen years. I was in a tight spot;
I didn't want anything *bad* to happen to you, just because you were your father's child. So that's
when I screwed up and left you with Marianna."

"How did you know Anna?"

"I didn't. She really is your father's aunt. She was his only living relative, so I contacted her and paid her to take care of you and keep her mouth shut. What I didn't know was she was playing me, planning to double-cross me by taking you and disappearing. She stopped seeing it as a job after a while, and ended up getting attached to you. She's the one who named you Charlotte, since she hated the name Ace. Anyway, when I figured out what she was up to I sent people after her. I never thought you'd get separated-"

"Let me see if I got this straight," Charlie interrupted. "Anna saw through your B.S. and wanted to get me away from you, so you sent people to our apartment that night to take her away. Only she ended up escaping you somehow but had to stay on the run so you wouldn't come after her again, leaving me to wander the streets of New York as a small child-"

"I didn't know that would happen-"

"Why didn't you just give me back to my mother?" Charlie wanted to know. "Why was it better for me to be on my own?"

"I didn't know you were on your own, not until I saw the surveillance photos later. I was too busy trying to track down Marianna, because she was working with your father."

Charlie blinked. "You said he was dead."

"Everyone thought he was because he just disappeared, which is exactly what he wanted. He took a page out of my book and let everyone believe he'd drowned his sorrows for the final time. Once he found out you were with Marianna he contacted her, and they started to work together on how to get you safely away. He stayed away, just to be sure."

"And you know all of this-"

"-just like I knew everything else and had those photos taken," he finished. "You were my Golden Ticket; there was no way I was letting you off my radar. Once I figured out what Marianna and your father were up to I had my men intervene. And you're right; she did escape, with his help I'm sure. And they've been impossible to find ever since."

"Why have they been running from you all this time?"

"Because they're working on putting me away," he explained. "And then they'll come after the rest of my family. Their hatred for me must be more important than their love for you."

"More likely they're just trying to keep me safe," she snapped. "From a maniac who likes to play God with peoples' lives."

"So judgmental," he said, shaking his head.

"I want to know why you've kept track of me. Is it because you're waiting for the right time to strike, to lure my father out of hiding?"

"I kept track of you in the beginning because you were a tool, a very important one. But it didn't take long for it to become more than that. I'm fond of you," he admitted. "For almost four years you were like my daughter. I hired people to keep track of you even when I was out of the country, so I've gotten to see your whole life. And you've amazed me, Charlie Booker. You've handled yourself like a true Montenillo."

"Excuse me?"

"You're tough, smart, quick on your feet, and a survivor. And look at what you do for a
living-you're a bounty hunter, for God's sakes. That carries the same disgrace as 'mobster' to all the ordinary people, and by ordinary I mean cops."

"You mean my father."

Stevens nodded. "It doesn't always fall on the side of legal, very few people understand, and most consider it criminal. Do you really think your father would understand or approve of the life you lead? If you weren't his own flesh and blood he'd hunt you down himself. Cops only see black and white, never shades of gray. Not like we do." He leaned in closer to her. "You're more like me than you'll ever be like your old man."

"I inherited my strength and capability from Diana," Charlie said through clenched teeth, choosing to ignore everything he said about her father and her line of work. "Everything else I learned from Anna, Melinda, Rita, and Bob. And my father's ability to completely disappear? Believe me, if I had to I could pull off something similar." She paused. "I'm nothing like you," she told him emphatically. "When you compare the two of us it makes me sick. And I owe you nothing."

"I disagree," Stevens countered. "You owe me your life. Anyone else in my position-like my old man, for instance-would've killed you a long time ago for being a liability. But I didn't, because of my soft spot for you."

"That's a crock," she snapped. "You kept me alive to barter with. He's getting close, isn't he? To taking all of you down? You want to use me as leverage again. That's why it's now, that's why all the theatrics and head games. You want me off my game so you can use me for whatever your planning against my father. You do know, that even if you stop him there'll always be another cop. Someone else who hears the name Montenillo and vows to dismantle the family at all costs."

"That may be true. But it's personal with Avery."

"Avery?"

"Paul Avery," Stevens clarified. "Your father."

"You've been more than cooperative," she said suspiciously. "Freely telling me everything I want to know after your ridiculous ploys to get me here. Why?"

"I brought you here because it was your first home. I'm telling you the truth so you'll do the right thing and help me stop the man who's only your father in name only."

"Because you stole me from him!" Charlie yelled. "And my mother. You robbed me of a childhood, you sick son-of-a-bitch. I went through hell because of you and because of that-" she aimed her gun again "-I should kill you where you stand."

"You're smarter than that, Charlie," he told her. "Did you really think I'd just let you leave after how hard I worked to get you here?" He made no move for it but Charlie knew there was a weapon somewhere, most likely in close reach.

"No, I didn't. Which is why this entire conversation has been recorded," she informed him, feeling the device in her boot. "My partner's been listening in, transmitting everything to the police as we speak."

"You're bluffing," he accused, just as sirens could be heard in the distance.

"I never bluff." Taking advantage of his surprise, she bolted down the hall.

Stevens was on her shortly, blocking off her route to the back door. Charlie ran down a different hall, leading away from the kitchen and saw a medium-sized window as she ran. It was
solid, with no latch. Looking around quickly, she shattered the glass with the handle of her gun, and kicked out the shards. Then she hoisted herself up and jumped out of it.

She rolled down the muddy hill on the side of the cabin, watching as uniformed officers began to storm the cabin. Charlie looked up to see T.J.'s victorious expression looming over her. "You did it," he told her, offering her his hand.

She accepted, allowing him to pull her up. "We did it," she corrected. Then they both broke into a run, hurrying away from the cabin before the police could question them.

***

"What a rush," Charlie declared, leaning against the Chevelle and trying to catch her breath.

"Nothing quite like it, when you pull off something like that," T.J. agreed, coming to stand beside her. "I would've given anything to see his face."

"It was priceless." Then her expression sobered. "It's still not over. He's got people out there watching. I don't know when it will be safe for Avery to come home."

"How are you?" he asked curiously. "Now that you finally know the truth?"

"Relieved to finally know, sickened by what Stevens has done."

T.J. was about to comment further when he frowned suddenly. "Your leg," he said, examining it with his gaze. "It's bleeding."

"Must be from the window." Charlie looked at the blood-soaked stain on her jeans, then slowly lifted the pants leg. "I've had worse," she commented, starting to walk off.

"Wait." T.J. touched her on the shoulder, then took a look for himself.

"It's just a scrape-"

"It's a lot worse than a scrape," he argued. "We need to take care of it before it gets infected."

Charlie heaved a sigh of defeat. "If you insist..."

T.J. got a First-Aid kit out of his trunk and quickly went to work on her leg as Charlie watched. "You're good at that," she grudgingly acknowledged. "But I still think you're wasting your time. It's not bad until you start to lose feeling."

"Because that means you've lost too much blood. I know, I know. You're used to the big stuff. But even small stuff can knock you off your ass if you're not careful." He finished putting on the bandage. "Done, he announced, standing.

"We should get going. I really want to see Diana, let her know what I found out," Charlie said, starting to walk around to the passenger side of the car.

"Let's go home then." T.J. tossed her the keys.

"Are you serious?" she asked incredulously.

He nodded. "I'd say you've earned it."

Charlie drove away from the cabin, leaving the cops and Stevens behind. T.J. settled back, playing with the stereo and they started the trip back to New York in mollified silence. By the time they were approaching the state line T.J. finally broke it. "This will seem incredibly juvenile after what just happened…but I think we should talk."

"About what?" Charlie asked, though she was sure she knew.

"You know what. Us. What's been going on."

"We've been in an intense situation," she told him quickly. "Close quarters and all that. It's bound to affect us a little bit."

"It's more than that, and you know it." He turned toward her. "There's something here, Charlie. What we have in common gives us a connection, something neither of us has had before."

"What exactly are you saying?" she asked, keeping her eyes trained on the road ahead and refusing to avert them.

"That I like spending time with you," he answered. "And I think you like spending time with me."

"What do you want to do about it?" she asked, though she already knew the answer.

"I think you know."

Charlie pulled over on the side of the road, in an area surrounded by trees. *This is insane,* she told herself. *I just got the revelation of a lifetime and now I-* She shook her head slightly. *And just this morning I was embarrassed because we woke up spooning.*

Stop thinking about it, another voice urged. *Being impulsive doesn't always have to get you into trouble.*

But she knew that it would.

Charlie turned off the motor and they were on each other in a second, kissing each other greedily. "I think it's safe to say our professional relationship is effectively ruined," she said in between kisses.

"In that case, I'll consider myself fired," T.J. said, kissing her back.

Charlie let the seat back and they continued to kiss, T.J. above her with one hand entwined in her long hair. For the first time in a long time Charlie could feel herself completely let go, switch off her over-analytical tendencies and just enjoy herself in the moment…because the moment felt really good.

Afterward they laid in the chair, staring up at the roof of the car and listening to the faint music coming from the speakers. "Car sex," T.J.

stated. "Did we get caught in a time warp and suddenly become teenagers again?"

"If we suddenly feel the urge to do the Macarena, I'd say we should worry," Charlie quipped. She turned to face him. "You're really not freaked out by all my scars," she told him, impressed. "That's definitely a first for me."

"Why should I be, when I've got plenty of my own? It's kind of refreshing, huh?"

"Definitely," Charlie said with a nod, leaning over to kiss him again.

When they finally got back on the road they cranked up the stereo once again, singing as loudly as they had on the way, leaving Massachusetts.

Chapter Nine

Pleased to see they'd gotten back in tact, Diana invited T.J. and Charlie over for a late dinner that night. They spent the meal joking and catching up and after they were finished, T.J. left to give Diana and Charlie privacy.

"I bet I know what this is about," Diana said as they cleared the table.

"You do?"

"I saw the way you and T.J. were looking at one another at dinner," Diana said knowingly as they went into the kitchen. "I hope I'm not stepping out of line but it seems like this trip brought the two of you a little closer."

"You're very perceptive," Charlie told her. "And we can talk about that later if you want. But I need to tell you something first."

Charlie sat at the kitchen table across from Diana, the dishes forgotten, and proceeded to
tell her everything she learned from Stevens. She watched her expression go through various stages until Charlie was finished, and her eyes seemed to sparkle with tears.

"We met at a frat party I snuck out to," Diana began. "I didn't come out and lie about my age but I didn't stop the guys from thinking I was in college too. I'd had a huge fight with my parents that night and a friend of mind suggested we crash a frat party…and I met him. He introduced himself as Johnny Black, friend of Raphael Montenillo, the youngest and only member of the Montenillo crime family to attend college. Johnny was his bodyguard-though about the same age-to please Raphael's father, Francisco. We all knew about the Montenillos and couldn't figure out why Raphael was in college but knew not to mess with him. Anyway, we spent most of the night talking…and then we started seeing each other. In secret from my parents, because I admitted to still being in high school. It didn't take long for me to become crazy about him, even though I knew he worked for the mob, which made him dangerous. Like most teenage girls, I found that highly appealing. But it became about more than that; as I told you before, he was the only person in my life to treat me with respect.

"Then one day, shortly after I found out I was pregnant, I saw on the news that Antonio Montenillo had been arrested by an undercover cop. I couldn't believe it when they showed Johnny's picture and called him Detective Paul Avery. I just sat there, frozen, not having any idea what to do. I was already struggling with how to tell him about my pregnancy and then I found out everything he ever told me had been a lie. He was probably just using me as part of his cover. I felt so hurt and betrayed but still thought he should know. But when I got up the courage to tell him he had disappeared, and I never heard from him again. Now I know that that's when he faked his death to stay hidden; he found out I was pregnant from this Stevens guy?"

Charlie nodded. "Stevens found out everything he could about you to use it against him."

"Instead, he used you. I can't believe that man stole you from me, pretending to be an adoption agent, and took you with him to raise for the first few years of your life. What kind of person does that?" Diana demanded shakily. "What kind of monster uses an innocent baby to get what he wants?" She shook her head. "He's the reason your life turned out the way it did, the reason Johnny-Paul-disappeared for all these years…"

"I'm going to find him," Charlie told her firmly. "I'll do whatever it takes to make it safe
for him to come back."

Charlie could tell the toll the conversation had on Diana so she changed the subject. "You were right about T.J.," she admitted. "I hope it's not weird for you-your friend and neighbor being with your long lost daughter."

"Actually, I think you're well-suited for one another," Diana told her. "But you're not as convinced, are you?"

"I'm not good at this," Charlie blurted. "Dating and men. My past is sketchy and I've never let anyone get close enough to really see-" She broke off. "He's a good guy."

"Too good for you?"

Charlie didn't respond.

"My opinion might not count for much since you've known me all of two minutes, but there's a lot more to you than you realize, Charlie Booker. You're not as damaged as you think you are. And I know T.J. very well. I haven't seen him this happy in a long time. Don't you think it's time you finally let yourself off the hook...and let yourself be happy?"

Charlie thought about it, trying to let the words sink in. She'd never admitted to not feeling good enough before, at least not out loud or to another human being. She knew she was a tough, capable person but somewhere along the way she stopped having confidence in her relationships with men. It had always been the same: she was up front about her job and her life and they couldn't handle it. But as she really thought about it, she never gave them a chance to know. Maybe she'd pushed them away by asserting how tough she was...so they wouldn't see how vulnerable she could really be.

As Charlie was leaving she gave Diana a kiss on the cheek. "Thanks for dinner," she told her. "Next week, my place, we're on for Italian and you can try my famous chicken parmesan. I'll even show you the secret ingredient Rita used."

"I'd be honored," Diana told her. Then she squeezed her hand. "I'm very proud of you, for what you did today. That couldn't have been easy, facing that man. But from what I hear, you handled yourself brilliantly."

"That would be from T.J., huh? So I guess it was you he was talking to on the phone when I came back from paying the gas station attendant."

"Guilty."

"Uh huh." Then Charlie paused. "I'll think about what you said," she promised. "And I'll let you know how things turned out."

"I'll be looking forward to it."

As Charlie walked out the door she saw T.J. exiting his apartment with his trash can, obviously preparing to roll it to the dump out back. "Hi," she said awkwardly.

"Hi," he said back.

They stood there for a moment and then burst out talking at the same time. "I wanted to tell you-" Charlie began.

"I'm glad I ran into-" T.J. started. Then they both laughed. "You first," he told her.

"I just wanted to tell you again what a great partner you were," she said. "You talked me down when I was losing it, and I really appreciate that. Thanks for having my back."

"My pleasure. We make a good team."

Charlie nodded. "What were you going to say?"

"Just that...I enjoyed our time together. And I'd like for it to continue...but I won't pressure you. I get where you're coming from about being burned so I'm leaving it up to you."

"What do you mean?"

"I mean today can mean whatever you want it to mean," he told her. "It can just be what it was, which was great, or it can be more. It's your decision."

"Mine?" Charlie asked in surprise. *He's leaving the ball in my court?* she thought incredulously. *That really happens?*

He nodded. "You know where I stand. Whatever happens next...is your call." He kissed her on the cheek. "Good night." He turned and started down the hall.

Charlie stood where she was a moment before heading in the opposite direction. As she went out to the parking lot she thought about what Diana said, and how she felt when she spent time with T.J. *He's a great partner,* she reflected. *Our working chemistry's great. I never thought I'd work that well with anyone aside from Bob. And...we have another kind of chemistry as well. Maybe it's time I take a risk in my personal life, instead of just in my professional one.*

Maybe it'll be worth it.

***

Charlie spent the next few days in her the non-working routine she sometimes employed, which included a lot of exercise. She did keep her ears open about the case against Stevens; so far, he was still in custody awaiting arraignment. Since his true identity was revealed he was deemed a flight risk and would most likely stayed locked up until his arraignment. Charlie made the decision not to take on any new jobs for the time being, just so she could stay on her toes in case something should happen. She also started looking into tracking down her father and Anna, wondering if he had been in Australia as well.

She checked in with Bob, updating him on all that had happened. He was as astounded as she was, and just as ready to break into Stevens' cell and take care of him personally. He was glad that Charlie finally knew the truth, finally had the answers she'd spent most of her life searching for. He took her out one night to celebrate, inviting Diana since they were each interested in meeting the other. Diana especially liked hearing about Rita, and all they'd both done for Charlie.

Soon a week had passed since the Cape Cod trip, and Charlie still hadn't spoken to T.J. She'd told Diana it was because she'd been so busy and preoccupied with Stevens but Diana saw it right away for what it was-a stall tactic. Though Charlie decided she wanted to give it a shot with T.J., she wasn't sure how to go about doing it. She did have a reminder of their time together, however, every time she looked down at the halfway-healed gash on her leg.

She stopped by Diana's apartment one overcast night to drop off a book she'd been telling her about and ran into T.J. "Fancy meeting you here," he joked, pulling his door closed.

Charlie nodded nervously, unsure of what to say.

"Diana's not home," he told her, noticing the book in her hand. "But you could probably stuff that through the mail slot."

"Alright."

"Good seeing you, Charlie," he said, then walked away.

Charlie walked over to Diana's door and slid the book through, her heart pounding. Then
she ran down the hall and out into the night, just as a rain started to fall. She looked around the
parking lot for a Chevelle, grateful that he had a car that would stand out. She finally saw it toward the back under a grove of trees, and took off as the rain started to pound harder.

T.J. was getting in the car when she called out to him, hoping to be heard over the roar of the rain and wind. He finally looked up, shutting the open door. "What are you doing?" he called back. "You're getting soaked!" He stopped at the side of the car.

"So are you!" she yelled back, running up to the car and stopping on the passenger side. "I made up my mind," she told him. "I'm sorry it took so long, it's just I'm really bad at this…but then I realized I'll keep being bad at this if I never take a chance on giving something a try." She began to walk over to him. "You know everything about my life, so you know what a mess I am…and you don't care. You don't try to change me, you don't wish I was different. You just like me, for me. And that scared me at first, because it was so foreign. But I don't want to be scared anymore. I want to do this." She went over to him and began to kiss him where he stood.

He kissed her back for a moment, then pulled away. "Does this mean you want to be with me?" he asked softly.

"Hell yeah it does," she replied, then started kissing him again. T.J. lifted her off the ground, wrapping his arms around her as the rain continued to pour down on them, neither one of them seeming to notice.

***

A few nights later there was a knock on Charlie's door while she was quickly pulling on her shoes. "One second!" she yelled, running down the hall. She stopped at the hall mirror, taking one last look before heading to the door to let T.J. in to pick her up for their first official date.

When she opened the door she was surprised to see him holding a bouquet of lilies. "I thought if we're going to do this, we should do it right," he said, holding the flowers out to her.

"They're beautiful," she told him, inhaling the sweet scent. "Thank you."

"You look great," he told her as they headed down the hall. "Green's definitely your color."

"Thanks," she said, looking down at the dark green halter top she'd just bought on a whim. "You look great too," she added, taking in his snug black T-shirt. "So, where are we off to?"

"It's a surprise," he told her. "And I promise, you're going to love it."

They drove out of the city until what appeared to Charlie to be the middle of nowhere. T.J. turned onto a dirt road that led directly to a lake surrounded by trees.

"Where are we?" Charlie asked curiously when they stopped. "Is the surprise going for a moonlight swim? Except there's no moon tonight," she observed, looking out at the star-studded sky.

T.J. took her hand and led her to the back of the car, where they both hopped onto the trunk. "There's a meteor shower happening tonight, and you have to be away from all the lights to see it," he explained. "You mentioned once you were curious about what one looked like, so I
thought you might like it."

Charlie nodded as they both leaned back, laying side by side. "When I was a kid I used to
look up at the sky all the time, particularly when I felt alone, and the moon and stars always reassured me, always made me feel like someone was watching out for me. When I got older I became fascinated with astronomy, always wondering about the universe filled with stars and moons and planets...and maybe even little green men," she added with a grin.

"Maybe we should watch for spaceships instead of meteors," T.J. suggested.

"Which reminds me." Charlie pulled something out of her jacket. "Diana might've let slip you're a closet Trekkie so I thought these would be perfect for you." She handed him the small bag.

"Spock ears?" he asked, pulling them out of the bag. Then he shook his head. "She didn't. Please tell me she didn't."

"She may have told me about the time you snuck out as a kid to go to a Star Trek convention...in full costume as Spock."

"Is this what I get to look forward to from now on? Diana sharing all the embarrassing stories she knows about me?" T.J. shook his head. "Note to self: no more dating my friends'
daughters."

"I thought it was hilarious. I've been trying to picture it-" She closed her eyes, then burst out laughing. T.J. pushed her away in response, then decided to start tickling her. Charlie shrieked and retaliated until they were both laughing, gasping for air.

A while later the shower started and they laid in silence watching it, Charlie taking it in completely amazed. "It's beautiful," she murmured as they watched the last strands of color streak across the sky.

"It is," T.J. agreed, turning toward her. Then he kissed her. "What do you want to do now?"

Charlie looked past him to the lake, then back at him. Wordlessly they both jumped off the car and ran toward the water.

Charlie kicked off her shoes and stripped down to her bra and underwear and ran into the water, splashing as she did so. "I haven't done this in years," she announced as T.J. ran in behind her.

"Neither of I," he said as he swam toward her. "First car sex, now stripping and swimming in a lake in the dark. We're on a roll."

"Definitely." Charlie swam out a few feet, waiting for him to follow. Then she jumped on top of him, trying to shove his head under the water. He broke away, splashing her in the face and trying to do the same to her. They did this for a while, laughing and yelling, then stopped long enough to start kissing.

"So," T.J. asked as he walked her to her apartment later. "Was it a good first date?"

Charlie nodded. "Yes, it was. I had a great time, and your surprise was perfect. You were right, I loved it." She kissed him as they stopped at her door.

He pulled back after a moment. "I know now is the awkward part when we talk about whether or not I come in and what happens afterward, so I'm going to save us by telling you good night now."

"You don't want to come in?"

"Of course I do," he told her honestly. "But this is our first date, and even though we've already been together, maybe we should take things slow, do things right. We've got plenty of time...there's no need to rush for anything. Why don't we just enjoy it?"

"Maybe you're right," Charlie told him. "Maybe the mistakes happen when you're trying too hard too fast. And this was a good night, so maybe we should just quit while we're ahead."

"Okay." He leaned forward, kissing her on the cheek. "Good night, Charlie. I'll call you tomorrow."

"Good night," Charlie said as he started to back away. Then she unlocked her door and went inside, smiling to herself.

Chapter Ten

"You do know how ridiculous all of this is, don't you?" Charlie asked, peering through her binoculars at the apartment across the street. "All this time we've spent waiting here when we could've just popped over and took this guy straight to your client-" She broke off, shaking her head gently.

"Unfortunately, that's where our professions differ," T.J. informed her as she passed the binoculars to him. "P.I.'s don't go and collect the cheating spouse for our client. We just provide evidence and present them with all the facts. Even though it would make my life a lot easier to do it your way," he added.

"Yeah. The more *effective* way."

T.J. laughed. "No argument there."

Charlie and T.J. were sitting on a rooftop in the Village, staking out the apartment across the street. Charlie was sitting in on one of T.J.'s cases, a possible cheating spouse. Several weeks had passed, and Charlie had spent the time she normally would have on jobs on tracking down Paul Avery and Anna instead. She did consent, however, to help T.J. on his cases now and then-though he didn't really need it-so they could spend some time together.

Bob had been helping her with her search; so far they found out that Anna lived in Montreal for a certain length of time, before relocating to Australia. Her time before that was still a mystery, as was how she got away from Stevens' men all those years ago and where she went right after. As for Paul Avery they did find evidence that he had indeed been in Australia with Anna, but now both their whereabouts were unknown.

Stevens' arraignment was set for early October, which meant he was to remain in lockup until then. Charlie had considered visiting him several times but was always talked out of it by someone, telling her what she already knew-she wouldn't be able to get anything out of him, and it would just be wasting her time. She couldn't admit to anyone the real reason why but she couldn't hide the truth from herself, which was that Stevens' comparison of him and herself bothered her more than just about anything else he said. It probably had to do with the fact that he was right about one thing: her father would never understand or accept her profession and was undoubtedly disappointed in her. It didn't make sense to care about the opinion of a man she'd never met, but knowing all he'd done to protect her and Diana made it matter, made her want him to be proud of her, to see that his efforts hadn't all been in vain. It didn't take much for her to understand that it wasn't likely to happen.

After all...what cop would want a bounty hunter for a daughter?

She shook her head abruptly, trying to rid her mind of those thoughts and concentrate on the present. "Well, I don't see how you stand it," she told him. "All we've seen so far is a middle-aged man practically drink himself into a coma."

The woman who'd hired T.J. told her husband she was leaving town while she'd really checked herself into a hotel nearby so T.J. and Charlie could catch him in the act. After several hours of watching the man drink and glue himself to the television, Charlie was starting to feel restless.

"I don't always get the thrill rides; boring cases pay the rent too. But it helps if you're
prepared." He reached into his bag.

Charlie's eyes lit up. "More of those little strawberry cakes?"

"Better." He produced a small bag of caramel coated popcorn and peanuts. "It'll help us enjoy the show." He held the box out to her.

Charlie reached into the box and pulled out a large handful, munching contentedly. "Oh, here we go," she said, sitting up straighter. "Check it out."

They turned their full attention to the apartment door, which was opening to reveal a large-chested young blonde wearing go-go boots, heading straight to the man on the couch. Without a word she sat in his lap and they began to kiss.

It didn't take long for it to turn into much more than that. Charlie just shook her head while T.J. took the photos, wondering how some people could be so predictable. "No imagination," she muttered.

After T.J. had enough photos he turned to Charlie as he was zipping up his black bag. "So? What'd you think?"

"I think you should charge a boredom fee. Also damages from pain and suffering, after what we just had to watch," she added, standing.

"Settle for a nightcap at my place?" he asked as they left the roof.

"Absolutely."

When they arrived back at T.J.'s apartment he went down the hall to put up his equipment, leaving Charlie standing by the window in the living room. Though they'd been dating nearly a month now they still had yet to spend the night together at either of their places. They were standing by their original decision to take things slow, and that meant they hadn't been together since the first time in Massachusetts. Now that she was here in T.J.'s apartment...that might change.

It's ludicrous to be nervous, she chided herself. *You've already slept together. Why should you be anxious about it now?*

But she knew why: because it was quite clear to her that this was different than anything she'd ever been involved in before, and that every decision seemed to really matter. And she didn't want anything to happen that might blow it.

In other words, she was rapidly falling for T.J.

In some ways it felt completely sudden, too sudden to admit and yet, at the same time, it also felt right. It didn't matter that she'd known him less than two months, it didn't matter she had no idea what she was doing, it didn't matter that they weren't officially a couple yet. All she knew was she feeling and behaving in a way she hadn't before...and she had no intention of putting on the brakes or looking back. She did, however, suffer from a case of extreme pride and kept those thoughts and feelings safely to herself.

When T.J. returned he walked over to the bar and poured each of them a drink, gesturing for her to join him on the couch. "That wraps up my workload for the week," he told her, pulling her back against him as they sat. "As soon as I call Mrs. Sutton in the morning. What about you? Anything new come up?"

"Not since the last time we discussed it," Charlie told him. "Everyone's working their asses off so we should be finding out something soon. Right now my biggest concern is the Montenillos, if they're prepared to retaliate in some way because I got Stevens arrested. I'm sure he wasted no time fingering me."

"Maybe not. Maybe that's why you haven't heard so much as a peep from them."

"But why would Stevens keep it to himself? What has he got to lose now?"

"Something tells me he didn't expect for this to end with him in prison," T.J. said. "After all he did to get you to that cabin for whatever master plan he had in motion...for it to just stop-"

"I know," Charlie interrupted. "It makes me nervous too."

They let the subject drop after that, just sitting in the silence for a while. Charlie later noticed the clock on the wall across from them, letting her know it was nearly one a.m. "I guess I should probably get going," she said, sitting up.

"What's the hurry?" he asked quietly.

Charlie turned and looked back at him. "Is that your way of asking me to spend the night?"

"Maybe."

Before she could say anything else he started kissing her. Charlie kissed him back and he wrapped his arms around her and they rose from the couch, starting to move down the hall. Then T.J. stopped, looking at her intently. "Are you sure?" he asked. "I know we agreed to take things slow-"

"We have," she interrupted. "If we went any slower we'd be going backwards and...I don't know about you, but I'm tired of looking back."

"So am I." Without another word he lifted her in the air, causing her to cry out in surprise.

Then they resumed kissing, continuing down the hall and to the bedroom.

Afterward Charlie started to get dressed but T.J. stopped her, pulling her back toward him. "Stay," he requested.

"Are you sure?"

He nodded.

Charlie dropped her shoes and crawled next to him in bed, letting him pull the covers up around them. "You have a nice room," she commented once they were settled, looking around.

T.J. laughed. "Just are noticing?" he asked teasingly.

She shrugged. "I was preoccupied earlier."

A short while later Charlie heard T.J.'s rhythmic breathing and closed her eyes, letting herself finally drift off, feeling happier than she had in a while. *Maybe Diana's right,* she thought, rolling onto her side. *Maybe I'm not so damaged after all.*

***

After running for what seemed like a while Anna stopped, breathing heavily. They'd made it to the park, and Anna collapsed onto a bench, hugging Charlie to her chest. Then she pulled back. "I need you to listen very carefully to what I'm about to say to you, okay?" Charlie nodded. "If we get separated for some reason I want you come back to this park and hide. If anyone comes up to you, run as fast as you can and scream as loud as you can. Do you understand?"

"Yes...but why?"

"I'm going to do everything I can to stay with you, Charlotte," Anna vowed. "But if
there's a reason I can't...the most important thing is for you to be safe. We've been to this park a lot, so I know you can find your way back to it if you have to. And when you do, and you're sure no one's following you, I want you to come to this bench and stay here. And I promise I'll do everything I can to meet you back here, tomorrow morning. Do you understand all of this?"

Charlie nodded. "Come back here, hide, stay on this bench until tomorrow."

"That's right. You're such a smart girl." Anna kissed her on the top of the head, and they started running again.

They ran to an alley and then Anna stopped; it was blocked by a tall chain-link fence,
with barbed wire at the top. Anna slowly turned around to face her pursuers, seeing that they were trapped.

Anna put Charlie on the ground as the men advanced her, grabbing her by the arms and trying to carry her away. "Run!" she screamed at Charlie. "Go!"

"Anna-"

"Go!"

Charlie began to run as the men dragged Anna away, sobbing loudly.

Charlie's eyes flew open and she blinked rapidly, instantly awake. It had taken twenty-three years but she'd finally remembered everything that happened that night; it was no longer a giant blank spot in her memory. Once and for all she knew what had taken place, and how she and Anna were separated.

She rolled over to tell T.J. but saw that the other side of the bed was empty, except for a small note left on the pillow. Charlie sat up, reading it to herself:

Had to go see Mrs. Sutton, she called right at eight demanding news and I didn't want to wake you. I've got to go into the office today, but you're welcome to stay as long as you want and raid my fridge-I just went shopping a couple days ago. In any case, I want to see you tonight if you're free. Call you later.

T.J.

Charlie got dressed, deciding to go ahead and go home, see if there was anything she could be working on. She turned the note over and quickly wrote on the other side *Had to go home and work on the search but I will be free tonight, if you want to catch up for dinner. See you soon, Charlie.* Then she made the bed, put on her shoes, and grabbed her bag off the floor, heading down the hall and out of the apartment, locking the door as she shut it.

"Looks like rain this morning," a cheerful voice came from behind her.

Charlie quickly turned around to see Diana sitting in front of her, an umbrella perched in her lap. She was watching Charlie in amusement, smiling broadly.

"Hi," Charlie greeted her, walking over and kissing her on the cheek. "How are you doing?"

"Not as good as you seem to be," Diana said knowingly, the subtext in her words apparent. "Where's my favorite neighbor?"

"Work," Charlie replied, knowing there was no need to keep up pretense.

Diana nodded. "Well, I won't keep you since you look like you're in a hurry. I'll talk to
you soon." She started to wheel herself toward her door.

"Wait," Charlie called after her. "I've got some things to check on today but they can wait until this afternoon, if you want to catch up." Since she'd been so busy lately Charlie hadn't had many opportunities to spend time with Diana.

"I'd like that," Diana said, unlocking her door. "Come on in and I'll make some tea."

Charlie got the mugs out of the cabinet at Diana's direction while Diana put the kettle on the stove, then wheeled herself back to the kitchen table. "I guess you might want to talk about why I'm here this morning," Charlie began, taking a seat.

"I only want to talk about whatever you want to talk about," Diana told her. "You have free reign, or discretion if you choose," she said with a wink.

Charlie laughed. "I don't really know how discreet I can be when you caught me red-handed. Yes, I spent the night last night."

Diana nodded. "First time I gather?"

"Yeah. Is this weird?" Charlie asked abruptly.

"Not for me. Is it for you?"

"Surprisingly, no," Charlie admitted. "I really don't mind you knowing at all."

"Good. I don't mind listening."

They spent the most of the morning talking, mostly about Charlie's relationship with T.J. Diana even shared some stories from her romantic past-after Charlie's father-and Charlie was surprised to discover that though there were differences in the circumstances of their lives, Charlie and Diana had a lot in common, even when it came to relationships. As they continued to talk, Charlie felt like she was really getting to know her birthmother and was starting to feel close to her.

Afterward Charlie was privy to Diana's sketchbook, something she'd only shown to T.J. Charlie felt honored and was quite impressed at how good Diana was. She promised to draw something special for Charlie and have it ready the next time they met, which she wanted to be the upcoming weekend.

"I don't know if it's something you'd be interested in or not, but I've always loved the theater," Diana confided. "Ever since I was in my early twenties I went as often as I could. Would you like to come with me to a show this Saturday? I promise it's not as boring as it sounds."

It Charlie was being truthful she'd never had any desire to see any kind of play; she never really had the patience to sit still that long, which was why she didn't frequent the movie theater. But it was hard to refuse Diana, so she agreed, telling herself to keep an open mind. She also proposed they go shopping, since Charlie didn't really have anything to wear to the theater. As she suspected, Diana was eager to comply. Charlie found herself liking the idea as well though she'd never been much of a recreational shopper-there was something about the idea of shopping with her biological mother that seemed like kind of a rite of passage.

Charlie left Diana's that afternoon feeling even better than she already did, which was definitely something she could get used to.

***

That evening Charlie was looking over the file she'd assembled on what she knew so far
about Anna and Paul Avery, checking and re-checking all the information she'd accumulated-including some background she found out about Paul a couple hours ago-to try and make some kind of make-shift timeline. T.J. had called and was on his way to her apartment,

where they'd decided to order in, and Charlie wanted to wrap things up before he got there.

She leaned back in her desk, staring at the chart she'd just made to make sure everything was correct:

<u>Marianna Thompson Marquez, a.k.a. Anna</u>
(Born 8/24/41 in Boston)
-only child
-married Daniel Thompson 3/15/61, moved to Atlantic City
-worked at the casino
-Thompson dies of stroke in '71, she moves to Jacksonville (age 30)
-marries Christian Marquez shortly after
-parents relocate to Jacksonville, Marianna cares for them until their deaths
-marriage to Marquez ends after five years, divorce volatile, Marquez gets everything
-Marianna leaves Jacksonville and moves to NY in the early eighties
-Marianna is hired by Stevens to care for her great-niece (me) in 1986
-Marianna meets up with Paul in 1987, work together on getting us away from Stevens
-Stevens sends his men after her, I escape
-somehow she escapes Stevens' men, likely with Avery's help
-ended up in Sydney for the past ten years, Montreal just before that
*1987-2000 is a mystery

<u>Paul Avery</u>
(Born 2/6/58 in Hartford)
-only child
-parents divorced in '70, moved to Queens
-enrolled in the police academy straight out of high school
-was known for his strong dislike of organized crime
-went undercover in the Montenillo organization at 22, posing as 20-year-old Johnny Black, bodyguard to Raphael Montenillo (Francisco's son, Stevens' cousin), at NYU
-became trusted employee and friend to Stevens (a.k.a. Hector Montenillo)
-in '82, 2 years after he went undercover, Avery cracked the case that led to Antonio Montenillo's arrest, and the deaths of Andre and Joaquin Montenillo (Stevens' brothers)
-there wasn't enough evidence to go after Francisco or his three sons (Carlos, Diego, and Raphael)
-Hector faked his own death and became Andy Stevens

-Stevens began to blackmail Avery after I was born, Avery complied until he started working with Anna on an escape

-Avery led everyone to believe he'd drank himself to death so he could get the upper hand on Stevens

-Avery presumably helped Anna escape Stevens' men and hasn't been heard from since (1987)

Seems accurate enough, Charlie thought as she slid the paper into the folder. *Now I just need more.*

T.J. arrived shortly after and Charlie grabbed all the take-out menus she had in a drawer, holding them out for him to pick. They both agreed on Chinese, so Charlie got on the phone to
place their orders. As she did she noticed T.J.'s phone was ringing and he walked away from her slightly so he could answer.

After Charlie hung up she could still hear him on the phone and went to join him in the living room.

"...not really workable right now," he was saying, walking the length of the couch and rolling his eyes to show Charlie his annoyance with the caller. "I know it's their thirty-fifth anniversary...yes...but you did kind of spring this on me..." He stopped, listening. "See?" he asked a moment later. "Holly can't jet off to Palm springs either. I-" He broke off. "Would they go for that? Are you sure you're okay-yeah. Call me back after you talk to her. Okay. 'Bye." He hung up, coming to sit by Charlie on the couch. "That was my sister," he told her. "Kari."

"Is she the Vegas one?"

"No, that's Holly. Kari's the aroma therapist who lives in Minnesota with a man who could do denture commercials. She's also the one who thinks everyone can just drop what they're doing just because she asks them to, like we don't have lives or something, says we need to stop having such selfish auras. Or something screwed up like that." He sighed.

"What'd she want?"

"Our parents' thirty-fifth anniversary is coming up," he explained. "I've known it for months but neither of my sisters have said anything about a big party or anything so I just assumed we'd all be stopping by Palm Springs whenever we could. But, for some reason, Kari decided to throw a big party for them last minute in Minnesota-which I doubt they'd want to drive up there for, they hate going there-" His phone started to ring again, cutting him off. "Hold on," he told her, answering. "Hey Holly. Just finished talking to her too? Yeah I know..."

He was still fielding calls back and forth between both sisters when the doorbell rang, and Charlie went to answer it with her wallet in hand. She paid the delivery guy and took the large, hot bag into the living room, then went to the kitchen to get the beer.

"So? Has anything been worked out?" she asked when she got back, seeing that he was now off the phone.

"We decided against the big party and opted to have dinner instead," he told her. "And each of us can bring a guest." He looked at her meaningfully.

Charlie looked back in surprise. "You want me to come to your parents' anniversary dinner, meet your family?"

He nodded. "If you feel comfortable with it. And you'll never believe the timing-my parents told Holly they were thinking about coming up this way soon for a visit, so we all talked it over and decided to have the dinner here in New York."

"Are you sure about having it here? It sounded like your sister was dead-set on having it in Minnesota-"

T.J. snorted. "Like that would ever happen. Our parents hate Minnesota. They're not too keen on Jeremiah either but he's Kari's plus-one so they'll have to deal with it."

"Jeremiah?" Charlie repeated. "Really?"

T.J. nodded. "Told you they're crazy. So. You want to meet them?" He looked at her intently.

Charlie nodded. "Of course I do. You've met my family," she pointed out, indicating Diana, Bob, Jack, and Megan. "The more important question is...do they want to meet me?"

"Why wouldn't they?"

"Oh I don't know." Charlie flipped her hair over her shoulder and gave him a wide-eyed look. " 'So what is it Charlie does again? Goes around kidnapping people for money?'"

T.J. shook his head. "That's not what you do," he told her with a laugh. "Although your impression of my mom is spot-on," he teased.

"Ha ha. I'm serious. Or trying to be anyway. You're an accomplished P.I. in the city-"

"-and the woman I'm involved with has that city by the horns," he finished. "You've survived it here better than people twice your age. That's an accomplishment, too. And don't worry so much about them. My parents are pretty open-minded; they'd have to be after having daughters like Kari and Holly." He looked at her, suddenly understanding. "You've never made it to this point before, have you?"

Charlie shook her head, unnerved as usual by his eerily accurate perception. "Pretty pathetic, huh?"

"No, pathetic is getting divorced before you turned thirty," he corrected. Then he sat up. "Enough of this self-deprecation. I'm starving, and I know you are too." He reached for the bag as Charlie opened the beer, pulling out the carton of mushu pork and it handing it to her. "They'll love you," he assured her. "No question."

***

After her run Saturday morning Charlie met Diana at her apartment so they could leave to go shopping. Diana was concerned about keeping Charlie from her work but Charlie assured her that anyone could reach her if they needed to.

They went to a store that sold formal wear, one that Charlie had passed often but never entered, not having reason to. As they began to look around Charlie discovered there was more to her mother than simply being a former wild child and daredevil at heart: she also had an inner girly-girl that Charlie never would've suspected before. She truly came to life as she selected dresses and accessories for each of them to try on, her face lighting up every time Charlie tried on something new.

Maybe it's not so much about being a girly-girl as it is making up for lost time, Charlie realized. *She's never had the opportunity to bond with me this way...and it's a first for me too. She's making up for all the dates and proms and other formal occasions but so am I; I never went to any dances, never had a high school prom. I never thought I wanted it and maybe I didn't...maybe all I really wanted was this.*

After spending several hours in the changing room Charlie and Diana each choose their attire for the play that evening. Since it was her idea for the shopping trip, Charlie treated.

They went to lunch afterward, Charlie taking Diana to the infamous diner she'd told her about. Charlie didn't expect to run into David since it was the middle of the day, and was grateful; that chapter had finally been closed, and on a good note. There wasn't any need to go back now.

The afternoon went by quickly; they spent most of it at the park. When they finally made it back to Diana's apartment it was time to start getting ready for that evening.

As they went out into the hall, pausing so Diana could lock the door, they heard footsteps coming up behind them and a low whistle.

"Look at the two of you," T.J. said, looking at them both. "It's the hall of hot women."

Diana chuckled as Charlie just shook her head. "You always were such a flatterer," she told him, shaking her head. Then she gestured to her deep blue evening dress. "What do you think?"

"I think you're beautiful," T.J. told her, kissing her on the cheek.

"I agree," Charlie said, studying her. She'd helped Diana fix her hair into an up-do, that, in Charlie's opinion, made her look at least ten years younger. And the color of her dress went with her complexion very well.

T.J. walked over to Charlie. "I think you're beautiful too," he told her, wrapping his arms around her and taking in her long, closely fitted black dress with a plunging necklace and silver sequins lining the bodice. He gave her a kiss. "You guys have fun at the theater tonight," he told them as he pulled back. "See you later."

Charlie and Diana left after telling him good-bye, heading downtown.

***

"I'm impressed," Diana said as they exited the theater several hours later. "You said you have a problem with staying still...but you didn't move an inch."

"I'm just as surprised as you are," Charlie told her as they headed toward Diana's SUV. "To be honest, I never really thought the theater or a play would ever be for me...but I really enjoyed myself. I wasn't bored at all; it was great. Kind of makes me want to see another one."

"It's addictive, isn't it?" Diana asked knowingly.

Charlie nodded. "I've lived here in the city all these years...and I never knew the kind of stuff I was missing. Until now."

"But now you're getting to make up for all of it," Diana pointed out. "It's never too late to start over."

Charlie wholeheartedly agreed.

Chapter Eleven

By mid-August Charlie had learned that Anna spent some time in Nova Scotia before relocating to Montreal. She also learned that Avery had been with her in Sydney for the past ten years, on and off. His time before that remained a mystery, and there was still a considerable chunk of time in Anna's life that still hadn't been accounted for. She'd also made little progress on how to get in touch with either of them now, although she was hearing rumors from her Australian contacts that they might be leaving soon. They were both spotted at the passport office, which nixed Charlie's plans of possibly flying out to Sydney.

She and Bob were also working closely together on trying to anticipate any possible moves the Montenillos might make, although everything seemed to be quiet on that front. It was that precise fact that had them both worried, but neither were sure what could be done about it until someone made a move. Charlie kept her promise to Bob about not visiting Stevens in lockup, though it was getting harder and harder for her to honor that promise when all she wanted to do was grill him for answers.

T.J.'s case load had been light and he'd also pitched in, although there was little more for him to come up with. The anniversary dinner for his parents was rapidly approaching, only a week from the upcoming weekend, the weekend before Labor Day weekend. To Charlie's surprise, she wasn't anxious about it all anymore, most likely because of all the more pressing matters to be anxious over. She found herself looking forward to meeting T.J.'s family, though she'd only been dating T.J. a little over a month and they had yet to make their relationship "official".

Things were also still going well with Diana; she'd kept her promise about sketching something special for Charlie. Using the photos of all the women involved in Charlie's life, Diana sketched a kind of "mother" collage of Anna, Melinda, Rita, and herself. Charlie was not only impressed by how good it was, she was also incredibly touched; Diana had definitely delivered on the "special" part. Charlie had it framed and it sat on the center of the mantle in the living room.

When she had some down time she went ahead and organized the baby shower for Megan, setting it for the coming Sunday afternoon. Megan was highly impressed with her for having the time to plan it and was concerned Charlie was pushing herself too hard; Charlie assured her that she could handle everything, since after all, she was used to a lot of juggling.

The afternoon before the shower T.J. took Charlie out for a surprise, giving her no hints whatsoever. The only thing she had to go on was the whispered conversation she'd accidentally interrupted between him and Diana a few days earlier.

"You keep doing special things for me," she said as they drove through town. "It's starting to make me feel like the scorecard's uneven."

"Are you kidding? You're going to meet my wacky family in a week," he reminded her. "It doesn't get much more special than that. And it's not a contest, you know. We don't have to keep score...we just do whatever we want to do. Besides, this wasn't even my idea; it was Diana's."

Now Charlie was even more intrigued. "And I don't even get a hint? I'm dying of curiosity here," she complained.

"You get one hint," he conceded. "Remember when you told me you wondered what it was like to have 'normal' things growing up? Well, you're about to find out now."

Charlie sat in the passenger seat, puzzled. *What was I saying I was curious about?* she thought, trying to remember. *Siblings, family dinners...I have no idea.*

"We're here," T.J. announced a short while later, pleased to see Charlie gaping as she read the sign in front of the building.

"An animal shelter?" she asked with a frown. Then she remembered-she'd mentioned wondering what it'd be like to have grown up with pets. She looked at T.J. in surprise. "I'm getting a pet?" she asked in confusion.

"Diana suggested it," T.J. explained. "She said everyone should get a chance to own one, and since you didn't during your childhood you can now. She also said something about it never being too late."

Charlie recognized the line. "But...there's a reason I've never gotten a pet, and that's because I don't have time for the responsibility," she explained. "I'm gone all the time, sometimes for months-"

"That's where Diana comes in," he broke in. "She's agreed to take care of your pet whenever you have to go out of town."

"That's a lot of trouble-"

"She wants to do it," T.J. told her firmly. "And like you've said before, you don't know what the future holds. You might not always be a bounty hunter, you might have more time."

"I guess that's true-"

"It's up to you now. Would you like to finally own a pet?"

Charlie looked at the building that housed so many dogs and cats who'd never had homes or had possibly been mistreated and abused. She knew exactly what that was like, and she also knew what it felt like to be taken in and given a new life, a better life.

"I'll do it," she told him at last. "But it has to be a cat; I've always seen myself as a cat person."

"I can't imagine why," he said as they got out of the car. "It can't be because you're stealthy, quick on your feet, picky about who you like, curious, always getting into trouble, or because you have nine lives."

"Smartass," she said, following him up the front steps. "You forgot independent."

A half hour later they emerged with Charlie holding a small, black-and-white kitten who she'd named Harley. They stopped by a pet store on the way back to Charlie's apartment to get food and supplies and a few toys, then headed back to get everything set up.

Charlie put the food dish on the floor in small walk-in pantry, then set up the small pillow-bed in her room. Harley was about four months old and had been found abandoned near a gas station downtown just a few weeks earlier. Despite his rough start in life he instantly warmed up to Charlie, with whom he seemed to feel safe. He fell asleep in her lap while she and T.J. were watching the news, appearing completely content.

"This was a great idea," Charlie said, looking down at him. "It's one of the things I never got around to doing since everything's always so up in the air, but now…" she trailed off, looking over at T.J. "Things finally start to feel like they're falling into place."

Charlie invited Diana over the next morning so she could meet Harley and Diana instantly fell in love; it wasn't difficult, seeing as Harley was an undoubtedly charming kitten. Diana agreed to stay and keep an eye on him, since was still so young and not used to his new home yet, while Charlie went over to Jack and Megan's house where the shower was being held.

Baby showers and female-dominant gatherings were not Charlie's expertise, being a novice on both counts, and she didn't have a clue how all of it was going to come off. Luckily Megan's mother, Mrs. Hunter, seemed to know what she doing and was happy to take over when Charlie felt overwhelmed. When the guests arrived everyone was curious to meet Charlie, the pseudo-sister-in-law who Megan often mentioned but no one had actually met, other than Megan's mother. Whenever talk strayed toward her line of work Megan quickly deflected, and it was clear to see that she knew what she was doing. Charlie wasn't surprised since the same thing was bound to come up when discussing Bob.

Charlie hated to admit it to herself but the shower wasn't nearly as torturous as she'd imagined it would be. She was completely out of her depth, no question, but because it was for Megan-for whom she had a sisterly affection-she managed, and almost felt normal doing so.

As the last guests were leaving and Mrs. Hunter was busying herself with gathering all the gifts and matching them with the appropriate cards, Megan approached Charlie as she was cleaning up the kitchen. "So?" she asked, walking over to the sink. "Was it the nightmare you were imagining?"

"It would've been if I had to endure any of those ridiculous games I've seen them play on TV at baby showers," Charlie answered, wiping off the counter. "Luckily your mom's intelligent enough to know that would've been a deal-breaker."

"She is completely fascinated by you, I must say," Megan said, reaching over and opening the dishwasher. "She's never met anyone like you. You've always had her intrigued."

Charlie stopped. "Is that your way of saying I have no idea what she says behind my back?"

Megan shrugged. "I wouldn't take it personally. She's as mainstream as they come, Charlie. It's her nature to question what she doesn't understand. But, that being said, it doesn't mean she doesn't like you. And it doesn't mean she doesn't appreciate what you did today."

Charlie reached over her and took the plates from the sink. "Stop. I told you I've got this." She started loading the dishwasher. "So I'm on her good side, huh?"

"Definitely. And I want to thank you too. I know none of this was easy for you and I know how stretched you've been lately. Thanks for spending your highly coveted free time on us." She patted her belly.

"That's what aunts do."

"And godmothers," Megan added.

Charlie stopped. "Are you serious?"

"Who did you think we were going to pick?"

Charlie blinked. "I don't know. I guess I hadn't really thought about it. I keep forgetting how Catholic everyone is."

Megan burst out laughing. "You've been a part of Jack's family for ten years, you know how Italian Bob and Rita were…how could you possibly forget that?"

Charlie shrugged. "Maybe because they never seemed to mind what a heathen I am," she
said, winking. Then her expression grew more serious. "If that's what you and Jack want, I'd be honored," she told her graciously. "And it means a lot that you would choose me."

"It was never a choice," Megan said, putting her hand on Charlie's shoulder. "There's no one better suited to be our baby's godparents than you and Bob."

As Charlie drove home she thought about her conversation with Megan, and about how things had been going lately. Her life was slowly in the process of doing a complete one-eighty from what it'd once been. She'd always been so closed off, so alone, and now she had a real family, real people who cared about her simply because they wanted to care about her. She was in a relationship, she had her first pet, and now she was going to become a godmother. If she didn't know any better, Charlie might think she had what would pass as a normal life...though she was still as abnormal as could be. And the even bigger surprise was that she found herself really wanting it.

***

The week passed fairly quickly, but was fairly unproductive in the information front. Everything seemed to come to a standstill the subject of Anna and Paul Avery, and with Stevens' arraignment still over a month away Charlie was growing impatient. She couldn't help but feel that something big was going to go down in October, and had a gut instinct that the Montenillos would want Avery to be a part of it. Since Charlie was certain that he was aware of that, why had he still not tried to contact her? Why were he and Anna still hiding?

As pressing as those questions were Charlie managed to put them on the backburner for a while so she could concentrate on the upcoming dinner with T.J.'s family. In lieu of a present since she had no idea what to get them, Charlie decided to make tiramisu and invite everyone back to her apartment for dessert. She knew it was a somewhat risky move, if the dinner didn't go well, but knew she had Harley to help break the ice. Nothing was a better tension-breaker than a cute kitten.

As she was putting the finishing touches on dessert Charlie realized she still had time before she had to get ready, so she called Diana for moral support. "I'm completely clueless," she greeted her. "I've never met anyone's parents before."

"Charlie-"

"They're going to ask me what I do for a living and I'm going to freeze up and start telling them how much I know about guns. I mean, what else do I know about? How to get out of tight spots, how to disappear if need be...on second thought, those two things might come in handy..."

"Charlie!" Diana cut in. "Will you relax? This isn't as bad as you're making it. I've met T.J.'s family and I can tell you, you're going to be fine."

"How do you know?"

"Because it's pretty damned obvious how much you care about their son and brother," Diana replied. "That counts for a hell of a lot more than your job or anything else you don't think they'll understand."

Charlie sank onto her bed. "I'm acting like a complete idiot. Worse than an idiot. I'm
acting like a-"

"-girl?" Diana finished.

"Yeah. Something like that."

"Welcome to the club," Diana told her. "It only gets more crappy from here on."

"Thanks for the motherly pep talk."

"Anytime. And save me some of that tiramisu."

After Charlie hung up she showered and dressed, leaving Harley napping on his blue pillow-bed. She was just finishing with drying her hair when T.J. called to let her know they were running behind because his parents' flight was delayed and that they would meet her at the restaurant. As soon as he let her go her phone began to ring again.

This time it was an unknown number, a number that didn't look like a cell or a home number. Suddenly she had a hunch and snatched up the phone quickly. "Booker."

"Good evening, Charlie."

There was no mistaking the voice. Part of her had been expecting this for some time; though she'd managed to talk herself out of going to visit Stevens she had the suspicion that he'd try to contact her. Even prisoners were allowed phone calls. "What do you want?" she asked coldly, continuing to get dressed.

"I want to see you."

"Well, that's not going to happen," Charlie told him, hunting for her purse. "So you might as well just tell me now what it is you want to say."

"I don't have a lot of time, and I don't exactly have a lot of privacy. I'd rather talk to you in person."

"I don't give a damn about what you'd 'rather'. You have two seconds to say something interesting, or I'm hanging up."

"What if I could tell you where your father is?"

Charlie shook her head at his weak attempt to play her. "That's a crock and you know it. First of all, if you knew where Avery was you would've set that trap in Massachusetts for him, not me. Secondly, if you somehow found out where he is I wouldn't be your first call, your uncle would have that honor so he could order your cousins to take him out."

"It's so sad how your life experiences have jaded you," Stevens told her, a note of pity in his voice.

Charlie could feel the anger welling up inside her, threatening to completely take over. "You contributed to my life experiences," she told him through clenched teeth. "And I don't have time for your games. I have somewhere to be." She left her bedroom and headed toward the front door.

"Ah yes, the ever-important meet-the-parents dinner."

Charlie's blood began to boil. "Let me guess: you have your family's cronies still tailing me, right? How predictable can you be?"

"I really think you should come see me, Charlie, before visiting hours end. You wouldn't want anything to spoil your plans, would you?"

Her hand froze on the doorknob. "Are you threatening me?" she demanded.

"I don't threaten," Stevens told her. "I merely...suggest."

"Fine," she snapped, jerking the door open. "I'll come. But I hope you understand that if

anything happens to someone I care about I'll be doing a hell of a lot more than just *suggesting*."

By the time she arrived Charlie was informed that she only had ten minutes before visitors had to leave. Taking a deep breath she walked over to the only remaining empty seat, sitting across from the glass and waiting for Stevens. After what felt like hours she saw him being led over to her by a guard, a pleased expression on his face.

Charlie picked up the phone when Stevens did, regarding him in what she was sure appeared to be a professional manner. She hoped she was doing a good enough job of concealing how she really felt or the guards might be inclined to lock her up as well. "I'm here," she stated crisply. "Now will you tell me what you want?"

"I was telling the truth before," he told her. "About knowing where your father is."

"Alright, I'll bite. Where?"

"South America."

"And how did you happen upon this information?" she asked with mock politeness. "Still in touch with your contacts south of the border?"

"Maybe."

"Do I get to know why you're telling me and not your family?"

"Who says I didn't?" His expression, if possible, grew even more smug as if there was something crucial he knew and had no intention of sharing with her.

"I've had enough of this," she told him vehemently. "Do you really think your mind games are going to work on someone like me?"

"You're tough, Charlie, but you're not invincible. Don't make the mistake of thinking you don't have weak spots, like everyone else."

Charlie stared at him for a moment, trying to see beyond the amused expression. "You know, I just can't figure you out," she said finally. "You went through a lot of trouble evading the law by faking your own death, and it went pretty successfully. No one was the wiser except my father, and you made sure he wouldn't breathe a word by using me as leverage. So my question now is why did you make it so easy for me? You barely put up a fight. If I didn't know any better," she continued, leaning forward, "I'd think you wanted to get caught."

"You never cease to amaze me," he told her. "How quick you are…it's a shame you never wanted to be part of the organization."

"Oh yeah, why didn't I think of that? Why didn't it occur to me to get in bed with the people who separated me from my family?" she asked sarcastically.

Stevens chuckled. "Did anyone ever tell you what a spitfire you are?"

"You really don't have anything to tell me, do you?"

"I might, if you ask the right questions."

"Alright." she leaned forward. "Tell me how Anna escaped from your men."

"I told you how; Avery helped her."

"Why did they go on the run?" Charlie continued. "Why didn't they ever come back from me?"

"You're stepping out of my territory now," Stevens replied. "I can't answer for what happened after they eluded my men. But I do know there's a good chance Avery's in South America now."

"What makes you so sure?"

"People talk in here," he said, gesturing with his head behind him. "I'm not the only one
with a score to settle with Avery."

"Alright, let's say I believe you. You still haven't told me why you're telling me."

"Because I want him to come back, and you can move him along." His expression had finally begun to harden. "I want this finished."

"There's no way I'll lead him back into a trap."

"Even if it meant it would all be over?"

"You know, I'm not buying any of this. I haven't figured out why...but it was really important to you to get me here tonight," Charlie told him. "I know there's no chance of you telling me why...so I'm leaving." She pushed back, about to rise from the chair and hang up the phone.

"Have a good time tonight," he told her pleasantly. "If it's not already too late."

Charlie couldn't help but sense the double meaning in his words. "Don't call me again."

"Remember, South America."

Charlie ignored him and hung up, walking away without looking back. As soon as she exited the building she immediately starting calling people she knew just to make sure they were safe, since Stevens had been so elusive. She was convinced more than ever that getting her to come was the goal, not what he actually told her. She stopped by her apartment to check on Harley and make sure no one had broken in; a quick look showed no sign of forced entry but she looked further, checking the place from top to bottom to make sure a more stealthy intrusion hadn't taken place. Then she called Bob, filling him and getting his take on the situation. After his initial annoyance at her for caving in and going to see Stevens he went into professional mode, doing everything he could to help her out.

By the time she was finished Charlie was worn out; she collapsed on the couch in the living room, trying to regain her bearings. After an hour of intense grunt work she couldn't find anything that had been disrupted, or anyone. Everything seemed to be okay: all her information was safe, as well as the people she was certain would be targeted in order to get to her. Though she was grateful nothing had happened, she was more puzzled than ever as to why Stevens wanted to see her. Normally her mind was well-equipped to handle a situation like this, string together unlikely clues and scenarios to figure out an end game. But now the only thing happening was she was thinking in circles, whether it was because she was personally involved or re-hashing everything to death she didn't know. Letting out a long sigh, she closed her eyes as Harley quietly crept into the room and jumped up on the couch, curling up next to Charlie's stomach.

A few minutes passed before her eyes flew open and she was realized where she was supposed to be. Careful not to disturb Harley, Charlie rose from the couch and took off in search of her cell, which she was certain dozens of messages were waiting for her.

It turned out to be two, not a dozen, and both were from T.J. as she expected. She ran a brush through her hair as she listened to the first one, telling her they'd all arrived at the restaurant and were ordering an appetizer to hold them over until she got there. The next one was half an hour later, in which T.J. sounded concerned and curious, wondering where she might be. He also said his parents were starving after their flight and they had to start eating without her.

Charlie jumped onto her bike, not caring that the ride was going to destroy her hair and
make her look rumpled; her bike was a hell of a lot faster than taking a cab.

She spent the whole ride there berating herself for getting sucked into Stevens' games and
still wondering why he wanted her there in the first place. Since she wasn't successful in figuring that out, all she'd managed to accomplish was ruining the first meeting between her and T.J.'s family. For a fleeting moment she considered that as the reason Stevens' lured her away but it was too minuscule, too petty. There had to be another reason, something more significant. And even though she was sure it was a bunch of B.S., she was going to check the South America lead just to be safe.

Charlie arrived at the restaurant in time to see T.J. exiting with his family, heading toward the parking lot and taking out his phone. Smoothing the fly-aways from her hair, Charlie quickly sprinted over to catch up to them.

As soon as he saw her he could tell something had happened, and sent her an expression that clearly read *what happened?* and *are you okay?* She shook her head slightly, indicating that it could wait.

Before she could open her mouth to apologize a woman with short, curly light-brown hair who Charlie assumed to be T.J.'s mother stepped forward, extending her hand. "I'm Miranda Mackenzie," she said, regarding Charlie with the same piercing blue eyes as her son. "You must be the young woman we've heard so much about this evening."

"Charlie Booker," Charlie said, shaking her hand. "It's good to meet you, Mrs. Mackenzie-"

"Please, call me Miranda." Mrs. Mackenzie gestured for the others to come forward. "This is my husband, Thomas," she continued as Mr. Mackenzie stepped forward to greet her. He was a tall man, taller than his son, with the same thick dark hair; the only difference was it was streaked with silver.

Charlie shook T.J.'s father's hand as his mother went on to introduce the rest of the family: a young woman a year or so younger than her with long, wavy dark hair and misty eyes who turned out to be Kari, the aroma therapist who lived in Minnesota; her long-time, live-in boyfriend, Jeremiah Brown who did indeed look old enough to appear in a commercial for dentures; T.J.'s youngest sister, Holly, who appeared to be about twenty-four with the light blonde hair, striking dark eyes, and full figure that enabled her to have the career as a Marilyn Monroe impersonator; and, lastly, Holly's new boyfriend Adam Garrett, who looked like he was T.J.'s age but had the build of the Incredible Hulk. Holly quickly explained that he used to play college football.

"I'm so sorry I'm late," Charlie told them all after the introductions. "Something…came up that I had to take care of. I'm sorry I missed dinner, but would still like to invite everyone over for dessert."

Everyone agreed and then split up, with T.J.'s family calling cabs and Charlie heading to her motorcycle, which Adam seemed to be staring at in interest.

She arrived home first, which gave her time to get out the tiramisu, dessert plates, and silverware. She also found a bottle of wine in the back of the cabinet above the sink that she'd long forgotten about and went searching for the wineglasses Jack and Megan bought for her last Christmas.

She set up the table in the small dining room, which was really just an extension of the
living room that had a chandelier, and a table she set up near the sliding glass doors that led out to the small balcony. By the time she'd finished T.J. and his family had arrived.

Harley promptly ran to Charlie's room at the sound of strangers, and Charlie escorted them all through the living room and to the table, where she began to serve the dessert and pour the wine.

"This is Rita's-my surrogate mother's-recipe passed down through her family for generations," Charlie explained as she passed the plates around. "They're all Italian and pretty stingy about sharing their cooking secrets but Rita said she'd make an exception for me."

"Charlie's a great cook," T.J. spoke up, standing next to her. "You guys enjoy it while I borrow her for a moment." He reached over and grabbed her by the arm, starting to lead her away.

"We'll be right back," Charlie said, following T.J. from the room and down the hall.

They stopped in Charlie's room, waking Harley from his doze. Charlie sat on the bed and began to stroke him as T.J. shut the door. "Okay," he said, joining her on the bed. "Spill. What happened?"

Charlie hesitated. "I heard from Stevens," she said, not meeting his eyes.

"He called you?" T.J. demanded. "What did he want?"

"To see me-"

"That's where you were?"

Charlie nodded, looking up at him. "It was a complete waste of time," she admitted. "All he did was jerk me around. And claim that Paul Avery is in South America."

"South America?" T.J. repeated. "Where did he come up with that?"

"He said people talk in lockup," Charlie answered. "I know it's a load of bull. Everything is: calling me, wanting to tell me something, talking in circles when I get there. I got the distinct impression he wanted me there for a reason and that's what made me late, trying to figure out what that might be. I had to make sure there was nothing to the veiled threats he kept making the whole time I was there."

"You're not checking into the South America tip are you?"

"I am, just to cover all my bases." She stood. "I'm really sorry I was late and missed dinner. God knows what kind of impression that made-"

"They understand," T.J. told her. "I've told them how busy you are, how much you've got on your plate right now and that sometimes you have to leave unexpectedly. I'm a P.I., so they get it. Besides, if there was any kind of ill feeling toward you that tiramisu will take care of it, believe me." He kissed her on the top of the head. "Come on," he said, standing. "Let's get back in there before they drink the whole bottle without us."

Before they could leave the room Charlie's phone rang, and she answered it quickly. "Hey Carter, you got anything for me?" She listened for a moment, then her expression went from surprised to grave in a matter of seconds. She just sat there, listening for what seemed like a long while. "Alright. Thanks." She hung up, facing T.J. slowly. "You'll never guess what happened while I was visiting Stevens in lockup."

T.J. frowned, unable to ignore the uneasy feeling rising inside of him. "I'm almost afraid to ask."

"The Montenillos attacked a shipment that belonged to a rival crime family, the first time they've done anything major in twenty-five years. They've been laying low ever since Avery busted the organization and sent Antonio to prison. I'll give you two guesses as to where that shipment was going."

"South America?"

Charlie nodded. "Argentina, to be exact. The family is the DeMarco brothers, one time associates of the Montenillos. There hasn't been any known hostility between them over the years although they stopped doing business together a long time ago. Anyway, it seems that the DeMarcos have been in contact with someone unknown recently, someone who wants to take down the remaining Montenillos. The Montenillos found out about it and retaliated by taking out the shipment tonight, at the exact time I was visiting Stevens."

"And let me guess: the mysterious unknown ally of the DeMarcos is your father."

Charlie nodded. "So it would seem."

T.J. shook his head, starting to pace the length of her bed. "You realize that none of this makes any sense," he told her. "If it was the Montenillos' plan to fire back at the DeMarcos, what did it matter to them if you were aware of it or not? And, if it was Stevens' aim to distract you from that event why did he tell you about South America? He had to know you'd check up on it, just to be sure."

Charlie stared straight ahead without really seeing, deep in concentration. "He wanted me to," she said slowly. "He told me about South America because he wants me to run down there and find Avery, they track me, and then they have a clear shot. Why they can't find him on their own-"

"Maybe they think he won't be able to resist making contact with you if you come down there."

"Except that he's had plenty of time to contact me over the years, and he hasn't yet." Charlie stood. "So the Montenillos are prepared to start a mob war. The DeMarco brothers...I don't know a lot about them since they rarely leave Argentina but they'll definitely fight back if they're provoked."

"And what about you?" T.J. wanted to know. "How do you know the Montenillos won't come after you to get to Avery?"

"Wasn't that all part of Stevens' plan all along? He set us up in Cape Cod in the hopes of using me to get to Avery."

"Only he got interrupted by the cops."

"Right." Now it was Charlie's turn to pace. "It's not over. They're planning something, I know it. And it will definitely involve Paul, possibly Anna. I guess it depends on how much she's helped him work against them over the years." She groaned. "This is so damned frustrating! I'm used to doing, taking action. I'm also used to having all the facts, and this time I couldn't be more in the dark. And this is something big, I can feel it."

"You do have good instincts," T.J. agreed. He put his hands on her shoulders. "We can't do anything about it now, so why don't we go back out there and let my crazy family get to know you. We can pick this back up first thing tomorrow."

"Sounds like a plan."

When they went back to the dining room, Charlie and T.J. saw that most of the tiramisu had been eaten and the Mackenzies were bursting to compliment the cook. Charlie sat next to
Miranda at her insistence, pouring herself a glass of wine and listening to T.J.'s mother talk about the recipes and cooking tips she picked up while she was in Europe for a summer trip
during college. Charlie was fascinated, telling Miranda how she'd always wanted to go overseas, prompting Miranda to give her an in-depth guide to all the places she had to see if she ever got the chance.

T.J., his father, Jeremiah, and Adam all went out on the back porch to smoke the cigars T.J. bought for the occasion, suddenly giving Charlie the urge to run down to the nearest gas station and buy a pack of cigarettes, though she hadn't touched one in years. Instead she started to clean up with Miranda's help, while Kari and Holly were entertained by Harley, who decided to make his debut now that the crowd had dwindled a bit.

After the cleaning was finished, all the women progressed into the living room where Miranda continued the story about T.J.'s tenth birthday, and how he spent it up on the roof of the school after his friends dared him to climb up and he injured himself, unable to climb back down. "We were looking everywhere for him," she was saying as Harley climbed up into Charlie's lap and began to purr. "He was only supposed to be gone for the afternoon, playing with his friends, so by the time it got dark we were frantic."

"How did you find him?"

"His friends finally had the sense to contact us and tell us what happened. Needless to say, he didn't have much of a birthday celebration after we found him."

"Grounded?" Charlie asked with a grin.

"For a month."

The men came back in then and the conversation turned to Mr. and Mrs. Mackenzie, with their children sharing memories of their parents over the course of their lives. Charlie listened with real interest, completely intrigued by what it must be like to grow up knowing who your parents were and being able to celebrate their thirty-fifth anniversary with them.

A short while later things began to wind down, T.J.'s family tired from their long flights. As they all started to leave to head back to the hotel they all bid Charlie and T.J. good night, with Miranda bringing up the rear. "We're going to be in town for a few more days," she told Charlie, "and we'd all love to see you again."

"Sounds great," Charlie said, slightly surprised when Miranda hugged her. "I'll call you tomorrow and we can set something up." She pulled back. "Happy anniversary."

"Thank you, hon," Miranda said as she stepped up to hug T.J. "We want to see you too," she told him. "It's been too long since our last visit."

"I know. I'm glad you guys got to come up," T.J. said, kissing her on the cheek. "I'll stop by tomorrow. Have a good night."

When they were alone Charlie plopped onto the couch with T.J. close behind, resting his head in her lap. Harley curled up next to his feet. "What a night," Charlie said, closing her eyes.

"Yeah," T.J. agreed. "They loved you, by the way. I could tell."

"That's good," she said, sounding somewhat surprised. "It was a lot easier than I thought it'd be."

"You did great," he told her. "You were the perfect host, and then you got all domestic and feminine, talking over cleaning the dishes-"

"I take it that's something women do often?"

He nodded. "Seems like it. If I didn't know any better, Charlie Booker, I'd say you're becoming domesticated."

"Oh really?" she asked, raising an eyebrow. "Care to wager on that?"

"Name it."

"Okay." she sat up partway. "We go to the shooting range tomorrow. Whoever gets the most targets buys the loser a drink and admits to being domesticated. Deal?" she asked, sticking out her hand.

"Deal," he said, shaking it. Then he kissed her.

Chapter Twelve

"It's official: Paul Avery was definitely sighted in Argentina," Bob told Charlie and T.J. the next morning, gesturing for them to sit on the couch across from him. "Do you remember our South American contact we used on the Gilbert case a few years ago?" he asked Charlie.

"Enrique? Of course," she replied. "I've actually worked with him since then, since he has a lot of connections abroad."

"He's the one who confirmed it, which is how I know it's legit," Bob continued. Bob was very picky about who he trusted, so if he put his faith in someone Charlie knew that person was reliable. "He's in the process of getting the photos ready to e-mail to us, photos that put him in the small town near the DeMarco estate."

Bob had called Charlie early that morning to invite her over to his apartment so he could share what he'd found out. Since T.J. spent the night he came along, just as interested in Bob's discoveries as Charlie. Bob and T.J. had met on several occasions since T.J. started dating Charlie but had yet to collaborate professionally. Charlie was grateful for the added input.

"What does he know about the DeMarcos?" Charlie wanted to know.

"That they're notorious gamblers, for one. Everything they do they do in style, and are very concerned with appearances, which is why they have the flashy estate. They're very picky about who they do business with; Enrique described them as either being great allies or dangerous adversaries. Once they're crossed, they don't usually forget."

"Which means they consider the Montenillos adversaries now."

"They probably felt that way for a while, which is why they were eager to assist Avery. The DeMarcos also throw large parties about once a month, to generate publicity in the circles of their choosing."

Charlie nodded. "Okay. What about Avery?"

"Enrique doesn't know much," Bob replied. "Just that he's been seen with the DeMarcos, and it was regarding the Montenillos. He's keeping his eyes and ears open though, ready to inform us the minute he finds out anything else."

"What about Stevens?" T.J. spoke up. "What's your take on him?"

"Professionally speaking, the man likes to appear as though he's an enigma but his style's easy enough to figure out. It's all about family for him, and revenge. The way he goes about getting what he wants, however, is entirely a different story. He couldn't be more unpredictable in the way he pursues his goals, or how he plans to achieve his end-game. It's obvious he enjoys a certain modicum for the dramatic, and elaborate displays. He'll never come right out and tell you what he wants unless he thinks it'll benefit him. It also seems like he has a sort of attachment to Charlie," he added, his voice hardening. "Which is why he didn't kill her or use her further in the first place. But don't misunderstand that," he warned Charlie, turning to her. "I don't believe for a second that he wouldn't hurt you in order to bring down Avery, now that everything seems to be falling into place for him and his family. You're probably in more danger now than you ever were as a child."

"Is that also spoken from a professional standpoint?"

"No, it's spoken from a paternal one," Bob answered honestly. "You ought to know by now that I can see it both ways."

Charlie and T.J. left a short while later, having plans to meet up with T.J.'s family for brunch at the hotel. "So you've worked with this Enrique guy before?" T.J. asked as they walked down to the parking lot. Charlie nodded. "Does that mean you've been to Argentina before?"

Charlie nodded as they walked down the sidewalk. "About three years ago Bob and I had a job in the Bronx, hired by a lady trying to find where her ex stashed money from an account that was rightfully-and legally-hers. We ended up in South America; that's where he was hiding out. While we were down there we met Enrique, who was referred to us by Bob's old boss who'd had successful dealings with him in the past. He turned out to be very good to us, really helping when we needed it."

"Have you been back since?"

Charlie shook her head as they approached T.J.'s car. "No, I've just worked with him over the phone. He's very thorough, very productive. He's also a nice guy, which doesn't hurt. The old adage is if Bob trusts someone they're usually worth trusting."

"Does Bob trust me?"

Charlie looked at him in surprise as he unlocked their doors. "Of course he does. If he didn't, he never would've let you into his apartment the first time you met. Or sit in on a meeting like today." She opened her door. "Now. Can I ask *you* something?"

"Go for it," he replied, getting in.

"Why the sudden curiosity about my old jobs?"

"I was just curious about South America," he told her. "I didn't know you've ever been there before. I was under the impression that you'd never left the country."

"Just that one time. You probably thought that because I've never been to Europe, and that's where I really want to go," Charlie told him. Then she looked at him as he pulled out of the parking lot. "Do you feel like you don't know enough about me?"

"I do," he told her. "I investigated you, remember? But I didn't do it twice," he muttered under his breath, smiling.

"No, you didn't have to; I was up front with *my* intentions," she teased. "But I don't mean things you'd find in a profile. I mean...is there anything you want to know? Anything you're curious about?"

"While we're on the subject...have your jobs taken you out of New York? Other than the South American one."

"I've been up and down the Eastern seaboard," she replied. "But I've never been out West, not yet anyway. What about you? Where have your cases taken you?"

"The farthest was Los Angeles," he told her. "A teenage runaway, about five years ago."

They fell silent for a moment, giving Charlie's mind a chance to buzz and whir, trying to fill in what wasn't being said. "Is this your way of telling me you don't want me to go to Argentina?" she asked finally.

He looked at her, startled. "Where'd you come up with that?"

"Come on, neither of us are amateurs here. You started questioning me about my jobs because you think I'm going to jet off to South America."

"I was asking you questions because I was curious," he said defensively. "But since you brought it up...are you planning on going to South America?"

"I knew it!" she said triumphantly. "What does it matter if I did?"

"It matters because it's dangerous."

"True," she agreed. "But no more dangerous than staying in New York. T.J., I might as well be wearing a neon sign that reads 'Montenillos, come and get me' because of my connection to Stevens and Avery."

"That's different," he protested.

"How?" she challenged. "How am I any safer-"

"Because you're not alone here."

Charlie blinked. "I wouldn't be alone there either," she reminded him. "If Avery's still there that would be the best protection there is-if I was someone who needed it. The man fell of the map for almost thirty years, and he used to be a cop."

"But he could be gone by the time you get there."

Charlie turned in her seat so she could get a better look at his expression, which remained unreadable. "First of all, I haven't decided to go down there. Not yet anyway. I need something a little more substantial to go on first; you don't go off half-cocked without so much to go on as a photo, even if the source is reliable. You know that." She paused. "I can tell something's bothering you. I'm not good at guess-the-emotion, so why don't you just save me a lot of trouble and tell me what's really going on."

T.J. stopped at a red light. "It's nothing," he told her. "Just forget I ever said anything."

"Oh no you don't," she protested. "You're not going to bring something up and then leave me hanging. I want answers, Mackenzie," she said forcefully. "Now."

He looked at her, his expression somewhat amused despite himself. "Did anyone ever tell you how sexy you are when you're barking orders?"

"Flattery does not deflect me," she warned. "Now tell me, what's going on?"

They were nearing the hotel now, and Charlie was becoming increasingly curious. Everything had seemed to be going well between them, especially since meeting his parents had been such a success. But when they got to Bob's this morning things began to change, as soon as they'd started discussing South America.

T.J. pulled into a parking space and cut the motor, turning to her. "You're making this bigger than it should be," he told her. "We have to go in there and see my family, so now's really not the time-"

"I swear if you evade me one more time I'll be using *you* for target practice instead of going to the shooting range," she threatened.

"Fine," he relented, "fine. I just think that sometimes...you forget you're not single anymore."

Charlie frowned. "What the hell does that mean?"

"It means that when something important comes up you automatically going into solo-mode," he told her, not meeting her eyes. "I mean, yeah you call Bob and all the people you know for info but when it comes to the action, you're a solo act."

"But I haven't been, until recently," she reminded him. "Bob was my partner for ten years."

"I know. But this is different. This isn't about letting a colleague or even a father-figure in. It's about letting the person you're involved with in. Not necessarily for professional backup,
but for emotional backup. Also for someone to watch your back."

"You don't think I'd let you watch my back?" she asked, frowning.

"I think you want to, and you have to an extent. We started working on this together-professionally-and you've let me into the inner circle since then by letting me tag along to Bob's today. I just think that when it comes to the big stuff-"

"I'll run off unprepared, shoot first, and ask questions later without thinking about my safety?" she guessed, finishing. "I always think about my safety, T.J. I am good at what I do."

"I know you are," he told her. "You blew me away when I first met you. You're a pro down to the letter, and anyone would have a hard time knocking you down. But that doesn't mean it can't be done."

"I know I'm not invincible," she said. "And I get where you're coming from. If the situation was reversed and I thought you were being too rash in a case I'd probably speak up too." She reached over and squeezed his hand. "Thanks for being worried about me. But I promise, no matter what happens, that I'll take care of myself and definitely give the Montenillos hell. Alright?"

He smiled tightly, kissing her briefly on the forehead. "Alright," he agreed quickly. Then he reached for his door handle. "Let's get going, we're running late."

As Charlie let him lead her into the restaurant she had a feeling that something was still off between them, that there was something that T.J. wasn't letting go of. But she didn't have time to figure it out as they walked over to the table where the Mackenzie family was waiting.

After everyone's plates were full of food Charlie asked Miranda what their plans were for the day. She told Charlie it had been a while since she'd been to New York and that she and the girls were planning on going shopping. She made it clear that Charlie was more than welcome to join them but Charlie had to take a rain check, telling Miranda she had a previous engagement with her son at the shooting range.

"This is what you guys do for fun?" Kari asked, raising an eyebrow.

"It's one thing we do, yeah," Charlie answered with a shrug. "Got to stay at the top of our game. And a little friendly competition is always a good thing," she added with a wink.

Holly was interested in hearing what else they did for fun, and seemed to get a kick out of the stakeout they had recently for T.J.'s cheating spouse case. Miranda also chuckled when Charlie described the snacks they brought as if they were watching a show.

"In a way, we were," Charlie said with a grin. It surprised her how at ease she felt around T.J.'s family; it was nothing like she'd been expecting. They seemed to accept her no matter how unusual her lifestyle was, and constantly encouraged her to reveal more of it to their curious ears.

A while later, when they were all sufficiently stuffed, T.J. and Charlie prepared to leave, with Charlie promising to go on a shopping spree with the Mackenzie women before they left and T.J. inviting the guys over the next day to watch the all-stars.

Their next stop, as planned, was the shooting range. T.J.'s heart didn't seem to be in it at first but things picked up shortly, and for a while they were neck and neck. At last they called up their targets, comparing each. "Well, well," T.J. said after a moment. "It seems like you've beaten me, Oh Not-So-Domesticated one." He held out his hand. "Ready for that drink?"

Charlie grinned, her concern for his earlier attitude forgotten. "Absolutely."

***

T.J. had to go into the office later that afternoon so Charlie was on her own in the search. Even though she knew how necessary all of it was she missed being out working, constantly on the move. Her refusal to take on any new jobs was key in clearing her schedule for the search for Paul and Anna, but it was doing little to satisfy her craving for adrenaline. She needed something to do, and she needed it now.

So instead of sitting home in front of the computer as had been the norm lately, Charlie took off on her bike, deciding to be proactive. If she wanted to be ready when the Montenillos went to war, since they'd undoubtedly be pulling her into it because of her father, Charlie decided to check out the competition. The actual DeMarco brothers lived in Argentina but the few associates they had in New York weren't that far out of reach, so she headed to the Village just as the sun was starting to sink into the horizon.

There was a small warehouse that read "Coffee" near a truck yard, which Charlie knew was a front. She killed the motor and walked her bike over to a grove of bushes near an old dirt-and-gravel road that hadn't been used in years, undoubtedly leading to a dead end. She shouldered her black leather bag and took off, just as the last strands of sunlight disappeared into the golden-red sky.

She waited, hidden, until it grew completely dark and started toward the side of the building, where she could see the faint flurry of activity. Pressing herself flat against a pillar she waited for the right person to pass, the person who would unknowingly give her an inside view of what was going on.

At last a short, thin young man walked past, about eighteen or twenty. He didn't appear to be overly observant, which worked in Charlie's favor. As he passed she waited for the right moment and then, taking a cue from T.J., dropping a listening device into his shoe. A listening device that also happened to be a tracker.

When she was sure she was alone she made a run for it toward the trees where her bike was hidden, leaning against it as she set up her computer. Her tech had shown her a while back how to operate the equipment she was about to use, and Charlie was pretty sure she'd gotten the hang of it.

This proved to be the case when she got it set up successfully, putting in her earpiece so she could listen as she tracked the unsuspecting guy's movements. He was heading inside the warehouse, asking for someone named Peterson.

At last he seemed to have found him, and they began to discuss his fee. As she listened Charlie deduced that the boy was a loader, meaning he transferred merchandise from the warehouse to the large semis in the lot next door. He seemed low-level, operating only on a need-to-know basis. Charlie hoped that he would talk to someone soon who could clue her in as to what was going on.

A couple hours passed and Charlie remained stationary, not learning anything of consequence. She was about to call it a night when she heard something that made her sit up a little straighter.

"...the shipment that was destroyed?" the boy was asking.

"It was a big deal," a second voice replied, reasonably older. "They're saying the
Montenillos did it."

"Who?" the boy asked.

The second voice chuckled. "You really don't know who you get in bed with, do you kid? The Montenillos used to work with the DeMarcos," he explained. "Until recently."

"What happened?"

"Don't know," the man replied. "It's above my pay grade. All I know is the Montenillos go around thinking they're people who don't need to be messed with. What they don't know is the DeMarcos, though a smaller force, are just as lethal. If a war's what they want, a war's what they'll get."

"Who's this Avery guy?" the boy asked, and Charlie was immediately on the alert. "I heard some guys talking about him on the pier last night."

"Avery?" the man repeated. "Now that I do know. Long before you were born there was this undercover cop that infiltrated the Montenillo organization. There was a big fall-out and somehow he ended up on the run. He's not a cop anymore, but he still wants to bring them down. That's why he's been meeting with the DeMarco brothers in Argentina."

"He's actually meeting the DeMarcos?" the boy asked, obviously impressed. "That's huge."

"I know. People like you and me will never see the likes of them; we're underlings. But Avery's the real deal. I don't know everything, but I do know they're taking him seriously. I also know he's got a daughter."

Charlie's breath caught in her throat. Apparently she'd struck gold in choosing to listen to the grunt workers.

"A daughter? She a cop too?"

The man chuckled again. "Oh no. There are stories about her; she's famous, around the Brooklyn area especially. Or should I say infamous."

"Why?"

"You'd never believe me if I told you, kid."

"Try me."

"Alright. She's a bounty hunter."

There was an obvious pause. "A bounty hunter?" he repeated. "Like Boba Fet in Star Wars?"

The man spoke again, undoubtedly amused. "Yes, like Boba Fet. Except it's her profession, her actual job and means of putting food on the table. She's slick, that one. Heard all kinds of things about her."

"Like what?" the boy asked. It was clear he was fascinated.

"Like she gets away with what would put most of us in the slammer. Which is kind of ironic, considering her old man used to be a cop. I don't know the details but she didn't grow up with him. Actually, as far as I know, they've never met. Anyway, this girl's tough. Most guys I know wouldn't want to screw with her. She can hold her own." There was a hint of admiration in his voice. "It's kind of a shame, though. As good as she is there won't be any getting out of what's coming."

"What's coming?"

"War," he replied bleakly. "And I don't have a clue which side's gonna pull through. I do
know she's as important as Avery. The difference is, she probably doesn't know it."

"How do you know all this stuff?"

"I listen. You'd be amazed at what you can pick up on while you're part of the background. When almighty important ones think you're not paying attention they'll let anything slip. Makes for interesting conversations later on."

"It helps what we're doing go by faster, that's for sure," the boy said. "So this girl. Is she hot?"

After that the conversation took a far less informative turn when the subject drifted from her to bikini-clad women who apparently looked like her, going down that path until they were discussing swimsuit models and Playboy centerfolds. When she heard the older man start to describe his fantasy woman she decided to pull the plug.

It had been quite an enlightening evening. Though she hadn't really learned anything new she did know that someone-either the DeMarcos or the Montenillos-had big plans for her. Plans that began and ended with Paul Avery, who Charlie was more intent that ever on finding. Which meant, despite T.J.'s misgivings, she would most likely have to go to South America.

Instead of thinking about the argument that would ensue she thought instead of the way the elder man described her, as someone most men wouldn't want to mess with. She was interested to know what people considered as stuff that would get "most people sent to the slammer". Though she'd definitely pulled quite a few misdemeanors in her day for the sake of the job, she'd never done anything people would include in the big leagues. But then, that's how rumors and stories began: with a grain of truth, accompanied by vivid imaginations and water-cooler talk.

As she started to walk her bike a safe distance away she suddenly heard shouting coming from inside the warehouse and froze, making sure she was still safely hidden while scoping out the area. Her blood pumping loudly in her ears, Charlie remained on alert, feeling the adrenaline pump through her veins that she earlier craved.

It turned out to be a false alarm; someone had an accident in the warehouse-merchandise was damaged-but there was no risk at all for her. Standing again she took her bike and began to walk it in the opposite direction. As she drove back to Brooklyn she felt better than she had in a long time, finally feeling like herself once again instead of the muted version she'd been forced to become lately. This was the life for her, no question. It was painfully obvious that she couldn't be content with anything less. *Which is a good thing I don't plan on retiring anytime soon,* she thought as she sped along under the starlit sky. *And that I have a boyfriend who understands, who craves the rush as much as I do. It's who we are.*

And most likely who we'll always be.

***

"It sounds like he was half in love with you," T.J. commented later that night, lifting his bottle of beer to his lips. "Trying to sell you as some badass femme fatale."

Charlie raised an eyebrow. "Don't think I fit the bill?"

"Oh you fit the bill alright," he assured her, reaching for the deck of cards. "It's just I never knew you had such a die-hard fan."

Charlie had stopped by T.J.'s apartment just as he got back from the office. While playing cards, Charlie told him all she'd overheard earlier at the DeMarco warehouse.

T.J. shuffled the cards. "Up for one more round?"

Charlie nodded and he dealt.

At T.J.'s invitation she stayed the night, curling up next to him in bed and thinking-unsurprisingly-about South America. She'd all but decided to go, though no one knew about it yet. Now she had to figure out the best way to break the news to T.J. when she knew it was a touchy subject for him. Although it was getting really hard for her to understand why: he took risks all the time, as did she. Why should this time be any different?

Yet there was a part of her that knew it *was* different, because it was bigger than anything she'd ever faced before. And that was saying something.

Days passed and soon it was near the end of the week, which meant the Mackenzie family's trip was coming to a close. They all went out to lunch Thursday afternoon and Charlie and T.J. rode with them to the airport afterward.

As they said their good-byes, Miranda pulled Charlie aside, telling her once again how glad she was that they met and how much she was looking forward to seeing her again. Charlie found herself saying she felt the same way, and she really did. Their meeting had gone so much better than she ever thought it would.

"I also want to say," Miranda added, "that I think you're really good for T.J. I know we haven't known each other for very long, and I hope it's not too premature for me to say so but...you make him happier than I've ever seen him."

It might've made other women in her position feel uncomfortable but not Charlie. She took at as the highest compliment, and thanked Miranda for saying so. Secretly she wondered if she was right; if that was the case, Charlie was definitely heading into uncharted territory.

After saying good-bye to T.J.'s sisters and Mr. Mackenzie-all of whom also expressed their desire to see her again-the Mackenzies departed, Miranda making T.J. promise he'd come down to Palm Springs as soon as he got the chance. When they disappeared from sight, T.J. put his arm around Charlie's shoulders and steered her toward the exit. "They had a good time," he stated, as much to her as himself. "I could tell. It all worked out pretty well, huh?"

"I guess it's not hard, when you're meeting good people," Charlie told him as they walked out into the sunny afternoon. "Speaking of good people, Bob invited us over for Labor Day. Diana too. You game?"

"Sure," he agreed. "You just spent time with my family, of course I'll spend time with yours."

He was in such a good mood the rest of the day that Charlie considered bringing up the trip but ultimately decided against it. Instead she set it up with her travel agent and started getting her gear together over the weekend. She also spoke to Enrique, who would be expecting her at the beginning of the week.

She was cooking spaghetti Bolognese Sunday night when she heard a knock at the door. Looking at her luggage strewn around the living room, she called through the door to ask who it was.

"It's T.J.!" his muffled voice came through the door as she quickly gathered her bags and tossed them into her office, shutting the door. She called back for him to hold on.

"Hey," she greeted him, kissing him quickly on the cheek. "You're just in time, I'm cooking dinner." She took his hand and led him inside and to the kitchen.

After letting him taste the sauce and getting the proper reaction, Charlie brought the food to the kitchen table and they began to eat. When they were both full they sat on the couch and watched a movie of T.J.'s choice, Charlie's mind on her luggage in the office.

When the movie ended T.J. seemed to want to play around, which started when he tickled her and they chased each other around the living room and ended up in the shower, staying in long enough for the hot water to run out. Then they went into Charlie's bedroom, flopping side-by-side on her large bed, facing one another and staring intently. "So, what do you say?" he asked quietly, brushing a strand of her wet, coppery hair out of her eyes. "It might be a little late in asking, seeing as how we've met each other's families and everything...but do you want to be an official couple?"

As she looked back at him everything else was driven from her mind. She'd been waiting to have this conversation since they hadn't actually discussed it...but it seemed as though it was heading in that direction. Now Charlie was glad to finally have it out in the open. "I thought we already are," she told him, pulling him close to kiss him.

She woke up early the next morning and did something she never did: cooked a full breakfast. Protein shakes, granola, or yogurt were her usual meals of choice but after the night they'd had she felt they deserved something a little more filling. Also, it was fun to make; she hadn't made pancakes or bacon in years.

When T.J. entered the kitchen the table was covered in plates filled with bacon, eggs, pancakes, and fruit. "All this for moi?" he asked, surveying the food in surprise.

Charlie breezed over to him, kissing him on the cheek as she set the orange juice on the table. "Don't thank me yet; we're going for a run right after," she warned.

That afternoon they picked Diana and went to Bob's apartment, T.J. bringing a case of Bob's favorite beer. He was already firing up the grill on the back porch and they all joined him, talking and drinking while they waited for Jack and Megan.

Once everyone had arrived they began to eat the hotdogs and hamburgers Bob had grilled, as well as the potato salad Megan had made. As Charlie excused herself to go to the bathroom her cell rang, and she answered on her way down the hall.

It was her travel agent confirming her one a.m. flight for that morning, and Charlie received all her information quickly, thanking the woman and telling her she'd be ready that morning. As she was hanging up she ran right into T.J., who was rounding a corner. "Sorry," she said quickly, falling back. She looked at him for a moment, wondering if he overheard her conversation.

If he had, he made no sign of it. He simply kissed her on the forehead and went on to the bathroom, joining her on the porch with the others a short while later.

As the evening was winding down Charlie realized she needed to let Bob in on her plans, and T.J. too. She wanted to tell them separately, so she waited until she saw T.J. was busy talking to Diana before pulling Bob away from the group.

"I figured as much," Bob said when they arrived in the kitchen and she told him what was going on. "I know Enrique will take care of you, but you really need to be careful Charlie. I'd feel a lot better if someone was going with you."

"Like who, you?" she asked, only half-teasing.

"Like the guy out on my back porch. You know, your boyfriend?"

"I can handle this," Charlie insisted. "I don't need backup, not yet anyway. Besides...this isn't a job or a case. It's my life. I need to be the one who handles it."

"You let him help you in Massachusetts," Bob pointed out. "You've said it yourself: you make a good team, Charlie. Why not let-"

"Because," she interrupted impatiently, "I want to find my father myself. Don't you think I've earned that?"

"Of course you have, but this is bigger than some family reunion. We're talking big league mob players-cutthroat, bloodthirsty, vengeful mob players. This is something I wouldn't even take on solo. Having backup is smart, Charlie, not a sign of weakness."

"This isn't about weak or strong; it's about answers," she argued. "This whole thing started with Stevens and Avery-I was pulled into it by result-and it's going to end with them. With people connected to me, which means the fewer people I care about involved in this, the better."

"For who?" Bob wanted to know. "Them or you?"

"I don't think you're really-"

"Hey," T.J. interrupted, walking into the kitchen. "Jack wants to talk to you about the coming weekend," he told Bob. "Something about some kind of trip."

Charlie looked at Bob, somewhat surprised. "Trip?" she repeated.

"Jack wants to do some male bonding over a campfire. Not really my scene, but you suck it up for family." He looked at Charlie meaningfully as he walked past. "And they do the same for you," he said quietly, then disappeared through the frame.

"So," Charlie began, leaning against the counter, "how much of that did you hear?"

"The two of you weren't exactly being quiet about it," T.J. told her, standing by the far wall. "But I didn't need to hear to know what you were arguing about." He looked at her. "I know you're planning on going to South America."

"What gave me away?"

"Are you kidding? I figured it out as soon as you found out Stevens' lead was real, and that Avery was really down there in Argentina. The longer you kept quiet about it, the more convinced I became. Then there was last night, and the homemade breakfast this morning-"

"What about it?"

"You were softening me up before you dropped the bomb," he answered matter-of-factly. "It would've been pretty effective if I hadn't already figured it out."

"There wasn't some kind of plan or conspiracy; you came over last night, and what happened, happened. I made you breakfast this morning because I had a good time last night and was glad we made a decision about us. Yes, I thought it might make things easier...only because I knew that you would have a problem with me going, though I still can't figure out why."

"Of course you could, if you really thought about it," he told her. "Bob nailed it on the head: you won't take backup. That's dangerous, reckless even. As a pro, you should know better. But you're not thinking like a pro, you're thinking like a daughter wanting to connect with her long-lost father, and there's nothing wrong with that, Charlie. No one could blame you for wanting to track down Avery, see what he's like, and let him fill in the gaps of all you still don't know. But this isn't an ordinary situation. We already know you probably mean something to the Montenillos. If you go down there you might find out you mean something to the DeMarcos, too."

Charlie waited a moment before speaking. "I'm aware of the danger involved," she said finally. "But it's nothing compared to the danger Avery and Anna have been in all these years. Taking down half the Montenillo crime family was huge, and it'll follow him for the rest of his life, no matter what happens next. If he could do all he did to keep me safe-without even have met me-I can do this for him. And don't say he wouldn't want me to risk my life going down there because as I've already established, I'm in just as much danger here. We all will be, until this is over. Avery knows that. And so do you."

"You still don't get it, do you? This isn't just about Avery, or even the Montenillos or the DeMarcos-"

"What's it about then?"

T.J. shook his head. "You," he said simply.

"Me?" Charlie repeated. She pushed away from the counter in annoyance, walking over to him. "I don't get you. You pretty much do what I do, live how I live. I have more in common with you than just about anyone on this planet, and that's no small thing. I never thought

I'd meet someone who really got me, who understood where I'm coming from. You can empathize in so many ways...and we make a good team because we complement each other, too. You have this uncanny ability to see the positive in everything, and you have no idea how good that's been for me." She stopped just a few inches in front of him, reaching out to touch his arms. "We're alike, you and me," she said quietly. "If anyone could understand why I need to do this, it should be you."

He looked at her with an expression she couldn't interpret. "I do understand," he told her, a twinge of sadness in his voice. "And we are alike, except in one significant way."

"And what way is that?"

Before he could reply the back door opened and Jack and Megan came in, stopping to tell Charlie and T.J. good night. Charlie forced a smile as she hugged them both, determined to hear the rest of what T.J. was going to say.

That didn't appear to be in the cards, however, because Diana came in shortly saying she was ready to leave. They were both silent on the way back to T.J.'s and Diana's apartment complex, a fact that didn't go unnoticed by Diana but she remained respectfully quiet.

After Diana wished them both good night T.J. and Charlie were standing in the hall, neither making a move to speak. At last T.J. spoke up, clearing his throat. "I'm beat," he told her finally. "I'm going to call it a night. I'll call you tomorrow."

"My flight's in a few hours," she told him quickly. "And I don't know how long I'll be gone."

T.J. nodded and wordlessly walked over to her, kissing her lips briefly. "Have a good flight," he said quietly. "And good luck in Argentina."

She nodded, watching as he unlocked his door and gave a slight wave in her direction before shutting it behind him. Charlie stood where she was for a moment, trying to figure out what had just happened. Unable to come up with any viable explanations, she turned and walked out of the lobby, heading into the overcast night.

Chapter Thirteen

The photos Enrique promised arrived just as Charlie was checking her e-mail on the way to the airport. There were several black-and-white shots of a man who appeared to be in his early fifties, his back mostly to the camera. He was too far away to be seen clearly, but Charlie knew it was the best Enrique could do; Paul Avery didn't seem to be the kind of man easily captured on film.

As she looked Charlie tried to find a resemblance; she'd seen photos, albeit not good ones, of Avery when he was young in the police academy, and some after he became a detective. Since the photos were public ones, they didn't really do justice if one was trying to find physical similarities. But, from what she could tell, the old photos she'd seen seemed to correlate with the ones she was looking at now, which meant Avery had definitely been in South America. The question was, was he still there?

Bob had called her right before he went to bed to wish her luck, hoping that she had "come to her senses" and asked T.J. to come along. She assured him she had everything well-handled and would let him know as soon as found out anything. He promised to continue to keep his ears open about Anna.

As Charlie expected, she hadn't heard from T.J. She considered calling him to say good-bye but it was clear when they said good night that he'd said all he wanted to say. So she took a cab to the airport, right on time for her one a.m. flight, and tried to put their argument out of her mind.

JFK was packed as usual, and she had to weave her way in and out of the throngs of people as she headed toward Gate 18.

She looked around one last time as she prepared to board, surprised that she found herself wishing T.J. would've shown up so they could part on decent terms. *I really need him on my side,* she thought as she walked forward. *Who knows what I'll be walking into down there.*

But it seemed he didn't mind how they left things because she so saw no sign of him, walking to the attendant to present her ticket. Without another glance backward, Charlie boarded the plane.

The in-flight movie was some kind of girly romance flick, which made Charlie happy she hadn't wasted money on headphones. Instead she turned her attention to her computer, going over all the intel and looking up all the other contacts referred to her in the area. She knew the chances of Avery still being in the exact place Enrique told her about were very slim, but it was possible that he was in the same general area. At least she could find out about his patterns and possibly his motives for being in South America-other than meeting with the DeMarocs, if he had any-even if she didn't find him.

When she soaked up all the information she could Charlie decided to try and get a few hours sleep, so she'd be alert and ready to deal with whatever was waiting for her.

When she finally landed she checked into a motel and got cleaned up, then immediately arranged a meeting with her contact, Enrique Sabados, at a small outdoor restaurant outside the city in an hour. She checked her voicemail and e-mail and discovered she had no messages. Her I.D. in one pocket, her gun in the other, Charlie headed into the small village where the restaurant was located.

She arrived first, ordering a drink while sitting at the bar and having a quick look around. *Mostly families here,* she observed. She also noticed the high fence running around the perimeter and several of the men nearby casually looking toward it from time to time. Obviously something important was on the other side but she didn't feel the immediate need to check it out. Yet.

A short while later Enrique arrived, kissing her on the cheek in greeting. He was a tall, well-built dark man with graying hair and a matching beard in his late forties. Originally from Guatemala, he spoke with a thick accent and talked frequently about his wife, Consuela. Bob knew him through his former boss, who'd worked with him once years ago and spoke highly of him. Bob and Charlie, in turn, could say the same.

"Charlie," he greeted her warmly. "Welcome back to Argentina."

"Thanks," she told him, giving him a tight hug. "It's good to see you again."

They sat across from each other at a small table, and Enrique pulled out a thin file. "It's not much," he said, sliding it over to her. "But it's all I have."

Charlie opened the file to see several more black-and-white photos similar to the ones he'd e-mailed her earlier. It was still too hard to tell exactly what Paul Avery looked like but Charlie thought she maybe she could see a resemblance. Then again, it could be wishful thinking.

"Did you find out why he's here? Is it just about getting the DeMarcos on his side?" she asked, setting down the photos..

"As of late he's brokering a truce," Enrique told her. "The families here who are in business with the Montenillos are getting restless, concerned about their interests. Word is that Paul's trying to assure them he's not interested in putting any of them away. He only cares about the Montenillos."

"Because it's personal."

Enrique nodded. "As you know, he's not a detective anymore; he's his own free agent. All he seemed to care about over the last twenty-something years was Hector Montenillo. Or Stevens, as he's also called. At least that's what's been said."

"How long has he been here?"

"About six months. But he's been here before, on and off over the years. Never stayed too long so Stevens wouldn't have the chance to track him here. Other than Australia, his whereabouts before now have been a mystery." He pulled out a map, pointing to the area he circled in red. "This is where he was recently spotted, at the DeMarco estate."

"Do you have any more background on them?"

"Nothing different than I told Bob," he replied. "Except they can be especially dangerous."

Charlie nodded, finishing her drink. "Anything else?"

Enrique looked at her solemnly. "You're thinking of approaching them?"

"Have to. They're the only lead I've got." Charlie stood.

"You can't just show up at their home uninvited," he told her, standing also. "They're incredibly paranoid and know nothing about you."

"Are you saying they'll greet me with a cigar and a semi-automatic?"

"Yes, but without the cigar. Charlie, I really must insist that you rethink your plans. I know you want to find out about your father...but have you considered that he might think it's
too dangerous for you to do so right now?"

"If he thought it was that dangerous, he would've contacted me himself, tried to stop me from coming after him."

"Perhaps he thought you may not listen to reason, and take his warnings as a reason to come anyway."

"Have you been talking to Bob?" she asked suspiciously.

Enrique shook his head. "I like you, Charlie Booker. I don't want to see you get hurt."

"Thanks, Enrique, but I'll be fine. You've worked with me before, you know I can handle myself."

He nodded. "Yes, that's true but-"

Charlie held up a hand to stop him. "I'm already here," she pointed out. "I might as well make the most of it. You said they have monthly parties. When's the next one?"

Enrique hesitated. "This Saturday," he told her reluctantly.

"Can you get me an invite?"

"If you sure that's what you really want..." he trailed off. "I'll find a way."

"Thanks," she told him. "You've been a big help. And for the record, I wasn't exactly sold on the idea of going in with such little info, basically unprotected. Contrary to popular belief, I don't have a death wish."

"I'll contact you when everything's ready," he promised. "You should probably lay low until then."

"Agreed. Don't want to rouse suspicion until I have to."

They parted ways, Charlie looking toward the fence one more time with interest before heading back to the motel.

***

Charlie stayed true to her word and laid low for the next couple of days, staying in her motel room and getting in touch with all her contacts to see if anyone had anything new for her, disappointed when she found out they didn't. On Thursday afternoon Enrique came through, bringing over Charlie's invitation as well as a long hanging bag. "I assumed you didn't bring any formal wear with you; this is Consuela's," he explained, draping it over an armchair near the window in Charlie's motel room.

"How is Consuela?" Charlie wanted to know. "This is the first time we've worked together that you haven't mentioned her right away."

"She is fine; she is visiting family in Buenos Aires," he told her. "When I mentioned that you had to attend a party she suggested I let you borrow this," he explained, indicating the hanging bag.

"One of these days, I'm going to meet her," Charlie said as she walked over to the chair where the dress was draped. "So, what did you tell them about me?"

"The DeMarcos know you're a bounty hunter but don't know about your connection to Avery or Stevens. They think you're just working a job and have a few questions for them. It's safer for you if they continue to believe that."

"Agreed," Charlie said, unzipping the bag and carefully pulling out the dress. "Wow," she
said, whistling in amazement. "This is really beautiful. Tell your wife thanks for me."

"I will. Good luck tomorrow night. Let me know if you need anything else," he instructed as he was leaving. It might've been Charlie's imagination but she could swear that he really had deep misgivings about her going through with the plan. He didn't say anything else about it, however; he merely wished her a good night and was on his way.

Charlie spent the evening going over all her notes, info, and photos on her computer one more time in preparation. She also tried to investigate the DeMarco brothers further but didn't come up with anything she didn't already know.

Before she went to bed she bit the bullet and called T.J., though she knew with the time difference he'd be probably be working. As she suspected, it went to voicemail. "It's me," she greeted him. "I've got an important meeting to go to tomorrow night, in the form of a formal party. I'm hoping it will give me the answers I need. I still haven't sighted Avery so this party's all I've got to go on." Her tone sobered. "I'm sorry about how we left things. If I wasn't so stubborn you'd be here too and we'd make a great pair showing up at the DeMarco party together." She paused. "It's not easy for me to admit when I'm wrong. I really do think it should just be me tracking down Avery...but maybe I was too quick to exclude you. Anyway, we can talk more about it soon. Wish me luck" She hung up, laying back against the pillows.

The hours passed quickly the next day until it was late afternoon, and Charlie started to get ready. When she was finished she looked at her reflection in the small bathroom mirror, taking in the long emerald green dress that hugged her body as though it were made for her. She'd fixed her hair into a fancy up-do, the first time she'd ever attempted such a feat, and was pleasantly surprised that it turned out well. She grabbed her small purse, dropped her phone inside, and left the motel.

On the way to the DeMarco estate she realized she hadn't checked her messages in a
while and wanted to see if Enrique had any more advice for her. She had four messages, but none of them were from Enrique.

They were all from the same number, T.J.'s number. Curious, Charlie checked the first message just as she was starting up the front walk of the DeMarco property. "Good luck at your party, I hope it'll be informative for you. And you're right, we would've made a good pair. Maybe next time." A brief pause and then, "I'm sorry I didn't come see you off. We'll talk more when you get back." She checked the second message. "Something about that name, DeMarco, stood out to me the first time you mentioned it. I'm doing a little digging to what else I can find out; for some reason I'm sure I've ran across it before. How much do you know about them, other than what Bob found out? How reliable is your contact down there? I'll call you when I remember how I know the name." She was listening to the third message when she had to stop, waiting in the line of guests waiting to have their invitation checked so they could enter. "It's me again. I ran the name DeMarco and couldn't find much so I started checking my old case files. I was right, I have heard the name before. You really need to call me back, I can't tell you everything in a voicemail. You need to be careful."

Charlie was growing concerned as she started to listen to the last message, arriving at the door. "Don't go to that party tonight, Charlie. I figured it out, who the DeMarco brothers are. They haven't just been suppliers to the Montenillos; they worked for Stevens when you were born. They were the men Stevens hired to come after you and Anna, before they made it big in Argentina. They're the ones who grabbed her off the street-"

"Senorita?" a voice interrupted. "Invitation?"

Charlie looked at the man at the door and wordlessly showed him the slip of paper, lowering her phone in confusion. As soon as she got inside she ducked into a small hallway and tried T.J.'s cell. When she couldn't get him she tried Enrique. "It's me," she told him when he answered, looking around to make sure she was alone. "I just found out the DeMarcos worked for Stevens and were the ones after Anna and me that night. That means they would know my name-"

"-which means they know who you are," Enrique finished in alarm. "They know you're not just a bounty hunter; they know all about your connection to Stevens and Avery...you've got to get out of there, Charlie. Now."

"But-"

"Listen to me," he interrupted. "I did not know about this. From what I found out about Paul Avery and your great-aunt, the men he helped her escape from weren't the DeMarco brothers, but that doesn't mean it wasn't them who were hired to grab her in the first place. They know who you are, Charlie. They know you're Avery's daughter and have known it when they were in talks with him to team up against the Montenillos. This isn't a good development; something is seriously wrong-"

Before she could respond she heard footsteps approaching. "I gotta go," she told him quickly. "I'll call as soon as I can." She hung up despite Enrique's protests.

Charlie quickly replaced her phone in her purse and started straightening her dress, acting like the hem had gotten caught in her shoe. She straightened up in time to see a man she recognized immediately from the photos she saw earlier. It was Javier DeMarco, the younger of the DeMarco brothers. "Can I help you with something, senorita?" he asked pleasantly, looking at her in such a way that let Charlie know he recognized her immediately.

"Just trouble with my dress," she explained, smoothing it down. "Good evening, Mr. DeMarco."

"Buenos noche, Senorita Booker," he replied steadily. "Won't you join my family and me at the bar?"

Charlie wordlessly followed him into what appeared to be a ballroom, crowded with dancing couples as live entertainment played. He stopped in front of another man Charlie recognized as his older brother, Emilio DeMarco, standing next to an attractive woman who must have been his wife. "Senorita Booker," he greeted her warmly as she approached. "I'd like to introduce you to my wife, Isabella."

"Good evening Mrs. DeMarco," Charlie greeted her, shaking her hand. Javier went to another woman standing nearby, introducing her as his wife, Katerina. As they all exchanged pleasantries and started small talk, Charlie kept her eyes open, trying to figure out her next move. As long as she was in the general population of the guests she was relatively safe. As soon as they found a reason to ask her to leave with them, she was in trouble.

Charlie looked quickly around, scouting all possible exits. The only problem was most of them were blocked by groups of guests, cutting off her routes if she had to get out in a hurry. She also saw security milling around, though she was sure they were oblivious to the other guests. To the untrained eye they were simply well-dressed men casually wandering around but Charlie could immediately spot them due to the way they walked, their discreet observation tactics, and the obvious weapons hidden under their long formal jackets. *Think,* she silently ordered herself. *You've been in countless situations, some worse than this. You can figure out what to do.* The problem was, unlike those she'd had to deal with on the job, she had limited knowledge of the DeMarcos, and she wasn't used to an enemy she didn't know.

The moment arrived that she'd been dreading, when Emilio asked his wife and sister-in-law to excuse them while they discussed business. Having no choice, Charlie followed the DeMarcos through the ballroom and out onto the back terrace, which she quickly saw was completely deserted.

"Why don't you have a seat," Emilio requested, gesturing for her to sit across from him and his brother. Charlie did so warily, briefly wondering just how vastly the DeMarco property extended. "Would you care for a drink?" he offered.

Charlie leaned forward. "I think we can skip the polite host routine. We all know why I'm here, so why don't we just get on with it."

"Straight to business," Javier spoke up. "I like that."

"As do I," Emilio agreed. "Very well, Charlotte Booker. It's nice to see you again; you've grown into quite a beautiful woman. Talented too, from what I hear."

"A lot can change in twenty-three years," she told him evenly. "I understand I have you to thank for taking Anna from me, leaving me to wander Central Park alone that night as just a scared little kid."

"So you know the truth then, about who we are? Just as we do about you. How long have you known Paul Avery is your father?"

"How long have you been in talks with him?" she deflected.

"Long enough," Emilio replied. "His main concern is destroying the Montenillos. At least, that's what he says. But we've known all along that you are his daughter, though he was careful not to mention that fact, and that you are what he's concerned about most."

"Do you have any intention of honoring his request?" Charlie wanted to know, bypassing his last comment.

"We worked with the Montenillo family many years ago," he told her. "Particularly Hector. Or Stevens, as he calls himself now. He did hire us that night to procure Marianna, separate her from you, since she was planning on double-crossing him. What we failed to factor in was Avery's diligence; he helped Marianna escape from our associates and they both fell off the radar after that. Until this year, when he showed himself to us, letting us know of his plans. His most recent visit, the one that brought you here, was fairly productive. We agreed not to interfere with his…mission."

"And how much did that cost him?" Charlie wanted to know.

"It's easy to see what we've heard about you is true," Emilio observed, his tone still pleasant. "You're very bright, very professional."

Charlie ignored the compliment. "How involved are you, now that the Montenillos retaliated when they found out you were talking to my father?"

"We're extremely involved; we don't take the destroying of one of our shipments lightly," he declared.

"So now you're completely on board with working with Paul?" she asked. "You might
not have had much of a reason to take him up on his offer at first, but you do now," she pointed out. "What exactly are you and my father planning to do?"

"You ask a lot of questions," Emilio told her. "But I'm afraid I can't give you the answers."

"Then why am I here?" she challenged. "Why did you agree to the invitation? Why did you insist on speaking to me in private?"

"I doubt you realize just how valuable you are," he told her. "You're linked to some fairly powerful people."

"You consider an ex-cop valuable?" she asked, slightly confused. Then it hit her. "He's doing something for you, something big. He promised you something, didn't he?"

"Let's not get ahead of ourselves. I'd much rather talk about you."

"What about me? Are you planning to hold onto me as an incentive for Avery to hold up his end?"

"As if his hatred for the Montenillos isn't enough?" Emilio asked in amusement. Then his expression sobered. "The thought crossed my mind when your friend Enrique gave me the call. I must say he didn't seem too enthusiastic about making sure you were invited, but he came through like any good informant," he said, shrugging. "Yes, the idea of using you was appealing to us, to make sure Avery followed through. But no, we won't be using you as a bargaining chip. That is Stevens' style, not ours."

"Then what is your style? Why was it so important you talk to me tonight?"

"We wanted to make the acquaintance of another Montenillo foe," he replied. "What is that saying you have in your country? 'The enemy of my enemy is my friend?'"

"You seem to be forgetting that they weren't always your enemy," Charlie reminded him. "In fact, your participation in Anna's abduction all those years ago makes you *my* enemy. And you better believe, I'm not someone to cross."

"Oh I know that, all too well," Emilio told her with a smile.

Something was incredibly wrong; Charlie was as sure of it as she was her own name. She couldn't put her finger on it exactly, but there was something about Emilio's manner, the way he oozed charm and refinement, that she didn't trust. There was definitely more going on than she knew about, and it was making her increasingly aware how trapped she truly was out on the terrace.

And then it hit her. It was so amazingly obvious that she didn't consider it before; it was a rookie mistake, one that might cost her if she didn't play her cards right. She decided truth, for now, was her best option. Let them know she was no fool, and that she always stayed on her toes. "You didn't arrange this meeting because of Avery," she said slowly, as if it was just coming to her. "You told him everything he wanted to hear, about how he has your support. And when the Montenillos attacked, it gave you even more reason to be on board. Too much reason. It was too convenient, all of it: Stevens' tip about Avery being here in Argentina, the attack on your shipment while I was visiting him in lockup. It was all a trap, and Avery was the bait," she said, shaking her head. "Blowing up the shipment was a set-up, as is our meeting tonight. You're not holding me as leverage for Paul; you're delivering me to the Montenillos. What you get in return is beyond me-"

"What we get in return is peace," Javier spoke up, stepping forward. "The situation
between your father and Hector-Stevens-has been building for years. We've all been ready for it, what the takedown of the Montenillo organization will do to the rest of us. It all comes down to who's side your on-which is the winning side. We plan on standing by the

Montenillos, who've always been good to us. Avery should've known better."

"They laid the trap, and you fell right into it," Emilio added. "Why Avery couldn't see this coming..."

Charlie shook her head, leaning forward. "You know I won't go quietly. I'll give you the fight of your life."

"I know how good you are at fighting, especially when your back's up against the wall," Emilio told her, his tone still pleasant. "Or a boxcar," he added casually.

Charlie felt white-hot anger bubbling up inside her chest and it was all she could do not to let it take over. "Mr. DeMarco, I've had all the run-around I can stand," she said, rising from her seat. "And unless you want an unpleasant scene at your party, you'll let me walk out of here unharmed."

"You're bold, Senorita. Too bold for your own good. If you're not careful, it might backfire for you someday," he said, rising as well.

"Is that a threat?" she snapped. "You better be careful, if I'm Montenillo merchandise. You don't want to *damage* me."

"There's no need for this get...unpleasant."

"Of course there isn't; you're only about to hand me over like some kind of business transaction-"

Suddenly a sound ripped through the night, overpowering the music and the buzz of conversations from all the guests inside. Muted screams could be heard from inside as the sky appeared to erupt in flames, on the other side of the fence that surrounded the DeMarco property. The brothers stood transfixed for a moment, trying to figure out what had just happened.

Charlie took advantage of the explosion and lifted her dress, pulling her gun out of her leg holster and pointing it directly at Javier DeMarco's head. "I'm leaving," she spat venomously to Emilio. "If you want to stop me, you'll just have to shoot me. But not before I take out your brother." She held her head high, staring at him boldly in the eye as she walked away from the table, not breaking her gaze, her gun still trained on the younger DeMarco.

"How do you know I won't shoot you first?" Emilio countered.

"Because you were cocky enough to assume I wouldn't be that much trouble-which was foolish, considering how much you know about me-and failed to arm yourself. A very common mistake," she chided, edging farther from the terrace all the time. "Relying too heavily on your security detail...and they're no where to be seen. Kind of sad, considering you used to be more hands-on."

"You might walk out of here tonight, Charlotte Booker," he began, his tone low, "but make no mistake: you have a target painted on your head, and the Montenillos are relentless when it comes to getting what they want." He paused. "You're a worthy opponent, that's for certain," he added, with grudging admiration as Charlie continued toward the fence.

"And you're a twisted son-of-a-bitch, Mr. DeMarco," she shot back. "If we ever have the misfortune of meeting again I hope it's with my .45 jabbed in your back." She continued to have her gun trained on Javier as she reached the fence, her hair standing on end until she safely made it up and over, landing flat in the dirt. She could hear the shots fired behind her as the DeMarco security team finally emerged and she hauled it, running the length of the fence on the abandoned lot next door, peering into the darkness to figure out her best escape route, and leaving the burning inferno behind her.

"Charlie!" a voice called insistently from the darkness.

"Enrique?" she called back, moving toward the direction of where his voice came. She saw movement a few yards away and yanked off her shoes as she ran toward him. "Damned good timing," she panted, leaning against a tree.

Enrique nodded his agreement, walking up next to her. "The explosion will keep them distracted for a while."

"How did you know I needed a diversion right then?" she asked, looking over at him.

Enrique pointed to the large green jewel on her bodice. "That's a microphone."

Charlie was impressed. "You were very well-prepared, weren't you?"

"Not well enough," he said, his expression darkening. "I fed you to the lions."

"You didn't know," Charlie told him. "No one did. Not even Avery." She let out a long sigh. "I've got to find a way to let him know he's being double-crossed."

"Don't worry about Avery, I'm sure he'll figure it out soon enough." He rested a hand on her shoulder. "Come. Let's get out of here."

"You don't have to tell me twice." Charlie began to follow him across the dark field to the spot where his truck was waiting. "I didn't know you knew your way around explosives. And it's a pretty safe bet this dress wasn't wired when your wife wore it," she added, looking down.

"I wanted to give you backup," he told her with a shrug. "Even if you wanted to do this alone."

"I should've known better," she muttered. "How did we not see this coming, that the DeMarcos are just as in bed with the Montenillos as they ever were. And they wanted to trade me off like I'm some...Ace in the hole," she said, remembering what Stevens had once called her. "Stevens," she said bitterly. "That manipulative son-of-a-bitch. Prison's too good for him."

Enrique dropped Charlie off at the motel, promising to call her if there were any updates as to Paul's whereabouts. Charlie let him know that she was catching the first available flight out tomorrow; she was certain Paul was no longer in Argentina. She couldn't help but notice how infuriated Enrique seemed with himself as he left, and she reassured him that he was in no way to blame but he was single-handedly responsible for making sure she got out of there alive tonight.

After he left she walked slowly toward the bed, throwing her ruined shoes across the room and looking down at the soiled dress; she'd have to find a way to get cleaned and back to Consuela as soon as possible. She caught her reflection in the mirror next to the TV set; her hair was falling and hanging at an odd angle, her face was smudged with dirt from her landing when she jumped over the fence. Instead of going straight to the shower she collapsed on top of the bed, thinking about how lucky she was to have gotten out of there in one piece. She also had to digest that she had now become a priority to the Montenillos, which meant her life just got a lot more dangerous.

Her eyes opened a few moments later when a knock sounded on the door. "I'm coming, I'm coming, Enrique," she mumbled as the insistent rapping continued. She unlocked the door, wondering what he'd forgotten.

But it wasn't Enrique standing on the other side. "T.J.?" she asked in disbelief. "How did you-"

"As soon as I figured out who they were I got on the first flight," he informed her, barreling into the room. "I've been trying to get in touch with you ever since."

"I've been a little preoccupied," she explained, shutting and re-locking the door. "With narrowly escaping a screwed up trade."

He frowned, studying her appearance more closely. "What happened?" he demanded. "Are you hurt?"

Charlie shook her head. "Thanks to Enrique, I dodged a fairly large bullet." She quickly explained what had happened.

T.J. just stood there, shaking his head. "This is unbelievable. What kind of father would put you in harm's way like that?"

"T.J.-"

"This is Avery's fault," he interrupted angrily. "He should've got in contact with you a long time ago. He should have known the DeMarcos would double-cross him; it's his responsibility to make sure you're safe, seeing as how it's his fault you're involved in this at all. Not to mention the fact that he's your father, assuming that counts for anything."

"Stop," she said, walking up to him and taking his arms in her hands. "This isn't his fault; it's mine. I should've been better prepared but I got cocky, and I got impatient. I wanted to find him, T.J., and I wanted to do it on my own." She sighed. "But now I have bigger things to worry about. I have no idea how the Montenillos are going to react knowing their ploy to get to me failed; DeMarco was right about one thing, they're going to come after me full-force." She started to pace. "I've got to figure this out. There must be-"

T.J. stopped her, pulling her to him and hugging her tightly. "You're okay," he murmured into her hair.

Charlie let herself stop and hugged him back. "I'm okay," she echoed.

They stayed that way for a long moment until Charlie finally pulled back. "I really need a shower," she said and started to limp toward the bathroom, wincing slightly. Apparently jumping over the fence in a split-second's time in heels wasn't good on the ankles. She paused in the doorway. "Want to join me?"

He nodded wordlessly and followed her into the tiny bathroom, having the grace to not utter a single "I told you so" like a lesser man would have done.

***

Charlie was wide awake for the flight home, watching the mundane movie being shown with T.J. in silence. Neither felt like talking any more about what happened, and Charlie was too tired to try and figure anything else out. When the plane touched down at JFK they were both eager to get back home, ready to put the trip behind them.

But Charlie knew it wouldn't be that easy. As much as she didn't want to, she had to fill Bob in and let him know what was going on. She could only imagine what kind of reaction he would have but she knew he'd never forgive her if she left him in the dark.

So, after taking a day to catch up on sleep, she let him know she was back in town and he invited her over for dinner. She accepted, bringing his favorite cigars to help with the uproar she was sure would follow her recounting of the events that took place in Argentina.

She managed to dodge the subject until they started to do the dishes, and decided to just go for it and tell him everything. As she talked she watched Bob's expression, saw the lines on his face harden. He was gripping the dish he washed so tightly that by the time she'd finished it shattered.

Charlie bent down and began to clean up the shards while Bob started to pace the kitchen, getting more furious with every step. "I'm calling Sabados," he declared, heading for the phone, "and I'm tearing him a new one for letting you go in there-"

"It's not Enrique's fault," she interrupted, standing. "Besides, I'm alright. Even though those bastards are twisted as hell and I still feel like I was some kind of toy there for their amusement while they waited to hand me over to the Montenillos...I got out of there, Bob. I aimed my gun at Javier's head and just hopped over the fence, no worse for the wear. Do you have any idea what kind of rush that is?"

"Do you have any idea how much I can see through you right now?" he countered. "You're standing here acting like it's just another notch in your professional belt but we both know they did a number on you, preparing to use you just like Stevens used you when you were a small child-which you haven't recovered from yet by the way. And here's the thing: *that's the way it should be*. When are you going to remember you're more than a trained bounty hunter? You're still human, Charlie, which means you bleed like the rest of us. And as for you being alright...that remains to be seen."

"What are you talking about?"

"Are you conveniently forgetting what you just said, about have a target painted on your back by Francisco Montenillo, one of the most ruthless crime bosses ever to rule the East coast?"

"It's kind of hard with everyone reminding me every few seconds: Enrique, T.J., you..." She pushed away from the counter.

"There's a lot more to be thinking about right," she said, abruptly changing gears. "Like where Avery is now."

"And what the Montenillos plan to do to you," he added. "While we figure it out you're staying out of South America," he ordered. " And don't go anywhere that has even the slightest connection to the Montenillos."

"Yes, sir. And can I stay out till midnight tonight, please, please?" she clasped her hands together, pretending to beg. Despite the gravity of the situation she couldn't help herself.

"I'm serious, Charlie," he told her, not cracking a smile.

"I know, and it's insulting. I'm a grown woman, and we both know I can take care of myself. Yes, this is turning out to be bigger than anything we've ever dealt with before-"

"That's an understatement-"

"-but I can handle it," she finished undaunted. "Have faith in yourself. You're a great teacher."

"Teaching only goes so far."

"What else do you need, life experience? I've got plenty of that," she reminded him. "We
all just need to take a step back and let all of this settle down while we wait for Stevens' arraignment."

"You realize he probably won't make it until then," Bob pointed out. "Antonio's
connections on the inside have long dried up and prison's full of enemies of the Montenillos. He's lucky to have lived this long-"

"-which is probably why his family's gearing up for battle, which explains the 'assignment' they gave the DeMarcos, in the form of holding on to me. What they plan to use me for exactly is anyone's guess."

Bob looked at her in concern. "That's priority number one. The second one is paying close attention to Stevens, because there's a strong possibility Francisco will be arranging some kind of escape," he told her. "But hopefully the cops are anticipating that."

"Yeah well..." Charlie trailed off, drying her hands on the dish towel and turning to face him. "If they're not...all of this is really going to go to hell."

Chapter Fourteen

"Thanks again for taking care of Harley while I was gone," Charlie told Diana on the phone the next morning as she quickly made her bed. "I know he's a handful right now, getting into everything."

"He's definitely very active," Diana agreed. "Can't sit still for two seconds. Kind of like his Mama."

"Kind of like mine."

Diana laughed. "Touché. Now. When am I going to hear about this exotic South America trip?"

"It wasn't that exotic; it was a train wreck," Charlie told her bluntly. "And I guarantee once you hear about it you'll be just one more person who's barely speaking to me."

"T.J.?" Diana asked knowingly.

"And Bob. They're both acting like…my protectors or something. It's completely suffocating, and a little offensive."

"Now you've got me really curious; talk," Diana ordered.

"Fine. But don't say you weren't warned," Charlie said and proceeded to tell the story once again.

"Wait till I get my hands on this Enrique," Diana fumed once Charlie had finished. "Where does he live again?"

"Why does everyone keep blaming him? He is the one who saved my ass, remember?"

"It never should've needed saving in the first place-"

"I've been in danger most of my life," Charlie interrupted. "Which is what everyone seems to be forgetting."

"Then I really don't understand how Paul can still keep his distance after all of this."

"Neither do I, but what do I know? Just because the man shares my DNA doesn't make him any less a stranger."

Diana grew uncomfortably quiet, as she always did whenever Charlie mentioned Avery, so Charlie quickly turned the conversation in a different direction. "So. Do you want to yell at me too?"

"No," Diana told her quickly. "I understand where you're coming from, Charlie, I really do. A lot of this spirit that seems to keep getting you in trouble came from me you know. And I know that you're more than just an average person on a quest to find the truth: you're smart, quick, well-trained, and you're more than capable of taking care of yourself. Which brings me to the other side of this, which I can also see. Just because you're capable doesn't mean you should take on the world alone. I know finding Paul is important to you, as is filling in the remaining gaps in your past. But I also know your judgment is slightly clouded; Paul's not the only one with a score to settle. You hate that family as much as he does, and that Stevens man even more-"

"I have every right-"

"I'm not saying you don't," Diana cut in. "But just consider for a moment what it feels like for the people who care about you to be relegated to the sidelines. Would that sit well with you if it was T.J. in your shoes? Or Bob, or me for that matter?"

"No," Charlie admitted. "But it doesn't come naturally for me to ask for help. Not when it comes to my personal life."

"I know. That's why there's still time to learn."

After her run Charlie heard from Enrique, who had nothing new to report and wanted to know how she was doing. She jokingly told him she hadn't acquired any Montenillo bullet holes yet but it only seemed to make him more agitated. She assured him she was taking the situation seriously and was doing everything she could to arm herself, not just with weapons but with information. He seemed appeased by that and told her he'd keep up the search for Avery on his end.

Remaining true to her word, Charlie spent half the day at the shooting range and the gym, and the other half at home glued to her computer soaking up as much information as possible on the Montenillo family. Stevens called her twice that day and both time she ignored his call, refusing to get sucked into his twisted mind games any further.

That evening she decided to go see T.J., with whom she'd had little contact with since their return to the States. Not wanting to announce her arrival she went to Diana's to see if she knew where he was. She told Charlie he was working a new case and had been out all day, which meant he probably went to the place he sometimes went to unwind, and Charlie knew exactly where that was.

She drove out of town, away from the city lights and into the moonlit night to the place she remembered well, though she'd only been there once before. When she got to the narrow off-road she slowed down, looking for any sign of a Chevelle.

Just as she'd suspected, it was parked under a grove of small trees a few yards from the lake they swam in on their first date. T.J. was stretched out on the back of the car, looking up into the sky and doing something Charlie rarely saw him do; he was smoking cigarettes. The all-too familiar smell drifted over to her as she pulled up beside him, killing the engine and removing her helmet.

T.J. looked over at her in surprise but didn't rise, so Charlie went to him, leaning up against the back bumper. "Mind if I bum one?" she asked, though she instantly regretted it: she'd been a non-smoker for some time now. But in light of everything that had happened recently she felt it was okay to indulge at least once.

Reaching into his pocket, T.J. pulled out a pack and wordlessly handed it to her. She took one and he leaned over, taking out his lighter and lighting it for her. "Thanks," she said, taking a long drag. He nodded and quickly stuffed the pack and the lighter back into his pocket.

They smoked in silence until they were finished, each dropping the cigarette butts on the ground and grinding them with their feet. Then T.J. looked at her as though she'd just arrived. "Did Diana tell you I was here?"

"I guessed," she replied. "It wasn't too hard to figure out. When we came here last time it seemed like a place you've been to several times before."

"When I first moved into my apartment, I went out driving that night," he started, his eyes on the sky again. "Even though I'd calmed down a lot after I met Diana I still needed to get out, blow off some steam. Come to grips with the fact that I was now divorced. So I drove around aimlessly, not really paying attention to where I was going, and found this place by accident. Ever since that night, whenever I've had a lot on my mind or just needed a break after a case I'd come back. It always seemed to calm me down."

"And that's why you're here now?" Charlie asked quietly. "You need to calm down?"

He shrugged. "I needed to think."

When he didn't offer anything else she decided not to pry, exactly. "How's that going for you?"

To her surprise he gave a small smile. "Not bad. No nuclear explosions, no global chaos. And I don't think anything's imploded yet." Then his smile faded. "Are you sure being a couple is something you want?" he asked abruptly.

Charlie blinked in surprise, caught off guard. "I guess I deserve that, after the way I've been acting," she said slowly. "But yes, it is what I want."

"Are you sure? I mean, I know this is uncharted territory for you. It's uncharted territory for me, which is why I've been giving you such a hard time. The truth is...I've never felt this way about anyone I've been involved with before, not even my ex-wife. And that scares me." He looked at her carefully. "Does it scare you?"

"Yes," she told him honestly. "But not enough to run away."

"Me either," he admitted. "So I guess we're just crazy then, huh?"

"Better crazy than self-destructive," she told him, moving in closer. "So what do we do about it?"

"Just keep being crazy I guess," he replied, kissing her.

They went back to Charlie's apartment shortly after, and T.J. stayed over for the first time since she'd told him she was going to South America.

***

The next couple of weeks passed quickly, with Stevens' arraignment quickly approaching. Charlie had been on alert but there was no sign of any threats from the Montenillos toward her, which made her start to wonder if they'd ever had an arrangement with the Demarcos at all; it was more than possible that they just wanted her for their own purposes and conveniently blamed a more likely suspect. Still, she kept her guard up and took as many extra precautionary measures as she could.

During this time she approached both Bob and T.J., finally relenting and letting them in on it all the way, including the parts about her safety. She found it wasn't as hard as she thought to ask for help in this situation, and as a result she was getting along with everyone better and they, in turn, seemed to be appeased.

It also gave her a chance to see what a true asset having T.J. on board was. She knew he was good, from his time working with her in the beginning and accompanying her to Massachusetts, as well as the cases she'd assisted in, but now she was greatly reminded.

Out of the information they all had procured it seemed to be certain that Paul had vacated Argentina and his whereabouts, once again, were currently unknown-as were Anna's. Charlie wanted to assume he'd let himself be known as soon as he felt the time was right, but couldn't help but think that time was now. If anyone could help her figure out what the Montenillos were planning, it'd be Avery; she was sure he made it his life's business to find out everything else he didn't already know about them. She just couldn't figure out why he still felt it necessary to remain in hiding.

On the last weekend in September Charlie was supposed to meet T.J. in a bar near his office after he'd finished for the day-he'd just completed the paperwork on the case he just wrapped up-and when she arrived she saw that he wasn't alone. There was several men sitting around him at a small table, a large pitcher between them, laughing at something T.J. was saying. Charlie walked over and kissed him quickly in greeting; since there weren't any available chairs T.J. pulled her into his lap and introduced her to his friends: Jake Larson, Sonny Parker, and Joel Remar.

They were guys T.J. had met over the years in the course of his business, all of whom happened to be in the neighborhood when they saw his unmistakable car in the parking lot. They all seemed eager to meet Charlie, offering to buy another pitcher so she could drink as well.

After an hour had passed the men were more than slightly inebriated; after listening to Charlie's story they started playing a drinking game and were quickly proven to be notorious losers. Charlie felt more relaxed than she had in a long time; it was nice to be able to kick back with T.J. and his friends, bonding over beer and similar stories. It didn't hurt that his friends seemed quite impressed with her, especially about how she wore a leather jacket when it was still hot out, owned a motorcycle, but most especially because she was a bounty hunter. They also seemed to admire her ability to hold quite a bit of alcohol without seeming the least bit drunk.

As the night wore down and her fatigue began to set in Charlie was leaning against T.J. as Joel started talking about a case he worked on years ago. He was getting to the part about his client remembering a certain date that ended up holding the entire case together when a light suddenly went off in her fuzzy brain.

She wasn't sure if it was the alcoholic haze that was making her think of things she hadn't before but she realized, in any case, that the key to the entire mystery behind the Montenillos secret plan might have something to do with a single date, a significant date. Not something obvious, like when Antonio Montenillo was incarcerated or the death of two of his sons, but something more obscure, something that only had meaning to one of the family.

She excused herself to the bathroom, and once she was inside and closed the door she took out her phone, which had internet access. She got into her e-mail and checked over the long passages of information she had on the Montenillos and the brief ones she had on her father. She didn't know what she was looking for exactly so she just kept her eyes open for any dates that might stand out.

She was about to quit when suddenly she found something near the end, something she hadn't paid any attention to before. Now it all seemed blindingly obvious, as everything began to click into place. She knew what the Montenillos were waiting for, why they hadn't tried to break Stevens out yet. They were waiting for a certain date most likely on his orders, a date that meant a lot to him. And that date was mere weeks away.

    Charlie headed back out, noticing everyone was standing and divy-ing up the tab. Since T.J.'s friends still seemed influenced Charlie called them a cab and they all went outside to wait.

    T.J.'s friends insisted that they all hang out again and told Charlie how glad they were to have met her. Charlie smiled faintly and wished each of them a good night, not able to say much more due to the newfound discovery weighing on her mind.

    After following T.J. home to make sure he made it okay Charlie told him she decided to
sleep at home that night because she had a lot to do the next day. As she was driving home a plan began to form in her mind, and she started figuring out the best way to proceed. By the time she
got home she had everything mapped out in her head and had a clearly-lined plan. Unfortunately it was a plan that wouldn't go over well with anyone, and had the potential to destroy fragile relationships that had already been under enough strain.

    But this was something that had to be done, something that couldn't have any unforeseen deviations. This was the way things had to be, and even though it was going to be met with a lot of hostility and anger at least the people involved would be alive to keep holding on to that anger.

***

    Charlie put her plan into action that Monday, a few days after its conception. She invited everyone over-Bob, Jack, Megan, Diana, and T.J.-with the pretense of having a family barbeque to test out her new grill. After everyone started eating she planned to let them know what was going on, and what had to be done about it.

    Bob arrived first, bringing the beer and Jack Daniels to season the marinade. Charlie led him out to her back porch and let him inspect the grill she'd recently purchased while she brought the meat out from the fridge.

    "So how are things going on the recon front?" he asked a short while later, leaning back in a lounge chair and opening a beer. "I haven't heard from you in a few days."

    "It's been about the same," she lied, keeping her back to him as she laid the meat on the grill.

"You want to put our heads together before everyone else gets here, hash things out?" he offered. "Maybe we can pick something up we missed before."

"I don't think we'll have time; I've got to watch the food." Charlie knew of he kept pressing her he'd end up seeing right through her, and she wasn't ready to tell him yet; he'd yell less if they weren't alone.

"Fine. You cook, I'll get your computer." He got up from the chair, tipping back his beer and draining the contents.

"No don't," she said quickly. "You'll wake up Harley and scare the hell out of him."

"Cat's gotta warm up to me sooner or later," Bob said with a shrug. "I'll be careful-"

"Stop!" she said, turning around. "I don't want you to get my computer."

"Why not?" he wanted to know, frowning.

"Because...there's something on there I don't want you to see," she said, knowing the time for pretense had ended. "I lied. I did find something out, something big."

"I know," he responded, leaning against the wall and watching her carefully. "I could tell as soon as I brought it up."

Charlie let out a sigh, closing the lid of the grill. "I should've known I couldn't keep anything from you. And I was going to tell you, as soon as everyone got here."

"Why wait?"

"Because I wanted everyone to hear it at once so I don't have to repeat myself," she replied. "Because once you all hear what I have to say, none of you are going to be very happy with me."

"Now you're starting to scare me," he said, his frown deepening. "I don't want to wait until the others get here; I want to know now."

"Fine," she relented. "But don't say I didn't warn you." She took a breath. "I started thinking that we were missing something, something huge, something most likely right in front of our faces but we didn't see it because we've been working so hard, thinking it all to death. Then I thought, what if it wasn't something obvious? What if it was something more personal, which would make it harder to figure out? So I went over everything again, for what seemed like the thousandth time, and I found what I was looking for. Suddenly, it all made sense. It's the glue that holds everything together, proof that it really is Stevens running the show."

"What is it?" Bob asked quietly, obviously able to tell from the direction the conversation was taking that everything was about to change.

"I think the Montenillos are going to break Stevens out," she revealed. "His arraignment is set for the twenty-second but it'll be earlier than that. It's going to happen the fifteenth." She sat down on the edge of a chair. "Most likely they have someone inside on the payroll, which will assure it goes off without a glitch. Once he's out he'll join his family, and not only will the war with my father start but I'm pretty sure something else is going to go down too, something business-related. Maybe it has something to do with the DeMarcos, maybe it's just about making sure the other crime families know who's the head honcho. Either way, it'll be big and it'll get ugly-"

"Why the fifteenth?" Bob interrupted. "Why is that date important to Stevens?"

"All of this is just a theory," she said quickly, "but I've really thought it out and it all makes sense." She paused. "October 15, 1980 was the date Avery went undercover as Johnny Black in the Montenillo organization. This year marks thirty years of the beginning of it all, the first event that had a domino-effect on everything else. The first day of the betrayal, in Stevens' eyes."

"You really have thought this out," Bob observed. "And I think you might be right. It makes complete sense, and since this is about revenge for Stevens it would explain the date and probably how much damage he intends to inflict in honor of his late brothers and locked-up father."

Charlie nodded. "Which means we're sitting in the middle of a soon-to-be war zone. Everyone connected to Stevens and his family or my father is in danger, big-league danger. It would make sense for the people who aren't participating in this fight to take cover, hightail it out of here as fast as they can until it's over. Until it's safe." She looked at him meaningfully.

"And what you don't want to tell me is that list of people doesn't include you," he said, leaning forward.

"They need to be safe, Bob. They've got to get out of here so they won't get caught in the line of fire."

"He'll be expecting that," Bob protested. "He's watched you all your life Charlie, so he knows how you think. He'll be banking on you to count on me to get them out, leaving you alone and exposed."

"I know."

Bob pushed away from the wall, his expression darkening. "You suicidal, reckless, crazy moron," he said, his voice low and shaky. "You want to offer yourself up as bait."

"Not exactly. Look, we know I'm a marked woman, which means anyone around me will be marked too. The best thing to do is for me to stay in plain sight, because whatever's going to go down we know, somehow, I'm going to be a part of it."

"You're out of your damned mind-"

"Think about this, Bob. I can do more damage if I stick around."

"You think that's what this is about?" Bob asked slowly. "You have it in your head that you're going to take these animals down?"

"Not just me."

"Who-Avery?" he asked in disbelief. "You're counting on a man you've never met, the reason you're in this mess to begin with? That's your grand, master plan?"

"Not entirely," Charlie said defensively. "Do you want to hear what I have to say, or would you rather insult me every five seconds?"

Bob crossed his arms over his chest and gave a slight nod.

Charlie told him what she thought was going to happen, and what she planned to do. After she finished she waited for his reaction, not sure of what to expect.

He seemed to be taking it all in and looked at her a long moment before speaking. "The only way I'll agree to this plan and if I stay here with you," he told her finally.

Charlie shook her head. "You can't. You have to get the others out of here-"

"I will. I'll get them somewhere safe and then I'll come back."

"That's not good enough," she argued. "I don't want them alone and unprotected-"

"I'll call somebody, have someone I trust set up-"

"No!" she cried angrily. "I don't want anyone but you. You're the best, Bob. I'm counting on you, and I'll beg if I have to."

He stepped away from her, shaking his head. "I won't do it. I won't leave you here like this, on the off-chance that your so-called father might show up and help you out."

"Bob I have to-"

"Enough!" he yelled, so loudly that Charlie flinched. He walked directly up to her, standing toe-to-toe. "You are not allowed to put on the martyr-hat, you hear me? I didn't find you that night ten years ago just to turn my back on you now while you march straight to the slaughterhouse." He took a breath. "You've been more than a partner to me, Charlie Booker," he said, his voice breaking slightly. "You're family. You're...like a daughter." It was the way their relationship had always been but he'd never spoken the word out loud before. "I already lost one," he continued quietly. "Don't ask me to stand by and do nothing while I lose another one."

Tears were stinging Charlie's eyes as she put her hands on his shoulders. "You won't be doing nothing," she told him firmly. "You'll be taking care of our family, and yourself. I can't do what I need to do if I'm worried about everyone else. If they're with you, I won't have to."

Bob merely shook his head, unable to speak.

"I know how much I'm asking of you," she went on, her voice gaining strength. "You've always been there for me, without me having to say a word. I'm only asking now because I really need you. You are the best, which means the people I care about will be safe." She took his hands in her own. "I'm going to be okay. Just like you, I had a hell of a teacher, and he taught me everything I ever needed to know." A tear trickled down her face as she smiled, giving him a quick wink. "You know me. I won't make anything easy for them...and I'll do everything in my
power to make it back."

"I never could say no to you," he said gruffly, kissing her on the forehead. "I'm going to hold you to that," he said as he pulled back. "If you do anything stupid, like get yourself killed...I'll never forgive you."

Charlie nodded. "No getting killed, got it." She brushed an impatient hand across her face. "Come on and help me get this dinner together. The rest of the guest list will be here shortly, and I'm going to need backup when I let them in on the real reason why they're here."

"Hmph," he grumbled, but followed her over to the grill as she handed him a pair of silver tongs.

Jack and Megan arrived shortly, followed by T.J. and Diana. As everyone was seated around Charlie's table, Bob helped her bring the food in and wordlessly started to serve. Charlie was careful to avoid T.J.'s eyes, knowing hers would only give her away.

As everyone began to eat Jack tried to start up a conversation but it was easily noticed how quiet both Bob and Charlie were, and everyone's curiosity to know what was up was becoming apparent.

Finally Jack appeared to have had enough, looking from Bob to Charlie. "Alright," he said, dropping his fork onto his plate. "Something's going on between the two of you that you're not sharing. Out with it."

Charlie and Bob exchanged a glance. "I wanted to wait until everyone finished eating-"

"Wait for what?" Megan interrupted, looking concerned. "What's going on, Charlie?"

Diana looked at her daughter carefully. "You didn't invite us over to test out your new grill," she said quietly. "That was just a ruse to get all of us here. Something's happened, hasn't it?"

Charlie was waiting for T.J. to jump in but he only stared at his plate, pushing the meat around with his fork listlessly. "Yes," she said, shifting her gaze to Diana. "Something has come up that I need to talk with you all about. Something that's going to be…difficult." She looked at Bob, who nodded encouragingly.

"Just say it," Jack said, his eyes darting back and forth between his uncle and the woman who was so like a sister to him. "We don't keep secrets in this family. Not about the big stuff."

"It's not a secret," Charlie assured him. Then she took a deep breath and told them everything she'd told Bob.

The room was dead silent as she talked, and dead silent when she finished. Everyone at the table looked either angry or devastated, or both. All except T.J., who remained expressionless and refused to meet her gaze.

Finally Jack shot up from the table, throwing his napkin down angrily. "Just who the hell do you think you are?" he demanded, glaring at Charlie. "And you," he said, turning to Bob. "How can you let her go through with this?"

"Jack-" Megan began warningly.

"No," he interrupted angrily. "I heard what she had to say, now she's going to hear me." He turned toward Charlie. "I get that you're a risk-taker, and you've spent ninety-five percent of your life living on the edge, starting from a very young age. And I know it wasn't your fault then. But you're more than capable of making your own decisions now. And you have no right to make ones that put your life in danger."

"Don't get upset with Bob, he was just as angry as you are. I didn't give him a lot of choice about this. And as for putting myself in danger, I do that every day," Charlie reminded him quietly. "For my job."

"This is different, and you know it," Jack shot back. Then his expression sobered. "You're not a kid anymore, Charlie," he said quietly. "You're not alone now, and you haven't been for some time."

"This isn't about that, Jack," she protested, rising as well. "I need you safe. All of you. And there won't be a safer place than wherever Bob chooses. As long as he's with you, you'll all be alright."

"But you won't," Megan spoke up softly. "How do think that makes us feel, knowing we're safe while you're out here risking your life?"

"And for what?" Jack added. "A father you've never met?"

"This isn't about Paul!" Charlie yelled, her self-control wearing thin from all the emotions coursing through her. "This is about a man who decided to play God with my life, a man who used me as a bargaining chip to get what he wanted. Used a little baby who had a mother-" she looked at Diana- "out there looking for her, praying every night that one day she'd find her again. He cost me everything, the kind of life you had growing up," she said, looking at Jack. "But it's not just about revenge; the Montenillos are a crime family, a dangerous crime family who have been wreaking havoc for decades, ruining a lot more lives beside my own. Don't you see that all of this needs to stop?"

"But why is it up to you to stop it?" Jack wanted to know. "Don't you get it, Charlie? You couldn't be my family any more if you actually had my blood running through your veins. We've already lost enough; Mom's gone," he said, his voice cracking. "Do you really want me to lose you too?"

"You're about to have a baby, Jack," Charlie said softly, looking at Megan's large baby bump. "You and Megan are about to be parents. You need to be thinking about your kid, not a grown woman who can take care of herself. I know it's my fault you're in this situation, that any of you are in danger at all. It's all because of me, so let me be the one to make it right."

No one spoke for a long time. Jack and Charlie continued to stand, neither meeting the other's eyes. Finally Diana cleared her throat, and all eyes turned to her. "Charlie is my daughter," she said, addressing the group. "And I don't want her to do this. But she's earned the right to make her own decisions, for better or for worse. There are few people more equipped to handle something like this than her. And if she thinks it'll make it easier for her to focus if we're all safely out of the line of fire, I think we should respect her wishes." She looked Charlie in the eye. "I can't fault her for doing the exact same thing that I would do."

After that no one voiced any more objections, fought back with any indignation. Everyone wordlessly cleared the table and Bob decided it was time to fill the others in on his plans for their safety, that would start almost immediately. While he went over everything Charlie excused herself, asking T.J. to join her on the back porch.

Charlie shut the sliding glass door behind him, huddling her arms to her chest and joining T.J. by the porch railing, looking out at the nearby apartments and roads, all lit-up as a backdrop under the night sky. "I heard from everyone in there but you," she said quietly. "Now that it's just the two of us, you feel like sharing?"

"What do you want me to say, Charlie?" he asked, not taking his eyes off the horizon. "It's your life. And just as Diana said, you've earned the right to make your own decisions. Even if those decisions include signing you own death warrant."

Charlie winced slightly. "I know what the Montenillos are capable of, but don't you think that's a tad melodramatic?"

T.J. shook his head. "Don't insult my intelligence by trying to play this off like it's nothing when we both know it's battle, a battle you can't hope to win. You're great at what you do but even you can't outrun bullets, and even you don't have a chance when it's a hundred to one."

"I know what this must be like for you," she began, "and I'm sorry to have to put you through it-"

"Do you really?" he interrupted, finally turning to face her. "Do you really have the faintest idea what this is like for me? We've been working side-by-side for the past month on this, after the South America fiasco. Remember, when you said you'd change and finally let me in enough to help you? Or was that all a pack of lies?"

"Of course it wasn't a pack of lies," she said defensively. "I meant every word. I did want your help, and you gave it to me, and we worked very well together. But that's not what this is about."

"Oh no? What's it about then?" he asked, folding his arms over his chest.

"Can't you just try to understand?" she pleaded, dodging the question. She wanted to tell him what she was really feeling, that she wanted him safe as much as she wanted the others safe. She didn't want him staying behind putting his life on the line for her, but she knew if she told him that he'd fight her, insist the odds were better if they stay and fought together, and eventually she'd cave in. But she couldn't, so she had to try a different tack. "You and I are risk-takers," she began, "reckless by nature. We're not typical nine-to-fivers; we spend most of our time in the trenches, as evident by all our battle scars. We've both had dozens of close calls on the job and I have in my personal life. Outsiders think we're crazy because they run from danger, and we run toward it. If anyone should be able to understand this...it's you."

"I do understand," he said, his voice rising. "Which is why I don't understand why you wouldn't want me to stay with you. This isn't about asking for help anymore; it's about survival. We make such a good team, and you know it. I can back you up now, but you won't let me. I want to know why that is." His eyes searched hers. "What aren't you telling me?"

So badly she wanted to scream out the truth, that she had no right to ask him to risk his life for her. He didn't need to be involved in this; she wasn't going to risk something happening to him because of her. If things were different, she would want his help: the irony of the situation was that she'd finally learned how to ask for it when it came to her personal life. She could see the two of them fighting this out together...and she could also see him not coming back. "Just go," she said quietly. "Get on a plane and fly down to Palm Springs, spend some time with your parents, and be glad you don't have to worry about any of this."

"You're not making any sense," he protested. He walked up to her and took her arms in his hands, squeezing gently. "Talk to me," he pleaded.

But she couldn't. Instead she took a deep breath, knowing what to say to make him go. "This is just between me and Stevens," she said, trying to make her tome flat. "You're not a part of it."

T.J. staggered back as though he'd been stung. "That's what you think?" he asked incredulously. "You don't think it's not between the people who care about you too? All those people in there-" he jerked his head toward the door- "and out here?" He continued to back away. "But you can't see that, can you? You're too blinded by your hatred for Stevens and-" He broke off.

"And what?"

"And you still think you're that little girl Anna left on the park bench," he told her, sadness etched into his expression. "And the teenager roaming the streets of the city after Melinda died, who ended up nearly beaten to death in a boxcar-"

"Stop!" Charlie cried, squeezing her eyes shut. She knew she deserved everything he was saying but she couldn't handle hearing it.

"You think you're still alone," he continued, undaunted. "That you have to handle everything by yourself because that's all you've ever done. You're a survivor through and through...but you're also a lone wolf when it comes to the personal stuff. You may have let Bob and Rita help you all those years ago but it was temporary, just until you got back on your feet. All so you could do it yourself again. Now it's finally coming to a head and you're determined to finish it alone, even if it kills you. Do you have any idea how sad that is, when it doesn't have to be that way?"

"That's not true," she whispered, though she knew that it was.

"Yes, it is." He shook his head sadly. "You came so close to truly letting me in. I really thought you had, until you invited all of us over here tonight. I knew that something was up as soon as I saw you and Bob but I kept my mouth shut, hoping I was wrong. And I wish I was." He was edging closer to the back door. "I'm sorry...but I can't keep watching you do this to yourself."

"What?" she asked, though she already knew the answer.

"Pushing everyone away so you can fight alone...because that's what you think you deserve. Even after all this time you can't see yourself any differently than the kid living on the street doing whatever it took to survive. You never thought you were good enough to deserve more than what you gave yourself. But you do. You deserve everything. You deserve to know who you really are, the person I came so close to-" He broke off, shaking his head. "But now we'll never know."

Charlie couldn't take it anymore; it was all she could do to hold herself together, her arms wrapped tightly around her sides. "I'm sorry," she managed, unable to look at him.

He nodded. "I know." He put his hand on the door handle. "Good-bye, Charlie," he said softly. "And good luck."

Charlie just stood where she was, unable to move. Everything he said had been true; even though she wanted him to leave to protect him she couldn't deny that he'd nailed everything else right on the head. Here it was at the end, and she still had to go at it alone. He was right about being the ashamed kid who never thought she deserved better, and he was right about how close she'd been to truly letting him in. And now they would never know how it could have been.

But he'll still be alive, she reminded herself. *That's what's really important. You made sure of it...there's no way he'll stick around now. He'll be safe.*

But knowing that didn't make the punched-in-the-gut feeling go away. The truth was, he really did understand her, better than anyone else ever had. But it turned out that she'd been right all along.

She was far too damaged to ever have someone like that-someone good-be in her life.

Chapter Fifteen

The next morning was gray and cool, the sun hidden behind large patches of dark clouds. Having slept little, Charlie was up early, going for her usual run and stopping at the gym after. After stopping at home to shower she drove over to Bob's apartment, where everyone was meeting.

No one said much as they gathered in the parking lot; Bob and Jack were loading the luggage in the van Bob rented, while Megan carried a cat carrier, a dish, and Harley's pillow-bed. Harley was sleeping peacefully in Diana's lap, curled up in a ball.

After the van was packed it was time for good-byes, all of which were emotional. Charlie hugged Jack first, squeezing him tightly. "I'm sorry I'm disrupting your life," she told him, pulling back. "You and Megan should be doing baby stuff, like putting final touches on the nursery. Not heading off into the unknown, cut off from your life."

"It's okay," he assured her. "We both had vacation time coming up so it's not a problem. Don't worry about us…worry about yourself." He looked at her for moment. "I didn't mean to jump down your throat last night," he apologized quietly. "But I think you know how much you mean to me, and I couldn't stand the thought of you-" He broke off with great effort. "Just watch your back, okay?"

She nodded. "Always do." She stepped up to hug Megan, who'd also come forward. "You guys watch out for one another, and take care of that baby." She eyed Megan's belly. "Listen to Bob and you should be alright."

They got into the van before giving one last wave, and Diana approached her, gently stroking the top of Harley's head. "I'm not saying good-bye," she told her abruptly. "I already did that once, twenty-eight years ago, and I never intend on doing it again."

"Agreed," Charlie said, giving Harley a quick pat on the head. "Thanks for agreeing to take care of him."

"That was part of the deal." Diana looked at her carefully. "I'm not going to lecture you because, as I said last night, this has to be your choice, and I get why you want us out of the way. That being said, I have to tell you that I think he's completely right."

Charlie frowned. "Who?"

"You know who. He told me everything when he took me home last night, everything that you said. I get why you're doing what you're doing but I don't get why you won't let him help you."

"Diana-"

"Do you have any idea how much that man cares about you?" she interrupted. "How much it's killing him to watch you self-destruct?"

"I'm not self-destructing!" Charlie snapped. "I thought we discussed this last night, when you claimed to understand. And I'm not just doing this for me, you know. I'm doing it for you too, for everything Stevens put you through by separating us all these years. He has to pay for that."

"So you are looking for revenge; this isn't about the greater good at all is it?"

"Damned straight I'm looking for revenge, but that isn't the only reason. I am doing this for everyone. It needs to be finished."

"But what good is it if you end up dead?" Diana challenged. "You think Stevens or any of
this will matter then? You think Paul will care what happens to him if you die?"

Charlie knelt down in front of her. "You need to have a little faith," she said, taking one of Diana's hands. "You and I both know I'm no Girl Scout; I've been working on this, and I have a plan. And I'm sure Avery is going to show up. When you start to get worried, just think about yourself, and what you would do. You might not have raised me, but I'm still your daughter through and through. Have in faith in that. Have faith in me."

Diana nodded wordlessly, squeezing her hand and then pulling Charlie toward her for a hug. Then she sat up straighter. "I guess we need to get going so Bob can beat traffic. You find a way to contact me when this is over, you hear?" she asked, looking at her sternly.

Charlie nodded. "Yes, ma'am. Good-" She stopped, remembering. "See you soon," she said instead.

Diana gave a brisk nod. "See you soon," she echoed, then turned and started to wheel herself toward the van. She almost disappeared from sight when she stopped suddenly, turning around slightly. "You and T.J....the most stubborn people I've ever met." She shook her head, then disappeared around the back.

Once everyone was settled, Bob pulled Charlie aside. "I've found out a little bit more," he told her, "since last night. I've sent everything in an e-mail, but just to sum it up there are some associates of Stevens that you should keep an eye out for. He's got two we know of from the Bronx: Joe Welbourn and Timothy Freelan. They've been working with Stevens under the radar for the past several years, and they're fairly discreet for the most part. Not much in the brain department but they're big, beefy, and have a penchant for following orders to the letter. They'll be Stevens eyes and ears while he's on the inside, and will be his muscle when he gets out."

Charlie nodded. "Got it. What else?"

"You also need to watch out for Stevens' cousins-Francisco's sons: Carlos, Diego, and Raphael. They're the ones basically running the show; Francisco's more of a figurehead since he's hit eighty. Even before that he was known for sending his sons to do the dirty work while he kept a low profile. So low in fact, that that's why there's never been any evidence to secure a warrant, which is why Avery only went after the other half of the clan. Antonio was a lot sloppier."

Again Charlie nodded. "Sounds good. I'll add it to what I already know."

"Alright then," he said, shifting slightly and looking as though he wanted to say something more. Finally he added, "You know Stevens is unpredictable when he gets going, so be prepared for anything. Fight dirty if you have to...and remember everything you've done for the past ten years." He stepped forward, embracing her quickly. "You be careful, kid. I'll contact you when we've made it."

"You better." Charlie pulled back. "What you said last night, about me being like your daughter...you know that you've always been more than just a teacher, a partner, or a mentor."

He nodded. "I know. And it's been an honor."

After she watched the van pull out of sight she mounted her bike and took off, not exactly sure where she should go next. She still had some time before the fifteenth, which left her schedule wide open. Since she'd already done her exercise for the day she decided to just drive around, blow off some steam, and get her head together.

It had the opposite effect than the one she'd wanted. Instead of her thinking becoming
more focused it dwelled on the people who'd just left, the people she cared about more than anything in the world. She knew they were safe; Bob was better protection than the F.B.I. She tried to concentrate on that, knowing it made breathing a lot easier and that she didn't have to worry.

But then her thoughts went to T.J., causing her stomach to twist itself in knots. Stevens and everything else was shoved onto the back burner as she thought about everything he'd said the night before, and how right he'd been.

As the days passed, Charlie spent all her time on preparing, both physically and mentally. However when she had a free moment she thought about other things, things she shouldn't be thinking about right now because she couldn't afford the distraction. Still, it seemed to take on a life of its own no matter how much she tried to stop it.

A week before the fifteenth Charlie decided to go to the diner, though she'd previously decided she wouldn't go back any time soon. David wasn't there, to her relief, but she couldn't stop herself from thinking about him as she ordered and when her food arrived. As she was finishing she started thinking about all the memories, about how they has their last conversation as a couple at this very counter. She'd accused David of not being able to accept her job, which meant he couldn't accept her. He admitted that it had become too much: the stress of not knowing where she'd disappear to and if she was alright, all the trips out of town, the danger and the close calls...but then she remembered something she'd long blocked out. David told her he could deal with all of it, though it'd be hard, but what he couldn't deal with was constantly being kept at arm's length, shut out. And that was the way T.J. felt now.

Apparently they had more in common than their looks.

But it *was* different with T.J. because she didn't want to keep him at arm's length anymore and if she wasn't so afraid of losing him things would be completely different now. But she couldn't tell him that.

After she paid her bill Charlie got on her bike and took off, heading for T.J.'s apartment complex. Since it was getting down to crunch time she wanted to make sure he'd gotten out of town while he had the chance.
***

Strategically hidden from view, Charlie looked at T.J.'s empty back porch, continuing to stare at his back windows as she had for the past twenty minutes. His car was in the parking lot but that didn't mean he was home; if he really was leaving town he probably took a cab to the airport so he wouldn't have to leave his car in the lot. At one point she considered breaking in but ultimately decided that was going too far, so she settled for staking out his apartment from a safe distance.

As she continued to stare at his back porch she thought about all the ways he'd changed her life, all the ways he'd changed her. There were a lot of ways in which she was incredibly mature; hard events in life had made her grow up very quickly. She was definitely wise to the ways of the world, but the one thing she never really learned was how to successfully conduct her personal life, particularly in relationships. In that way she was very inexperienced, and young in a sense, when she met T.J. But being with him had made her grow up, made her mature as she had in all other areas of her life. Only now she didn't feel like it, resorting to camping out across from his apartment like some kind of stalker. But she couldn't help it; she had to make sure he'd gone.

More time passed and there was no sign that anyone was home, so Charlie decided to leave. As she started toward where she parked her bike she thought she heard movement nearby and froze, standing still long enough to really listen and figure out what was going on. The moment passed, however, and when she turned around she saw she was just as alone as she had been the entire time. With one last glance at T.J.'s window, Charlie headed across the parking lot without looking back.

When she woke up the next morning she thought about something she'd started a while back but never finished, though she'd been given plenty of chances. But since the stakes were higher now than they'd ever been before, it was time to take action.

Charlie contacted the lawyer Rita used, Mr. Parkman, and he agreed to squeeze her in later that afternoon. Until then Charlie spent her time at the gym; she'd been there so often lately all the trainers knew her by name. She particularly liked kick-boxing, and repeatedly kicked the bag with such a vengeance that she acquired an audience, who applauded when she was finished.

On the way to *Harmon & Morris Attorneys at Law*, Charlie thought about her decision, knowing it was the right one. Even if she wasn't about to face incredible danger what she was about to do was a smart, responsible decision, something someone in her line of work should have taken care of a long time ago. But it wasn't too late, which was why she was going.

"Miss Booker," Mr. Parkman greeted her, shaking her hand and gesturing for her to sit across from his desk in his office. "It's good to see you again. The last time we spoke about your decision you were still undecided-"

"It's different now," Charlie interrupted, taking a seat. "Which is why I'm here."

He nodded. "I took the liberty of drawing up the paperwork you requested over the phone," he said, handing her a thick manila file folder. "If you'll look over it, you can ask questions you might have."

Charlie opened the folder and read the words LIVING WILL printed in bold across the top. "It seems pretty straightforward, which is good," she said as she flipped through the paperwork. "What I said before still stands, about Bob, Jack, and Megan receiving the bulk of my estate. I also wanted a provision for their baby, my godchild; I'd like to set up a college fund for him or her. Also, there's someone new in my life since the last time we spoke, and I want her included as well. Her name is Diana Sullivan, and she's my birthmother. When I get home I'll type up the specifics, of what I want everyone to inherit."

"That's all listed here," he told her. "I made a note of it when we spoke this morning. I also added a Thomas James Mackenzie."

Charlie nodded. "There's something special I want to leave for him, if anything should happen," she said, quickly scribbling it down. "Can you take care of that?" she asked, sliding the small card across to him.

Mr. Parkman read it, nodding. "Absolutely. The only thing left to do is to get the papers filed, signed, and notarized. Then you'll be set."

Charlie nodded, standing. "Thank you, Mr. Parkman," she said, shaking his hand. "I'll be in touch with the rest via e-mail."

Charlie went straight home and spent the early evening dividing her assets and deciding
who would inherit what. She also decided to follow in Rita's footsteps and leave each of them a letter, including one for Jack and Megan's unborn child.

The last and most difficult one was her letter to T.J. She hardly knew where to begin, and spent a long time just staring at the blank piece of paper. Finally it all came to her, and once she started writing she was unable to stop. She ended the letter by telling him what she'd left for him, something she knew he'd appreciate and take of as if he'd bought it himself. Something she trusted to no one else.

She'd decided to leave him her bike.

***

The days ticked by, slowly and methodically. The early fall weather seemed to mirror Charlie's current mood: it remained chilly, with occasional strong gusts of wind, all under a continuous gray sky. Though it didn't rain the gloom everywhere was apparent, as if the universe knew exactly what to expect in the coming week, which would be a definite reason to be gloomy. Among other things.

Charlie's head was crammed so full of facts, yet she kept going, refusing to be slowed down for a second or distracted in any way. It wasn't too hard to be focused, considering everything in her life that could potentially distract her had been removed.

She focused less on trying to pin down Avery's and Anna's location and more time on the Montenillos, the DeMarcos, and any other probable key players. So thorough was her homework that she felt almost as though she could pass for mobster herself, with all she'd found out.

All her digging cemented her theory that something big was going down on or near the fifteenth, aside from Stevens imminent breakout. For a short time she considered warning the police what was going to happen but knew if anyone in the department was on the Montenillo payroll it would only tip them off as to how aware she truly was, and she couldn't have that. Flying below the radar for the time being was her best course of action, at present.

She half-expected Paul to leave some kind if sign that he was on his way; no matter how untrustworthy he appeared in Bob's eyes, Charlie was certain he'd be making an appearance soon. It was the only thing that made sense, the only way this battle was going to go forward.

On the thirteenth Mr. Parkman had gotten back with her and assured her the paperwork was on track, and soon the documents would be legal and binding. Charlie felt an odd moment of peace in knowing that everything was taken care of if the worst should happen. Though she had no intention of dying she knew she had to be prepared, just in case.

It was down to the wire now, and Charlie found she had no fear, only determination. Her mind wasn't going anywhere else, anywhere that could make her feel fear-like thinking of the ones she cared about. Instead it was all business, and she knew she was as ready as she was ever going to be.

Chapter Sixteen

Charlie woke up on Thursday, the fourteenth, in full planning mode. She forgo-ed her usual run in lieu of kickboxing, something that always calmed her nerves and sharpened her focus.

It wasn't too long ago that Bob had contacted her-discreetly-to let her know they'd arrived at their destination and were all safe. She knew he wasn't expecting her to reply back; the less contact they had, the better for everyone involved.

That afternoon she assembled all her gear, including every weapon she'd ever owned, as well as listening devices, her computer, and a long-lensed camera. Then she got dressed for the evening: she put on a pair of faded black jeans, a black tank top, and her leather jacket. She also laced up her favorite black sneakers, the ones she'd dubbed "lucky" since the night on the job she outran a large drunk man with a baseball bat and unbelievable temper while wearing them.

After pulling her long hair into a high ponytail she gathered all her gear and packed it into her leather pack, then locked up and headed downstairs to the parking lot where her bike waited.

If the sky had been cloudless she would've been able to see the setting sun as she drove downtown, the cold wind feeling good on her face as she went. By the time she arrived at her destination it was twilight.

The bar was called Shaker's, and she'd gone there quite often over the years. A lot of her informants preferred to meet there, at a place both inconspicuous and comfortable. Charlie bypassed the bar, however, and headed straight for a vacant pool table in the back near the emergency exit.

As soon as she arrived Charlie was aware that she was being watched. She wasn't surprised; this bar was directly in Montenillo territory. She came on purpose, to draw them out. It was clear, however, that they weren't going to make the first move. There were two of them in the corner opposite her, and she could feel their eyes on her with every move she made. She feigned ignorance and continued to play, acting as though she hadn't a care in the world.

Based on the intel Bob gave her, Charlie knew the men were Freelan and Welbourn. Freelan was the elder of the two, thirty-seven; he was also six-foot-four and brawnier than most football players. Welbourn was thirty-five, shorter, and stockier but every inch as muscular. When it came to physiology alone Charlie only had a few advantages, one being that she was small and lean, which made her light on her feet, and she was younger, though she wasn't positive that she was in better health. *I thought I took care of myself, kept myself in good shape…but they make me look like Jell-o,* she thought, racking once again and starting over. Luckily she had speed on her side; she'd come a long way from being chased down by several beefy guys at a train yard. This is what all her training over the years had truly been about: this night, starting this moment. She was about to see if all her hard work paid off.

When Charlie sank the eight ball for the third time she glanced up casually to see if her audience was still there, blending into the background. They were but had changed their stance; no longer were they leaning casually near the far wall. They'd started to advance her, slowly and discreetly, but continuing just the same.

She casually walked over to the nearby table where she'd hung her jacket and grabbed it, slipping it on carefully. As soon as she zipped it a shadow fell over her, and she quickly reached behind her.

She swung the pool cue around, jabbing Welbourn in the gut several times, which caused him to finally double over. As she swung the other end at Freelan's face he grabbed it, jerking it from her grasp and flinging it to the side. He lunged at Charlie but she ran at him full force, knocking him to the ground and proceeding to punch him repeatedly.

Wellborn pulled her off, throwing her backward and sending her crashing through the small table and tumbling to the floor. By now everyone in the bar was watching in shock, the men in particular looking more than a little vexed.

Charlie gingerly touched her bloody lip as Welbourn and Freelan loomed over her. "Better watch your temper, boys," she chided. "Your boss wants me alive, remember?"

"Alive, yeah," Welbourn said, reaching down and grabbing her by the neck of her shirt. "In what condition...he didn't say."

"Hey," a gruff voice ordered from behind him. "You let her go, right now."

Wellborn and Freelan turned around to see all the men in the bar grouped behind them, a tall burly man standing in front. The man looked past him to Charlie. "I don't know where you're from...but around here it isn't okay to attack a woman."

"That's right," a voice echoed from behind him. "We're tired of you Montenillo scum coming in here, scaring our patrons." The crowd cheered and echoed their agreement.

Wellborn and Freelan looked at each other and then ran toward the crowd, chaos quickly following as Charlie hoped it would. She used the brawl as a chance to escape, stopping at the counter. "Here," she said to the bartender, throwing a wad of bills her way. "That should cover damages. And call the cops," she added. "Those men are definitely wanted."

"No problem," the bartender told Charlie, accepting the money. "No one around here likes the Montenillos and their goons."

Charlie knew that, which is exactly what she'd been counting on. Now that Welbourn and Freelan were sufficiently occupied, she could go forward with her plan.

She went out the back exit and to the alley where she'd parked her bike. Unfortunately her discreet exit turned out not to be so discreet after all.

Three men were grouped around her bike, their faces shadows in the dim light. As she quickly assessed them Charlie could tell the man slightly apart from the others was Raphael Montenillo; the other two were no doubt faceless minions.

"Raphael Montenillo," she called over to him, not moving from where she was. "And company," she added. "What can I do for you this fine evening?" She had two knives in her left jacket pocket and a gun shoved in the back of her pants, and was debating over when the right moment was to grab something.

Montenillo and his men didn't make a move either; it appeared as though they were at a standoff. "Charlotte," he said simply. Then he seemed to be studying her for a moment. "It's strange," he began at last, "you don't look exactly like him: you have different hair, different eyes. But something about the way you conduct yourself, something about the way you operate, how cool you always appear to be, how methodical...you are definitely Paul's daughter."

"Touching. But I'm guessing you didn't follow me here to compare/contrast me with my father."

Something in Montenillo's expression changed then; gone were the forced politeness and refined manners. "You know he's a rat, don't you?" he asked softly. "He came into our organization with all the right qualifications, earned the trust of my father and Uncle Antonio-enough to be assigned as my bodyguard, because I foolishly decided to go to school. I wanted more than what my family had to offer; I thought I was better than they were, because I aspired to be more than just the average 'mobster'. And my good friend and bodyguard Johnny Black was a big part of that. He was always telling me that I could have a life outside my family, that I could go anywhere, do anything that I wanted, and that I should never have to apologize for that. He told me it was too late for him, that he was in too deep, but I still had a chance. And that I was on the right track, by going to school." His expression darkened. "Then one night, while I was at a football game of all places, the police raided my family's business, arrested my Uncle Antonio, and murdered my cousins, Andre and Joaquin. We thought Hector died that night too; it was a while before we learned he faked his own death and became Andrew Stevens. We lost nearly everything that night, all because of an undercover cop. A liar-" he took a step forward- "a fraud-" another step- "an opportunist-" another step- "and a traitor." He stopped a yard away from Charlie, his features twisted by underlying rage. "He was Hector's friend, my confidante and encourager...but it was only to take us down; he never gave a damn about any of us. When I found out the truth I vowed that someday he would pay and spent years preparing for it, finally becoming a man my old man could be proud of. Now I rightly take a stand with my brothers as we finally take Paul Avery down, and you along with him."

Charlie drew her gun just as he drew his and hit him square in the shoulder. Montenillo cursed, staggering backward and holding his arm close to his side. The two men behind him sprang into action, beginning to fire back as Charlie dived to the ground, looking for shelter.

She crouched against the wall behind a corner, breathing heavily and waiting for the slightest sound to give away their position. "You might as well come out," Montenillo called. "We're going to catch you sooner or later, so why not make it sooner? After all, the longer you drag it out, the worse it'll be for your boyfriend."

Charlie froze.

"Got your attention now, don't I? If you keep trying to fight us, he's dead."

"You'll never catch him," she called, pulling out her knife and hiding it under her sleeve. "He's halfway across the country by now."

"You sound pretty sure of that. But if you knew it for a fact you'd jump out and take us out right now."

Charlie jumped up and faced them, her gun aimed at Montenillo's other shoulder. "Want a matching set?" she asked. Just as she was about to pull the trigger again Montenillo fired first, hitting her on her right shoulder.

"Now we're even," he said as she fell back a few steps. "Hector always had a soft spot for you," he said as he moved closer, his men not far behind. "I've been telling him for years it was a mistake, a mistake he couldn't afford. Personally, if it were me in his position...I would've killed you a long time ago."

Before he could do anything further shots rang out, and the men on either side of him crumpled to the ground, one after the other. Montenillo looked up in surprise as a hand came from the darkness and pulled Charlie to her feet. The hand continued to fire until Montenillo retreated, disappearing into the darkness.

Charlie lowered her gun with her uninjured shoulder; she'd fired second-hitting the guy on the right-after her unknown assistant fired first. She slowly turned around, squinting in the darkness in order to make out his shape. "T.J.?" she asked carefully.

He stepped forward from the shadows, tucking his gun back into the back of his jeans. "Thought you might need the assist, though it seems you were handling yourself just fine. Not that I had any doubt," he quickly added.

Charlie just stared at him for a long moment. "How did you know where I was?"

"You have your informants, I have mine," he said with a shrug. "I put feelers out, got everyone in the area I know to watch out for you.

I got a call a short while ago from my favorite bartender, Maria, who told me you were at her place in the midst of a bar-brawl. Nice move by the way; Freelan and Welbourn were both picked up by the cops, so you have two down."

Charlie looked at the men lying on the ground. "Four, actually." Then she turned around, looking back at him. "Montenillo told me they were coming after you," she said quietly. "I didn't think it could be possible, because I didn't think you'd be stupid enough to stick around." She shook her head. "Why didn't you go to Palm Springs?"

"You really expected me to go soak up the sunshine while you were out here fighting for your life alone?" he asked incredulously. "I think you know me better than that. And I know you better than you were counting on."

She frowned. "What are you talking about?"

"I have to admit, it took me a minute to figure it out. At first it was really easy to believe that you just wanted to go at it solo, that you still hadn't learned how to let anyone help you. But then I remembered how far you'd come, how much that was appearing to change. Then you said what you said about me getting out of here, going to Palm Springs with my parents and I realized then that you weren't trying to get rid of me so you could go on some crazy kamikaze trip. You were doing it so I would be out of the line of fire like everyone else."

She shook her head, starting toward her bike. "I don't have time for this," she said, wincing slightly from the pain streaking down her arm.

"Wait!" he called after her, jogging to catch up. He touched her on her good shoulder, slowly turning her around. "We need to talk about this."

"I'm in the middle of a battle here, in case you haven't noticed," she snapped. "It's not the time or the place for some 'share our feelings' convention."

"Admit it," he ordered, not releasing his grip on her arm. "Come on, Charlie. Don't I at least deserve the truth?"

Her expression softened. "Of course you do."

"Then tell me."

"Fine. Yes, you're right," she confessed. "I said what I said to get you out of town like the others. I sent them away not just for their safety, but for me as well because I can't handle someone getting hurt because of me. And that includes you."

"But I'm like you," he reminded her. "I'm trained, which means I can help you. I'm not some civilian you have to protect, who will distract you from doing what you need to do."

"I know. But don't you get it?" She started walking toward her bike again, and he followed behind her. "Bob warned me about this a long time ago, but I didn't really listen then because I was young and didn't have any attachments." She took a breath. "He told me our line of work isn't dangerous just because bullets fly or people fight back; it's also dangerous because it affects the people we care about. We do can hurt them, if people try to retaliate and use our loved ones to do it...but it also hurts us, because if anything happens to them because of us..." She leaned against her bike, breathing heavily. "Family, friends, lovers...they're all liabilities. Rita was a liability to us both, as were Jack and Megan. And now you are, for me. Liabilities make you lose your focus, get distracted, and you can get sloppy as a result, which is something we can't afford. That's something you shouldn't have a problem understanding."

"I do understand," he told her. "But I was under the impression that I was a lot more to you than a liability you couldn't afford."

"You are," she told him impatiently. "That's why it's a problem." She let out a long breath. "The truth is, I really have changed. I wanted to let you in from the moment I figured out the fifteenth meant something. But I also knew what it would mean: this is bigger than anything either of us has ever faced and probably will ever face, if we survive. I'm good and so are you but we're not invincible." She paused. "Do you know how I spent the past weekend? Planning."

"You should have," he said reasonably. "So you'll be ready."

Charlie shook her head. "Not for this. Planning for the future, in case...in case I don't make it back."

T.J. stopped. "You did...what?" he asked slowly.

"Truthfully, it should have been taken care of a long time ago. I've known ever since I was a little kid that my life expectancy was most likely far shorter than everyone else's. But yes, I had a living will drawn up. I even included you. That's how serious this is, T.J." She looked at him. "It's not too late for you to make a run for it."

He shook his head. "No way in hell. I'm not going anywhere."

"Who's suicidal now?"

"I appreciate how you feel, but just as you expect others to respect your decisions, you need to respect mine. It's my choice, Charlie-"

"It's not your battle-"

"It is my battle, because I'm making it my battle. You were right; the Montenillos are a blight on the entire Eastern seaboard. If there's anything we can do to take them down, we should at least try."

"But-"

He walked up to her, putting his finger to her lips. "My choice," he repeated. "So you might as well get used to it."

"No letting me got out in a blaze of glory, huh?" she asked, attempting humor.

"Absolutely not."

"Alright," she relented grudgingly. "I have a storage space on Tenth, just a few miles from here. Follow me there; we'll need as much fire power as possible." She mounted her bike then, starting the engine.

"Hey," he called over the roar of the motor. "Answer something for me."

"Yeah?" she asked, grabbing her helmet.

"What were you going to leave me?" he asked curiously.

Charlie let out a half-laugh. "You really want to know?"

He nodded.

"I'll tell you," she promised, her expression sobering. "As soon as we make it out of
this."

***

They raided Charlie's storage space, taking all they could fit into their packs. As she was about to lock up the building she caught T.J. staring at her bike. "What?" she asked, wondering if he'd figured it out.

But instead he looked deep in thought. "We should probably leave it here," he said, resting a hand on the handlebars. "They'll be expecting you on your bike."

She nodded. "Good thinking."

Together they pushed the bike inside the storage place; it only barely fit. Charlie reached up to pull down the door, almost crying out in pain from the sharp twinge she felt in her shoulder. She covered it up quickly, however; T.J. didn't know she'd been shot.

They got into the Chevelle and drove away, T.J. noticing the needle on the gas gage was dangerously low. They stopped at a gas station to refuel, and while T.J. was pumping the gas Charlie excused herself to the restroom inside.

She didn't go to the bathroom, however. She went in search for some ibuprofen and a bottle of water. *Hydration and warding off infection are key for gunshot wounds,* she thought, using her past knowledge to help her now. *So I guess this is scar number thirty-two,* she mused as she located the medicine. *It would've been nice to stop at thirty.*

She made her purchase and stopped in the bathroom to doctor up her wound. She carefully removed her jacket and started to inspect it. From what she could tell she was lucky; the bullet seemed to have passed through. She cleaned it as best she could with water from one of the bottles she bought, washing off as much blood as possible. She couldn't find any antiseptic, so she'd had to settle for rubbing alcohol to sterilize the wound. Clenching her teeth tightly together, she poured some of the clear liquid on the open wound and felt her skin cry out in pain; she groaned loudly though her teeth were still clenched. Afterward she took a medium-sized bandage-the only size she could find-out of its packet and carefully placed it on top of the bullet-hole. Then she replaced her jacket and headed out the back exit.

She was around back, leaning against the wall. Surprised and angry that her hand was shaking she opened the bottle and shook two of the small brown pills into her open palm. She opened the remaining bottle of water and tipped it back, swallowing the pills. Then she stood where she was for a moment, closing her eyes and commanding herself to breathe deeply. *This was nothing,* she told herself. *It's not like you've never been shot before. Although in the past you had access to a needle and thread thanks to Bob and were able to stitch yourself up. This wound is still open, so you have to pray it doesn't continue to bleed.*

By the time she re-joined T.J. he was already sitting back in the front seat, looking at her expectantly as she approached. "Took you a while," he commented as she got in. "Everything okay?"

"Yes," she lied. "Everything's fine. Let's go."

The wind was cool, coming through the open windows as they drove back into the city. Charlie told him her plan was to go down to the main Montenillo warehouses, where she was certain some kind of business meeting was going to take place, before whatever they had planned that night. Since it was after midnight now and officially the fifteenth, Charlie was sure all the Montenillo plans were about to be revealed.

"Alright," she said when they were a mile out from the warehouses. "Park here, and we'll get ready. The goal is to do as much recon as we can; we've got plenty of equipment to set up to help us out."

They opened the trunk and Charlie began pointing everything out to him. "It's your pick," she said when she'd finished. "You want to say here and set up base? Or do you want to go closer, be on the move?"

"I'll take base," he told her. "You're good on the move."

She nodded. "Alright then. Keep your phone on for emergencies, but our main form of communication will be these." She held up two earpieces and a small box. "We'll be able to talk to each other, and listen to what's going on inside once I get close enough to plant the bug. That'll be our ears, and I'll be our eyes. I'll tell you everything I see. And if all else fails-"

"Shoot first, ask questions later," he finished. "Pretty straightforward."

She nodded, handing him an earpiece. "There you go. Good luck."

"You too." He kissed her quickly on the lips. "Find what we need and we can get the cops here in no time, shut this operation down."

"That's the idea. Then we focus on the other part of the plan, the part they want me and my father for."

Charlie took off for the first warehouse, crouching low and using the heavily wooded area for cover. There were two men posted out front as guard, and she was certain there was also a guarded back entrance as well. From her position she could see little; she had to get closer to drop the listening device.

She snuck around the side of the building, judging the distance to the top. She started to climb, using the wood siding for footing. She finally hoisted herself up to the roof, which was relatively flat, and she had no problem walking across.

Charlie looked down through the glass window, peering through all the dust and grime until she could get a layout of the inside of the building. From what she could see the area around her was unoccupied; taking advantage of her momentary good luck she carefully opened the window, her shoulder tensing under the strain. When she had it open just a crack she dropped the device through the opening and it fell, unnoticed, resting next to a large stack of unopened crates.

After shutting the window she stayed where she was; she had a fairly good glimpse of what was going on inside. As she suspected they were starting some kind of meeting; Raphael Montenillo was standing in the corner looking perplexed, lighting a cigar. His jacket was draped over his shoulder while the other, the one Charlie shot, had been bandaged. His brothers were a few yards away, talking to some of their employees in hushed tones. As they started to move closer, Charlie could start to catch what they were saying.

"Everything's on schedule," the man she recognized as Carlos Montenillo, the eldest of the brothers, addressed the others. "The DeMarco brothers have just informed me that their shipment arrived down at the pier a short while ago and is currently en route via truck-transportation. These warehouses contain all the product we're shipping to them, which is why all of you are here tonight. We have to make sure this stays under wraps, which means we need your discretion. All of this product needs to be loaded up tonight; our father will be here shortly to oversee."

"Are you getting all this?" T.J.'s voice suddenly sounded in her ear. "This is huge."

"I know," she said back. "Think we've got enough?"

"Definitely. I'm calling the cops as we speak. Just make sure no one leaves until they get here."

"Of course; I get the easy part," she said sarcastically. "You know, this explains the DeMarco connection...but what about Avery? And why did they want me?"

"They're talking again," he told her. "Check it out."

Charlie stopped talking and started listening, watching Carlos and Diego as they approached Raphael. "This looks like it's well-handled," Raphael told the other two. "Shouldn't we get going? After Pop stops by we're all supposed to head to-"

"Charlie," T.J.'s voice broke through urgently. "Francisco Montenillo just got here."

Charlie turned around, watching as the approaching headlights suddenly shut off and a driver got out, opening the back door to the black limo. Francisco Montenillo stepped out, followed by two bodyguards. "He's going in," she told T.J. "No, wait." She watched carefully as the guards suddenly changed direction. "The guards are sweeping the perimeter. T.J., they're coming your way," she told him, her heart pounding. "Get out of there, now."

"Don't worry about me, just keep an eye on-"

"They see you!" she interrupted, rising to full height. "They're coming right toward you! Get out of there!"

"Alright! I'm going! Meet me at the next warehouse."

"I'm on it!" Charlie looked one last time through the window before running to the roof's edge, carefully lowering herself down. She ran around toward the back, in the opposite direction of the guards, and as she rounded the corner she caught T.J.'s form running ahead of her. What he couldn't see was a guard running behind him, his gun raised.

Charlie jerked her own gun out from under her jacket and fired; the man crumpled and fell, and T.J. spun around in surprise. "Go!" she yelled. "They had to have heard, they'll be coming!"

"Charlie-"

"I'll meet you! Go!"

As Charlie expected the warehouse doors burst open and Montenillo men ran out, following by Carlos, Diego, and Raphael. Francisco's guards urged him out of the way as everyone began to sweep the area, looking for the direction from which the shot came.

Charlie froze in a grove of trees, watching. Before she could react two guards caught T.J. and walked him back to the Montenillos, calling that they caught the intruder.

"Come on out Charlotte!" Carlos called, looking around the area. "We caught your boyfriend! Show yourself or we put a bullet in his head."

Charlie jumped out from the trees, landing unsteadily on her feet. She could feel herself continuing to bleed through the bandage; it'd been happening for some time but she had to just keep going. Now the blood loss was starting to catch up to her but she ignored it, concentrating
on the scene before her. "Alright, I'm here," she said, holding her hands up in the air. "Let him go."

T.J. was watching her with an expression she couldn't interpret; she met his eyes briefly, hoping to give him some assurance. "That's what this is all about, isn't it?" she continued, slowly walking forward. "Catching me for Stevens and luring my father out of hiding. You wanted bait...well here I am."

"Why should we let him go?" Raphael spoke up. "Both of you have killed our men tonight. Why not make it even?"

"Oh, come on now. You really expect me to believe you care about a few faceless employees, low-level minions who are easily replaced?" she asked, her heart continuing to pound.

"Loyalty is not something we'd expect you to understand," a voice spoke up. Francisco Montenillo stepped out from behind his bodyguards, coming to stand next to his oldest son. "Your pig of a father knew nothing of loyalty, of family," he continued, addressing Charlie. "We accepted him into our fold and he repaid us by betrayal. As the saying goes, the sins of the father..." He trailed off. "It doesn't surprise me that his daughter would be just as treacherous, or have the same regard for allegiance. My nephew had a weak spot for you but I can assure you, Ms. Booker, that I do not. We owe you nothing." He nodded toward the guards.

Charlie knew if she started shooting T.J. was a dead man; she had to think of a way to distract them. "Wait," she said suddenly, pulling out her gun. "We're doing this on my terms, Montenillo. Stevens wants me, he can have me. But only if he-" she looked at T.J. "-gets a running start out of here."

"You're not in any position to bargain," Francisco told her, his tone slightly amused.

"Oh yeah?" She moved her gun from pointing in his direction to her own temple. She saw T.J. pale and she managed a discreet wink in his direction. "If he dies, so do I. And we both know that's not what your precious nephew wants. At least not before his so-called big plans for me and my old man. So, you have two seconds to let him go or you get to explain to Stevens why the plan he waited thirty years to execute got cut off at the knees on the count of your arrogance."

"You're crazier than your father," Francisco said, the amusement gone from his voice.

"Haven't you heard?" Charlie asked, making no move to withdraw her weapon. "I'm a reckless, thrill-seeking, danger-loving bounty hunter. I put myself out there more in a week than you suits do in a year, which means you better believe I'm more than capable of pulling this trigger. What's it going to be? What's more valuable to you? Loyalty toward your nephew...or trying to punish me?"

Francisco turned toward Carlos and gave a slight nod. Looking disappointed, Carlos called the guards off and T.J. was released. "There," Carlos said to her, gesturing toward T.J. "Your boyfriend's still breathing. Now you can lower the gun."

"I lower it when he gets out of here," Charlie said, still holding her position. "Unharmed."

"Alright," Carlos said. "He gets out of here."

No one moved as T.J. started forward, looking at her desperately. She gave him a slight reassuring smile as he started up the hill toward where his car was parked. As soon as she saw him disappear she lowered her gun, dropping it on the ground in front of her.

Two guards stepped forward, each grabbing one of her arms. Carlos ordered them to take her to the nearest car and meet up with Stevens. Charlie let them take her; it wouldn't be too hard for her to try to escape but she didn't want to go back on her end of the deal until she knew T.J. was safely away.

As they started toward the closest black car parked in the gravel, shots began to ring out all over the area. Charlie instinctively dropped to the ground, looking for where the gunfire was coming from. *The cops,* she thought. *They're here.* But as soon as she thought it she knew it couldn't be true; cops didn't shoot without announcing themselves and giving a perpetrator chance to surrender. *Then who is it? What's going on?*

Before you could contemplate it further she was roughly hauled off her feet and dragged toward the car. She twisted and squirmed, trying to fight back, but she was starting to have bouts of dizziness and her strength wasn't what it should have been. She was overpowered easily and thrown into the backseat, the driver taking off as fast as he could while he screamed at his partner in the front seat, trying to figure out what was going on.

"Where are you?" T.J.'s voice suddenly came into her ear. "I'm at my car."

"Get out of here," she whispered while her captors argued. "I'm in the car with two guards, heading toward the road."

"Alright, I'll meet you. Were you okay? You looked a little gray out there, which most people would've done if they threatened to take their own life to save someone else. Which I'm grateful for, by the way, but it was completely stupid-"

"You're welcome," she interrupted. Then she decided to tell him the truth. "I was shot earlier," she admitted.

T.J. cursed. "Just hang on, okay? I'm going to follow you."

"You really shouldn't-"

"Who the hell are you talking to?" the guard in the passenger seat barked. He lunged toward Charlie and she began to fight back, the earpiece falling onto the floor.

As the driver pulled onto the road Charlie and the other guard struggled. Their scuffle began to get out of control as the passenger accidentally hit the driver while trying to grab her, causing the driver to lose control of the wheel. Charlie tried to jerk it back so they could stay on the road but he fought her, and the car started to slide off the road and into the deep ditch.

Panicking, the driving cut the wheel hard to the right, causing the car to tip upward. He desperately tried to regain control but it was to no avail. He slammed the gas and continued to try to turn and the car couldn't handle the rough action. It flipped over, sliding across the road until finally coming to a stop.

For what seemed like a long moment all Charlie could see was white, faintly hearing voices she shouldn't be able to hear. She heard Anna call her Charlotte, Melinda singing her "Happy Birthday", Rita tell her how proud she was for graduating, and Diana telling her she'd see her soon.

Then the white light vanished, replaced by partially crushed and splintered glass that was once the windshield. But the road beyond didn't look right; it appeared to be above her.

It was then she realized she was upside-down in the front seat of the wrecked car, unable to move. There was no movement on either side of her; both men were still enough for her to believe they were dead. Her eyes flicked over to the smashed door, trying to figure out how she was going to get out.

Her face was warm and sticky and her mouth had a metallic taste in it she recognized as blood. She couldn't feel her legs, her arms were in severe pain, and a dull ache crept up the base of her skull. Still, she seemed coherent enough. If she could only manage to get to the door...

Suddenly a pair of shoes appeared in front of the window, and Charlie looked up to see T.J. kneel down in front of her, his eyes terrified. Then he tried to open the door.

As he worked Charlie began to smell it. "Gas," she managed to croak out.

"What?"

"Gas," she said a little louder. T.J.'s face drained of color as he continued to work, trying to pry the door open with the crowbar she recognized from his car trunk.

The door finally budged and he dropped the crowbar as Charlie began to slide to the side. A fire ignited as she gently lifted her out of the car.

As T.J. started to carry her away the car burst into flames behind them, lighting the sky like fireworks. He could feel her slipping away; her legs dangled like a limp rag doll's. He hurried toward his car.

He quickly threw open the back door, laying her out flat across the backseat so he could assess her injuries. There was a large gash on her forehead where blood flowed freely and her face was contorted as though she were in severe pain.

"How bad is it?" she managed, her breathing labored.

"I'm getting you to a hospital, now." He stood.

"But Stevens-"

"I don't give a damn about Stevens!" he yelled. "Or the Montenillos or Paul Avery or any of it. All I care about is you, and I'm getting you help." He started to close the door.

"Wait," she called weakly, beginning to cough. "I have to tell you something."

"It can wait."

"No," she protested, "now."

"What?" he asked quickly, his brow furrowed with worry.

"You mean a lot to me," she managed, continuing to cough. "If were a regular chick I'd tell you right now that I love-"

"Stop," he ordered, bending down over her, his face only a few inches from hers. "Don't you start talking like that. You're not dying on me, Charlie Booker." He slammed the door shut.

Charlie could see him outside the window, his blurred shape starting to blend in with the backdrop behind him. The world was slowly starting to slide out of focus, and all sounds seemed to come from miles away. She felt removed from the scene, as if she were watching it unfold from a far-off movie screen.

Then she heard a sound that startled her back into consciousness, a sound that could have been fireworks. But she knew that didn't fit; the sound seemed to have come right outside the window, and when it happened T.J. had fallen backward to the ground.

The door slowly opened, revealing a large, shadowy figure looming over her. He was dressed all in black and he blocked anything that could have been going on behind him. Except for a pair of feet, lying one on top of the other, clad in boots Charlie recognized to be T.J.'s.

Her eyes slowly traveled up the man standing before her, past the gleaming silver gun in his hand and all the way up to his lined face and menacing eyes. His eyes also seemed triumphant, as if he wanted to celebrate his victory. After all the years he spent planning it had finally happened, and he'd won.

Charlie felt anger like she'd never felt before shoot through her as Stevens leaned down toward her. She twisted away as best she could, which only resulting in excruciating pain shooting down her side, causing her to cry out.

This couldn't be it, couldn't be the way it ended. She knew her chances of surviving that night were slim but she never intended to make it so easy. She planned to go down fighting, give them all hell like they'd never dealt with before, and let her name by synonymous with a spirit who'd never given up until the very end.

But that didn't seem to be the way it was going to go. She was stuck lying on the back seat of a car after being in a near-fatal car accident, and all she could do was watch Steven smile his arrogant smile and just lay there while he took her to who knew where. She couldn't fight back, she couldn't try to escape, she couldn't avenge what she was sure happened to T.J.

She wished desperately that thinking it would be enough, that somehow her body would translate her fierce thoughts and determination into raw strength. But try as she might, she couldn't move, couldn't yell, couldn't break free. She was completely stuck.

"You bastard," she managed to whisper as he continued to stare at her like she was some kind of treasured conquest. "I'll kill you."

She could see him moving toward her, feel him lift her off the seat. She was having a harder time staying coherent, but she could remember the knife in her jacket pocket as Stevens started to carry her away. With the arm that hurt the least she felt with her fingers inside the fabric, until they gently ran over something cold and hard. She quickly drew her weapon, slicing Stevens on his exposed forearm.

She felt immense pleasure when he let out a cry of pain, though she'd like to do much more to him than nick him on the arm. Still, it was something, and she felt slightly more satisfied as the world around her began to fade and she slipped into the gray that awaited her.

Chapter Seventeen

T.J. blinked slowly, his eyes struggling to adjust. He tried to sit up but there was still a sharp pain in his chest that made breathing difficult, so all he could manage was to prop himself up against the side of his car.

When his breathing finally returned to normal he leaned forward, examining the bullet-holes in his jacket. He carefully shrugged out of it, then pulled his shirt over his head to see the three bullets in a triangular formation caught in his bullet-proof vest.

He lifted it up to inspect the red and purple marks on his chest, then shook his head slightly and reached for his shirt and jacket.

Once he'd dressed he pulled himself into a standing position, his eyes quickly sweeping the area. Then he looked back at the backseat, knowing it would be empty. Unsure of what to do next, he began to pace.

He could hear a car approaching from behind him so he got out of the street to let it pass. Instead of continuing on, however, it cut the lights and began to slow down. T.J. looked up at the black SUV in interest, then thought of the Montenillos and drew his gun.

The last thing he expected when the driver side door opened was to see a woman emerge, steadily approaching him. She appeared to be in her late sixties/early seventies, her white-streaked gray hair pulled behind her in a simple bun that reminded T.J. of an old-time schoolteacher. Her eyes were dark and piercing, as was her expression, and as she got closer T.J. recognized a few distinct features in her face, since he'd seen them before. It wasn't just because he'd seen photos of Marianna Marquez in his and Charlie's research; this woman had

Charlie's nose and high-cheekbones, as well as a similar manner in the way she carried herself. Without a doubt, this woman was Charlie's great-aunt.

"I'm Marianna Marquez," she greeted him, stopping about a foot in front of him. "But you can call me Anna."

"What are you doing here?" he demanded. "How did you find me?"

"We were at the warehouses," she explained.

"You're the people who opened fire on the Montenillos," he said, understanding at once. "It was your intention to stop the shipment as well."

Anna nodded. "But it looks like we didn't get here in time to stop the rest of their plans."

T.J. nodded his agreement, starting to feel angry. "He took her. Where, I don't know. But it would've been nice to have a little help before all of this got out of control. Where's her father? Why didn't he stop Stevens?"

"Like I said, we didn't get here in time," she answered him calmly. "I understand that you're upset, Mr. Mackenzie, but I'm here to help you get my niece back."

"How?" T.J. wanted to know.

"What kind of fire power do you have?"

T.J. led her to his trunk and showed her what he and Charlie had brought along. "Looks good," she said, nodding. T.J. shut the trunk. "Follow me."

"Wait," he said, grabbing her by the arm to stop her. "There's still a lot you're not telling me, like why you're here now and where you and Avery have been all these years. And how, exactly, we're going to go up against an entire organization."

"I know you have a lot of questions, which I'll answer when we get to where we're going. Let's go."

T.J. started his car while Anna started hers, and he waited for her to pull out onto the road before following behind her.

***

Before Charlie opened her eyes she could feel the razor-sharp pain shooting down her arms as something pulled on them tightly. White-hot pain coursed through her entire being and she began to yell in agony before she could stop herself.

"One arm broken," a voice said, breaking through her haze, "one dislocated shoulder, one gunshot wound, gashes, loss of blood, possibly a concussion. I'd say you've been through the mill, haven't you Ace?" He chuckled softly. "There's no way you're getting away from me now."

Her eyes opened, revealing a large, windowless room that was completely empty except for the chair she was tied securely too and Stevens, standing a few feet in front of her. She blinked in the harsh overhead light, fighting back the dizziness that threatened to engulf her. She managed to glare at the man across from her through all her pain. "Go to hell," she snapped viciously.

Stevens chuckled again. "I should've expected you to be angry after I killed your boyfriend. Though I couldn't understand the attraction; he was beneath you, Charlie. But I guess it doesn't really matter now."

The image came back at once, the significant one before everything faded. T.J. had fallen to the ground...because Stevens had shot him.

Rage welled up inside of her like an uncontrollable volcano, far more powerful than any physical pain she was in. "You murdering son-of-a-bitch," she growled, blinking back hot tears of anger. "It wasn't enough, was it? To kidnap me, keep me away from my family, use me to barter with, stalk me most of my life, torture my father...no. You had to go beyond that and kill the only man who-" She broke off, squeezing her eyes shut.

"Come on now, Charlie. That's not any way to talk to the man who raised you for four years."

"Because you kidnapped me," Charlie snapped, overcome with fury and grief. She looked down at her ropes. "No parent would ever do this."

"I tried to do right by you, but you wouldn't cooperate. All you had to do was help me trick the information out of your old man that will free my family...but you wouldn't agree." He shook his head sadly. "Now you have to be bait."

"That's a step up from being a bargaining chip."

"Such a feisty thing." He took a step toward her. "I wonder if your father appreciates what you've done for him."

The dizziness once again tried to overpower her, and she fought it as best she could. "He won't fall for any of it," she told him. "He fell off the map for almost thirty years. He's too good for you...and so was

T.J." She clenched her jaw. "You shot him like a dog, you unbelievable coward. You deserve to burn in hell for that."

"So judgmental." Stevens began to walk away. "See you soon, Charlie." He turned off the light before shutting and locking the door behind him.

Once Charlie was alone in the darkness she let herself break down, crying quietly. She could hear Bob's voice repeating in her head over and over about liabilities, as well as relive all her own fears she'd had. She should have been firmer, should have found a way to throw him on the plane if she'd had to. But now it was too late. She gave in, and T.J. paid for it with his life.

The truth was, *she* was the liability. He got too close to her and her fight, and now he was dead. Her greatest fear had come to pass.

When the dizziness kicked up again she didn't fight it this time; she let it consume her instead so she didn't have to feel. She began to experience sweet freedom as she faded yet again.

***

"So Stevens hired you," T.J. said as Anna unlocked the back door of the SUV. "And you agreed to keep your nephew's daughter from him."

"Sounds really bad, doesn't it?" she asked, standing aside to reveal numerous boxes stacked up in the back. "But there's more to it than that."

They arrived at their destination a brief moment ago, and Anna was starting to answer T.J.'s questions. He still didn't know where they were except that he saw a small abandoned shack in the woods, and even from a distance he could see the lights on inside. Then he turned his attention back to Anna. "So tell me then," he said.

"Paul faked his death, as you know, and I, like everyone else, thought he was dead. So when Stevens contacted me, telling me about Paul's daughter, I heard him out. Even though Paul and I lost touch over the years he was still family, as was his daughter, and Stevens led me to believe she had nowhere to go. He told me her mother was dead and that she had no other family. And, I'm ashamed to admit, I needed the money. My ex got everything in the divorce and I'd been struggling ever since. Stevens offered me a nice salary; all I had to was keep quiet and take care of the child for as long as he wanted me to. So I agreed to the arrangement."

"He told Charlie you got attached."

"I did. Here was this beautiful little girl, who had no one in the world but me-so I thought-and she didn't even have a name. So I named her, after my grandmother Charlotte, who I'd adored. And from then on...it stopped being a job." She shut the car door and began to walk toward the trail in the woods.

T.J. followed her. "When did you start working with Avery?"

"When he found out where Charlotte was," she replied. "He found out she was living with me and he contacted me, revealing that he was alive and wanted his daughter back. I had already started to think of ways I could disappear with her, get her away from Stevens, because I could start to see what kind of man he really was. When Paul told me Stevens' true identity, I knew we had to act immediately so we started planning, working on a safe escape. But Stevens caught on to what we were doing, and he made steps to stop it."

T.J. nodded. "He sent the DeMarco brothers to your apartment."

"That's right," Anna said as they approached the shack. "The DeMarcos were arrogant, thought it beneath them to keep an eye on one older woman. So they left me with their underlings, which turned out to cost them."

"And Avery helped you escape."

Anna nodded. "Yes, he did."

"Where have you been all this time?" T.J. wanted to know. "Why haven't either of you tried to contact her? Do you have any idea what she's been through over the years? You both could've prevented that."

"We know," Anna said quietly. "And we regret that more than you could ever know. But we stayed a away for a reason, and that reason wasn't just to save our own necks from the Montenillos. It was to plan, to mobilize, and organize. To prepare for the showdown we knew was to come."

T.J. frowned. "You make it sound like the two of you were building an army," he said slowly.

"That," Anna said, knocking briskly on the wooden door, "is exactly what we were doing."

The door opened to reveal a large group of men between the ages of twenty-five and forty-five, all well-built and milling around getting weapons together and talking amongst themselves quietly. They came to a stop, however, when Anna and T.J. entered the room. "This is

T.J. Mackenzie," she addressed the group, indicating him next to her. "He's going to help with the raid."

They all nodded their greetings which T.J. returned, still slightly confused. "Who are all these people?" he asked her.

"Either ex-cops or ex-military," she replied. "Recruited from all over the world by Paul and myself. Some of them have personal stakes in this-someone they know has been hurt by the Montenillos or the DeMarcos-but most are here because they want to be, because they see what a blight those families are and want to stop them. They've already spent their time serving their communities and their countries...now they want to serve the greater good."

"All of these men...are fighting? With Paul?"

"And you," Anna told him, "if you wish. We've spent years training for this night; these men are the weapon the Montenillos will never see coming. When Paul gives the go ahead, they're going in."

"We're going in," T.J. corrected. "What do I need to do?"

"Talk to Mac," she said, pointing to a man a few yards away handling ammo. "He's in charge of the operation."

"Alright." He looked at her. "Thanks for finding me, letting me be a part of this."

Anna nodded. "We want the same thing, and we can use all the help we can get. Go on now."

T.J. approached Mac, who formally introduced himself as Malcolm Garrett, former Navy Seal. They began to work together, Mac outlining the layout of the building they'd be storming. As T.J. listened he began to feel hopeful, like they might actually have a fighting chance.

* * *

"Charlie."

Charlie walked down a long hall, toward the voice that beckoned her. She had no idea
where she was or how she got there...or what the occasion was for her to be wearing a simple white cotton dress.

Her name was called again and she quickened her pace, hurrying down the wood-paneled hallway. The voice sounded incredibly familiar...

She ran down the hall that never seemed to end, her long hair streaming out behind her in a coppery blur. She finally got to the end, stopping at the corner.

She was staring into a large, ornate dining room with a high-vaulted ceiling and extravagant chandelier, which shone brightly on the long, polished mahogany table underneath. The table was set with fine china and crystal glassware, and long, lit votive candles lined the center. Fresh flowers were in vases behind the candles.

There were also heaping platters of food, food that appeared more appetizing than any other Charlie had ever seen. She couldn't figure out what holiday it was or what dining room she was in; she'd never been here before in her life.

Then she noticed, for the first time since arriving, that there were four high-backed chairs spread sparsely around the table, and two of which were occupied. As she walked closer she could see Melinda sitting on the right and Rita seated across from her, on the left. The chairs at the head and foot of the table were both empty.

"Would you like to sit down?" Melinda asked, gesturing toward the head of the table.

"If you're ready, we'd love to have you," Rita added.

Charlie looked from one woman to the other. "I don't understand. How can either of you be here? What's going on?"

Before either woman could reply the far door opened, and someone else joined them in the dining room. "Don't get started without me," he said, bringing with him a large basket of rolls. He placed it at the foot of the table but did not sit down.

"T.J.?" she asked in disbelief as he stood before her, completely unharmed. "You're alive?" She started toward him, reaching out to touch him. Then she withdrew her hand, looking back at Melinda and Rita. "I get it," she said slowly, feeling deflated. "All of you are dead, and you're asking me to join you in...wherever we are."

It made sense now: the chairs around the table all occupied except for T.J.'s: his hands rested on the back of the chair slightly, staring at it with deep contemplation. And the remaining chair, the head of the table, was reserved for her.

"If I sit down," she began quietly, "Does that mean I'm dead too?"

"You're close," Melinda said. "That's why you're here. You have to choose."

She looked around at their faces. "You're all dead,' she whispered, more to herself than for their benefit.

"Are we really?" T.J. spoke up. "All of us?"

Charlie knew what he meant; not all of them were dead. She was still alive, but in some kind of limbo.

"You have to choose," Rita said, repeating Melinda's earlier words. "No one can force you to join us at this table."

"Unlike us," Melinda continued, "you still have a chance. You can still keep going, keep trying. If that's what you really want."

"Or you can join us," Rita concluded. "So which is it?"

"Sit down…or fight?" Melinda asked.

Charlie's eyes flew open, adjusting to the over whelming darkness. The right side of her body felt completely numb, while pain repeatedly shot down her left. She knew it was her right arm that was broken-the same one that had been shot-and it was her left shoulder that was dislocated. She also felt dizzy, groggy, and disoriented, but even in her haze she knew what she had to do.

She had no intention of sitting down at that table without a fight.

Since her right hand wouldn't budge she concentrated on her left, which still had some movement left in it. The lightness in her jacket pockets revealed that her knives had been taken as well as her guns but she still had one left in her shoe; she could feel it pressing against her ankle.

It was hard to believe how clearly her mind was working, considering the dizziness and loss of blood, but her determination was pushing her forward as she started to rock back and forth in the chair, going from side to side. She squeezed her eyes shut, bracing herself for the impact as she hit the floor.

She waited for a moment, expecting someone to come running. When no one did she looked down at her left boot and began to shake and kick it furiously.

Come on, she silently begged. *Let one thing just work in my favor…*

Then she could see the tip of the handle. She raised her foot higher until it started to slide out before clattering to the floor.

It took her about ten minutes to reach it, twisting and turning and kicking as much as possible. When she finally got it in her grasp she slid it carefully through her fingers and with her good hand, started to work on her ropes.

It wasn't an easy task with a dislocated shoulder but she finally managed, grateful that no one had walked through the door at that time. She knew there was a guard outside her door but the walls were thick, and chances were that he couldn't hear much of what was going on inside. The fact that there was nothing in there to help her escape undoubtedly lulled him into a false sense of security, which was to her advantage.

She carefully made her way over to the air, ignoring her pain. She had to come up with a way to pop her shoulder back into place, and also how to get the guard to unlock the door. She looked down at the knife in her hand-her only weapon-and began to feel overwhelmed. *You can do this,* she told herself firmly. *You've been banged up before...you have to keep going.*

Suddenly she heard the last sound she expected to hear, the sound of the door unlocking. Charlie quickly pressed herself up against the wall as flat as she could, waiting breathlessly for the door to open.

The guard came in, unable to see the vacant chair across the room. Charlie quickly darted past him, using the element of surprise, and out into the bright hallway.

Her shoulders ached as she ran, her broken arm flopping limply beside her. She rounded a corner, keeping her eyes open for all possibilities. Her knife was out and quickly accessible; it was the best she could do, but she knew it wouldn't be enough.

Suddenly there were footsteps behind her and shots were fired; she dove to the floor, landing on her left side and screaming out in pain; the force of the fall had popped her shoulder back into place.

Charlie rolled onto her back, feeling numb all over. She saw the fuzzy form of an unknown guard looming over her, about to reach down and grab her before suddenly flying backwards, slamming into the far wall.

Charlie's eyes caught the faint shape of a shotgun and the man carrying walked over to her, kneeling down next to her. Her vision returned to focus and she made out the distinct features of Enrique Sabados. "Enrique?" she asked in confusion. "What are you doing here?"

"I came for you," the voice replied, the kind face appearing concern. "There's no where else I'd be tonight, Charlie."

There was something strange about his voice; it didn't sound quite right. Her brain felt fuzzy but she commanded it to work, trying to figure out what was off. "Your accent," she said slowly. "It's gone. You sound American; you sound like a New Yorker." She began to frown. "I don't understand."

"There isn't time to explain," he said, putting his arm through the strap of his gun and hoisted it around his shoulder. "We need to get you out of here."

"Who are you?" she demanded as he helped her up. "You're no more South American than I am." It was true: with a cleanly shaven face he looked like a completely different person. He also wasn't wearing traditional South American garb like Enrique usually wore. Instead he was dressed in dark clothes, complete with a dark leather jacket not so unlike her own. And as she carefully stared into the concerned face she suddenly found it very familiar. The mustache had hidden it before but now she could plainly see the nose shaped exactly like her own, as well as a similarly shaped face. And though his eyes weren't the same color as hers they were the same shape, large and round. It was too impossible to believe and yet, the proof was right in front of her. She felt incredibly foolish for not being able to figure it out long ago; now it was painfully obvious.

"Paul?" she asked quietly as he got her to her feet, letting her lean on him heavily. When he saw that it wasn't enough, that she could no longer support herself even with his help, he carefully scooped her up and checked the hall to make sure it was still empty.

"Yes," he said finally. "I'm Paul Avery."

"But how did-why-"

"I don't have time to explain now, but I promise I will later," he told her, picking up his pace. "I've got to make contact with the team and we've got to get out of here."

"But you're my...you pretended to be my contact...Bob found out about you through his old boss..."

"A man who owed me a favor," he replied, rounding another corner. "He set me up with your partner-who I had checked out thoroughly by the way," he added. "He's a good man."

"The best," Charlie said. "But that doesn't explain why the subterfuge; why didn't you tell us who you were? And when I was in Argentina...that would've been a perfect time to say 'hey guess what, I'm your father'."

"I couldn't tell you then. I'm sorry, but it wasn't safe. It wasn't safe before then either. But it was my way of keeping an eye on you. I just wished I'd known more when you got to Argentina. I didn't want you to come at all but I knew I wouldn't be able to stop you. You're too much like-"

"You?" Charlie interrupted shortly.

"Your mother," he said simply. Then his tone changed. "We're almost there. You just need to hang on until we can get you to a hospital."

There was so much she wanted to say, so much she wanted to know. She wanted to express her anger as well but she knew it wasn't the time or the place. She also knew she needed to conserve her energy. So as Paul hurried through the building she let herself relax, having no choice but to count on him to get them out of there safely.

***

T.J. followed the group of men he was assigned to around the left side of the building, bringing up the rear. Anna had stayed behind, setting up base, while the rest went out to the old Montenillo cannery, the place of Antonio's arrest years ago. Mac had organized everyone into small groups, and T.J. was glad to end up with him. He had a no-nonsense attitude he'd no doubt developed in the time he served in the military and was well at ease giving orders and coming up with strategies.

T.J. had asked Anna about Avery before they left and she told him he should already be at the cannery trying to get to Charlie. She couldn't be positive, since they'd lost contact a while back. The plan was to meet up with Avery, get Charlie out of there, and take down the Montenillos from within. Two of the groups had been given explosive charges to set all over the building and would wait for Avery's signal before setting them off. Mac's team was in charge of locating Avery himself.

Mac signaled for the others to follow him cautiously through the side door. They entered a semi-darkened area of the building and began down a long narrow hallway, remaining on alert.

T.J. listened out for anything unusual but the area seemed relatively quiet. Too quiet for his comfort.

As they turned a corner Mac suddenly yelled for them to fall back, and though T.J. was too far back to see what was going on he could guess why. They turned around and he led the retreat, only to be stopped by more Montenillo men.

They were trapped.

***

"I can walk now," Charlie assured Paul as they descended a flight of stairs.

"Are you sure?" he asked doubtfully. "With the way your injuries look I don't know how you're even still conscious."

"I'm tough," she said as he started to let her slide down. "I've had some time to get some strength back. I can make it," she insisted.

"Alright," Paul relented, eyeing her warily. "But don't overdo it, okay?"

Charlie nodded. "Deal. So what's the plan exactly?"

"Get you out, then blow this place sky high," Paul told her matter-of-factly. "My men are in here setting up charges now."

"Your men?" Charlie repeated, following as he led the way.

Paul nodded. "You didn't think I'd come back here without backup, did you? That's what I've been doing all this time," he explained as they started down a new corridor. "Recruiting."

"Where?"

"Everywhere."

Charlie knew it wasn't the time but she couldn't help it. "I get what you were doing, staying underground these years so you could build your own army," she said quietly. "But I still don't understand why you went through the trouble to become my contact. Or why you didn't reveal yourself in Argentina."

"I nearly did, when I found out what was really going on," he admitted. "Those double-crossing lowlife DeMarco brothers had me fooled, and I should have known better. I never should have let you go in alone."

Even though she was still angry she found herself feeling slightly bad for him. "I would have found a way, with or without you."

"I can see that. It was hell of a risky move, what you did tonight. You were really planning on taking them down all by yourself?"

Suddenly Charlie sobered quite a bit. "I wasn't alone," she said softly.

"That's right," Avery said. "The P.I." When she looked at him in surprise he shrugged. "I've been watching you your whole life," he confessed.

"You weren't the only one," she said bitterly as they kept on.

"I know, and I'm sorry. I have a lot of explaining to do, and a lot of apologizing. And I promise I will, as soon as we get out of here." He pointed to the left. "Turn here."

Charlie obeyed. "You seem to really know where you're going."

"I should. This is where it all went down those years ago," he explained. "Where I arrested Antonio...and started the chain of events that led us to the mess we're in now." He shook his head. "I was a stupid, hot-headed kid who had no concept of the future. It never occurred to me that attempting to take down such a notorious crime family would have serious consequences. But it should have." He sighed. "And I should've thought the future as far as your mother was concerned, too."

"Did you care about her?" Charlie wanted to know. "Was she important to you? Or did the only thing that mattered come in the form of a badge?"

"You have a right to ask that. And the answer is yes, I cared for your mother very deeply. And when I found out about you...it was the most profound moment in my life. And I vowed then and there I would do whatever it took to get you away from Stevens, and that he would pay for all he'd done." He paused. "I'm sorry that I let my need for vengeance affect you. You shouldn't have ever had to wander the streets and do whatever you had to survive. You deserved more than that. Better."

Charlie couldn't say anything to that, so she just continued behind him wordlessly.

"But you finally he got it," he continued. "Bob and Rita...very good people. And that P.I. you've been seeing. Speaking of," he said as they neared the end of the hall, "he should be meeting up with us soon."

Suddenly Charlie leaned up against the wall, squeezing her eyes shut and holding her side. She wasn't sure if it was just the physical pain she was in or the combined effect of it and the grief she was dealing with, but she suddenly felt overpowered. "I'm okay," she managed, clenching her left fist. "I just need a second."

Paul looked at her in concern. "Maybe you are as injured as I first thought. You said you were in a car accident?"

Charlie managed a nod. "We flipped over and I was thrown around before we stopped. And I did get shot earlier," she added, opening her eyes. Then she took a deep breath. "Let's go."

Paul looked at her warily one last time before starting again. "There's something I should tell you. When we meet everyone back at the rendezvous point my partner will be there, the one working by my side all these years and helped with the recruiting."

"Your partner?"

"Marianna."

Charlie let out a gasp of surprise before she could stop herself. "Anna's here?" she asked in disbelief.

"Like I said, she's organizing everyone. Got them set up while I was in South America. She made a pit-stop on the way back to the guys, to pick up your boyfriend after you were separated."

Charlie felt her anger return, more sharply than before. "He won't be there," she said bitterly, her body beginning to shake in fury. Then she swallowed hard. "He's dead," she told him softly.

Paul stopped, turning back to face her. "Dead?" he repeated.

Charlie nodded. "Stevens...shot him."

"I'm sorry," he told her sincerely.

Charlie nodded again, trying to ignore the lump developing in her throat. "Let's keep going," she said, starting to move again. "Where are we, the back? There's hardly any activity here," she commented, ready to change the subject.

"We're actually about to near an exit," he told her. "And coincidently, this section is rarely used. Even tonight it seems."

"Lucky for us then-" Then Charlie broke off, grabbing Paul's shoulder. "Someone's coming," she whispered.

Paul handed her a gun before taking one for himself, nodding for her to remain where she was while he took off in the opposite direction. Charlie flattened herself against the wall, listening carefully.

A moment later Paul returned. "We've got to go," he told her, grabbing her gently by the arm. "They're coming-"

"We're here," a voice broke in from behind them. A few yards away stood Francisco Montenillo, flanked on either side by a guard. "So glad you could finally join us, Avery."

"You?" Avery asked in surprise, moving protectively toward Charlie. "I didn't think you'd deign to grace us with your presence."

"We've already had the honor," he said, looking at Charlie. "And I thought it was quite fitting, since this is the place you arrested my brother and we all found out who you really were. Now you can lose your daughter at the same place. Kind of...poetic, is it not?" he asked with a smile.

"Go to hell Montenillo," Charlie spoke up.

"Not before you dear," he said, nodding toward his men who drew their weapons.

***

For a moment no one moved, as T.J. and the others were blocked on both sides by Montenillo men. Luckily the other groups found them, and the shooting and fighting began.

T.J. saw several of Avery's men fall, as well as Stevens' men. T.J. covered Mac and Mac soon returned the favor, as T.J. moved forward.

"There's something going on down the hall!" he called to Mac. "Looks like some kind of standoff."

"Do you see Avery?" Mac called back.

T.J. tried to get a better look. "It must be," he told Mac. "He's talking to someone but I can't tell who." Then he could see that Avery wasn't alone. Charlie was standing next to him, looking as though she were about to fall over. "He's going to need help!" he called urgently to Mac.

"Go on!" Mac told him. "We'll catch up when we're finished here."

T.J. looked at them one last time before taking off down the hall, stopping far enough back where he couldn't be seen. As he listened to the conversation he could identify the voice of Francisco Montenillo...who was talking about killing Charlie. He saw Avery step in front of her and heard his quiet voice say, "You stay away from my daughter."

T.J. waited until he had a clear shot and fired at the guards, killing them both. Montenillo stared at him in surprise. "You," he said, breathing in sharply.

"Where's your nephew?" T.J. demanded, aiming his gun in Montenillo's face.

Charlie knew for sure that she was hallucinating now. She saw a blurry image of the man who couldn't be T.J. run up and kill the guards and threaten Montenillo, while Paul assisted, adding plenty of threats of his own. Charlie leaned back against the wall, completely confused.

Then she saw Paul force Montenillo forward, jamming his gun into Montenillo's back. He and the man who looked like T.J. started talking quickly, Paul telling him to get her out of there. The other man assured him he would and told him to meet outside. As Paul shoved

Montenillo roughly down the hall the man who couldn't possibly be T.J. ran toward her.

"I don't understand," she mumbled. As many times as she blinked, the image didn't change. It couldn't be possible, it couldn't be real.

There was no way T.J. could be standing there in front of her when he was dead.

Chapter Eighteen

"It's okay," he told her. "I'm here, and we're leaving right now." He reached over to touch her but she recoiled.

"I'm not going anywhere with you," she told him, shrinking away. "You're not here to take me to the hospital, you're here to take me to the table."

He frowned. "What are you talking about?" he asked in confusion.

"You're dead," Charlie whispered. "I can only see you because I'm almost dead too, right?"

"Dead?" he echoed. "I'm not dead, Charlie. I promise."

"But Stevens said...I saw him shoot you-"

"I was wearing a vest," he explained. Then he took her hand and placed it over his heart. "Feel that? I'm real."

"You are real," she whispered, feeling her knees give way.

T.J. carefully lifted her up and started down the hall toward the exit. "We're not dying," he told her. "Not tonight."

By the time T.J. got her out the door Charlie felt more coherent. It was amazing how it was working, boomeranging back and forth ever since she first lost consciousness. But it might have had something to do with the fact that her boyfriend hadn't died. She felt as though an enormous weight had been lifted from her shoulders.

But though she seemed to be doing better T.J. refused to put her down and let her walk. "At least give me my gun," she complained. The gun she had earlier had fallen from her fingers when she first saw T.J. "I promise I'm still a hell of a shot."

T.J. rolled his eyes. "Always such a tough guy. If I didn't know any better I'd swear you had testosterone."

"Bet you're glad I don't, huh?" Charlie asked with a grin as he walked away from the building, near a small grove of trees. "Now give me my gun." She held out her hand.

T.J. laughed despite himself. "Who are you going to shoot?" he asked, pulling it out of his back pocket. "The doctors in the E.R.?"

"No," she told him darkly, her eyes suddenly narrowing. "Him."

T.J. stopped and followed her gaze. Stevens was approaching him, looking angry and disheveled. As he got closer they could see how wild his eyes were; he was definitely past the point of reason.

"Your father is killing my men," he snarled at Charlie. He came to a stop, running his hand back and forth over the gun in his palm.

"Good," she said, drawing her gun.

"We both know you're too weak to use that," he said, taking a step forward. Then his expression darkened. "My family is in there."

"Then why are you out here?" T.J. wanted to know. "If they mean so much to you, why aren't you helping them?"

"That's simple." He took another step forward. "I want Charlie."

T.J. stiffened. "For what?"

"My uncle planned on killing her all along, said she was a loose end we couldn't afford.
Said my soft spot for her put us all in unnecessary danger...which is why I'm taking off. And
she's coming with me."

"Like hell she is," T.J. snapped, turning to go.

Stevens aimed his gun at T.J.'s forehead. "Smart move, wearing the vest. But this time I can assure you I won't aim anywhere but your head."

Suddenly Charlie dropped her gun and it clattered to the ground, causing Stevens to jump back. Her eyes rolled into the back of her head as T.J. sank to his knees, calling her name over and over again and shaking her gently.

Stevens stepped forward. "What happened?"

"She was shot, in a major car accident, and kidnapped," T.J. snapped, still trying to wake her. "Not to mention all this time she'd been losing blood when she could've been at the hospital." Then he stopped. "No," he whispered.

"What?" Stevens demanded. "Is she alright?"

T.J. looked up at him, his face a mixture of shock and disbelief. "She's dead," he whispered.

Stevens stopped cold. "What did you say?"

T.J.'s face hardened. "Charlie's dead," he repeated, his voice full of fury and grief.

Stevens' expression darkened with uncontrollable rage. "Then there's no reason for you not to be."

Just as Stevens was about to fire, Charlie reached over and pulled out T.J.'s gun and shot Stevens directly in the chest.

Stevens' eyes widened in surprise as he pitched forward, looking up at Charlie with what appeared to be admiration. "Never con...a con," he managed, his eyes glazing over.

T.J. looked down at Charlie. "That was a hell of a risky thing to do," he told her. "What if he hadn't fallen for it?"

Charlie smiled at hearing the same words a second time from a different person. Apparently, she'd done a lot of risky things that night. "I'm just glad you didn't."

"Not a chance. No going out in a blaze of glory, remember?"

"Speaking of a blaze...Paul told me about the plan, about the explosive charges," Charlie told him. "Do you think they're alright in there?"

"They should be," he said, but his tone wasn't too convincing.

"They might not even know we made it out," she added. Then she looked at him. "I want to go in after him but I can't; it's pretty clear my part is over in the action portion."

"I'll go," he told her quietly. "I'll find him and we'll get everyone out."

"This is big," she said, taking his hand quickly. "For me. I'm not the type who stays outside waiting while everyone else risks their lives...but I have to learn to accept help sometimes, don't I?"

He nodded. "Yes, you do."

"Then do me a favor. Don't go and get yourself killed-for real this time-and make me regret ever asking."

He nodded. "Deal." He kissed her quickly, then he took off.

As she watched him start to run away she called out after him. "I'll tell you now what I was going to leave you!" she yelled after him.

"What?" he yelled back.

"My bike!"

She thought she heard him laughing. Then he shouted back, "Thanks!"

It was hard for Charlie to believe after everything that had happened that night that there wasn't more she could do. Part of her felt infuriated for voluntarily benching herself but she knew she'd never make it; she'd only slow everyone else down, and time was of the essence.

Her eyes fell on Stevens' body and she decided to move away. Standing was out of the question, so she half-crawled, half-scooted over to the nearest tree so she could prop herself up against it. She was too keyed up to process the fact that the man who'd caused her so much pain and misery was finally dead, and that it was almost over, so she leaned against the tree instead, looking out at the horizon.

Night was slowly ebbing away; the first strands of dawn were approaching, though all the stars were still visible. *The sky finally cleared up,* she thought as she continued to stare at it. *Maybe that's a good sign.*

It was incredibly frustrating not to know what was going on inside, and more frustrating still not being able to help. She thought instead about how, if everyone got out in time, it would all finally be over; she'd finally be free. Maybe she'd even get to see Anna once everything had settled down.

There was still so much to be said between her and Paul. He owed her explanations, and he was going to have to deal with all the pent-up anger she felt...but there was something else she was thinking about, something that Stevens said when they had the standoff at the cabin. It was true that Paul was no longer a cop but he still acted the part, organizing those men the way he did, most likely running things like a prescient. If he still believed in what he once did, about upholding the law...how would he really feel about having a bounty hunter for a daughter? Could he ever really be proud of her?

Unbelievable, she thought, shaking her head slightly. *You barely know the man and already you're thinking about gaining his approval. Add that with waiting out here doing nothing constructive to help and you've got...a girl. How-*

Suddenly a deafening explosion shook the earth and she looked across the field to the cannery, which was now ablaze with flames miles high. "Oh God," she whispered as she watched it burn. "Please let them have gotten out."
***

Paul, T.J., and Paul's remaining men jumped backward at the explosion, standing a safe distance away from the raging fire. "We did it," T.J. said in amazement. "We made it out."

"And the Montenillos didn't," Paul murmured. "Even after we gave them fair warning," he added with a shrug. Then he stared at the burning building for long moment, all the memories rushing back from the last time he'd been here so long ago, and everything that had happened since. After thirty long years...it was finally over.

"We should get out of here," T.J. said to Paul as Mac led the others away, planning to meet Anna back at base. "Charlie's not too far away."

Paul nodded, letting him lead the way. "By the way," he said as they went, "you look

pretty good for a dead guy."

"Vest," T.J. explained as they hurried along. "It came to me just as I was leaving my apartment."

"Good thinking, Paul said. "You're quick on your feet, I'll give you that."

T.J. shrugged. "I doubt it's any different than what you would've done."

"Yeah, well..." Paul trailed off. "You know, most men would've done what she wanted, got out of town. Especially if it wasn't their battle to fight."

"Well, sir, I'm not most men," T.J. said. "And if Charlie's involved, it is my battle."

"Good answer," Paul said approvingly. "I might like you yet." Then he stopped, seeing that T.J. was looking around. "What is it?"

"I left her right there," he said, pointing to a spot not far from Stevens' body. "Where-"

"There," Paul said, pointing to a tree a few yards away.

They hurried across the field, T.J. getting to her first. Her eyes were open but glassy; she was staring straight ahead at the horizon, barely registering their presence. "Sun's coming up soon," she murmured, not shifting her gaze. Then her head turned slightly, her eyes struggling to focus on T.J. "No blaze of glory for you either."

"Not tonight anyway," he said, grasping her hand and giving it a squeeze. "Can you feel that?"

"Kind of." Her gaze drifted to Paul. "You got out too," she said. "Good."

He nodded. "The ambulance is on its way," he told her. "Shouldn't be long now."

Charlie didn't seem to hear him but continued to stare at him. "You were a cop," she said abruptly. "But I'm...I'm a bounty hunter," she stated, her expression unreadable. "If I wasn't your daughter would you come after me?"

The question took both T.J. and Paul by surprise. T.J. never knew she ever questioned her job, and it seemed to be the last thing Paul was expecting as well. "Of course I wouldn't," he told her in surprise. "Why would you ask such a thing?"

"Because," she said. "You could've had anything: a doctor, a lawyer, a teacher, a businesswoman, or a cop-carry on the tradition. Instead you got me."

"Charlie Booker," he said softly. "Do you think I'm not proud of you?"

Charlie said nothing but her gaze held firm.

He took her other hand. "I wasn't there to see your first steps, hear your first words, watch you go to school, or teach you how to ride a bike. I missed your birthdays and school dances and didn't get to teach you to drive...but I saw your life, though but from a distance. I saw how difficult that life could be, how it would've destroyed a lesser person. But not you. You were unbelievably tough and strong, smart and sure, and you did more than survive; you thrived. It took you a long time but you found your place in the world...and you met good, loving people along the way. I don't see how any father could be prouder of his daughter...just for being you, Charlie."

Charlie's face lit up and her eyes began to sparkle with tears. "Thanks," she whispered. "That's really good to hear." Then she turned toward T.J. "And you...I'm really glad you're alive."

He nodded. "I'm glad you are too. I wasn't ready for the bike anyway."

Charlie gave a small smile.

The rescue team arrived shortly after. Paul was the only one allowed to ride in the ambulance since was a family member, so T.J. got a ride from Mac back to his car and met the ambulance at the hospital.

T.J. parked in the parking garage, pulling into the nearest available space. He sat where he was for a moment, gripping the steering wheel and staring blankly ahead at the gray wall, trying to absorb everything that had happened. The image that kept coming back the most was of Charlie, leaning against the tree and looking fragile for the first time since he'd met her.

When he walked into the waiting room he found Paul standing near the window talking to Anna, both their heads bent low as they were deep in discussion. Mac was a few yards away talking on the phone, nodding to T.J. when he saw him. T.J.'s eyes strayed to the TV, where coverage of the Montenillo downfall was already being shown. The cops didn't have any idea who was responsible for the tip-off and eventual fire, since there had been no witnesses, but with the remaining Montenillos all dead they had to recognize the definite end of the Montenillo organization.

As T.J. slowly sank into an empty chair, Paul approached him, taking the seat next to him. "We need to get in touch with Bob Holden," T.J. told him, his voice tired. "As soon as possible. He and the others need to know what happened...including Diana."

Paul nodded. "I'll take care of it." He paused. "I understand you're Diana's neighbor, and you know her very well."

T.J. frowned. "What *don't* you know?"

Paul smiled wanly. "Surely someone in your position isn't *judgmental* about keeping tabs on someone."

"I guess not."

"Okay then." Paul looked straight ahead. "I loved Diana," he said bluntly. "It was a long time ago, the situation wasn't ideal to put it mildly, and I know that I hurt her. But with all the events going on...none of it ever changed the way I felt about her. Or the way I felt about Charlie."

"I can see that," T.J. observed.

Paul turned to him. "And I'm not the only one, am I? You risked your life for her tonight. Maybe I haven't earned the right to say this yet...but I'm grateful."

"You risked yours too," T.J. pointed out. "I'm not saying you don't have anything to make up for but all the things you've done...that counts for something. Sounds pretty fatherly to me."

***

"I can barely stand to look in there, see her like that," Bob told T.J. quietly the next afternoon. As promised, Paul worked quickly to get everything handled so Bob could bring the others home. Bob and T.J. were standing outside Charlie's hospital room while the nurse was in with her, staring through the glass.

Charlie's right arm was in a cast, and most of her body was covered in cuts and gashes, some of which had to have stitches. She'd lost a lot of blood and received transfusions, which were helping. She also had a slight concussion but would make a full recovery, with rest and
time. For now, the worst was over.

"She's pretty banged up," T.J. agreed, "but you should've seen her last night. Even after the crash she managed to escape being tied to a chair and kill several men...including Stevens."

"No car accident could stop her," Bob said softly, a note of pride in his voice. Then he cleared his throat. "Anyway, she's going to be fine...and it's not like I've never seen her in here before. That girl has more lives than a cat, been in and out of the E.R. countless times over the past ten years-when you could drag her there-but it's never been this bad. Except-" He broke off, swallowing hard.

"The night you found her," T.J. finished, looking at the elder man.

"There are no words to describe...she was so still; I really thought she was-" Bob shook his head. "But she pulled through, just like she did now." He paused. "I've thought about that night almost every day for ten years to justify my reasons for why I wanted her to work with me. But I managed to block out the worst of it, the sitting in the hospital and waiting part. Until now."

"Can I ask you something?" T.J. asked quietly, facing the other man. "Charlie told me you tracked those guys down that attacked her and let her decide how to handle them...but she never told me what she chose to do. She said you were a big part of it, and I was just curious-"

"What would you have done?" Bob interrupted.

"I would've roasted them alive like pigs on a spit."

Bob chuckled. "Sounds like we think alike." His expression sobered. "It took a lot of convincing to make Charlie see that they deserved to be punished; she thought it was 'just business' because she couldn't pay what she owed." Bob shook his head. "When I finally brought them to her, though, and she saw them for the first time since...she lost control. She jumped on the ringleader and just started hitting him and wouldn't stop. When she finally did the guy was a mess and she regretted it, feeling like she was no better than them. So she ran, and it took me days to track her down. When I found her I told her I left them on the doorstep of the police department, but before doing so I impressed upon them how bad it would be for them if they spoke her name to anyone. They all had priors and ended up being convicted. Charlie, in the meantime, had a hard time accepting what she'd done. After that, we never talked about it since, and she's been careful to treat what we do as just business, and not get emotionally involved. And she's done really well. But now that all of this is over I think it's time for her to move on, start something new. She's the most capable person I know when it comes to starting over. She should do great."

As T.J. watched Charlie through the window he realized Bob was right. The years of not knowing the truth and the effects her career had worn on her, though it wasn't something easily seen. But now was the time for all of that to change.

Now was the time for her to be free.

***

Charlie's stream of visitors never seemed to end; her hospital room was a revolving door. T.J. was her most frequent visitor, Bob and Diana a close second. All of her loved ones were there except Paul and Anna, who were noticeably absent. T.J. assured Charlie that they'd been there when she was admitted and were calling constantly for updates on her condition. Charlie
suspected they wanted to stay out of the limelight and hoped when things calmed down she'd get a chance to speak with them.

By her third day as a patient Charlie had acquired a quite a number of stuffed animals, cards, and balloons. She'd finally convinced T.J. and Diana to go home, shower, and get some rest so she was alone for the first time, finally having a chance to read over the cards and study the stuffed animals.

She also had time to stare out the window and start to process all that had happened, and feel particularly grateful to be alive. After all the love and support she had surrounding her ever since she'd been admitted to the hospital she realized how lucky she truly was. Though she knew it was cliché to survive a brush with death see everything in a new light afterward, she found it happening regardless.

It wasn't easy for her to be confined to a bed. Though her arm was still in a cast she could feel her strength returning, and her impatience to waltz out of the hospital was almost tangible; she was certain she'd be able to leave under her own volition. The doctors, however, didn't see it that way so she was to remain a patient for the foreseeable future. It was difficult for her; she'd hated being in hospitals ever since her attack ten years ago, and did her best to avoid them ever since. She only stopped by the E.R. whenever Bob wouldn't take no for an answer but now she had to face it, finally deal with it, and put it behind her.

Though she was glad to have some moments' solitude for a while she was grateful when Megan arrived that evening. She went over to the table next to Charlie's bed and began to arrange all the gifts while talking about how she finally convinced Jack and Bob to have a guys' night so she could visit Charlie alone, figuring Charlie could use a female ear.

She was right; Charlie was glad to listen to Megan, to talk about everything she'd been missing since she'd been in the hospital. Megan was glad to inform her that while they were there she and Jack had an ultrasound and found out their baby was a girl. Charlie was truly happy for them, and Megan also let her know that her goddaughter was to be named Rita Charlotte Larson, after the two women who couldn't wait to meet her and the one who made sure she'd be safe.

Megan stayed for several hours and then Jack arrived to pick her up. While she was in the bathroom, Jack sat on the edge of Charlie's bed, looking at her carefully. "Are you really doing as well as you want all of us to believe, or is it just a show?"

"It's real," Charlie assured him. "I'm fine."

"Really? Because if I had been through what you have, had my life turned upside-down the way yours has been...I wouldn't be handling it half as good as you."

"Don't sell yourself short; you come from very strong people, and it's rubbed off on you more than you might think," Charlie told him.

"What about that guy, Avery? Has he been here to see you yet? And that Anna woman?"

"Not yet, but I think once things die down they'll see me. Why do you ask?"

"They owe you," he said simply. "They both have a lot of explaining to do." He paused. "There's something I've got to ask, though I might get my head bit off for it."

"What?" she asked curiously.

He took a breath. "Are you still going to be a bounty hunter?" he blurted, avoiding her eyes.

Charlie let out a half-laugh. "Is that all? You had me thinking it was something...well, a
lot more dire." Her expression sobered. "I've given it some thought," she confessed. "But I haven't come to any decisions yet. I promise when I do I'll let you know. Okay?"

Jack nodded. "Alright. But if you had any sense you'd retire like Bob."

"And who says I ever had any sense?" she asked, winking.

Days passed and Charlie had a long conversations with Bob about her career, still not coming to any decisions for the time being. She also had serious talks with Diana, wondering if she had any plans to see Paul, but she remained tight-lipped on the subject, so Charlie didn't press it.

The day finally arrived, a short time later, for her to be released. Given a clean bill of health, Charlie was ecstatic to finally be going home. T.J. was supposed to come that afternoon and pick her up, and she requested he stay at her place as long as he wanted. Diana planned on stopping by later to bring Harley home, who'd grown a lot in the time that Charlie had been away.

As she was waiting she began to pack, folding a shirt and placing it in her bag when a knock sounded on the door. Assuming it was T.J. she called for him to come in, her back to the door.

"Hello, Charlotte."

Charlie dropped the socks she was holding and slowly turned around. Paul was standing in the doorway but he wasn't alone; an older woman with gray-and-white hair stood at his side. Charlie immediately recognized her as Anna.

She only stare at the woman she hadn't seen in twenty-three years, unable to move or speak for the longest time. When the shock wore off it was instantly replaced by something she didn't expect.

"You never came back for me," Charlie accused, her eyes locked onto her great-aunt's. "You told me to wait for you on the bench and you never came back."

"I know," Anna said softly.

"I was five years old," Charlie continued. "I know that you were abducted but you escaped. You helped her," she said to Paul. "Between the two of you, you could've found a way to get to me, to save me from the hell of the children's shelter and living on the street. I mean, you knew everything about me. You watched me...but why couldn't you come get me?"

"By the time we started tracking you, you were older," Anna began, walking forward. "It took us a while to get tabs on you, and by the time we did you already had a family. You were adopted by Melinda Booker, and you finally had a safe, normal, good life. You were so happy, Charlotte. We couldn't bear the thought of taking that away from you."

"I was happy with Melinda," Charlie said quietly, "but I had questions. Questions both of you could've answered. I didn't have records or a birthday and had no idea where I came from. And, as you both know, I didn't get to keep my happy life with Melinda. After she died I was on the streets again, and we all know how that ended." She gestured around the room. "In a room just like this one, nearly beaten to death and completely terrified, with only a stranger for company."

"But that stranger became your family," Anna reminded her. "He and his sister made you a part of their lives, and you got ten good years to be with all of them."

"But I grew up to be a bounty hunter," Charlie pointed out. "Is that really what you
wanted for me?"

"We wanted you to be happy, and you were," Anna told her. "We wanted you to be safe, and Bob Holden took care of that. Not just because he was your partner and mentor, but because he gave you a family again."

"You were my family!" Charlie yelled. "Both of you! And instead of acting like it you went off to build an army." She turned to Paul. "And you still haven't given me one good reason why you pretended to be someone you weren't, earned my trust and respect, and still not tell me the truth."

"You have every right to be angry with us," Anna spoke up quietly. "And I wish we had the answers you deserve. But it was a long time ago, and nothing was what it seemed. We were hit from all kinds of directions, trying to the best we could to survive so you could survive. We knew the further we were away from you, the safer you'd be from

Stevens because the last thing you needed was to be connected with anyone the Montenillos had a score to settle with."

"I was selfish," Paul added. "I wanted to meet you, get to know you, but was too afraid to reveal who I really was. So I hid behind a fake identity, all the while trying to help you as much as I could." He paused. "And as for your profession, I already told you how proud I am of you, and couldn't be more so if you were a doctor or a lawyer. And please don't forget that I haven't been a cop in almost thirty years. I resorted to some...less than legal-or ethical-methods to take down the Montenillos."

Charlie looked from one family member to another, both of whom were nearly complete strangers. "I don't know anything about either of you. I'm not talking about what I can find out on paper; I'm talking about the real people you are, getting to know you. Am I going to get the chance?"

Anna and Paul exchanged a glance. "We'd like to give it to you," Anna began, "but-"

"You're leaving," Charlie broke in. Then she shook her head. "Unbelievable," she muttered.

"There are loose ends that need to be tied up," Paul explained. "Matters we can't attend to here."

"The DeMarcos?" Charlie guessed.

Paul nodded. "Then it really will be over, for good." He started to walk toward her. "We'll come back, Charlie. And when we do, we'll give you all the answers, time, and anything else you want. But before we go please know that everything we did, we did for you. I've been trying to protect you your whole life, but you ended up getting hurt anyway, and I'll never forgive myself for that. But I'd like a chance to make it up to you, if you're willing."

"So would I," Anna said. Then she pulled something out of her purse. "Maybe this will do for starters."

Charlie accepted the manila envelope and opened it quickly, pulling out a single sheet of paper. The words "Certificate of Birth" were printed across the top in bold letters, and underneath was a long blank line. Under that were two other lines; one had Paul's signature, and the other was for Diana. Across from them was the date, JUNE 6, 1982.

"As soon as Diana signs it and you get it notarized, it's official," Diana told her. "Then submit it to social security...and according to the state of New York, you will legally exist."

"All my life I've been a ghost," Charlie said, staring at the certificate. "Even when Melinda legally adopted me, and I became Charlie Booker, I was only the Charlie Booker that existed starting from August 10, 1992. But now..." She looked up at Anna. "Why isn't my name on here?"

"Because Charlotte was the name I gave you, and it wasn't my right to do so. It's up to you now, what you want. You should decided what your legal name should be; you've more than earned the right." She backed away. "I do love you, Charlotte. Take care of yourself."

"Wait!" Charlie called after her. "Bunny-shaped pancakes."

"What?" Anna asked, turning around.

"That's what you made me for breakfast," Charlie said. "Pancakes shaped like bunnies. They were my favorite."

"You remember that?" Anna asked in surprise, her eyes misty.

Charlie nodded. "I do." She took a breath. "I can't say I'm not angry, or that I understand everything...but you'll always be the first mother I had, the first one I remember. And you'll always be my aunt."

As Charlie watched her walk out the door, looking at her one last time before disappearing, she felt the last piece that had been missing from her past had finally fallen into place. She noticed Paul was still standing in the doorway. "What about Diana?" Charlie wanted to know. "Are you going to talk to her?"

"I don't know," he admitted. "I don't know of that would be better or worse for her." He nodded toward the door. "I need to get going."

Charlie nodded, unsure of what else to say.

"I wish I could tell you I made all the right choices, but we both know I didn't," he told her. "If I had found a way to get you away from Stevens I would've given you back to your mother, where you belonged. But we can't do anything about any of that now, all we can do is move forward."

"You're right," Charlie said. "So why don't we start over now?" She stuck out her hand. "Charlie Booker," she said formally.

"Paul Avery," he said back, shaking her hand. "Your father."

Charlie nodded. "It's nice to finally meet you."

***

When T.J. and Charlie arrived at her apartment later that afternoon Diana was already there, a sleeping Harley curled up in her lap. "I took the liberty of making us an early dinner," she said, as Charlie reached down to hug her and scoop up Harley. "You've got to be starving after all that hospital food."

"If you want to call it food," Charlie said, wrinkling her nose.

After they ate T.J. volunteered to do clean-up since Charlie was supposed to take it easy, something she knew wasn't going to last long. Diana joined her in the living room and Charlie produced the birth certificate and a pen. "Have you decided on a name?" Diana asked as Charlie passed the pen to her so she could sign the "mother" line.

"I've been Charlie as long as I can remember and Booker was a gift from Melinda, the only last name I ever had," Charlie told her. "So I want to stay Charlie Booker, if that's okay with you. But I still need a middle name."

"Of course it's okay with me. And I think you should choose your middle name."

"Well…Charlotte came from Anna, Booker came from Melinda, so my middle name should come from Rita and you. And as it turns out…you both have the same middle name."

"Rita's middle name was Marie?" Diana asked.

Charlie nodded, taking the pen from Diana and starting to fill out her name. "How does that sound?"

"Perfect." Diana signed her name under Paul's. "There you go, Charlotte Marie Booker," she said, passing her the certificate. "You officially have a name, birthday, and parents."

Charlie stared at the now-filled-out birth certificate, a large smile breaking out over her face.

Epilogue

Late that fall, Rita Charlotte Larson was born, and at her christening a few months later, Bob and Charlie were officially named her godparents. Jack and Megan took more pictures that Charlie could count, and T.J. and Diana were sitting side-by-side on the front row to witness it.

Paul and Anna returned to the States on Thanksgiving, and were invited over by Charlie to her apartment along with Diana and T.J. for the first Thanksgiving with her parents. The DeMarco threat had been handled, and afterward Charlie spent time getting to know them both, who each decided to put down roots in New York once again. Also, Diana and Paul had a chance to catch up and have a long-awaited heart-to-heart that resulted in their tentative friendship and re-ignited parental bond. Eventually they were able to find their way back to one another, despite all that had happened to keep them apart.

Anna decided to forgo retirement and found a children's center for kids who needed a place to go. Charlie fully supported her decision, and contributed financially. She also made a monthly appearance to teach the children about safety and strangers.

Charlie joined Bob in retirement from the bounty hunting business and made plans with T.J. to become partners. After Christmas *Mackenzie Investigations* became *Booker and Mackenzie, Private Investigators*. They solely handled locating biological family members. Bob was called in time-to-time for his input, but spent the majority of his time finally enjoying his retirement on a beach in Rio.

And, on New Year's Eve as they were laying on the hood of his car watching the fireworks, T.J. proposed to Charlie and she accepted.

SIX MONTHS LATER

Charlie stretched out on a beach chair, sliding her sunglasses down on her nose to watch the sailboats on the water. Then her eyes drifted to the slope beyond where a group of teenagers were preparing to go parasailing. The breeze ruffled her long, dark hair as she watched, making it swirl around her.

"I'm still trying to get used to that," T.J. said from his chair beside her, brushing her hair off her shoulder. "All I've ever known you as is a redhead…but I like it."

"I thought it was time I return to my roots," Charlie said with a grin.

He shook his head. "Even a foreign country doesn't improve your puns."

"It's so beautiful here," Charlie said, looking around. "Rita really would've loved the Greek Isles."

"Not a bad honeymoon, huh?" He turned to face her, propping up on one elbow. "So what do you say, Mrs. Mackenzie? We've got a whole summer ahead of us to do everything we've ever wanted. Where do you want to start?"

Charlie thought about sightseeing, trying out the food, and her eyes went again to the parasailers. There was so much they could do…plenty of it requiring high energy.

"I'd like to try parasailing later," she finally answered. "But for right now, the adrenaline junkie just wants to stay right here with her husband. And her incredibly girly drink." She sipped her Mai Thai, nudging the little umbrella out of the way.

"Sounds good to me," T.J. agreed, drinking his own. "Feels good to just relax for once, doesn't it? Just lay back, do nothing, and enjoy the scenery," he said, leaning back in his chair and closing his eyes.

Charlie nodded. "Absolutely. I've had enough excitement for one lifetime."

"Jana!" a voice called from behind them. A college-aged boy came running down the beach, stopping a few yards in front of T.J. and Charlie to talk to a dark-haired girl. "I just found out you can sky-diving a mile outside…" His voice drifted off as the couple began to walk away.

"Sky-diving," T.J. said, staring out at the water. "Never tried it before. Have you?"

Charlie shook her head. "No. It sounds like fun. For them, I mean. A good adventure for young-"

T.J. suddenly started laughing.

"What?" she demanded, sitting up to face him. "What's so funny?"

"You," he said, sitting up as well. "You're just itching to jump up and follow those kids to wherever they're going. Admit it."

"I'm not admitting anything."

"You're unbelievable, you know that?" he asked, shaking his head. "We haven't even been here a day, promising to kick back and relax, and you want to go sky-diving."

"I do not," Charlie protested. Then she paused. "So do you," she muttered.

They looked at each other for a moment before jumping up and running down the beach. "I call dibs on the red parachute!" Charlie called as she ran, T.J. close behind her.

THE END

Made in the USA
Columbia, SC
08 December 2022